I SHOT
THE DEVIL

RUTH McIVER

I SHOT THE DEVIL

BLACK STONE
PUBLISHING

Printed in the United States of America

First edition: 2024
ISBN 979-8-212-32074-0
Fiction / Thrillers / General

Version 1

Blackstone Publishing
31 Mistletoe Rd.
Ashland, OR 97520

www.BlackstonePublishing.com

For my brother, who taught me all about cars before I was even born; introduced me to AC/DC, horror movies, MTV, Jackie Collins, and punk rock, all while I was still in primary school

"I really don't know why it is that all of us are so committed to the sea, except I think it's because in addition to the fact that the sea changes, and the light changes, and ships change, it's because we all came from the sea. And it is an interesting biological fact that all of us have in our veins the exact same percentage of salt in our blood that exists in the ocean, and, therefore, we have salt in our blood, in our sweat, in our tears. We are tied to the ocean. And when we go back to the sea—whether it is to sail or to watch it—we are going back from whence we came."

—John F. Kennedy

PROLOGUE

RESIDENT ALIEN
BY CORMAC O'MALLEY

Why me? Why him? I asked the darkness.
Well, hell, because it's fun, the darkness answered.

At that moment, October 31, 1994, 11:11 p.m., the darkness had six heads, twelve arms, and twelve legs. The woods were all around, already knowing everything and swollen with our secrets.

You know that record *Rumours*, the one with the gaylord in tights on the cover that everyone's parents have? Well, that's how it all started. Someone said something to someone and someone's mother heard it and then it's all over the school, the PTA, and later, the news: Satan worship, group sex, animal sacrifice.

West Cypress Road Woods have a soundtrack. In the daytime, it's all Disney: hummingbirds and red-headed woodpeckers, the light footfall of deer. At night, the deep-bellied hoot of barn owls and nightjars and more sinister rustling deeper in the dark. There was an occasional homeless guy wandering through, kids parking, getting high, fooling around. Wildcats, you think; wolves, you imagine. Another layer of the soundtrack: the noises he made in the dark: gurgles, snorts, moans.

Feet shuffling in dirt, the crunching of sticks under boots and canvas sneakers.

Steve said that he'd killed a bear not far from there. He claimed to be a hunter, but all he had for evidence was a bearskin rug that none of us wanted to go near, let alone sit on.

We told Andre we had something for him. It was the only way to get him there that night without arousing his suspicion. Andre knew something was up—he was sweating, his eyes were unfocused, and he kept licking his lips and pumping his fist. Still, he came without a fight, slapping a mosquito and drinking a beer too fast, humming what sounded like "(You Gotta) Fight for Your Right (To Party!)."

Death's a lottery, Ricky Hell once said. Now Andre's number was up, everyone agreed. That's why he was smiling, Danny said. He compared Andre to a white cat: blond as a mouse and blind as a bat. It explained his resting aggression—natural disadvantages that made him both overly willing to please, but also extremely aggressive. He wheezed from asthma and wore contacts most days, but sometimes tinted glasses. He had a pear-shaped, near womanly body, and he almost always smelled like beer and plant matter; something botanical, earthy, rank.

I see it in a movie montage: faces, feet, and hands; kicking, breaking. The crack in his expression where he knows what's going to happen and he seems less afraid and even a little sad.

I rewind the tape, the bit where the reel is warped and baggy with wear, the break in Andre's voice. Why me?

You heard it all and you saw and you saw.

The worst bit is remembering before, the bits you can remember.

At Wendy's near the highway, all sharing the same Frosty and French fries in the back booth, before getting kicked out by some junior manager. Danny making devil horns and singing along in that deep growl of his, "Blood will rain down." Carole, still in her Dairy Queen uniform, smelling like Windex and sugar. Carole, grabbing you by your denim jacket, running her fingers down all the patches, like she was ticking boxes—yes, correct. Megadeth. Slayer. Metallica. The Crüe. Tick, tick, tick. Getting high in the parking lot in the back of the short-bed Chevy, with the tarp covering us, Hellhammer turned up so loud it was shaking the truck, and the smell of dope and menthols and Carole's lip balm. Smiling at each other. This little moment of belonging before everything breaks.

You didn't do it, did you? You just saw and you saw and you saw.

Some nights it knocks you out and you're on the ground, tasting blood, hands over your ears; yours, his, you don't even know. You don't know what you saw.

You don't even know if you made this all up. The same way you didn't feel real while you were in America. Whatever happened there feels like an MTV video clip, but one you keep editing and editing and then, in the final cut, Andre gets up and walks away.

1

SEPTEMBER 10, 2010

When my father was working a case, he used to say he was going underwater—a case had him by the leg, and sometimes, both legs at once. When he wasn't underwater, Raymond Paul Sloane, or RP to those unlucky enough to know him, taught me facts: the etymology of place names on the island; the life cycle of lakes and canals, the meaning of the word archipelago, that my name, Erin, means "from the island to the west." I learned that deep water is dangerous. Not only could a person drown, but it's a well-known phenomenon that rescuers drown alongside them. So, I tried to stay away from drowning men, but it was a lesson that never stuck.

Although RP had quit undercover work when I was in grade school, he was a phantom parent; an unclaimed seat at the dinner table, an empty chair beside my mom at school recitals. The only proof of his corporeality were the empty cans of Rolling Rock lined up on the coffee table, a TV set left on, a toilet seat in the up position.

Try as I might to resist turning into someone like him, I was spending most of my recent days in a liquid fugue, only I wasn't an investigator—I wasn't even much of a journalist anymore, except when I was writing for a glossy monthly magazine supplement called *Inside Island*. Long-form crime features that you could sort of sink your teeth into. Mostly I was at coffee shops, the kitchen counter, or bars until happy hour, churning out numbing copy for real estate agents, insurance companies, even school newsletters. I rotated bars in and around Suffolk County, largely sports bars around Massapequa with names like Paddy Power, careful to avoid being a regular anywhere. Life had become an ellipsis between the decade-long mistake of my twenties and the life I wanted.

It was duty that brought me back to the island. Months ago, I'd given up my apartment and my life in Brooklyn to care for RP, moving into his split-level bungalow on Oceanside Avenue. There were only three suburbs between Massapequa and Southport, a thirty-minute drive dependent on traffic, but they acted as a kind of geographical and psychic buffer between my past, which after all these years was almost like a lucid dream, an intense hallucination I could put down to youthful excess, if it hadn't left so many physical scars.

Denise, my editor from *Inside Island*, must have smelled my desperation, the animal ambition, underneath my all-day antiperspirant and the Dior Poison that I had been wearing since the nineties, because she was promising me a big story—something substantial. It was something close to hunger that resurrected me that morning and drove me, still half-drunk, to the Lyrebird Café in Rockville Centre to meet her. I wanted to become a "lifer"—a guaranteed full-time gig with *Inside Island*.

Even though the fastest route from Massapequa was the Southern State Parkway, my GPS told me there was an accident on Exit 37N, which meant I had to drive down Southport Avenue, past the train station that was just blocks away from Roosevelt High, my old high school.

At the lights, I looked out at the now fenced-off Old Res, as locals called it, a dried-up catchment filled with old soda and beer cans, scrap metal and, according to the adults, hepatitis. Aside from some new fencing and a different billboard (the old one had featured the obese man who got skinny on Subway holding his old fat pants, grinning), it looked the same. The Res backed onto Southport Station. I was surprised the place was still there. In freshman year, a classmate of mine, Linda Bauer, was dismembered from below the armpit to the groin, while clambering up an embankment onto the track, wasted on wine coolers. All the local papers, the floral tributes, acrostic poems that enshrined her picture—L is for lovely, I is for inspired and so on—forgot that she was N for nasty, D for diabolical and A for autocratic. Her death became an urban legend, just one of many in a community that felt like a sociocultural cul-de-sac.

I used to think that I'd escaped Southport, but as I got older I realized that I'd simply absorbed the town into my system, like when I ate a nickel as a kid and never saw it reemerge. Southport had become a part of my intimate geography, ingrained and shadowy. Near my heart: the library, where I hid and read *Les Misérables* until the German librarian kicked me out. Near my spleen: the Waldbaum's where I was busted for shoplifting. Take a right and you'll hit my liver, the nightclub Escapades, where I took my first drink, seriously underage. Over there by the gloomy underpass to Southport train station, my stomach, where I threw up the drinks, somehow glittery and foamy like I'd ingested a snow globe.

And yet all these parts that I'm showing you, all these were not the worst parts, not by a long shot.

I took out half an Ativan from my purse and swallowed it dry. I popped an Adderall and an orange Tic Tac and then spritzed a Frankincense-heavy space-clearing spray all over me that I'd got as a stocking stuffer at *Inside Island*'s Christmas party. I suspected it was from Denise.

It was 11:11 a.m. when I found the Lyrebird Café; I was either four minutes early or eleven minutes late, I honestly couldn't remember. Denise was a friend and she wouldn't sweat it—she was already in a booth drinking a cappuccino. I noted her little bottle of Sweet'N Low on the Formica table. Denise wasn't too much older than me, but she was literally twice my size. She styled herself in vintage dresses and wore her weight like an expertly tailored power suit—it wasn't just armor, it made her difficult to ignore; allowed her to break down doors.

If I'd learned anything about life, it was that you need padding; Denise had figured this out.

"Erin. It is so good to see you," Denise enthused. "Sit. You look svelte." She meant drawn, but was being polite. I shrugged in response and we smiled at each other.

A waitress with swallow and star tattoos on her neck took my order. The Lyrebird was what Denise might call "hyperlocal"—a concept she'd applied to the magazine to make it into a lifestyle magazine: the artisan ice cream, loft conversions and suburb profiles and, of course, tasteful gore were selling. In the aftermath of the GFC, *Inside Island* was not only still in print, it was glossier than ever.

I took my coat off; my face felt flushed. I caught a glimpse of myself in the mirror and winced. While at thirty-two my face was still unlined, I had lost some of that apple-cheeked youthfulness and my skin had taken on a slightly sallow tone. My lips were desiccated. I was a ghost in an old coat; in this case, one that had belonged to my mother, which still had the dry-cleaning receipt pinned to it from 1993.

"How's everything? How's RP?"

"He's dying and he's really pissed. The house goes on the market in October."

There was no way to sugarcoat it. If you'd met my father when he was younger, you'd know that it wasn't the Alzheimer's that had damaged the part of his brain that controlled empathy and basic human kindness, but he was especially miserable in care and verbally abused me when I visited.

My main goal was to keep him out of the state facilities. I toured one and the infernal moaning and occasional scream in various dialects, the smell of piss and shit mingling with disinfectant, was enough to make me write a living will.

"Sounds hard." Denise drove her hands across the table to touch mine. It was like they were warm liquid and my hands were a pile of autumn leaves.

"Thanks."

We'd worked together for a few years and she'd persisted in inviting me out for weekend brunch, evening drinks, afternoon coffee; I knew she liked me, and it was mutual, but I continued to hold her at a gracious distance. Denise was too canny, too intuitive—too warm. She would melt me.

My cappuccino and cake arrived. I couldn't really attempt the cake, so I sipped the lukewarm milky coffee, wishing I'd ordered an Americano. The Ativan had softened the edges of the morning, the lights in the café taking on a romantic glow, but the Adderall was making me drum my fingers on the counter.

"Erin, I'll get straight to the point. I've got a story for you. It's short notice for a feature like this, we were going to cover the Bethpage baby beauty pageant scandal, but we've had to scrap it." Denise leaned forward in her seat. I leaned in automatically, mirroring her—she'd lowered her volume, but her excitement couldn't be muted.

"This story—it got emailed to me by some true crime nut, who actually put your name forward, and even though a few supps writers have tried to claim it, I want you to have it. You've heard of the Southport Three, right?" She said it like you would a punch line. "In 1994, a high school senior called Andre Villiers was murdered by his group of friends in Southport, Nassau County . . ."

1994. I was sixteen. Words whispered to me by a boy, that I cannot forget, even if I tried to forget the rest: "*While in the wild wood I did lie, A child—with a most knowing eye.*"

"Maybe? Was it something occult and like, very stabby and violent?" Instead of sounding vague, I'm sure I sounded high, which I was. I could wear my buzz with the best of them, but the truth of the matter was, deception was not my forte. It was my father's. It was one of the reasons I chose not to be a cop like him. That and I was never going to pass a physical.

"No to stabby, yes to occult, and hell yes to very violent. It was sixteen years ago, on Halloween, and a satanic murder. You're from Southport, right, Erin? Were you, like, upstate or under a rock or something at the time?"

"Under a rock," I managed.

"You must have at least been permanently stoned at the time because it was a *huge* story." Denise ran with the pun.

"I was in Maine. Aunt Marnie didn't believe in TV." I didn't mention that I was tucked up in a white guest room with excellent linen, like an over-medicated and temporarily compliant injured bird. By the time I returned to New York, post breakdown, it was 1997 and the buzz had died out.

"Well, it was huge. A very photogenic Satanist by the name of Ricky Hell was the ringleader. He was shot dead on the scene, which was a major bummer, because he was like a star on the cover of *Rolling Stone* magazine—kind of a nineties Charlie Manson, but better looking. It's a very sexy case: think Satanism, celebrity lawyers, Geraldo Rivera, an essay in the *New Yorker*, opinion pieces about youth violence, drugs, video games, apathy, blah blah blah."

She slid her iPad across the table—it was cued to a true crime TV series called *Child's Play: Kiddie killers*. Klassy. The episode was titled "The Devil came to Southport: Ricky Hell and the satanic teen thrill-kill murder of Andre Villiers."

A beady-eyed man in a nylon suit and oversized spectacles, wearing a beige, old-school trench wandered around a wooded area. I recognized those woods—a mile from the Old Res. He reached a clearing, "the Spot," we called it—a ring of stumps that sat like makeshift bar-stools; old beer cans and cigarettes, candy wrappers and empty baggies littering the forest floor.

Denise provided me with a voiceover:

"Andre Villiers was eighteen when he was murdered, same age as Ricky Hell and nearly two years older than Carole Jenkins and Cormac O'Malley. Danny Quinlan-Walsh was seventeen, so he was placed in a secure facility in Westchester, a slap on the wrist, really. This is the only interview he gave, right before he went nuts and his lawyer told him to stop talking to the press."

Oh, I remembered. I didn't have the luxury of traumatic amnesia, and the pills I took only wiped out my short-term memory—receipts for impulse purchases I couldn't recall making, packages that appeared at my door, dinners left on the stove. But I remembered all right.

"I'll fast forward to the interview with him." Denise moved the cursor to 13:13. She sat watching me expectantly.

Danny in a starched Gap shirt; the hot WASP next door, with his long blond hair pulled into a neat ponytail. He looked like he was going to junior prom and not a murder trial, except for the part where he held Satan's horns above his head for one of the reporters. This became an iconic image in 1994. There was a constellation of zits on Danny's usually unblemished face: prison food. Despite that, he was healthy and strapping, a milk-fed, well-nourished middle-class teenager. I heard Danny's unreconstructed Long Island accent for the first time in sixteen years:

I mean, I just don't know how it happened, man. Ricky had a plan and we just did it. He changed form once we got there. We all did. And then it, like, started, and we couldn't stop. There was no stopping. Ricky, he, like, flew up and at the cop like a freakin' crow, and the cop, like, shot him, like: bang, bang, bang and Ricky was shouting: "Pray for us, pray for Satan." And then it was just, game over.

"Game over," Denise repeated. "Like Mario Brothers or something." You could hear the silent "tsk tsk" of reprimand that followed, but I knew she was thrilled. For someone with a little Zen garden on her desk and an out-of-office email signature that read *Namaste*, Denise liked true crime and, what's more, she liked gore. Throw in a murdered kid or a killer kid—or better yet, killer kids—and Denise was one happy editor.

Listening to Danny now, I realized that it wasn't a voice numbed by fin de siècle apathy; in fact, his voice crackled with emotion. I wouldn't call it remorse, but disbelief.

The DA remained unconvinced. So was I.

"But for Danny Walsh, it was indeed, game over," the narrator intoned. "The church-going quarterback was sentenced to fifteen years in a maximum-security Westchester County facility for the criminally insane."

Next, a collage of photos of Danny Quinlan-Walsh on the family boat, having lunch with his family. I was there that day; I remember Danny turning his unchristian Megadeth T-shirt inside out for the family photograph, so it was just plain black. Another photo: a sophomore dance photograph and I'm in it—even if my face is blacked out and all you can see of me is my clinging cherry-red velvet dress. His hands around my waist are the size of mallets.

Danny Quinlan-Walsh. The memory of him was like the skin of milk at the top of the bottle, the cream of youth: the smell of clean sweat, menthol cigarettes, double-mint gum. The taste of my own blood. The taste of Danny was in my mouth and I had to remove it. I swallowed my frothy coffee. I gulped down water. Denise watched me with naked curiosity, fluffing her hair up.

"It's cheesy, but you ought to watch it when you get home." Denise pressed pause. "After he'd served five years, his sentence was reduced to six years because of diminished capacity and good behavior. He was twenty-two years old on release, has never done an interview since. Carole Jenkins served three years in a juvenile facility. Same with her boyfriend, Cormac O'Malley. She wrote a book, *Dancing with the Devil: How I survived a satanic teen murder*. I've bought a copy from Abe-Books. Already on its way to you via FedEx. It was out of print; came out in '98, but by then the buzz around the case died down a bit. There were other crimes on the island that took over." They were mainly gun crimes: a sign of the times. A mass shooting on the train; a sniper at my old school, Roosevelt High, who only killed one person, but wounded many. They introduced metal detectors after that.

I remembered that Cormac O'Malley, Carole's semipermanent boyfriend, had been in my art class, but not much else. I thought about digging up my old yearbooks—except, of course, I'd burned them.

"There's a lot of innuendo surrounding the cop from Queens who shot Ricky Hell. A narco cop called Steve Shearer. Your dad was a cop, right? Did he know him?" Denise scanned me with scientific interest.

Hearing the name Steve Shearer was the mental equivalent of someone running a rusty knife down my spine. I remembered the name. I didn't want to.

"He knew *of* him."

"He was Cormac O'Malley's stepfather. He said Ricky Hell was resisting arrest and he aimed for his shoulder but missed, hitting the heart. Despite this injury, Hell continued to resist and was shot in the face. An

investigation revealed that it was a fair and lawful shooting—reasonable as opposed to deadly force. Ricky Hell obviously wasn't around to
dispute his role as ringleader. He was on hallucinogenic drugs, he was
a drug pusher, a Hispanic in an all-white area, and he'd brained a white
kid. There are rumors Shearer had a personal history with Hell but no
one investigated the connection further." Denise rolled her eyes. "And
Andre Villiers—I mean, he simply doesn't feature in any of this. His
parents were Jehovah's Witnesses, I think, and he was in trouble with
the law constantly. They condemned him, their own son. A meaningless death and then he sunk, like, without a trace."

Andre, the victim, was as one-dimensional and unsympathetic in
his death as he was in life. It was the only thing about the case that ever
made any sense.

"And Villiers had also been questioned by local police over a missing kid." The jangle of Denise's charm bracelet seemed impossibly loud
as she delivered this almost triumphantly. Denise loved missing kids.

I placed my palm on my solar plexus. Breathe. My heart was in my
throat. I tried to swallow some of the cake, but it was gritty and a little
stale. "Which missing kid?"

It turns out a town like Southport yielded a high volume of creeps
per square mile—three kids from Southport went missing, two were
found on Jones Beach in shallow graves.

"Cathy Carver. Know about her? Young blonde girl, missing, presumed dead since late 1993. The whole case had a touch of the JonBenét
about it."

I nodded. "My little sister Michelle was in her sixth-grade class.
They were friends."

Cathy disappeared in October 1993, just months before Mom and
Shelly died. She had never been found. I adjusted my scarf and tried to
appear cool as I looked up to meet Denise's laser stare. She could see
through a person; easily sniff out a lie from a text or an email, had a kind of
instinct that bordered on precognition. I could tell she wanted more, but
she knew that I was stubborn and secretive enough to not push the point.

"Wow. That's a crazy coincidence. Was Villiers really a suspect, I wonder? And if so, what about the other kids who went missing on the island? Weren't there a few?"

There were. During the nineties, children weren't allowed to walk or ride to school. Security systems became more sophisticated. The crimes changed the entire energy of the suburb. Wealthier families—and there were many, particularly on and around the water—hired extra help.

"Jason Weis went missing before Cathy, in like '92, but the other boy was later, like 2000, 2001. I think it's a serial killer type thing, so . . ."

"No, not Andre," Denise agreed. "So back to Satan allegedly compelling kids to kill in the woods in Southport. I mean, I know you—it's got your name all over it."

If she only knew.

All the pieces I had written for *Inside Island* were conversational, informative true crime stories that engaged with local cultural history and pop culture. I had two unspoken rules: I shied away from homicides, unless they were seriously historical, and I stayed the hell away from my old stamping ground. Now, Denise wanted me to break both rules.

While I had followed the developments in the abductions—leads mentioned in the newspapers always turned out to be dead ends—I had never researched, never even googled anything relating the ill-fated events of the past, the Southport Three and what happened that night in 1994. I never tried to locate old classmates or friends. I knew at the time that none of Andre's family had spoken to the press (nor had Ricky's) and that the public largely believed Ricky murdered Andre as a sacrifice to Satan. Someone had told me years ago about Carole's book. I'd never read it. Denise moved in for the kill—flattering my writerly ego.

"You grew up there, on the outside looking in. That's why you write the island so brilliantly. You're the only one who could write this story. I mean, you're getting a following. This will cement your reputation as the Ann Rule of *Inside Island*."

I long had an atavistic knowledge that the past was not going to stay contained forever, but it had managed to sit there, mostly undisturbed, for sixteen years. Now I realized, Southport had been coming for me all this time.

2

I found myself back in my gun-metal gray Chrysler LeBaron on autopilot to Roosevelt Field Mall in Garden City. I could have easily gone to the Barnes & Noble in Westbury to buy a new notebook, per my private ritual—new story, new notebook. This was not only a detour, but also my first return to Roosevelt Field Mall since '94.

As soon as I sighted the parking lot, I knew I'd made a mistake. Dread knotted my stomach, my palms began to sweat; even my feet seemed to perspire. I had forgotten how gargantuan the building was—it was the second largest mall in the state and spanned two stories, plus a concourse level. The directory indicated new additions and excisions of older chain stores.

In the nineties, Roosevelt Field Mall was like an airport and a destination in its own right—a kind of small, insulated country, where kids of all races comingled. It was also a coliseum; an arena where commerce and class lines blurred in what was otherwise a very segregated white-bread part of the island. There were people packing guns. There were record and bookstores, providing portals out of Southport, and the island itself; a jungle of hormones and subcultures seething and sedated by bright strip lighting and R&B auto-tune Muzak.

I exited the car and walked a half-mile from the parking lot to the entrance. I barely made it through the automated doors, which opened onto a Hannigan's family restaurant.

It was next to the cigarette machine at this Hannigan's that I reached first base with Danny—but more memorably, it was adjacent to the Burger King where I first met Ricky, who seemed to be getting to third with Carole Jenkins, his hand jammed halfway up her denim cut-offs as she perched, near catatonic, on his knee. Ricky, solemn and black-clad, opened his mouth to accept the occasional greasy spiral onion ring she offered, like she was feeding a depressed crow.

I recall him sitting on a backless swivel stool; his posture was poor. It occurred to me that he didn't know how to carry his height, but later I would learn that he had a problem with his back from a car wreck and he was sometimes hunched out of pain. He barely registered me, as his glassy eyes went straight to the book I had just shoplifted from the very same Barnes & Noble I was heading to now. It was a small book of poems by Edgar Allan Poe from the *Great American Poet* series. Ricky shifted Carole off his lap and seized the book, reading aloud while I squirmed with embarrassment: *"It was night in the lonesome October, Of my most immemorial year."*

The press only got hold of a few photos of the brooding, sneering teenage Ricky, with his cut-glass cheekbones and black eyes. In one, he's in a tux at a family wedding, where he looks more like an Aztec king about to attend a sacrifice, his fleshy lips pursed in a scowl of moral disobedience, displaying extremely white teeth lined up like tombstones. When I got to know him, I found out that despite conscientious brushing, the perfect veneer disguised a mouth of eroded enamel, molars riddled with painful holes and craters.

That day at the Burger King the white tops of his black eyes were showing and vicious acne scars marred his vaulting cheekbones. His AC/DC T-shirt read "Thunderstruck." (After lightning strikes, lights up the sky, residue will fall. Fulgurite, they call it.) Arrow, meet heart.

"'Ulalume,' huh?" He read the title as if tasting it. Then he looked at me. It was not my heart that took the hit, but somewhere lower: the gut—the small intestine even.

"Gay," Danny sighed.

"*These were days when my heart was volcanic,*" Ricky quoted. "Brutal assault," he added, nodding at me in approval. There was a white-blond figure behind him, wearing an army greatcoat and tinted John Lennon shades, holding a supersized milkshake that appeared doll-sized in his giant hand: Andre Villiers. He could have been Ricky's astral body—a phantom, a ghost.

Within a year, both boys would be dead.

———

I walked on, tapping my solar plexus and temple, trying to regulate my breathing. Despite much of retail going online, it seemed shopping at the mall was still a regular competitive sport. Although it was a mid-week lunchtime, teens on free periods or simply cutting class roamed in packs and pairs, wearing colorful puffer jackets and signature white Apple headphones. The gaggle of ye olde 1990s gum-cracking girls and braying boys in their baggy pants, which once clotted the arteries of the mall and beached themselves on the benches lining the concourse, had been replaced with kids who looked so professionally groomed and stylized, they resembled extras from a music video set who were playing misbehaving teenagers. I watched as they clowned and pouted in front of their smartphones. Some made out, some made war, draped on each other and vaping.

I found my way into the Barnes & Noble, scanning the aisles, walk-ing through the new releases into the literature and stationery section.

I decided upon a hardcover notebook: candy-striped along the spine, seaside-themed, high Americana. Small painted figurines waved from the shore; a boy chased a spotted dog. A diner advertised chowder. A seagull crested a lighthouse. This was the kind of idyllic New England I had dreamed of growing up in. The notebook was almost too pretty to write in, let alone depict a satanic thrill-kill murder that had haunted my life to date, but part of me relished the irony—the other part longed to escape into its landscape.

I paid the cashier and headed west to the exit. When I made it into the parking lot, I sat in my car with my purchase and lit a cigarette, taking deep breaths. Making lists normally soothed me; writing distanced me from emotion.

I wrote down the date, October 31, 1994; the story's anchor, my gateway to the past. The murder happened on Halloween. Yep—Halloween. Imagine how much the media loved that shit. RP moved us to Amityville in early '94 and had taken me out of Roosevelt High and into an all-girl Catholic institution called St. Mary's. The night Ricky Hell was shot and died in the dirt, I was on the cool bathroom tiles in a twilight state of consciousness, under the impression he'd ditched me. I was drunk on grief, rage, and cheap vodka, plus I'd taken a few pain pills. I was listening to "Anything Anything," a song by an eighties band called Dramarama, on repeat. Rewind and listen. Rewind and listen. I was taken to the hospital later the next day with severe alcohol poisoning.

Now in the car, I wrote my title:

Satan in the Suburbs: the Southport Three and the making of a satanic teen thrill-kill murder

Follow-up:

1. Interview the Southport Three.
2. Steve Shearer—look at arrest history/rep with narco cops; track down Ricky Hell's family; locate records of dealing/arrest sheet/juvie offenses.
3. Similar cases of minority kids being shot/satanic murders etc.
4. Andre Villiers (talk to living relatives)—victim profile, interest in Satanism and occult—and police interview re: Cathy Carver.

Panic hummed around me in the car. The writing wasn't helping this time—the drone of the radio, the sound of my jagged breathing. I winced as the radio announcer brayed that it was Flashback Friday! and the monotonous stream of Billy Joel's "We Didn't Start the Fire" commenced. I switched the radio off.

There were rumors surrounding Andre. Very loud whispers that suggested he liked to harass and sometimes hurt girls, that he liked it rough,
that his favorite kind of girl was young—*extremely* young. Before he died,
I'd heard that he'd been questioned over Cathy Carver's disappearance,
but I must have blocked it out. Why else would I forget something so
significant? Cathy had been my sister's friend. Her disappearance had
been a huge deal. And only months later, my sister died.

So, thinking of Andre Villiers as a victim, I experienced a genuine
episode of cognitive dissonance.

My father had seen multiple violent deaths, and as a rookie reporter
I had reported on homicides so vile, I still struggled to process the details. My father's adage was this: no one deserves to be murdered, but
some people were seriously asking for it. And over the last few years I
had come to conclude that he was right. Andre was one of those people.

One time, we were in the back seat of Danny's car, a skunk fog
around us, when Andre "joke-choked" me. I don't recall where the others
were, all I know is only he and I remained in the vehicle. One minute
we were talking, smoking; the next, "Auto-erotic" by local metal band
Hellbound came on, the lead singer death-growling:

> *Wrap my hands around your throat,*
> *My engine starts, at your death choke.*

It seemed like play: his lanolin- and weed-scented hands (not the
hands of a gardener, but the hands of a gamer or someone chore-adverse)
were on my neck, enacting the song's lyrics—perhaps even posturing to
be sexy. Guys hurt you as flirtation back then, maybe they still do. Something very serious passed over his face; like a cloud had moved over the car.
My instincts screamed that something terrible was happening. What did
his eyes look like? Rumor had it he wore tinted contacts—they were pale
blue and I could read nothing in them at all. I thought of *The Terminator*
movie afterward, because it seemed that whatever was happening was at
once mechanical and dangerous. Finally, my fist went out and connected
with his gut and it was like hitting Jell-O, which immediately firmed.

This took place in all of ten seconds; maximum fifteen.

He laughed it off and I joined him, after cursing him out first. I even stayed to smoke a cigarette. Then I left and sobbed into the bushes.

There were finger bruises around my neck that lasted for a week; bruises that were hidden by my mom's old arsenal of concealers and foundations. I knew not to revert to turtlenecks and scarves, because my friends, RP and Danny, would assume I was concealing hickeys.

Why did I stay? How could I have laughed it off? I guess I didn't want to be the "crazy bitch" who made trouble. I made sure not to be alone with Andre again and the occasion was forgotten. But nothing ever is, not really.

Now I felt the ghostly memory of his soft hands around my neck.

———

What Denise had said had hit home to me. Andre's murder was what the cops called "classically" motiveless—a relatively unplanned, haphazard sacrifice to Satan. The whole point of the murders was that there was no point. The crime was one of nineties nihilism: heavy metal, drugs, disaffected youth. And Ricky Hell had both a rep and a rap sheet for dealing drugs. He was a disenfranchised minority; he and his sister grew up in foster homes and suffered physical and psychological abuse. Ricky, who put a cup over roaches and took them outside—a boy who had attended every one of his sister's dance recitals, who told me he had shed silent tears at the end of *Beauty and the Beast*—was not the descendent of an Aztec king, the son of Colombian drug lord, nor could he shapeshift. Whatever story the media and the police coauthored was pure fantasy, fed by a buzz of gossip that surrounded Ricky. It had multiple chapters missing—not just the finale with the narco cop bringing down a satanic killer in the woods, but entire sections of that night. I always suspected it was Danny who incited and executed the attack on Andre—because I had seen the violence Danny was capable of. Satan had nothing to do with it. On the flipside, I could never see Ricky Hell crouched in the dirt, holding a bat streaked with fragments of blood and bone.

Now Denise positing that Andre—"Andre the Giant," the kids called him, he was 6'3—was a predator provided the kids with a motive and, yes, a reason to kill (no, not an excuse).

I dialed Denise's cell. She sniffed out my trepidation at hello.

"What's going on, Erin?" Her tone was a bit severe. "Don't tell me you're having second thoughts? I've just crushed three writers who are due a cover story. I might even have to take one out for margaritas later."

"I'm not." I lit another cigarette. Another bad new-old habit that had returned since I moved to Oceanside Avenue. "It worries me that it might be just a bit too close to home," I admitted. Talk about an understatement: here I was ripping off a psychic Band-Aid over a wound that had been inflicted in '94 and had infected my whole life, and I was doing it for a magazine story. "There's something I didn't mention. I knew those kids. I more than knew them.

"I told you I went to an all-girls high school called St. Mary's in Massapequa, right? Well, before that I went to Roosevelt High. I hung out with the metal kids and did breakfast bongs. My nickname was Eerie Erin."

Denise sucked in a breath. "Go on."

"Danny Quinlan-Walsh was my first boyfriend. And I knew Ricky Hell. Biblically speaking. When the murder happened, I'd already changed schools and I wasn't hanging out with the gang as much, but I was still officially dating Danny."

"Wow. Okay. This is big. This personal angle, it's just so perfect. We could dig out your high school diaries, notes Danny wrote you in class . . ."

"Mm, unlikely," I managed. Not only was everything burnt in a bonfire of my making, those notes were more like voodoo offerings: *DIE WHORE* written on the mirror in blood; a beanie baby with a noose around its neck.

"Did Ricky Hell confide in you? More importantly, was he really a Satanist?"

I swallowed, thinking of his brown callused hands and forearms, dotted with oil burns from being a short order cook. Kissing him and smelling oil and despair and fear reeking from his every pore. He even trembled in his sleep.

"All that Satan stuff was just Ricky posing; you know, acting out. Like teenagers do. Especially troubled ones. Even if the others were privileged. It was all bad sex, worse drugs, and heavy metal music, as far as I saw it."

"There's obviously no talking to Ricky now, but given your history, you could get to Danny Quinlan-Walsh, make him go on the record," Denise continued. "Maybe even the Villiers family would talk to you? If you work this personal history to your favor, it's gonna be your magnum opus."

My hands flew to my neck as if by instinct. I still couldn't say what I knew about Andre.

"Maybe I'm, like, already too much in the story, so to speak," I managed.

"You're an ex-metalhead misfit who made it out of Southport to tell the tale—Erin, you *are* the story. You are Satanism in the suburbs. Embrace it. Don't fuck this up and I promise you'll be a lifer at the end. If you file by October 18, we'll go to print on October 28. The Halloween edition again."

Barring Christmas Eve and the 8th of October—the date Danny and I had our last encounter—Halloween was one of the most traumatic anniversaries in my extensive back catalog. It was Ricky Hell's Death-versary. At the time, I'd hated him. I'd cursed him. I wanted something terrible to happen to him and it did. Recently I'd heard Ricky's voice in my ear. Sharp, like he was trying to get my attention. *Eerie!* Ricky was the only one who called me that. It had been sixteen years since I'd seen him; lost him. And now I was going to relive it all again; unfurl the tangle of feelings I had for Ricky. (*These were days when my heart was volcanic.*)

Danny Quinlan-Walsh, my alleged "first love," and I had never spoken since the night that Ricky Hell died, the very same night I had buried all my feelings, which were now in the process of being exhumed. But as for Danny, I did a quick body scan and found I still really had none. I decided to start with him.

3

It took all of five minutes to find him. Danny Quinlan-Walsh didn't have a Facebook or a Twitter account, but he was on LinkedIn. He was living on the island, managing his dad's boat storeroom in Southport. The Quinlan-Walshes, who were technically loaded, had lived waterfront on Bluebottle Way. I went out on the boat with them a few times and could see the appeal of life on the water. There was a quiet sense of otherworldliness; of being the only people out at sea.

To get to Prestige Marine Storeroom, the family business, I had to drive through parts of Southport that I hadn't revisited in sixteen years.

My appearance attracted a few stares. No one drove a secondhand car in Southport. My tailpipe leaked exhaust and my bumper was held together by rust. All the dimensions of the town seemed off—it was as if the buildings had shrunk in height, or the sky had become larger. It was azure blue and cloudless—and despite the changing season, a nearly too-warm, bright summer day.

I passed the old Waldbaum's, which had been bulldozed, a Gap outlet in its place, then Lake Angonjwin, which was also adjacent to Whitman Elementary School. Most people just called Lake Angonjwin "Whitman's Lake." Cathy Carver had lived opposite the lake, in a triple-tiered navy blue and ivory Dutch colonial mansion that resembled a very large and grand version of a dollhouse I had as a little girl, except her house had a fire-engine red front door.

I reached the breach between streets, where the Sound divided the suburb of Southport. Behind the corrugated iron fence, you could study the exteriors of luxury houses and their personal marinas, where their boats were docked. Pitch pines seemed to pierce the cloudless sky, which was the same perfect blue as the Sound.

Danny's family lived alongside the wealthier Southport residents and Prestige Marine. Turning onto Lake Drive would take me back to my first childhood home, which was significantly more modest than the Carver's lakeside mansion. It was on an oak-lined street that I hadn't visited since the night Mom and Shelly died: Christmas Eve, 1993. Winter.

I looked out at the Sound, the sunlight hitting the water in the distance. It was so blindingly bright and warm, but still, stupidly I wondered if it was snowing outside. It made me think my memory was like a snow globe—over the years, Southport had become miniaturized, shrunk, and trapped into a microuniverse. Now, I'd tipped it to one side and the snow cascaded. It was like I was ice-skating through time and trauma.

On impulse, I took Lake Drive and by the time I reached our old street, Helen Lane, I was feeling as I did when I was waiting for my SAT results; a sense of dread mingled with excitement. I idled outside 1100, straining to make sure the number was correct, mentally counting the houses, studying my neighbors' properties, which all looked the same— homogeneous, preplanned, and mass produced. I had been expecting to see our single-storied modest bungalow, with its thatched wood exterior and clogged gutters. I recalled the wrought-iron bench out the front, the artfully arranged pot of geraniums placed next to a Guatemalan welcome mat that my mom bought in the city, its colors and weave faded by a thousand entries and exits. I thought of tripping over Shelly's Rollerblades in the hallway, screaming her name as I fell through the doorway hours after curfew, my mom in her blue terry-toweling bathrobe with the red wine stains, looking grim and disappointed.

But it was all gone. Like an old tooth, it had been yanked out and remodeled, and only the garden remained. The current house was all sleek lines and display windows, rendered in silver cloud, with two ivory columns at the entrance. Inside, I was sure there would be skylights and white walls adorned with crappy modern art. I thought of the police tape and the way the emergency service lights had made silent patterns on the front of our house; a surreal lightshow. An inaudible aftermath to the equally silent tragedy.

I drove back to Lake Drive and parked for a minute at the lake. This ill-advised little scenic route down memory lane had shaken me up quite viscerally; I needed to collect myself before I faced Danny.

I got out of the car and lit a cigarette. Despite the movement of the waterfowl on the water, a young mom with a stroller alongside another woman who looked like her mom, and the subtle drone of a lawnmower, it was as if Southport itself was static and somehow soundless. While the day was deceptively bright and clear, there was ice in the air. There was a sense of total stillness as I walked the path, a glorious sheen on Lake Angonjwin. I could almost crack the image, like a spoon breaking a hard-boiled egg.

I returned to the car and drove on autopilot the rest of the way to Danny's workplace. Then it occurred to me; the night that my mom and Shelly died perhaps wasn't all that silent—I'd ruptured my eardrum. It had caused temporary deafness and intermittent ringing in my ears for days—and extreme vertigo. The world had tipped on its side. And the night they died, it had started to snow.

——

I barely recalled Prestige Marine from my teenage years, but from the looks of the empty parking lot, it wasn't doing well. Maybe it was just off season—perhaps rich people made after-hours appointments. Either way, I was buzzed through instantly by a heavy-set guy dressed in Hugo Boss but with a novelty tie. He was in his late twenties, blond like Danny, but with no bone structure to speak of. He didn't even ask my name, just started in on his sales pitch, gesturing to a boat called *Lady and the Tramp* that took up nearly the whole floor space. It was the marine equivalent of a Ferrari, but ugly. "That's a motor yacht," he said, "It's a Silverton 43, so very current—twin Volvo engines—"

"Safe," I suggested, rubbing my hands together.

He fiddled with his tie. He seemed uncomfortable with the adjective.

"But check out her dangerous curves. There's a salon on the main deck which features a convertible sofa, a loveseat for two, and an entertainment center that totally rocks. And that killer cherry finishing is featured throughout in high-gloss with satin accents—"

"Little Pat?" I cut him off.

"It's been preloved, so it's a regretful sale. A stockbroker. Finance is available." Then he paused. "What?"

"You're Little Pat, right? Pat Junior?" I remembered him now, a little boy at the dinner table being scolded for pouring too much American mustard all over his plate. "I'm actually looking for your brother Danny."

"Oh, you are, are you?" His tone went from flirtatious to a little wary.

"I'm Erin Sloane. I used to go out with Danny. I came to dinner at your house, a few times."

A slow, dippy grin spread over his face. While Danny was given a punching bag, karate lessons and therapy, and nerf balls and hand weights to squeeze to alleviate his anger, I remembered Pat as the complete opposite to his brother—sunny, hapless; kind of like a golden retriever.

"*The* Erin Sloane? Holy shit, I remember you! Good to see ya. He's in his office. First door on the right."

———

I walked down the polished concrete hallway and found the door ajar. Danny was on the phone. He put it down calmly. He mostly looked the same. I don't know if I had expected him to. He'd had his teeth professionally whitened and there were some sun and smile lines around his eyes. His office was Scandinavian minimalist—the desk an ugly meadow yellow with two industrial lamps on either side, and framed pictures of who I gathered were his family. He had a *Far Side* calendar, which was a tell—I'd bet money his dad had one before him. It was as if he'd gathered information on how to emulate an adult male and then replicated it. The room was a statement that he had a clean bill of mental health now; a monument to his newfound normality. I'd always felt he had the emotional complexity of a Twinkie: pretty package, hard layer, gooey, radioactive center. Now I knew that he was psychologically more complex and, thus, more toxic than ever.

"Erin," he said, devoid of emotion. It was like I'd served him the wrong coffee and he was deciding whether he'd send it back.

I sat opposite him and picked up the framed photo: Madonna and child. "Is this . . . ?"

His perfect jaw worked overtime. "My wife, Gina. And my daughter, Kelly."

My middle name.

Gina looked Southern Italian and was prettier than me, but the similarity was unmistakable. We shared the same round face and apple-like cheeks, a nose that was slightly too wide and flat—only her black hair probably hadn't come out of a bottle. Her eyes were very dark and seemed alive with joy in the picture, which drove a stake of pity into my heart. Danny's kid was adorable and a mirror of her mother, but with Danny's rosebud mouth.

"You want to get a coffee? The diner across the road?"

I couldn't get into a vehicle with him.

"Let's walk," I said.

"You're kidding?"

No one on the island walked anywhere. They drove down their driveway to collect the papers. I just stared at him and he shrugged on his overcoat.

I waved to Pat as we walked out of the storeroom.

"See you later, Erin," he said. "So bro, when should I expect you back? Before Christmas or . . . ?" he called jokily to Danny, who flipped him the bird. Despite the lightness of Pat's tone, the tension between them was old and frayed; an unraveling rope in tug-of-war sibling rivalry.

"You usually take long lunch breaks?" I asked Danny, watching Pat watch us through the glass, shaking his head.

"Pat's just not a creative thinker. I do my best business away from the office," Danny replied. He always was work-shy and arrogant. I scanned Danny's clothes. He was wearing a black cashmere wool coat and black pants, both well cut. His hair was still long and golden, but he'd tied it back into a neat ponytail. Just like he had for the trial. His button-up shirt was also black, as were his suede ankle boots—a metal-head clothed in Armani.

I could see that Danny had remained the golden son—not even a satanic murder could dull his shine.

Danny, an all-American quarterback with a touch of evil, had seemed to me to be a project, an emotionally defective fixer-upper for a wannabe-bad-but-basically-good girl. Sun-bleached hair, diamond-cut jaw, a deviated nose (a football injury) to give him character. Those cerulean eyes, pools for teenage girls to dive into and drown in. And I almost did.

"Business looks slow," I said, just to say something.

"Always is this time of year," Danny said, blowing on his fingers. He lit a cigarette and offered me one, which I refused, even though I was weirdly relieved to see he still smoked. Marlboros even. It was especially cold for September. Fear conditioning had alerted me to the prospect of snow in the air, in the same way you anticipate a bone breaking. The silence between us was equally sharp and only softened when we crossed the road and entered the diner. It was the jingle of the bell and the blast of central heating, Danny opening the door—a memory cue. He looked at me and felt it too; the amount of times we walked in together, hand in hand, or in furious single file, to sit over single cups of coffee and full packs of cigarettes.

Despite the clash between us, if we weren't making out, we were always touching; an endless, impossible game of sexual Twister. Mouth on nipple, orange. Hand on cock, red. From ages fifteen to sixteen, we were tied by the umbilical cord of the telephone, connected by hand and tongue. We were in each other's pockets (quite literally) around the clock. And yet, despite the pyrotechnic public sexual couplings, we were hardly Romeo and Juliet. More like Sid and Nancy.

I watched the waitress's hand shake as she filled his cup and I remembered when he was so attractive as a teenager that I'd seen a woman swerve her car when he crossed the road. I sipped the weak diner coffee. He ordered a bagel, plain, cream cheese on the side.

"You look thin," he said, when the waitress left our table.

"Yes, I am thin," I replied.

"You look good. Tired, though."

"Thanks again. You look rested. All that time in the mental hospital?" I brought the coffee to my mouth, wincing as if expecting a slap. Ricky Hell had been likened to Richard Ramirez, the infamous "Night Stalker," and Charles Manson, but no one had ever named Danny's serial killer doppelganger—Theodore Bundy. It was there in the prematurely creased forehead, the storm that passed his statue calm, perfectly proportioned face. I had weathered it.

Danny just smiled.

"You always had a way with words, Erin. I hear you're a writer now. I read a few pieces you wrote in *Inside Island*. Haunted houses, missing kids, that sort of thing."

"Mm. It's a new gig. And you took over your dad's boat business. Because of the criminal record. Or was it your choice of career?"

"Pretty much both," he said seriously. The swooning waitress returned with his food. He winked at her, buttering half his bagel carefully and spreading the other half with cream cheese, avoiding the salad leaves and tomato. I noticed he moved the pickle to the far end of the plate, for me to eat. He always hated pickles. The gesture was perversely intimate. Anyway, I couldn't take it now, not with my stomach twisted up like this.

"Partly because Dad got sick. I heard yours is now, too." He put down his bagel. "Like gone, in the mind."

I shrugged.

"My dad's dead. Cancer." Danny munched on the bagel. "Mom lives with us. She had a stroke, she's in a wheelchair." He shrugged in a glib "what are you going to do about it?" gesture.

"Sorry."

"You know . . . you look, like, the same. A bit thinner, but the same."
He seemed to be marveling at this.

I had nothing to say. I didn't need to supply any details of my life.
I wore no ring and must have reeked of spinster.

"Whatever happened to Carole and Cormac, do you know?"

"She married some old dude, moved down to Florida, works in real
estate. Cormac, dunno. Dude disappeared. I'm not meant to have contact with either of them, so it suits me fine. Your dad end up with his
partner, what was her name, Mona?"

Mona was the reason my parents slept in different rooms; the reason
my mom had been on antidepressants. I wonder if I knew about Mona
before my mom did. I was in ninth grade when Danny and I spotted
Dad and Mona at Nathan's in the mall, eating hot dogs and talking intensely. Hiding out at the Orange Julius, we studied them in the booth;
RP's arm behind Mona, a lazy, familiar gesture of possession.

"He's supposed to be doing a double," I'd said to Danny.

"He's doing her," he'd said.

"No," I said casually now, not taking his bait. I sipped my coffee
and looked him straight in the eyes. "But speaking of cops, you ever see
Steve Shearer before that night?"

"Steve Shearer?" Danny shrugged. "He sounds familiar?"

"Cormac's stepfather. He arrested you. He shot—"

"Ricky," Danny finished the sentence. "Yeah, like, not super well,
no. Also, the shrinks all said I had retrograde amnesia. Because of wit-
nessing and abetting the murder, you know. And all those drugs." He
gave me a look—bashful, but unapologetic—maybe even a little proud.

"I see." *Retrograde amnesia. How fucking original.* I can't believe he
used the word abetting. Danny had slammed that bat into Andre's head,
and hard. The killer blow. I shredded my napkin, drove my nails into
my palm. "I want to talk about Andre."

"Andre . . ." Danny went blank.

"You know, the guy whose head got caved in like a dropped water-
melon at West Cypress Road Woods."

"Erin, you gotta know, I don't really remember Andre . . ."

"Cut it out, Danny. This 'I can't remember anything,' this puff of madness shit won't work on me. I know who you are. I need to know about Andre. For real."

"May I ask why? After all this time?" He drank his coffee.

"I'm writing an article. For *Inside Island.*"

"Ah shit," he said. "And here's me thinking you were being senti-mental."

I pulled up my sleeve to show the row of burns.

"I'm not going to unbutton my shirt in here so that we can view your pièce de résistance—but just so you know, you have a funny idea of sentimental," I said, just as the waitress arrived to refill us. She looked down at my arm, visibly startled.

"I feel bad about that." He leaned back against the booth, looking out at the traffic, giving me his right side, his best side by his reckon-ing. With a nose like a child, a chin you'd want to chuck, his profile might never go on a coin—but front on, he was a pin-up, made for *Tiger Beat* and *Seventeen.* But what I once liked about Danny—because I did once like him—aside from an absurdist humor that came out when he was unguarded, was that while he was too canny not to be aware of his own good looks, they were also loathsome to him. Once when we were watching *Grease* with his siblings (his dad turned it off halfway through because of its adult content), he was transfixed by the charac-ter Crater-Face. "Scars are fucking savage," he'd kept saying. Was this a warning? In hindsight, I think it was.

"I had problems. I think of you all the time, you know."

"Some kids lose their parents. Some kids are foster kids. Some kids take care of their parents when they're up on multiple homicide charges. Some kids deal with real adult shit."

"Like you and Ricky Hell?" Danny stared. I looked away first.

I had gone into our meeting determined to be professional and was pissed at myself for betraying emotion, for giving anything away to Danny. The fact was, I wasn't a professional. It took every fiber of self-control I had not to upturn the coffee onto him.

"Listen, you could write a book about what you *don't* know about my life," Danny insisted. "Things that I never told you . . . well." Was he dangling his backstory as bait? I wouldn't bite, despite being insanely curious about what he would come up with. I had long suspected things were not what they seemed at Casa Quinlan-Walsh.

"I'm, like, you know, really sorry about the past. Things never changed for me. I mean, feelings wise, I still care." He looked up, showing me the china blue of his eyes, the whites exposed. "You're, like, in my heart."

Like, sorry. I quietly set my cup down. If Danny was convinced he loved me and I could exploit it for the story, I would.

"But you could do something now, Danny. I know that you're no Satanist."

I willed tears into my eyes as he squeezed my hand. I could feel his pulse. Only skin separated us.

"Danny, I know nobody at West Cypress Road Woods was there to do anything that night except beer bongs and maybe Carole Jenkins."

Danny smiled pleasantly. He remained silent.

"The only person who maybe believed in that crap was Andre . . ."

Danny looked at me like my math teacher did when I'd finally solved a problem.

"I feel like Ricky was playing a trick on everybody."

"Ricky was a poser plain and simple," Danny scoffed. "That jacket was the only metal thing about him."

I smiled. I'd got him to admit that much.

Danny flicked his pickles onto a napkin, then crushed the napkin in his fist. There was cream cheese on his lip. "He was weak. This is all off the record, right?"

"Sure. And agreed. Did you know Andre was interviewed by Nassau County PD about that missing girl, Cathy Carver?"

"Yeah. They talked to me. Ricky too. Your dad's friend . . ."

"Ox?" I guessed. Detective John Kovlozky, otherwise known as Ox, was an old friend of RP's. We hadn't spoken in a long time. I made a mental note to look him up after this meeting.

"They interviewed all the senior guys who hung out at Waldbaum's parking lot." Danny signaled for another refill. I held my hand over my cup. He appraised the waitress with naked sexual interest, but I knew Danny—it was a performance. "Don't get me wrong, the dude was a freak. But I heard on the news the cops think whoever took Cathy Carver took the Weis kid and Scott . . . whatshisname? And by then Andre was a bag of bones in the ground, right?"

"If that's their theory, Andre would be ruled out, yes. But who knows really? The cops don't. They haven't solved the case."

"Official theories aside, was he a fag, you think? Do those types go for both?" Danny's tone was casual but he was testing me, stirring me in the same way he did the creamer and sugar in his coffee.

"I don't know. I mean, I'm no expert. I guess I just wondered if there was another reason for luring Andre to the woods that night? Like, did you or maybe Ricky believe he'd done something bad? I know you guys both had sisters at Cathy's school."

"Cormac too," Danny mused. "And Carole Jenkins. What about this—come to Freeport with me, I'll tell you everything."

I looked up, genuinely gobsmacked. Danny was aiming for shy, but I knew he was just being sly.

"The motel?"

"I need to fix this. *We* need to fix this."

"I can't. You can't. You have a wife and child. Not to mention you treated me like a human punching bag."

He shook his head. His eyes seemed glazed. He must still be on medication, I thought. "There's a sense of incompleteness about us. An unfinished story." His lips began to tremble with the emotion of his poetics. "Maybe if I knew what happened, you know, between you and Richard."

Richard even.

"Were you intimate?" His tone had become cold. This was a pissing competition and I was the fire hydrant.

I knew this switch well.

"Yep," I said, knocking back my coffee. "We certainly were. But you knew, right?"

Danny's face went blank and then he smiled. It was a phenomenon, that smile, but he still made me sick to my stomach.

"If we go to the motel, I'll spill. On or off the record."

The thing about Danny was that he always wanted to win. I didn't trust him, not emotionally, not psychologically, and certainly not physically.

"It's the motel or nothing."

"You know what," I said, leaning across the table. "I'll take nothing."

"Just keep in mind, guys won't be lining up for forever. Tick tock, you're on the clock. And you know, you could do with a hot meal or two and a baby wipe—you'd shame a hooker with that eye makeup."

That was Danny in one—tears of contrition and then a slap in the face. If I was a less fucked-up person, I probably would have been offended. Instead, I felt a rush of euphoria. My lips tingled and became fuller. I glowed. I was beautiful, incandescent with rage.

"Thanks for the tips. I mean, you make marriage and children seem so fulfilling."

"Maybe I could place a personal ad," I continued. "'Emotionally disturbed succubus seeks callow hottie for meaningless dalliance. Must worship Satan.' What do you think? Score myself a hubby that way?" I added.

"I think you win at Scrabble, but you're lonely. You reek of it." He leaned in as if he smelled something foul and popped a stick of gum in his mouth. "Everyone needs someone, Erin." Or multiple someones in Danny's case.

"Did you ever like me?" I asked him.

He shrugged himself into his coat and had the gall to lean in and kiss my cheek. He smelled of Armani and leather and money. "Does anyone like anyone, really? People just belong to each other," he said. "But yeah. I always liked them crazy." Then he gave an involuntary twitch or, very possibly, winked. He left a pile of singles and his business card, with the waitress staring at his retreating back.

It was the back of a quarterback, the back of a killer.

4

After I collected my car, I drove down Southport Avenue to Danny's family house, about five blocks from the boat storeroom. Bluebottle Way was a typical tree-lined cul-de-sac, consisting of "splanches," two-story homes that retained a ranch house exterior. I was amazed to note that the same BMW SUV that Pat Senior drove, with the personalized license plate LVTHLRD, was parked in the driveway. I parked on the road, squinting through the French windows of the living room and saw the silhouette of a woman sitting on a couch in front of a large flat screen TV. The hunch of her shoulders, the Roman hook of her nose, told me it was Danny's mom, Cindy.

In Southport, the houses were laid out identically with a few variations. The layout of Danny's house was an alternative version of my house, the Shelbyville to my Springfield.

According to Tolstoy, *All happy families are alike; every unhappy family is unhappy in its own way*, but there's a common denominator. My mom was husky, into aerobics, binge eating, wine, and Ambien. My father had never been home for Mom's frozen and nuked dinners and lived like a medieval ghoul, in the dark recesses of the den, occasionally emerging, drunken, in his Homer Simpson tighty-whities. Sloane family unhappiness was manifest—it was soaked into the carpet and foundations of our house.

While the Quinlan-Walshes were rich and as Catholic as the Kennedys, their misery was told in small cues. The first time I was at their house for dinner (they called it *supper*), Danny's dad came home to the set the table, homemade lasagna steaming up his heavy black spectacles with their accountant frames. But Danny's dad wasn't an accountant. Dr. Quinlan-Walsh was a local physician—his boating business was a hobby, an earner on the side to his family practice. They had six kids (the eldest two adopted, the third a foster child, the rest biological). I noted Danny's mom's Marshalls pleather bag on the counter, his father's knock-off Casio watch. So, despite all their riches, Dr. Quinlan-Walsh, AKA Big Pat, was stingy. They wore no-brand sneakers, replica jeans and backpacks, which in Southport was a cardinal sin. And speaking of sin, you couldn't sit down anywhere without a Child of Prague simpering at you or the Virgin Mary casting down a pissed, prayerful look. Except of course, in Danny's bedroom, which was painted black and had matching satin sheets. "The devil sleeps in satin," his mother said once. "The devil's a smart dude," Danny replied.

His mom (*Please call me Cindy*) was unfashionably dressed. I spotted that underneath the superficial differences—her cinched floral dress and badly applied makeup, which covered acne scars, the pained smile permanently residing on her face—that our mothers were alike. After all, controlled despair was on trend with Southport moms—and the common denominator was Southport dads, to varying degrees.

Their unhappiness was told in their quasi loving exchanges recited with all the sincerity and enthusiasm of hostages reading a ransom letter. The chattering among the children that was silenced with a razor-sharp look from Dr. Quinlan-Walsh. The eldest three kids, named after biblical characters, fought endlessly. The fourth child's autistic rocking made me so anxious I chewed my nails and received a rebuke from Danny; a swift kick under the table. An infant and toddler clung to Cindy constantly, wheedling and whining, smelling of sour milk and Fruit Roll-Ups.

As the family started eating, Big Pat interrupted.

"Aren't we forgetting something? Let us give thanks," he intoned.

I swigged some milk and tentatively took Big Pat's unfamiliar fleshy, hairy knuckled hand and Danny's familiar one, noting each Walsh man had a ring—Danny's was a silver skull ring that I'd gotten him for his birthday; Pat's was a gold wedding band. We hung our heads down like evangelists at a prayer meeting. Even if I couldn't eat, I could do Catholic. I faintly recalled I was one.

"Bless us thy lord for these thy gifts . . ." As he spoke, I felt Big Pat's finger rubbing the inside of my palm, in a way that all girls understand is code for creep. *I can't touch you intimately*, the finger says, *but I want to. I'm imagining this is your pussy*. The finger rubbed and rubbed.

When we were getting along, Danny and I had played a game called "How much more could it suck?" The scenarios were mostly funny and always obscene, inserting historical and popular figures into the humiliation of the everyday—in Danny's case, masturbating to Candace Cameron when *Full House* was on and being caught by his mother was made all the suckier when Nancy Reagan and Celine Dion came in and made him sing "The Star-Spangled Banner." In French. My father getting drunk and crashing the car into my bike and then vomiting all over Christmas dinner was made worse when the New Kids on the Block came over, with a film crew. And had a gangbang with my whole family.

Danny whispered a particularly obscene scenario into my ear, and I sprayed out milk in a fine mist all over my flavorless, steamed-in-a-bag vegetables. Little Pat guffawed, Cindy gasped, and Big Pat squeezed my hand like a python.

"We are about to receive. Thank you, Christ Our Lord."

"Amen."

Underneath Big Pat's glasses, I saw eyes that were nothing like Danny's; the color of unshelled macadamia nuts, lusterless and brown, round as an owl's, and equally predatory. A cross glinted in the dark bed of his chest hair.

Cindy eventually excused us and we went up to Danny's room for "homework."

"Door open," Big Pat bellowed.

Danny's finger went up and the lock went on.

He paced the dimensions of the room, looking fit to punch holes in the wall, but he calmed himself down by taking out a bowl of weed and a pipe.

"Was my dad weird to you just now?" His tone was chilly; I noted his hands were clenched into balled fists.

"No. He just touched my hand," I said. I was pacifying him, but I felt a little shocked by the hand-molesting incident.

I sat on Danny's bed, a velour tiger-patterned bedspread covering it. He had an adult's ensemble, complete with side tables. I looked in the curved mirror above his bed. My hair was still good. I'd teased it and sprayed it so it stood up over my bangs on one side. My makeup was toned down for the family: eyeliner, blusher, lip gloss. I had put my Megadeth T-shirt on inside out so it wouldn't upset his mom (Danny's request). Despite sassing her, he was a Catholic boy after all.

"All that Christian shit just makes me hurl. I'm just happy I'm adopted, you know," he said, as he passed the pipe to me.

The AC hummed and the incense was lit. It was sage and, comingling with the weed, it created a ham-like aroma.

"Blow it out the window," Danny coached me. "They couldn't have a baby. They got me, Little Pat, and Joshua, and then started popping them out."

"Like Pringles?" I laughed, already blazed. "That doesn't make sense."

Danny didn't laugh. He flopped back on his tiger bedspread. He wasn't smiling. I put my hand on his stomach. His belly. His abs would be more accurate. This was the body of a teenager. He didn't go carb free or drink protein drinks. He lifted barbells—but his muscle was lean, carved out of surfing, skating, and his unknown genetic bounty. His mouth was, well, almost slutty for a boy—full, pink, and curling with possibility.

On the other hand, I had draped my newfound curves in cords and jeans, big T-shirts, and long hair. In retrospect, I was beautiful in that I was young; but nothing special to behold, not like Danny.

"Once you pop, you know? She couldn't stop . . . popping."

He held my wrists too tightly.

"Did you wash your hands?" he asked. In addition to a problem with containing his anger, Danny also had undiagnosed and certainly un-treated OCD. The grubbiness of my house, the rotaviruses that lived in our towels, the filthy soles of my feet could inspire hour-long funks and lengthy lectures, and usually ended in scalding showers and apologies.

"Yes . . ." I groaned.

"Sorry. I just hate the way you *touch* everything."

At first dope, then acid, smoothed the jagged edges of his OCD. I think that's why he liked drugs. And I liked him better high. But the comedowns came with writing on his skin, biblical condemnations, germs you could literally see. I liked Danny best undressed; the silk of his skin, sex and the cinnamon of his breath (Big Red gum, cigarettes), his semipermanent hard-on, the fact that he paid attention to me, not in a healthy way, no—but with the vigilance of a lion on the Serengeti guarding a gazelle's carcass.

Why did Danny, a kind of Golden God who had come down from Mount Apollo, choose to fraternize with me? Now I knew it was because of his predilections, rather than any notion of romantic love.

Because what started out as games like "How much more could it suck?" turned into a love of ropes and an understanding of knots that tran-scended the maritime, and we quickly escalated from traditional teenage fumbling into what I now understand to be hard limit sadomasochism. The introduction of the unimaginatively named "Light my fire" game, featuring lighters on the skin, and the "Take my breath away" game, auto-erotic asphyxiation, were prime examples of where he was headed, where *we* were headed. In the beginning, we were just two red-blooded Roman Catholic metalhead misfits doing things we'd seen on late-night TV. But Danny's appetite for pleasure was beginning to be rewired, new neural pathways informed and amused by my physical pain and my subjugation. As he lit a fire under my feet, I thought this must be what it feels like when you're being burned at the stake. Sometimes Danny would stare at me for what seemed like hours, staring into my eyes, asking things like "What are you thinking?" "Penny for your thoughts?" "Do you need me?" Sometimes this would turn into recrimination. Sometimes it would turn into a burning, ugly thing—very literally. People might think, for all my coldness, that I am tough, that I *was* tough. I was still a teenage girl. Once he slapped me, and more than once he used fists on me; once or twice, a car lighter. We called them smileys. And then he *really* hurt me.

In the beginning, I liked our games and I liked to play with him equally. In fact, I was beginning to understand the heady power that my sexuality engendered, without understanding the consequences. It was like owning a Ferrari but having no real idea how to drive it. All I knew was that I could incite in him a frenzy of feeling, fulfill a need for fetish that seemed to inspire a kind of unparalleled devotion. I didn't realize that I was careening straight into a head-on collision.

Because, despite all the sexual Twister, epic make-out rashes, crotch burn, and weird sadomasochistic games, Danny was a virgin, as was I. He was holding out on me. He wanted me to love him and thought he could force that love. And I was waiting for him to weaken. I was a furious, reluctant, and wrathful virgin. Which is why, he said, Ricky Hell became interested in me. And that is another story altogether.

———

I killed the car engine and was deciding whether to try to talk to Cindy Quinlan-Walsh when a sporty red Kia pulled up to the driveway. I knew who the driver was straight away. Gina, Danny's wife, was sans toddler and, like me, petite—5'3, 5'4 max. Unlike me, even dressed in yoga pants and a Champion sweatshirt, she was effortlessly chic. Gina caught my eye as she pulled into the driveway and parked. She got out and strode over to me, leaning into the driver's window with a brittle air-hostess smile—her makeup perfect. I couldn't see her eyes clearly through her tinted Chanel sunglasses. She was wearing discreetly expensive jewelry; small diamond studs, a tennis bracelet, and on her olive décolletage sat the letter "G" in white gold. Her naturally thick black hair had been professionally blow-dried. I wondered where their progeny was kept— maybe inside, with zombie Grandma Cindy.

"Like, maybe I have the wrong house," I brayed in an exaggerated Long Island brogue.

"What number are you looking for?" Her voice was surprisingly warm, like a spiced rum.

"My friend Cassie lives at 1125?" I made sure to inflect up.

"This is 1125," she said pleasantly, but her mouth drooped.

"The Glass residence? Is this Bottleneck Way?"

"Bluebottle," she amended. Something lifted in her expression. Then I realized: she was an old hand at this, the drive-by-mistress encounter. She was back from yoga or maybe even Pilates, high on adrenaline, ready to rumble.

"I'm sorry, wrong place." I guffawed. Gina was so beautiful, she'd turned me into a clowning teenage boy. She was gracious though, accustomed to the idiocy her beauty provoked.

"That's okay. Happens more than you think." She smiled at me, her wide photogenic face suddenly lighting up in a perfect smile, her teeth whitened just like Danny's.

No wonder Pat was so pissed at his brother—Danny was probably fucking around on a *Sports Illustrated* version of Snow White on his lunch hour. But why, I wondered? He was intensely loyal to me, but had been constantly convinced I was cheating on him. Jealousy, born of self-hate. Now he was enacting that self-hate, lost in a parade of women who would sublimate his loneliness and bad memories. Or maybe it was because Gina wouldn't play Danny's games.

I realized that Danny still liked me for what he'd originally responded to: I saw through to his wicked core. He didn't have to pretend with me. Because I was a little bit bad, too.

It's fall, I thought. *It's overcast. Why are you wearing sunglasses, Gina? Run*, I wanted to say. *Take that kid and run.*

"I'm really sorry," I said. I meant it.

"No problem. Good luck finding your friend."

Inside, Cindy moved to the glass of the French window, and for a second I was sure that she looked out at me in recognition.

5

I pulled into my driveway and my aging cat, Mister, ran from the house, trotting up to the car like a dog; flicking her tail rather than wagging. She'd been a rescue kitten who I presumed was male. By the time I took her to the vet for a check-up and discovered she was in fact female, the name Mister had stuck.

Our Oceanside Avenue house was another split-level bungalow which had remained completely unchanged since we'd moved in at the icy tail end of January 1994. The exterior of the house was the faded rust color blood makes after a few days on the sidewalk. The mailbox was like the yard: overflowing and perched on its decomposed hinge precariously. A few pizza parlor and nail salon flyers spilled out; leaves clotted the gutters. Spiderwebs had colonized the wrought-iron balustrades. I made a weak promise to myself to rake the leaves and call someone for the gutters. I collected the mail—a *Reader's Digest*, a few bills, and a gun mag that my dad subscribed to and which I read in the bathroom.

I took off my day clothes and dressed in my mom's coffee-stained ice-blue chenille robe; a relic from '93. It still smelled of fabric softener, Chips Ahoy cookies, and her perfume, Sunflowers. I had washed it since then, but the smells lingered. Wrapping myself up in her robe was like hugging her ghost. I cut up chicken livers for Mister, turning on the radio for company. Early AC/DC growled away in the background, which I took to be another omen. I hadn't listened to them since 1994.

I ate some antacids and sat down with Dad's Rangers mug and my seaside notebook. I also had on his old Rangers sweatshirt. The only sport he liked was ice hockey—it had just enough violence to keep him interested. I fired up my laptop at the water-stained oak table while I waited for the teapot to boil. Yummy Relaxer teabags contained traces of lavender, mint, cinnamon, and a natural sedative herb, and the packet depicted a family of teddy bears in patchwork smocks sitting at a kitchen table. From experience, coming down and hungover, the tea was the equivalent of pissing on a house fire—but it tasted okay and I needed all the help I could get with the twilight hallucinations.

I looked at the hot drink in front of me, knowing what this would turn into: while I had stopped taking illegal drugs, I ate prescription drugs like candy. While I told myself I was a social smoker and drinker, I hadn't been in a social situation for quite some time and I was managing to smoke and drink just fine. Things had escalated since moving into Oceanside Avenue; I could admit that. I wasn't quite at RP Sloane levels, but I was half past normal and a quarter to stupefied most days.

Know thyself, someone wise once said. And then a teenage boy quoted it back to me. But then he said something about how the knowing ultimately didn't help that much because you couldn't ever really help yourself. My dad's refrain to me was "You better wise up," and my answer became "Why?" And what he said to me, an unwitting teenage existentialist, was classic RP: "Because not knowing kills ya faster. What would you prefer?"

The fluorescents buzzed and flickered as I retrieved a very expensive vintage Murano glass, a wedding gift to my parents all the way from Italy, and filled the glass up with whisky. I picked up the phone and dialed Ox's cell. I left a brief message with a lump in my throat. It wasn't until I heard his brusque vocal prompt that I realized I missed him.

Ox's build was not the reason he was called Ox. He was solid physically—he ate a steady diet of hot dogs, cheeseburgers, and 7-Eleven

Big Gulps, but hadn't had as much as a cold in twenty years. Unlike RP, who was wildly unpatriotic and used his bad back to escape the draft, Ox had been to Vietnam, and would have gone to Iraq, had he not injured his hip and leg coming off his motorcycle while on duty. He had pins and a plate and sometimes dragged his leg, but he was a machine built on service to country, to the public. I'm sure he was in chronic pain, but he had never missed a day of work—maybe it's because he didn't drink. And although I wasn't exactly a flag waver, or even a very good citizen, part of me respected this unfussy sense of virtue—with Ox things were black and white, right and wrong, but I had lived in the gray area for so long.

I returned to the *Child's Play* true crime video on YouTube; the screen flickered and warped. It had the low res look and feel of the nineties, as if it had been recorded onto a VCR and uploaded recently. The reporter's Vincent Price–style narration would have been funny if it wasn't all so horrifying to me:

> *It was just a normal afternoon for Roosevelt High students Danny Quinlan-Walsh, Carole Jenkins, and Cormac O'Malley—meeting up in a local Wendy's parking lot to score tabs of acid from friend and dealer, Richard Juan Hernandez. Richard was known to the Southport stoner kids as Ricky Hell. A high school dropout, eighteen-year-old Hell was also a known misfit and a notorious Satanist. The group would regularly indulge in sex, drugs, and devil worship in the West Cypress Road Woods under his evil tutelage. And tonight was Halloween: Ricky Hell had big plans for his class.*
>
> *Andre Villiers, also eighteen, was known to have drug, emotional, and learning problems. The oversized senior was also heavily influenced by Hell—learning occult practices and sacrificing several small animals to Satan in the same woods.*

The narrator picked up a long branch and examined it, before he returned to his monologue. All the saliva dried up in my mouth. As I'd said to Danny, I'd never witnessed any of this small animal sacrifice; I'd never seen anything other than an upside-down cross scrawled in the dirt with a stick, a pentagram necklace or devil's horns made in tribute to bitchin' music.

Tonight, the sacrifice was to be human. Villiers was initiated into a fire circle, where the kids took magic mushrooms and LSD, mixing them with amphetamines. Police believed that the amphetamines were laced with PCP.

Former quarterback, Danny Quinlan-Walsh, a seventeen-year-old high school junior at the time of the crime, watched as Hell attacked Villiers with "superhuman strength" and then produced an aluminum bat for Quinlan-Walsh to finish the job on the 6'3, 220-pound teen. Hell struck Villiers first; Cormac O'Malley and Carole Jenkins, both just sixteen years old, ran and allegedly hid in the woods. They were later discredited as witnesses after Cormac O'Malley agreed that Ricky Hell "changed shape" or "shapeshifted" and Carole Jenkins' memories of the night proved too fractured to be credible. O'Malley called his stepfather, a local police officer named Steve Shearer, from a nearby payphone and allegedly returned to the scene to render medical aid to Andre.

The next bit of footage showed Andre Villiers' school photo—the narrator had called him oversized and he wasn't kidding. Andre was huge and very blond, almost like a Viking. When I put aside my revulsion he was, objectively speaking, almost a handsome dude. In another lifetime, Andre would have cleaned up on the lady front. But somehow the ladies did not like Andre. And given how easily his hands went around my neck, I'm not sure he liked the ladies all that much either.

Three blows, three kids; six in total, the number of the beast.

Imagine how much the media loved that shit.

The camera panned to a cawing crow.

There were no other witnesses except the woods.

I moved the cursor to pause.

I headed into the bathroom, ignoring Mister's outraged cries, shutting the door behind me as I undressed and hung up my robe. I stepped inside the shower, letting the hot water run so that it was scalding as I loofahed away the day, Danny Quinlan-Walsh, the memories that arose from our meeting—a collage of wincing body memories and words that I had long forgotten, words I had not been called, nor had I used myself, since.

The shower was normally where I felt calmer and contained, but today I began to tremble as the scalding water turned cold momentarily. It was a shock, and it enraged me. "Fuck!" I screamed aloud. I nearly put my fist through the glass, but instead began to howl. I sobbed as I scrubbed my meeting with Danny off me. I'd nearly forgotten how much I'd let him break me.

The venom in his tone when he used the name Richard, the mention of the Freeport Motel—where I held my secret liaisons with Ricky. Mental images of Ricky I had long pushed away: the hole in his cheek, his ruptured heart. The closed casket funeral I was not allowed to attend. The grief that had never formally commenced; had never officially ended.

I stood in front of the mirror with strip lighting that belonged to old Hollywood, looking at my reflection in the glass through the condensation. It reminded me of a subzero morning in February, when Ricky Hell drew *R 4 E* in the foggy windshield and winked at me, laying his head in my lap with a sigh.

I had loved someone once. Incredible: it was such a foreign statement to me now; it wouldn't translate into my current vocabulary. Anything beyond temporary relief, the most rudimentary physical needs being met, seemed to be inconceivable. I never looked at myself undressed or let anyone else look for that matter; I was a turtleneck and no pants in the bedroom kind of gal. I had a special swimsuit for ladies who were modest. Except I wasn't all that modest; it was just that my body told stories. All up my arms, like the Count of Monte Cristo's cell wall, the faint white scars of my imprisonment. My survival. But if I know anything about life, it doesn't divide us into victims, survivors, and perpetrators—we're all those things, all at once. I survived life so far, but it would win in the end.

My father always said it was lucky I took after my mom physically—I had the same green-gray eyes, wide nose, full lips. I had my father's jutting chin, however; a reminder of my stubbornness and all his bad habits.

RP never got a hangover when he drank whisky—leave the wine to the Italians, he said. I stuck with whisky and my mom's olive oil beauty regimen every night, I poured warm olive oil into my scalp, onto my face. My mom's skin at forty was creamy and thick, the color of burnt caramel. I know Shelly would have grown up to look just like her. She was the darker sister—black-eyed, curly-haired; a mermaid of a girl who lived for the water.

I lost my mom, Shelly, and then Ricky in the space of a year, so I spent a lot of time trying to conjure ghosts. There was an urban legend at my old school, called "Bloody Mary": you said the Virgin's name three times and she appeared.

I recreated the *R 4 E* in a heart on the steamy mirror.

Ricky, I said into my reflection. Ricky Hell, Ricky Hell, Ricky Hell. Nothing.

I cleared the condensation away.

6

The doorbell rang and I answered it, dressed in my robe.

"Ms. Erin Sloane. Express delivery." I nodded at the man through the locked screen door. He held an electronic tablet and a brown paper package with a sticker bearing the imprint AbeBooks. It was the book that Denise had promised to send.

"Sign."

I signed for it, holding my robe closed, conscious of my noxious whisky and cigarette breath. I took the package into the kitchen. Carole Jenkins' true crime book, *Dancing with the Devil*. The cover featured a teenage girl in a prairie frock with a survivor's grimace, a pin-up or a saint; either way, she sat in a position of supplication. I recognized that smirk—imagine a slutty Jennie Garth from *Beverly Hills, 90210* gone Christian. The first few lines of emotionally flat reportage droned and grated—it was a damsel in distress narrative. Chapters one and two seemed to mainly focus on Carole's early life—there was a glossy insert in the middle, with pictures of Carole, a copy of the original police statement, a few courtroom snaps. Carole Jenkins, who regularly put her fist in her mouth as a party trick; who watched a boy's brains get battered in and left her boyfriend at the crime scene, was born again after the trial in some tent at a church revival.

It was so easy to be found these days—and it seemed so many people wanted to be. They were eager to reconnect with old friends and classmates; with who they used to be. I used the *Inside Island* Facebook account to cyberstalk people's profiles and created aliases when I needed to use online forums. When people googled me, they'd find my byline—no picture.

Carole hadn't taken many measures to conceal her identity—she was now Carole Ruffalo, and her husband, the CEO of a brokerage for Ruffalo Realty, had an open profile too. She'd reinvented herself as a much fuller Florida blonde—but still very lean, now very tan, with plumper lips, eyelash extensions, boob job, lots of facial fillers. While she looked corporate, sophisticated in many of the images, her status updates—*Love Life write now!! Date nite with my man!!!! Why are ppl so inconsiderate GRRR*—were classless, penetratingly passive aggressive, and borderline illiterate. She'd clearly employed a ghostwriter for *Dancing with the Devil*.

I googled Carole's old flame, Cormac O'Malley. There were several Irish men of that name, two famous: a footballer, a folk musician. There were a handful on Facebook, none who looked like Cormac; an electrician from Cork; a Boston theater producer, wrong build, wrong age. Cormac O'Malley may not have a social media presence, but he would have a digital footprint—it would just be harder to trace.

Then I found an online résumé to an expired user profile on Jobhub Australia for a Michael Cormac O'Malley. I clicked on the Word doc and scanned it: his birthdate read 3/17/1978. I vaguely remembered Australians put dates around the wrong way. He was a Pisces then. The name was virtually the same. The birthdate sounded about right; he, Carole, and I were all born in 1978. Birthplace County Meath, Ireland. According to his résumé, he'd been in several schools in Australia, Ireland, and Canada. He listed conversational French as a hobby. He claimed he went to Belmont High, which was very close to Roosevelt. His last job, according to the résumé, was as a graphic designer at the University of Melbourne, Australia, in 2006.

I thought back to Cormac from freshman year. The first time I saw him was at an easel; he was drawing a very metal kind of illustration of a half woman, half panther with exaggerated breasts. I thought he was a very pretty girl until I heard him speak. His accent was nothing like

Crocodile Dundee or the incomprehensible Irish brogues I'd heard at Benny's, a cop dive bar that was my father's second home. His accent sounded nearly American but with a lilt; the musicality and intonation much like the way they spoke in the old Hollywood movies my mom liked. Maybe he'd learned American through movies and TV—or maybe all European people spoke like that. All I knew was the island.

It was all adding up. I saved the Word doc on my desktop. Then I skim-read Carole's banal observations and jumped to chapter three, her account of the murder:

> When I arrived at 6:30 p.m., Ricky, Danny, Andre, and Joe were at Wendy's but had gotten kicked out and they were hanging around the front entrance. They had a fight going on with the manager at Wendy's because Ricky used to work there, but got fired because he was tampering with the food and was suspected of stealing money. Some people said he was fired because he painted a pentagram in blood in the bathroom. Danny told me that Ricky once drew a pentagram with his girl-friend's menstrual blood to give it more power.

I laughed aloud and then remembered Ricky's lack of aversion to my menses. A hot tug of pride was met by a cold shower of jealousy.

> Ricky and his friends all listened to heavy metal music. Andre carried *The Satanic Bible* everywhere. He was the first to wor-ship Satan, but after the summer of 1993, Ricky said he was Satan himself. At first, I didn't believe him. I thought that Ricky was just trying to scare people and everyone said that it was because he dealt weed that he spread rumors, so that no one would try and turn him in to the cops.

This was probably the most insightful statement in the entire book. I also noted Carole was distancing herself from the gang: *Ricky and his friends*, even though she was in tight with us—after all, the first time

I met Ricky, she was sitting on Ricky's knee, handfeeding him onion rings. I kept reading.

> When I got into the car, Cormac gave me a beer and Danny passed around a joint. We listened to music and I smoked grass with them. We drove from the parking lot to the woods as it was getting dark. I think it was 6:06 p.m. I remember looking at the radio in the truck and thinking that was weird. We were there for several hours and I think it was around 10 p.m. when they all took LSD and did lines of what I thought was speed, but I think may have been PCP. Cormac gave me a few magic mushrooms.

No LSD for Carole thank you very much!

> I asked Cormac to open the door because the car was noisy and smelled like marijuana and I was nauseous. I went as far away from the car as I could and threw up.
>
> I turned when I heard a loud crack.
>
> I think that Andre was struck on the head with an object that looked like a bat and then he must have dropped, even though I did not witness that. I saw that there was a large pool of blood on the ground. I think that Andre had released his bowels because I could smell a bad smell. I think the person who hit him on the head was Ricky Hell, because the person I saw out of the corner of my eye was very tall and dark.
>
> All I could hear was "God is dead, Satan lives; let it rain down."
>
> I remember Ricky's arm was raised and, under the light of the full moon, I could see he was holding an aluminum baseball bat. It caught the light. His eyes were completely black. All the boys were there, I don't know who was hitting him, but it seemed like Danny and Ricky were screaming "Hail Satan, pray for us, pray for Satan" and things of that nature. It was so dark in the woods and because of the mushrooms I got so lost.

I thought about one of Ricky's favorite poets, Dante Alighieri and how he had memorized parts of the *Inferno*, in Italian, no less. One night he recited Canto I, "The Dark Wood of Error" to me on a damp mattress in a cold van, in both English and Italian, which might indicate that he was both a brainiac and a poseur:

> *Mid way in our life's journey, I went astray from the*
> *straight road and found myself alone in a dark wood*
> *What wood that was! I never saw so drear! So rank, so*
> *dark, so arduous a wilderness, its very memory gave*
> *shape to fear.*

I mean, talk about foreshadowing.

At first, I thought it was Danny who carried me out of the woods, but my church group says that it was God himself. And when I think of Ricky's black eyes, I realize that they are right. Because he, Ricky Hell, was the devil himself.

I think Ricky was following me, because I heard footsteps, but they stopped when I reached the road. Cormac was running behind me and he wanted to get to the payphone. I wanted to get away from him. He had blood on him and he was acting crazy, saying Ricky had turned into a crow. I reached the road and a car stopped and they helped me. I told them that my boyfriend and I had a fight and I needed to go home. I did not go to the police, because I was high and I was afraid.

Carole went on:

And there was another thing. Danny says that the crime was planned by Ricky before we went to the Spot, but I didn't know that. I never would have gone with the boys if I'd known. I'm not even sure that Danny is remembering that right.

I did not say this in the police report, because I couldn't be sure if it happened at all because I'd been so high, or because I was not sure if what he was trying to do was rape, but I think before Ricky turned on Andre, Andre had his pants down next to me in the car, his hands around my neck, trying to force me into a sex act. I accidentally hit Andre. I told my boyfriend Cormac, and left the car, to be sick. I think that's why Ricky attacked him, but I can't really be sure. The boys were just under his spell, as I had been, that's for sure.

I set the book down. Carole had tailored the story to meet the audience's insatiable appetite for Satanic mumbo jumbo—and to garner pity. Despite knowing this was deeply manipulative, I felt a distinctive and uncomfortable pinch of sympathy. I thought of Dante's dark woods again; the half-life of memories of what did or didn't happen in them. At the time Carole wrote *Dancing with the Devil* she lived with the trauma of a murdered boy who, moments before his grisly murder, had his pants undone and his hands around her throat. The act of remembering, or to try and remember, was to relive fear itself. I knew that. And the book would have been tough to write, even if it was total bullshit.

I instantly shook off my sympathy—Jesus, Carole was good. I mean, I had started to feel sorry for her. In Carole's rendition of "that night," Ricky was a cult leader and a premeditated murderer—a predator even. She made her boyfriend a blood-soaked hallucinating lunatic. One of the few details that I'd learned about the trial was that it was never suggested that Cormac had participated in Andre's murder—in fact his testimony had been temporarily halted because Cormac was rushed to the hospital with a migraine that landed him in the ICU: the kid had a mini-stroke from the stress.

While I didn't get the impression that Carole was (subtly) indicting Cormac in her version of the attack on Andre, she was implanting a seed of doubt—motive which had never been introduced in the formerly motiveless murder. I believed Carole that Andre assaulted her, but I knew Ricky and Danny would never have attacked Andre because of Carole, simply because it was the prevailing attitude of the time that if you weren't someone's exclusive girl, you were fair game. You didn't complain if you were attacked after you'd behaved provocatively, or if you'd gotten wasted. I knew not to tell anyone about what Andre had done to me, simply because I'd been stupid enough to be alone with him. Sick and sad, but true. And Carole and Cormac had dated for all of six months and it didn't seem like they were especially close. After all, Carole hopped in a stranger's car, abandoning Cormac at the scene of a satanic teen murder without batting a Revlon-covered lash.

I saw Carole's mouth form the words like a silent movie star, "Let's motor." Butter wouldn't melt in her mouth. Note also the hysteria— fainting Carole, the Dairy Queen, had left the scene, dizzy and nauseated from all the pot smoke and shrooms. Let it be on the record here: Carole was literally known as the Bong Queen in our sophomore year. Despite her stature, she could smoke and drink every boy under the table.

Really the only person who got off easy in *Dancing with the Devil* besides Carole herself was Danny Quinlan-Walsh. He may even have carried her out of the woods, like a teenage Jesus.

It was all an elaborate, fantastical lie with one truth written in (Andre)—because I believed that. It was the only part of the story I did. But one small detail confirmed her deceit. It was minor, but it mattered: Danny's truck had a ghetto sound system he had bought himself and he adored. It had been removed by his dad as a punishment for flunking his junior year. In another stroke of misfortune, a more modest car radio he'd borrowed had been stolen the week before in Freeport. Unless he'd got a replacement that day, they must have been using a boom box to listen to music that night. There was no way to tell the time in the car. Please, 6:06 p.m.? Give me a fucking break.

I drew a line under Carole Jenkins' name. LIAR.

My stomach was churning, so I chugged the remnants of the whisky in the glass, somewhat enjoying the esophageal burn. I heated up a tin of vegetable soup and toasted some freezer-burned gluten-free bread. I managed to eat a quarter of it at the kitchen bench and then topped up the whisky.

I thought about the survivors from the Southport crime: Danny, very much alive and malingering, continuing to lie; Carole, a Floridian real estate agent, skilled at lying too. Both were inclined to narcissism and were driven by self-interest. Cormac was perhaps somebody like me; someone who did not want to be found. If I smoked him out of his hiding place, all the way across the oceans that separated us, would he be the conscience of the Southport Three? Stranger things had happened.

7

Even though I was technically a crime writer, I was not a true crime aficionado by any means. I never understood the ghouls and ambulance chasers who traded body pics like baseball cards, dealt out grisly death details, and theorized airily about rape and homicide in online threads—in fact, they incensed me. It wasn't all that ironic that, as a survivor of crime, I stayed in its vicinity. The way I saw it, crime was my turf. I was here first, even though I'd never asked to be.

In anticipation of writing my last *Inside Island* piece on the Bethpage baby beauty pageant scandal, I had stumbled upon a virtual water cooler for victims of crime, survivors, and friends of the deceased: a site called "True Crime Happened to Me." The forum attracted some creeps and lurkers, but mainly it was the murder-curious; people passively affected by crimes in their area and some, more intimately involved, who blogged and commented. Any which way, it was a minefield of links and leads for a professional gravedigger like me, now known as EerieIsland78.

I thought about Denise's initial inference about Andre's involvement with Cathy Carver and how police had quickly dismissed that line of inquiry. Obviously, the police wouldn't tell the media why they were treating the missing kids as victims of the same perpetrator, but, given that Jason Weis and Trey Scott had been found buried in shallow graves not even three feet under on Jones Beach, a serial killer was most likely.

Cathy Carver's disappearance was legendary on the island—given she was a sweet blonde photogenic child, who lived on the water, so I expected numerous forums on her. I waded through many tribute posts and grief threads that had names like "Angel Wings"; with amateur artwork of Cathy with said wings; people had even made karaoke-style tribute videos. The first thought that occurred to me was that there was an element of fandom about these posters. It was fucking creepy. There was a lot less info and artwork of the boys; Jason Weis had lived on Beach Road. There was a picture of him, a smiling geeky-looking kid with a Mets cap and too-big front teeth. There was a very blurry image of Trey Scott, formerly known as Kim Lee, a small, grave-looking Korean-American boy. His house was not far from my old house on Helen Lane.

Some of the forum users were amateur sleuths who bandied around theories—dissecting the police's pet theories, the dribs and drabs of information that they had released to the public—some of the posters had salient points. Users speculated as to why Cathy had been taken by the same abductor as Jason and Trey—one user riffed on the kids being only children, shy and computer savvy, positing an early internet game as the common denominator.

Nassau County PD had set up a taskforce called Operation Lighthouse at the time. Detective Captain Robert Dolmer, who headed the unit, had since retired. The Police Commissioner, Bernard Sullivan, who had been heavily criticized at the time for delays, obfuscation, and lack of results in other unsolved cases, had also retired.

The crimes were featured on the Nassau County Crime Stoppers homepage, and there was a hotline for tips. I knew they would be inundated with everything from nosey neighbors to vengeful exes—so unless I had a lead, I'd bet anything my calls and emails about a cold case would go into the slush pile. I decided to hold off until I had a contact.

Unsurprisingly, there were numerous threads about the Andre Villiers murder—like Denise had said, it was custom-made for the media. There was even a forum called SP3: "SP3—three criminals, three kids—coincidence???!!! Three plus three is six!!!" Clicking into the thread was like descending into a rabbit hole of sub threads, documentary links, articles, online interviews—lots of pictures of Danny then and a few now, snapped outside the marina, looking charming, a middle finger raised. There were a few Ricky Hell related threads—all bullshit Satanism discussions. Another dedicated to contemporary ghost sightings of both Hell and Villiers in the West Cypress Road Woods. Then a thread called "Best Friends with the Victim" penned by a user called Seth75, who described himself as an ex-Roosevelt High student. The post was about four years old.

> **Seth75:**
> Andre was kind of my best friend. We went to the same grade school, junior high, and high school. We first smoked weed together.
>
> We used to go shooting. He was, like, scared of nothing. He was cool before he fell into the metal scene in Sophomore year. I told him to be careful man. I don't know, I didn't like those kids. Ricky Hell was bad news and Danny Quinlan-Walsh was a ticking time bomb.

Didn't I know it? It occurred to me I knew the thread's author. He was Seth Greene; I'd bet money on it. Seth was in a few remedial classes, as was Andre; I think Seth had ADHD. He dressed like a duck hunter and collected gun mags. Andre seemed irritated by Seth, though Seth's Ritalin prescription bought him an occasional invite to the metal kids' soirees. I recalled an evening at the woods where Seth was so out of it, Andre stole his wallet, spent the money in there on beer, and later he threw Seth's ID in the Res. Best friends indeed.

> **TrueCrime85:**
> Sorry about your friend. Was the Satan stuff real? Or were they all posing? I heard it was something the press made up cause the kids were alternative.

Seth75:

It was real. I think Andre's folks are the reason Andre
got into it. They were Jehovah's Witnesses or something
and they treated him bad. They're dead now, but they
never stood up for him when the press was saying all that
shit about him. He had all these books on black magic,
Anton LaVey, and *The Satanic Bible*. I even seen him put
squirrel blood on his mouth and chest and say this prayer
backward. I also saw him get possessed one Fourth of July,
I never seen anything like it before or since, he started
talking deep and growling. Ricky was into it too, but he
wasn't the ringleader.

The content of this thread was pretty much as I expected: urban
legend building, smoke blowing, wild rumors. I mean, squirrel blood
demon possession, talking backward? Those nights in the woods were
all beer bongs, psychedelics, and confused, semi-consensual sex in uncomfortable places. Andre did have a notebook that he lugged around;
he drew pentagrams and naked women in it. I faintly recalled he had a
copy of *The Satanic Bible*—but, as I said to Danny, no one took it or
Andre all that seriously. I had known Andre's parents were older and
Jehovah's Witnesses; now it appears they were deceased. I marked it
down next to item #4: Andre's family—parents dead? Living relatives?
   Then another poster.

Murderbabe66:

Yeah sorry man. I went to Belmont and used to hang in
the Res—didn't know Andre mega well, but I used to get
weed from him. All the kids said Andre's leather jacket had
a chalk X on it for a week before he died: fucking creepy!!
Like he was marked for death. Cormac had a little sister
who he was always with, they were like super close. I heard
Andre Villiers smoked her and a few of her friends out the
week before and she was only in middle school. My pet

> theory is O'Malley drew the X on his back, wanted the
> Giant dead. His sister posted here back in 2008, then she
> just disappeared, deleted her posts—it's all about a police
> conspiracy and how her brother and even Ricky Hell were
> innocent. Maybe it was the cop she was talking about took
> legal action but I think she's still got a Myspace and it's all
> up on there. www.myspace.com/AishyOm-.

Myspace? Wasn't that the social media equivalent of the Tamagotchi? Even so, I'd scored a virtual jackpot: a sibling of the Southport Three who was willing to talk—and an old friend of the deceased.

Murderbabe66's recollections were pretty dubious: The X on the jacket? Get real. Anyway, Andre only wore an army jacket, like a school shooter. I was, however, intrigued by her allegations that Andre, a senior, gave weed to Cormac's little sister and her friends. I mean, they were twelve, thirteen years old at the time—and it was strange in any context. Given Andre's nature, I suspected something might have happened.

Cormac had never been charged with or accused of hurting Andre. But if Cormac knew about Andre creeping on his sister, would that have enraged him enough to want to kill him? And, more importantly, who were Cormac's sister's friends? Danny, Ricky, and Carole all had younger sisters in elementary or middle school.

I looked in a few Southport threads—Seth75 wasn't an active user anymore. I made a post on the thread, asking if anyone knew his email address.

Cormac's sister might be the missing link I needed to find Cormac and get to the bottom of who Andre really was—which might explain why Andre's family had never spoken publicly about his murder or given any interviews.

I clicked on the Myspace link. AishyOm was short for Aisling. I looked up the pronunciation—it wasn't ice-ling as I thought, but ash-ling. Pretty.

Aisling O'Malley, 26
Actress, Dancer, Model
New York, New York

She was pretty, in an odd way, a model way; she was very thin, freck-
led, her ears stood out, and her lips seemed overly sensuous. She had
shamrock green eyes, wild red curls. Dressed in a red leotard, she resembled a young Kate Bush, circa "Wuthering Heights." She'd stopped
uploading videos in 2008, but there were several from before that. I
clicked on one of her in a monastic-looking bedroom, where she sang a
Norah Jones song, completely off-key. Then I skipped to another where
she sat in what looked like Central Park while she recited Shakespeare
by heart, eyes closed, completely earnest. The sound quality was terrible.

I clicked into a photo album called "3 Amigos." They were scanned
images, low res, grainy, with the look and feel of the nineties; confirmed
by the date in the corner, in red printed lettering from the drugstore:
10/10/1993. In one, a little girl with an auburn pageboy, crooked teeth,
and a nose and ears she never grew into, stares at the camera with an
ennui that belongs to a child in wartime. An older kid with obviously
dyed jet-black hair and a Ministry T-shirt and Doc Martens leans against
her. Cormac O'Malley.

The next, an eggshell and blue sky, a church looming in the background. The little girl is wearing a white dress that resembles a meringue.
If I looked closely, I could see the little prayer book. A confirmation, I
gathered, but judging by her size it could well be her first communion,
her first taking of the sacrament—the first taste of guilt and wafer. Beside
Cormac and Aisling was a woman dressed in a simple cheesecloth dress,
so young looking, they could all be siblings. The three of them holding
on to each other tightly.

"Aisling, Mac, Marion," the caption read.

The next photo nearly took my breath away: Julie Hernandez. She
had Ricky's bone structure, his slightly Asiatic dark eyes. She and Aisling
were wearing matching tan, stained, ugly roller skates with big orange
wheels, dressed in tiny fluorescent shorts and slogan T-shirts, big ugly
earrings. Very nineties. Julie and Aisling were clearly the centerpiece of
the photo. They were a year or two above my little sister Michelle. And
Shelly hadn't been allowed to play on the street, because Cathy Carver
had gone missing. Could she have been there with other friends?

I looked a little closer at the crowd of kids behind them in the next photo. They were at the United Skates of America rink. The kids were all Hispanic and black, kids from the non-whitewashed suburbs of the island, out on Friday night to skate. At the end of the night, when the rink closed for skating, they would dance to hip hop and reggae.

I used to go there, too. I scanned the date: 11/18/1993. Technically, I could have been in that picture.

Another photo showed Julie and Aisling and a bunch of friends at a table, eating junk food. Among them I spotted Carole Jenkins' little sister—Libby, I think she was called—and another set of teens photobombing them. Danny. His hair was the most distinctive thing about him; wavy, lush, and streaked with sun. His arms were hairless and muscular. You couldn't see the person holding up a V with two fingers, but I knew the stone in the ring. It was a tiger's eye. Ricky Hell believed in psychic protection. It didn't help him in the end. Andre, on Ricky's left, in his army jacket. I wondered if Cormac was standing away from the group, having stepped out just when the flash went off.

One set of teens, one preteen and gooey as caramel, another who allegedly sacrificed mice to Satan. Was this evidence of Andre grooming the girls?

I clicked to a hyperlinked interview with Julie Hernandez. She was thirteen years older, two babies in a stroller beside her, standing on a busy street in what looked to be Brooklyn, calm and self-possessed. Her hair was now ironed straight. I took a deep breath. Julie was so like Ricky it put me somewhere between laughter and tears. An emotion that could not be named. Or something similar, whatever Oscar Wilde said.

"Richard—Ricky—was troubled, right? We had a tough life. He was acting scary, talking about Satan, all that kind of noise. He never killed that boy, right, even if that kid was evil as all shit. Ricky, my brother, died in the arms of the Lord is what I'm sayin'. Those other kids got away with murder, right? Ricky died in the arms of the Lord and, with God's grace, his name will be cleared. Those people who trashed his name and the cop that murdered him . . . they all gonna be punished."

Julie swayed, her eyes closed, the babies blissfully unaware of their mother's distress.

I was also swaying in my seat. I checked the time: 10 p.m. Somehow, I'd lost myself in a true crime vortex for several hours.

Then I saw what Murderbabe66 had been talking about:

> The Southport 3 were victims of a police conspiracy!!!!

It was hard to read because the layout was crazy—lots of red, misspellings, screamy caps, and crank-style exclamation points.

> Andre Villiers murder was not a scarifice 4 Satan!!! A
> crooked cop was the real Devil in Southport. Steve Shearer
> murdred Ricky bc he was Ricky's supplier and Ricky was
> gonna Narc on him. Steve probably got the kids 2 kill Andre
> coz Andre knew 2 much!!!!!

Say what? Ricky dealing for a crooked cop? Ricky was a dealer—small time: acid tabs, weed, mushrooms. If he was dealing for a cop, why would Ricky narc on him? Andre as the victim of a hit by said dirty cop? Then I saw my father's name. The rest of the paragraph may have been written in Latin; I had to reread it several times to understand what Aisling was trying to say:

> RP Sloane key Homicide detective arrived at the scene
> intoxicated—leaving less qualified officers to handle it . . .
> he was a corrupt, fall-down drunk who was A KNOWN
> FRIEND to STEVE SHEARER and covered up for him!!!! Did
> Money change hands??!!!

It was a surreal experience, seeing my surname there. Thanks to RP, I had entered the story.

8

Aisling had attached a photo to her allegation about RP—I recognized the occasion—the Nassau County PD awards ceremony, 1992. Mom and Shelly died the year after. RP had a slightly beery smile stretching across his face. And next to him, Steve Shearer, who looked like the WWF wrestler Randy "Macho Man" Savage, with a nose that had been broken and set wrong. He had a dark, scraggly beard, a mustache that looked like a disguise. Maybe he was undercover as a biker but I could see his eyes were sharp, alert like a soldier.

I walked into the living room. We had a folding frame with photos of the same night on our old mantelpiece. Official photographs: one, my dad in full uniform, receiving his award; two, his arm around my mom and she's in an off-the-shoulder cocktail dress. I remembered that night. My mom called me into the hallway to zip her up—all her clothes smelled like mothballs and fabric softener—and she turned to me all dark shining eyes and lipstick-smeared teeth. Mona wasn't there that night, Mom must have been so happy to have RP to herself.

How do I look?

What I should have said:

Beautiful. I love you, Mom.

What I said:

You have lipstick on your teeth.

The memory made me curl in on myself.

Would it have killed me to be nice? Why was I so insufferable all the time?

And Shelly. I often kicked her out of the bathroom, my bedroom—yelled at her for being a kiss ass and a crybaby and stealing my lipsticks to kiss posters of boy-band crushes. The truth was that RP loved her so much more than me.

I never stopped to think how she might be feeling; how sad and scared she would have been after Cathy's disappearance, because all I cared about was myself and the calamitous love triangle I had found myself in. After Shelly died I went through her things and found a tape she and Cathy had made in a recording booth at a local amusement park. *Sing like the stars!* Its cover featured the two girls smiling awkwardly. It was a horrible version of the B-52's "Love Shack," punctuated with giggles and missed lyrics. Neither girl could sing. I played it a few times before the cassette was chewed.

Like RP, I was the worst. And I was behaving a lot like him now—unhinged, sentimental, free pouring, and smoking indoors.

My stomach lurched. I moved my hand to my solar plexus, the seat of my pain, and coached myself into deep breathing. I opened Carole's book, went straight to the glossy insert. I flipped the page over, leafing through pictures of Carole as a young teen; thin, with "Etch A Sketch" features—no sharp angles, no deviations from the custom-made WASP. Her high school yearbook pic. Enough Aqua Net to put a hole in the ozone layer, a Metallica tee, and a Maybelline pout. Then the trial. Carole, hair in a French braid, a middle-aged pantsuit (she had a good lawyer), looking like a sister wife from Utah. There was a picture of the Southport Three in the courtroom, Shearer giving evidence, with a Grizzly Adams undercover beard and a haunted expression. Steve Shearer, the object of Aisling's vitriol, alleged architect of the satanic teen murder, looked like a broken man to me.

Then I saw it; the police statement had been typed up on a Remington, headed: "Statement of Carole Jenkins, Nassau County Police Department."

It had been slightly smudged by a finger, but there was no mistaking the names:

Taken by Detective Sergeant Mona Byrnes and Detective Lieutenant Raymond Paul Sloane, November 1, 1994. Time: 3:33 a.m.

My father and Mona had taken the statement.

And now Mona fucking Byrnes, that bobble-headed Irish homewrecker, was in the story and back in my life. Typical.

———

I tried to convince myself that all these new revelations proved was that my father had neglected to tell me something crucial—he'd taken Carole's statement, he'd been involved in the investigation. Neither fact was exactly breaking news. Ultimately, the photo had simply evidenced my father knowing Steve, which was not really earth shattering. They were both cops.

It could be that Aisling had a vendetta against her stepdad. I had an inkling he was a bad dude. There was nothing outright sinister about him, but there was something else about the photo that nagged at me—it struck me that Steve Shearer looked significantly younger in the Nassau County Awards pic, which wasn't that long before Halloween in 1994. And what does that to people? Could it have been killing Ricky Hell? If Ricky was the animal Steve painted him to be at trial, why would that haunt him? I believe it's the thing that eats you up on the inside, like it did me. Secrets.

At the time of Andre's murder, RP told me that all he knew of Steve Shearer was that he was with the Queens precinct in New York, even though he'd moved to Nassau County; that he was a stepparent of one of the kids. But RP Sloane was a man with zipped lips when sober, and a penchant for mistruth; his moral compass had no true north. I considered Aisling's allegations. Could RP have responded to the scene, hushed it up, taken money? And the answer was yes, very possibly. The idea of Ricky Hell being stitched up for eternity by my corrupt-ass dad was painful and unpalatable, but not unbelievable. My mother and sister's death had cast a long shadow on the Sloane surname. In the late nineties, I thought about taking my mother's maiden name, but it never felt right. I wanted to absolve the problem of the Sloane name. But I couldn't, because I had inherited all the Sloane problems.

I knew, in my gut, that something was amiss.

———

I ran into the bathroom and vomited thunderously, bringing up brown-colored water, soup, and maraschino cherries, a gumbo of mostly undigested matter. I sat on the ground for a minute and then got to my feet, rinsing out my mouth, and looked in the mirror. I had the red-rimmed eyes of a reefer smoker. I was barely able to assimilate food, yet I expected to process and expose a fishy as fuck sixteen-year-old Satanic murder. If you believe in astrology, like Ricky Hell did, while I was a Capricorn by birth, my Taurean moon made me bullish and stubborn. Taking the bull by the horns may be an old Appalachian saying RP once told me—but it's smarter to lead it there.

9

RP was like the clichéd police captain from eighties cop shows, slamming shots of Pepto-Bismol and alcohol and chasing it with coffee and cigarettes. And because I'd inherited many of his habits, I'd inherited a few of his health complaints too—including the "Sloane stomach." I headed into the kitchen to take my cure, one of his half-assed home remedies for what he called a "twitchy gut"—the juice of a raw potato in room-temperature water, chased by half a bottle of Pepto-Bismol and then a slammer of diluted whisky for pain relief. I added my own touches: a crushed-up Percocet in the whisky, swallowed with the ever-ineffectual Yummy Relaxer.

Ten minutes later, I was ready to face the past again.

I sat at the kitchen table and typed out a quick email to Aisling O'Malley. Even though she seemed to be a ghost on the internet, she was a presence with whom I had things in common—bad dads primarily. We were both lodged in the past but, more importantly, we seemed to share a similar objective, even if our motives were unrelated: to clear Ricky Hell's name.

Hi Aisling,

My name is Erin Sloane, I'm a crime reporter with *Inside Island*. I'm writing a story about the Southport Three and the murder of Andre Villiers.

I found your Myspace page on a true crime forum. I'm getting the picture that Cormac O'Malley is your brother. I've been unable to locate him. I'm wondering if he might be living in Australia, using the first name Michael?

You said Steve Shearer was being protected by an RP Sloane and you made some allegations about Andre Villiers. I would really like to hear your side of the story, including your theories on why Andre was murdered and your understanding of Ricky Hell's relationship with Steve Shearer—and how RP was involved with Shearer. Incidentally, I should disclose here that RP Sloane is my father.

The man you're slandering.

I'd also like to get in touch with Cormac, as I've already spoken to Danny Quinlan-Walsh and will be trying to speak with Carole Jenkins, to get her side of the story.

Please get in contact to arrange a time to talk, either in person, by phone call, or Skype if that's more convenient.

All the best, Erin

Now my cell was buzzing. I took a guess—it was either one of two of my nocturnal callers, or let's face it—the *only* two people whose number was saved in my phone besides my father's care home and the pharmacy. It was Denise.

"Erin, you sound croaky. Wait, have you been crying?" She sounded alarmed.

"No. Something went down the wrong way and came back up."

"Uh huh." She didn't sound convinced. "Are you okay?"

"One hundred percent." Instinctively I closed my eyes as I lied to her. *See no evil.* It was all around me. Then I realized we'd spoken twice today, which was unusual.

"So, I got the book. Thanks."

"Great, but that's not why I'm calling." I noted an unfamiliar, sharp-ish edge to her tone.

"Well, I'm already making a lot of progress if that's what you're wondering. I've located Danny."

"Yeah, I know. He emailed me."

"Okay . . ."

"It was a largely litigious and threatening email, you know, suggesting that if we print anything defamatory about him, he'll sue the shit out of us, yadda yadda. Whatever. That's why we've got a lawyer on speed dial. He claims, though, that you went to his house uninvited—spoke to his wife, even harassed her."

"Well, that's just not true. I simply drove past his house and happened to bump into her."

"Oh my God, Erin, you're a horrible liar." I could almost hear Denise rolling her eyes.

"Okay, so I did talk to her, but how the hell would he know that? She doesn't know who I am. It was both discreet and uneventful. Except for the fact that Gina had a black eye and is a virtual clone of me, albeit way prettier, everything was nearly fucking normal."

Gina looked like I would have if I'd made better life choices. Except we'd both picked a banger of a bad one—Danny Quinlan-Walsh.

Denise made a sound of dismay.

"Danny has faux amnesia about the night in question, but his memory could be rekindled if I went to the Freeport Motel with him, as he suggested."

"Sexual bribery? And he's married. Quelle dreamboat."

I thought of Danny's maritime blue eyes, his love of ropes and rope burn. Unless Cindy, his zombie mom, had told Danny she'd seen his old flame near the front door, he was most probably following me.

"He's worse than you could imagine. And it doesn't begin and end at Andre either."

I could hear canned laughter drifting from a television next door, and a Spanish language program, both interrupted by a sudden sharp yowl and a growl, the sound of two things rushing at each other. Racoons maybe, or cats. I went to the window and looked out into the backyard and the sensor lights were on. My dad's aluminum beach chair that faced the pool had been knocked over. Despite the yard being half the size of our previous one, most of it was paved. A watery sheet of maple leaves congealed on the pool's cover. It had been raining at night—late summer storms. The yard was empty.

"There's more to tell you on the subject, but first I should probably come clean—this story is getting even closer to home if that were at all possible. RP and Mona Byrnes, his partner, took Carole Jenkins' statement."

"Shit." Denise exhaled heavily, as if she too had gained a heavy burden. "RP never told you this, obviously."

"Obviously," I agreed. "He never told me a lot of things though." I refilled my whisky glass—double shot, ice, seltzer. It gave me a warm burn as it went down. I told her about Aisling's Myspace and her theory about Shearer, Ricky—the drugs. Then, RP's rumored bribe taking. The picture of RP and Shearer together.

"What's your impression of Aisling? I mean, this is her stepdad she's trashing."

"I don't know. She could be legit. It does read a little like she might be a crank, because they're unfounded allegations; it's all a bit join-the-dots detective work. One thing's clear: she's got a huge-ass grudge against her stepfather."

"Who among us doesn't have a few daddy issues?" Denise agreed. "Erin, this stuff with your father . . . you've never talked about him in detail, or said anything about Southport. I know you lost your mom and sister, but I've been too polite to ask how. But now, as it pertains to the case and the story, I'm going to be rude, babe. RP is now in the story. You need to tell me what happened."

Southport and all its restless ghosts had come gunning for me. The past had a kinesis, a second life timetable of its own. All these secrets, held so close to my chest, were now spilling out.

"My father was suspected of being involved in the deaths of my mom and sister. It was formally ruled out, their deaths were deemed accidental but, you know, mud sticks."

I thought back to my dad's terrible, paralyzing despair, how he became unshaven and practically catatonic, drinking scotch, smoking, and drugging himself into unconsciousness. And what about me? Michelle was eleven, liked mint chocolate chip ice cream, the seaside, and horses. I told her once that they ate horses in France. For a week, I pretended that she was a ghost and that no one could see her except me. I was a bad sister; I was a bad daughter. I can't think of a time I thanked my mom for doing the laundry; in fact, I once threw a pair of underwear at her with a used pad inside them.

"We moved to Amityville in January '94 after they died, to get away from the house, the rumors. That's why I wasn't at Roosevelt when all this was going down. RP tried to blow his brains out about a month after we moved, missed by a mile. He said he was cleaning his gun. I wasn't there, so I didn't see it, but he left a note. I found it. *That's all she wrote.* And that's a direct quote." I lit a cigarette, heard Denise suck in her breath at the same time as I inhaled.

"RP never forgave himself because he wasn't home the night they died. He became a shell of a man. He lost his way, big time." I took another drink. "And then he sent me away for two years after Ricky's death, like he couldn't bear to look at me."

Disloyalty tasted like metal in my mouth. I washed it out with whisky.

"So, you think he could have taken a bribe?"

"I think there's a possibility."

"Let's get back to Andre, what did you find out there?"

"There's a guy who I think I know from Roosevelt High who is posting on a true crime forum claiming to be his old best friend. He says a lot of dumb stuff about Satanism, but he thinks Andre got Cormac's little sister Aisling and her friends stoned not long before his murder."

"How old?"

"She was about twelve. I mean, he didn't insinuate anything happened, but there were rumors that Andre was into little girls. And Andre tried to rape Carole. She says that in her book. I don't believe most of what she says, but I do believe that he hurt her."

And he hurt me. I couldn't say it aloud though.

"There's a photo of the kids at the skating rink near Roosevelt Field Mall. Aisling and her friends. Julie Hernandez, Ricky's little sister. And Libby, who is Carole Jenkins' little sister, is in the background. The metal kid gang were off on the side—Ricky, Danny, Andre, so the two groups knew each other."

"So, we have Andre hanging around Aisling and her BFFs, raising more red flags than a bullfighter, and then he's senselessly murdered by a bunch of kids you argue were about as satanic as KISS," Denise concluded. "How likely is it that the murder was more like retaliation? You know, kids doling out vigilante justice for kids? Or even killing for protection?" Denise was enthusiastic about this version of the narrative. "Cormac's Steve Shearer's stepson after all. Hell would be the perfect scapegoat—a cult leader who got them high, ordered them to kill in Satan's name."

"But why? Why not just tell the truth? Andre was a predator, he hurt Carole. We know that. And Danny did time for his part in killing Andre. I can't imagine Danny doing anything that wasn't purely self-interested. He didn't give a shit about his family. He was adopted— he talked about it all the time."

Danny was hardwired to hurt. He almost couldn't help it. No, it wasn't an excuse—but it was a reason. He beat Andre's head in. And I bet he liked doing it.

"Sentencing maybe," Denise said, in answer to my question. "It was a risky cover to adopt, but look at the lenient sentencing. Danny got a slap on the wrist and Carole did a stretch in a juvenile facility, so that's, what, three years? Cormac, the same. They could have done over twenty, life even. But with a smart lawyer, which they had, they got less time than a rational, organized execution-style murder."

I thought about this for a minute. The hero cop, the teen satanic cult leader, the quarterback killer, and a celebrity lawyer who knew how to make it saleable—to a courtroom, the media, and the public.

"Erin, if Shearer wanted Andre dead because he knew about Ricky and Steve's business relationship, it makes the devil in Southport outline a totally different story," Denise began. "The devil is not a mixed-race high school dropout but a narco cop. And that is HUGE. Book deal huge. Oprah huge. But you know the consequences. If RP had a hand in the cover-up, it's going to come out. You might implicate your own father in a crime. A few crimes, even. I know he's sick. Are you prepared to wear that?"

"I don't think I have a choice. And I think I have to find out either way." RP was so far gone now that he wouldn't know if a metaphorical knife had been stuck in his back, let alone be able to fight any allegations—but it was still going to hurt me to have to do it.

"I agree. So, suck the poison out while it's fresh. If you're going to tell this story, you're going to have to tell your own story. Your dad's. Whatever went down between you and Danny."

"Now you're being polite again. What Danny did to me, you mean. I can't even tell a therapist, Denise."

"Then write it out. And please keep a physical distance from Mr. Quinlan-Walsh. It sounds like you really poked the bear with your visit this morning."

It was an odd phrase—it reminded me of the testimony of the kids in the woods, all tripping and traumatized. I think it was Cormac who saw a bear on hind legs shooting stars. Ricky turned into a crow. The devil—a devil—appeared. Then I realized that it wasn't just Danny's arrogance and the sleeping violence between us that had been bothering me since our meeting. It was something he'd said about reading my articles in *Inside Island*. Although I'd said our conversation in the café was off the record, I'd taped it, if only for a personal archive of Danny's callousness about his own crime. I rewound it now, played it back to the part I wanted.

"You need to listen to something," I told Denise. I held the recorder to the phone.

Hearing Danny's voice in my room made me physically tense up.

"Do you get it?" I asked Denise. "'Haunted houses, missing kids.' He was provoking me, poking the bear."

"Missing kids?" she repeated.

"I never wrote about missing kids, Denise! Never Nassau County, never anything about missing children." I was aware of how shrill my voice had become. I brought it down a notch.

"Okay. So, it's a little weird, but it could be a slip of the tongue, no?"

"Nothing with Danny is a slip of the tongue, Denise. Danny isn't careless. He's trying to tell me something."

"No," she said slowly. "That's what the email was about. He's warning you off something. So now we know you're on the right track. Start writing now. Start at the beginning."

10

THE TESTIMONY OF ERIN SLOANE
DECEMBER 24, 1993: THE NIGHT OF THE INCIDENT

In December 1993, I was weeks away from turning sixteen and in the middle of a cold war with my mother. She wanted me to have a big rite of passage party, in a stupid dress with puffy sleeves, with friends and family. Sensing the calamity of cops and my criminal cohort of friends, I put my foot down. I won the cold war, because she died just short of two weeks before my birthday.

The death of my mom and Shelly was, I thought, the last block to topple the trembling Jenga tower of psychic suffering in my teen life. I was wrong. That fall would come later.

I had problems. My family life was deeply unhappy. I was curvy, my shoulders were too big from swimming and I wanted to look like Kate Moss. But number one was my boyfriend, Danny Quinlan-Walsh, a high school senior, star quarterback turned metalhead. For the first year I was reeling that he had somehow picked me, an auburn-haired, acid-tongued weirdo, over all the model chicks, waifs, and cheerleaders who were lining up to be his girlfriend. But when he went metal, he wanted a metal chick and that was me.

We'd been together a year when his mood swings had begun to

rapid cycle. There was a new sour aroma to his Ivory soap and pear smelling skin and hair. Despite his OCD, he was beginning not to wash because he said it retained his high better. His eyes were red-rimmed, and I had noticed he had begun picking at his chin. In fact, I noticed his eyes were all pupil these days—it was like the blackness inside him was consuming him. Gone was his quick wit and occasional bouts of good humor and creative gift buying. He was paranoid, mean, and equally needy.

I blamed the drugs. I mean, we were all taking them, but Danny really took to them. That December was like the opposite of the summer of love—it was the winter of hallucinogens. We'd spent most of the evening in Ricky Hell's van in Belmont, trying to score acid. The boys were tense. Danny had snapped at both Ricky and me a few times.

When Danny went to pay for gas and buy cigarettes, Ricky stared at me in the rearview mirror. It was a long look and not entirely polite. I gave him one back that was all deer in the headlights. He frowned and shook his head. Not like that, the look said. That's not it at all.

Partly why I was drawn to Danny was his big, quasi normal *Brady Bunch* family—their scheduled family outings, weekends on the water. Even though I knew, like my family, that the fault lines were profound. Our dysfunction was just more obvious.

I'd been told to come home by 10 p.m. to wrap presents and decorate the tree in Sloane family tradition. In Sloane family tradition I was late—it was closer to 10:30 when I got home and also true to Sloane family tradition, everyone had bailed. My mom had taken Ambien and was in bed with a bottle of red wine. I could hear the ethereal sing-song theme music of *The X-Files* coming from the master bedroom (my mom had a crush on Fox Mulder); my father was absent and Shelly had taken herself to bed.

I went up to her room to check on her. She'd been having nightmares recently. I sat on her bed, stoned—I did this nightly. I smoothed out *The Little Mermaid* bedspread she'd complained she was too old for. I, too, still had the pink-and-white girl's bedroom Mom had decorated years ago, despite pink being my most loathed color. I noticed her pillow was damp. She'd been crying herself to sleep. Michelle and I had this in common. I sat there for a while, then I kissed her and crept out of her room.

Danny and I went into my bedroom to do what we did—everything but. Danzig's "Twist of Cain" came on the radio and I hunted down Mom's stash of benzos, scored some Ambien. I rolled up a towel and placed it under my door. We had the window open as we blew the smoke from our shared joint out into the air. I fell into a shallow, broken sleep, which felt like two minutes, but when I checked the time it was after 3 a.m. Danny was up, pacing the room. He was already rolling another joint. I watched him tap something into the cannabis and tobacco—angel dust.

"Ricky's into you," Danny remarked in a "you know, it's snowing outside" kind of casual way.

"Okay," I said, knowing where this was heading. I watched him light up and I took the joint from him. I wanted to keep it away from him as much as possible, so I winced and took a deep inhale. I was actually scared of angel dust—it was circulating and people said it made you do crazy shit, like jumping off roofs thinking you could fly. But while I didn't feel like flying, I felt light. I felt like I was glowing, like the lava lamp in my room.

"He, like, knows you're a virgin. It's a turn-on for him."

"'Like a Virgin,'" I said to him, but I sang it. Then I laughed. "Whose fault is that?" I said. "Anyway, it's not a purity thing," I continued, "Guys just think they own you if they take it away."

"Is that what happens?" Danny said, taking the joint out of my mouth. "Quit bogarting it." I'd actually only taken a few hits, even though it felt like I'd been holding it forever.

"Of course not. But it's a kind of power, right? To have like . . . initiated someone?"

Danny inched across the bed, the quilt I was proud of—I made it myself in home ec on the sewing machine, a rich burgundy velvet. It was rippling and moving, almost like an exquisite sea creature. I thought of the song from *The Little Mermaid* that Shelly loved, "Under the Sea." I was underwater. But I wasn't drowning.

"It's about love," he said seriously. "And trust. I want to be able to trust you. To know it's like... you and me. Forever."

"It *is* you and me," I recited weakly.

"Why do I catch Ricky checking you out, then?" Danny's Pacific blue eyes were now as cold as the Atlantic. Mobsters died in those waters.

"You're, like, always pissed at me. You tell me I dress like a guy and to wear better clothes. Then you chew me out over guys talking to me or looking at me." I was getting deeply weary of this. I looked at my watch. 5 a.m. How was that even possible? We'd been fighting on and off since the last bell at school. Boyfriends were a giant pain in the ass, if this one was anything to go by. "Even if guys do that, it doesn't mean it's like... reciprocated."

"Stop using big words," Danny muttered blackly. "That's the way you try to win."

"Reciprocated? Right. A real *Jeopardy!* word," I said sarcastically.

"My father said you're Satan's main handmaiden," Danny told me, drinking milk, then dunking a cookie in it.

"Isn't that a good thing?" I said. "Wait—didn't Shelly leave those out for Santa."

He shrugged. "I just found them in the hall outside your room. And it means you're a slut. I've seen the way you act around him."

I rolled my eyes. I was losing patience, challenging the whole dynamic. I was so high I honestly didn't remember that I was supposed to be scared of him.

"Please. You wish."

Danny slapped me square across the face—my ears rang out and my sense of time and space warped and refracted. It would have almost been comical if it didn't hurt so much: my head snapped to one side, like whiplash. It caught my nose and I had to elevate my head to stop the blood.

The silence had a song of its own—the electrics in the room, the sound of leaves scraping against glass, the feedback in my ear all joined Danny's fire-engine loud wail. Much like a child, he cried out of fright more than remorse. After the first sob, he began to heave silently. He brought me Kleenex. His head on my lap mouthing: "I'm sorry, I'm sorry,

I'll never do it again. I love you, I love you. I'm adopted, I'm adopted." It was a whiny tune I knew too well. He fell asleep, somehow. I fell asleep too, from the dope and the Ambien, but it was mostly from the shock.

Then Danny was shaking me awake. He was grabbing and dragging me. I thought he was jealous with rage again and began my own whiny unconvincing solo: "Sorry. Sorry. I love you. I love you. Only you!"

"Erin! Get up, get up."

I was mumbling nonsense and he grabbed a coat, a denim jacket lined with fleece. Danny literally dragged me down the stairs by one arm. I was barefoot, no bra. The house smelled like rotten eggs. It was snowing outside, yet the subzero temperature did not clear my head. I vomited as soon as I hit the cold air. Steam rose from it and I was confused, dopey. Was it day or night? Suddenly, my dad was pulling into the driveway. Another cop car behind him. An ambulance, no sirens— just lights flashing on the front of the house, blue, red. A fire engine, also no siren. The soundtrack to whatever had happened was silence, except for the low-grade ringing in my ear.

Then I realized my mom and Shelly were still inside. It never occurred to me they might be dead.

The cold snap of air, the sulfur and marine smell of the Sound slapped me awake. I stood there. I had taken a few hits from a PCP-laced joint; I was still thick from benzos and booze, throwing up what looked like eggnog on the driveway, while a boy with no T-shirt and his jeans undone screamed at me. I had blood crusted around my nostrils and puke in my hair—but I couldn't care less. The ringing in my ear got louder. All I could think was: My father is going to kill me.

RP didn't shout, he just ran into the house. He reemerged, our dead dog Pluto in his arms. I knew Pluto was dead, from his staring eyes. And yes, RP attempted to rescue the dog first. My dad loved Pluto and the pool, in that order.

My little sister, my mom—were brought out shortly, on stretchers. I didn't think they were dead, in all the movies I'd seen, dead people had sheets over them. They had oxygen masks on. I also needed oxygen; a mask was placed over my nose and mouth. It smelled of plastic.

"Pumpkin. C'mon. We got to get away from the house."

Ox was there, he spoke to me in hushed tones, helping me put my Converse shoes and wooly socks on my feet one at a time; he held each foot in a gentle way that suggested he had raised children, but I knew Ox was childless. The kindness that he showed me, the softly delivered instructions, the reassuring repetition that I was okay, I was going to be okay.

I had helped my sister do this, every day of kindergarten.

Danny was wearing my father's velour slippers.

We walked up the road, the house was cordoned off with tape and orange cones. Our neighbors came out wrapped in bathrobes and slippers, brought me sweet hot coffee.

I watched my father talking to Danny. It was strange. They weren't fighting. He wasn't yelling or asking him what the fuck he'd been doing in his teenage daughter's bedroom or why she had blood all over her face. He was shaking Danny's hand and then hugging him, suddenly weeping. I had never seen RP cry. He gave me a look; the first time he'd made eye contact with me. It was so accusatory and full of loathing that I hung my head and gasped aloud.

Later I attended the first inquest hearing. I had been listening to Danzig and performing oral sex on my boyfriend when the carbon monoxide began to leak into the house; an odorless, lethal dose that killed my mom first in the master bedroom and Shelly, on the second floor, about ten minutes later. Both showed faint signs of life when the police arrived, but were pronounced dead at the hospital. I learned phrases like supine, asphyxia, aspirated. Expired. I learned that initially the police suspected a problem with the furnace, but it was a faulty flue in the pool heater that poisoned them. I had left the inquest in a fury when an expert witness on behalf of the pool maintenance company testified, claiming that the reason for Shelly's death was that her lungs had not developed normally—immature alveoli at birth. Nothing to do with their maintenance man.

I learned later that my dad had been a suspect. There were two compelling reasons. Number one: RP came speeding home. He ran a red light. He was caught on camera. He knew something was wrong when there was no way of him knowing. Nassau County PD thought he may have caused the gas leak, but felt remorse and sped home to rescue us.

Number two: my parents had a troubled marriage. He and my mom had a screaming fight the night before. She had even called her sister in Maine, who in turn told the cops something fishy was going on.

I shouldn't have survived; it should have been Shelly. It should have been Mom. Hell, it should have been Pluto. All three were dead. And Danny, who had woken up, gone to get us both water, realized something was terribly wrong. Danny, who had hit me so hard that my eardrum was perforated, had rescued me, and was now a hero.

When I saw my father embracing Danny I realized I had survived, so I was going to make my own choices now. That was when I decided I was going to Hell.

I found out later that Danny told my father he had slapped me awake. This was seemingly ok with RP. If I was Carole Jenkins, I might have written a book about it. It might have been called *PCP and Danny Saved my Life*. But I was not Carole Jenkins, I was Eerie Erin and I was working out a new version of the Southport Three story. In my story, Ricky Hell was maybe, just maybe, the doomed protagonist and Steve Shearer, the villain. What that made Andre and the other kids, I didn't quite know yet. But I was going to find out. And if I had my way, Danny Quinlan-Walsh would finally pay for what he did.

11

It was closer to midnight than morning, so when the phone rang I knew it was Ox—like me, he was naturally nocturnal. He started to think better when the sun went down.

"Hey Pumpkin," he said. "I just got in this minute and heard your voicemail. How's RP?"

I could tell the brightness in his tone was borne of alarm—Ox clearly thought it was a death call.

"Sadly, still hanging on."

Ox chuckled. He didn't mind my lack of social graces or graveyard humor. Compared to my father I was like "Dear Abby" or something.

"It's been a while. I got worried when I heard from you. You good?"

"I'm good. I'm sorry I haven't called. Work, you know."

"Yeah, yeah; it's okay. What do you need from me?" Ox got right to the point.

"Well, I need some intel on a story I'm working on. It's about a cop. A narco cop actually."

I paused.

Ox cleared his throat. "Go on."

"Detective Steve Shearer. He was from Queens North Precinct, I think. I'm investigating the Andre Villiers murder in Southport."

I could hear him light a cigarette, drag on it. I walked outside with my phone, looked up at the weirdly bright moon, a filmy blue ring around it.

"The Southport Three," he said, flat as a tack.

Like Pavlov's dog, I took out and lit up another Marlboro, which burned my raw throat.

"Yeah. I already spoke to Danny Quinlan-Walsh."

"Your old ball and chain?" Ox asked in a jokey but knowing tone.

"Yeah, the very same one. I'm going to try and locate the other two: Carole Jenkins and Cormac O'Malley. Cormac's abroad, I think. I found an online résumé for a Michael Cormac O'Malley. Birthdate's 3/17/1978. He claims he went to Belmont High, but I'm pretty sure it's Cormac."

"An Irishman born on St Paddy's Day," Ox used a terrible Irish accent. There was a clownish side to him that came out in odd times, namely during the small disasters of my life. Maybe it was a way to offset the horrors of his work. I knew he'd be alone, like me, in his basement apartment, lit up by the glow of computer monitors, occasionally answering calls and texts on his burner cells, reeling in cyber creeps on the *GRL Zone* friend forum. I laughed, humoring him.

"Yeah, but he's in Australia. His sister Aisling has a personal site where she names Steve Shearer as a kind of criminal mastermind behind the Southport Three."

"Yeah?" Only Ox's "yeah" wasn't really a question. "How's that?"

"Steve was a dirty cop, according to her, dealing drugs—Andre cottoned onto Ricky and Steve's relationship. I guess Ricky needed to be disposed of too."

"Not uncommon for a narco cop to make a few bucks on the side. And to ice a few people. But your old beau, the O'Malley kid and Carole Jenkins were all there and told the same story . . ."

"Yeah, the Satan thrill-kill story never worked for me."

Ox used pauses and body language to communicate. Over the phone, he was extremely difficult to read. His pause now seemed interminable.

"The other thing that's coming up," I continued, "is that Andre was a bit predatory. Sort of like the guys you go after. His name came up in the Carver case."

"Oh yeah?"

"That's another thing. I heard you interviewed him about that. In fact, Danny said you interviewed a bunch of kids."

"Danny's got memory problems, I think. I helped the taskforce with the cyber side. All the kids were in a computer club. They were using a chat room—a real primitive version of MSN, no graphics, just text. So, the police wanted to know who the kids might have been talking to online, that sort of thing."

"I read something about that."

"They caught a guy talking to Cathy Carver, but he was older than Andre—in his forties. He was ruled out for the abduction though. All I know is, the kids all seemed to fit a profile. They were eleven years old, kinda shy, only children, and they lived on or around the water. They liked to play with computers. That Villiers kid was interviewed a few times. I know they talked to a few other older kids, but Villiers was of interest because he lived right on the water, used to hang out at Whitman Elementary, talk to kids walking home. No reason for him to be there."

I thought of Andre, 6'3, standing there in his black army coat while all the kids in their colorful puffer coats passed him.

I wrote it down: *Kids protecting kids?* I thought about the taskforce that was assigned to Cathy, Jason, and Trey.

"Have you got a contact for anyone from Operation Lighthouse or anyone in their cold case division? I want to follow it up."

"No one from the Lighthouse days is still around and it remains unsolved, so no one will go on record. I know a Detective Marci Diaz in homicide who works cold cases. I helped them set up this online library where the public can search up and report on cold cases. Marci's next gen, maybe not around in the nineties, probably busy being born or something. I'll talk to her. No promises."

"Thank you, Ox, that would be amazing." I cleared my throat.

"What else is on your mind?" Ox prompted me.

"RP took Carole's statement with Mona. Aisling claims he was too drunk to attend the crime scene, but I've seen the statement, Ox. His name is on it."

"I was at Benny's with RP that night. He wasn't just buzzed, he was wasted." Being a teetotaler, Ox would know.

I picked up *Dancing with the Devil*. "Well, he sobered up and went to the station. I've seen the statement; it's RP's signature for sure. Aisling O'Malley has a photo of RP and Shearer together at a ceremony—we have a copy at home—insinuating that RP corroborated the details of the Andre Villiers murder and the shooting of Ricky Hell. And Mona would have done whatever Dad said."

"But, Pumpkin, why would he? Maybe RP and Shearer knew each other socially, but RP was in a different precinct, a totally different county."

"But in his undercover days with NYPD? Could he have gotten chummy with him?"

"There are seventy-seven precincts in NYPD, hon. RP wasn't in Queens North. He and Shearer probably crossed paths, but that'd be it. Listen, you could go down to Benny's on Sunrise Highway and hear all kinds of sick shit about your dad. Me too. No cop has an immaculate reputation. But the other stuff? Shearer inciting a group murder? Who is he, Charles Manson? Shearer has a big rep, I can tell you that already. He was a cokehead. A lot of narco cops were back in the eighties and early nineties. Coke was a recreational drug in New York then. Just like having a Jack and Coke."

"Okay. Thanks, Ox." It was as if an invisible fence had been erected; I was being dismissed. I was planning on talking to Mona next anyway, so I wasn't going to pump Ox for any more on Shearer or my dad and their relationship. I stopped breathing for a second as I heard another crashing sound around the side of the house. I took the phone with me to the kitchen window, looking over the gate and spotted the culprit—a bandit-striped face, an outraged sound as it clambered off the trash can so fast it was a streak of black and white. A racoon; not an incensed, grown-up Danny Quinlan-Walsh.

I had to tread carefully around Ox and his unwavering loyalty to RP. "I guess I'm wondering if you think RP could ever have taken money? Like a bribe from Shearer?"

Ox took a drink of what I knew to be a Big Gulp. "RP was a good cop. He had an impulse control problem."

I pictured an invisible pair of scales in Ox's hand, weighing it all up. "Your dad had a code of ethics that maybe doesn't make sense to you. Everyone did then. But blood money, backing a dirty cop, framing a kid for it? Nope. That don't mean he wasn't resourceful. If he did earn on the side, I'll bet he tucked it away for a rainy day."

"My father spent money like a drunk sailor at port on New Year's Eve," I countered. "I made sure he paid off the mortgage, and the car. There were a few stocks and bonds belonging to Mom that hadn't been sold by him, but my inheritance would have been decimated if Lenora hadn't put it into a college fund that could only be accessed by me, and only after I finished my degree."

"She was smart, your mom." Ox sounded sad.

"She knew me, and she knew RP. He didn't save—he couldn't save, Ox. It wasn't in his nature."

"RP always had something going—dice games, poker. But he was old school. I mean, down to the bone. So, if he did have money, he'd be keeping it somewhere, and not in a savings account." Ox cleared his throat.

I believed this. After all, RP had threatened to kill the bank manager for neglecting to remove Mom's name from the mail after he informed them of her passing.

"What are you saying, Ox? He's got a hidden stash?"

"Oh, I don't know," he breezed, but it sounded asthmatic. "If he does, it's close to his heart is all I'm saying. You're a smart cookie. You know what I mean. Talk soon." Ox didn't like to sign off, and for a moment we were both suspended there, breathing together for a few seconds.

I tried to think like RP—where might an old man have hidden a significant amount of cash before he totally lost his marbles? The house had a crawlspace and an attic, a Freddy Krueger basement slash boiler room, which was full of seed-smelling damp recesses and whining, sighing foundations. I avoided it for obvious reasons—I'd seen all the

Nightmare on Elm Street movies and the furnace scared me. There was the living room sofa, the photo frames, the recess under the floorboard.

My father had transplanted all my mother's clothes from the old house to one side of the mirrored built-in wardrobe when we moved. I sometimes went into the wardrobe and felt the plastic sheaths of dry-cleaned clothes, poking holes in the bags and fingering the fabric of good suits and formal dresses she'd never really worn. The real clothes she'd worn, the threadbare sweatpants and tangy sweatshirts, were all gone, bar the ones I wore still.

The closet also yielded shoeboxes of receipts and clippings; yellowing and musty, with the corpses of a few moths that had been embalmed with the paperwork.

I checked the toilet cistern, the first aid kit, the laundry hamper. I stood there in Dad's bathroom, reflected in the full-length mirror drinking whisky, wearing my mom's oversized sweatpants, my unwashed and lank hair in a bun, vomit splashed on my dad's Rangers jersey. Of all the low points in my life, this wasn't a valley or a trough or a nadir, rather a kind of peak, or pinnacle, of bat-shit crazy. I hesitated. If I went forward, over the edge, I would learn some terrible truths. My old self would die and with it, the truths I had held on to my whole life. I looked in the mirror and remembered Ricky Hell rephrasing a dead poet, Sophocles, I think:

"Knowledge is terrible when it brings no profit to the man that's wise. But you gotta get wise."

My head had started to thump.

Close to his heart.

RP's favorite saying was "Dogs are the best people." My mom and Shelly were in sealed urns on the mantelpiece. My father had cremated Pluto too. He hadn't wanted to leave him behind in Southport. But Pluto wasn't on the mantelpiece.

Mom had told me stories about my father growing up in care in Brooklyn: a foster home that dealt in quick, thick beatings, with kids not washing to deter any advances from older kids or the foster carers themselves, and foster carers who fed the kids the dog's food. My dad saved his and fed the dog, who became his protector, his best friend.

I went outside and located Pluto's shrine. I dug through the stones; they were smooth, but eventually the force of my bare hands digging cut the skin on my knuckles. A foot deep, under the stones; a layer of soil, dirt. Then a layer of plastic sheeting. I retrieved it, like a vet feeling for a foal, a long, shrink-wrapped block of money; so many stacks of green notes—more money than I had ever seen in my life. I gasped and shrank back.

RP didn't like banks, but why would he have a shrink-wrapped stash of cash that size unless there was something very dirty about the money?

Ox hadn't said it outright, but he knew there was money; whether it was an inordinate sum stashed in a pet dog's grave or not. RP described Ox as the kind of friend you could approach with a dead body and he would say without a beat: "Where's the shovel at?" I wondered how many "dead bodies" my dad had brought to him. Maybe this was one Ox couldn't bear to keep hidden.

The money awoke that part of me that said: *faster, louder, more; it's never enough.* That part of me that hunted endlessly for satisfaction, that was never sated. That would have spent her trust by her early twenties and ended up dead in a gutter, had her very savvy Mom not tweaked her will before she died. That same part of me understood why my father had never retrieved it, because he, too, was a constant hunter. That money would kill a person like him, like me. So he never touched it.

There was a small possibility that he had literally forgotten it was there, but that seemed unlikely. Sadly, until he went into the home, RP had remembered everything from his early life and about up to 2000; it was the present he couldn't manage. Then there was the more feasible explanation: that he couldn't bring himself to spend the money for some reason. Was it because it was blood money from Steve Shearer?

12

I finally fell asleep just before dawn, into that dreamless, iron-heavy sleep of sedatives and whisky and trauma. I was slapped awake by an impatient paw, the mattress still stripped, my mouth glued to the pillow. I checked the time: 10:30 a.m. There was a glut of unread texts on my phone:

> Did u come 2 my house?

> My wife is pissed.

> U need 2 bck off

> Like srsly

I didn't know how he got my unlisted cell, but I knew immediately it was Danny. I blocked his number.

Someone going by HSTN77 on the true crime forum had instant messaged me overnight.

> YO! Seth's email is greene.s.@gmail.com. FYI, we had a few beers once . . . dude is a bit fried from drugs.

I typed a quick thank you to HSTN77. It was no big surprise that Seth75 was cooked. Seth smoked a lot, making his last name, Greene, a bit of a running joke—and that crowd gobbled acid and shrooms like they were gummy bears. I sent Seth a quick email, letting him know I was writing a story for *Inside Island* and asked if he would be willing to identify himself and if he wanted to go on the record about Andre.

I attended to Mister and then took a thirty-minute scalding shower. Next, I made real espresso from a proper Italian coffee machine with an engine like a Ferrari. It was my dad's one concession to domesticity and I think he acquired it in a police auction—it was rumored to have belonged to a Gotti. Coffee was a form of food for RP.

I sat down in front of my notebook and considered the next portal into my story.

THE TESTIMONY OF ERIN SLOANE
VALENTINE'S DAY, 1994: THE DAY I WENT TO HELL

I found him at Wendy's—or rather, I allowed him to find me. Danny wasn't working nor was he with me—he was on his dad's boat on the Sound, on a family outing. Valentine's Day was his parents' wedding anniversary. I drank a diet cherry Coke with too much ice, watching Ricky watch me through the galley of the kitchen. I drew a heart and an arrow in salt on the tabletop with my black nails. I counted the steps that it took for him to come from the galley to my table. Sixteen. He smelled of ketchup, oil, and cigarettes. He steepled his fingers and I noted his knuckles were crusted with scabs. I wonder if, like me, Ricky ran his knuckles across walls while walking.

Like Persephone, the last few months of my life had been spent in the underworld with my dad playing Hades. I had become head of the house by default. I learned how to cook for two and to screen calls from creditors.

With Danny, after the apologies, it was like the slap had demarcated something in our relationship—a before and after. There were no limits anymore—soft or hard. That night I had stepped out of the relationship, the way you might imagine the soul leaves the body. More and more, it was like there was a slow fire inside me, gaining momentum. Danny tried to put it out; stamp me down, but I was out of his control, set on getting free. Then he tried wooing me. It alternated between a rose, a burn, a song, a fracture. Always an apology. And promises. No one noticed, no one cared. I was basically an orphan. When he was trying, he bought me gifts: a beanie teddy with a little latex skull on it, a troll doll with a face painted like Gene Simmons, lingerie (nylon, the cup size three times too small, a snap crotch) and a journal to write about him in. Then he wrote notes to thrill and frighten me; they only did the latter. He wrote little songs for me on the guitar, the most disturbing one he played me was to the tune of "Would?" by Alice in Chains, changing the last line to:

> I'll leave her body there
> In West Cypress Road Woods

Ricky sat down in the booth, soundless as a cat.

"Eerie Erin," he said and smiled, showing me his gray tooth. It was awful.

I watched his fingers in the salt. He'd used my Southport nickname. I would use his.

"Ricky Hell."

He had drawn a knife.

He gestured to the parking lot. "Let's get the hell out of here. Your chariot awaits."

We sat in his truck and he lit my cigarette. He took out his own pack. He smoked Marlboro Lights like Danny. The truck was not like Danny's though—expensive, new, hotted up, smelling like pine and cigarettes. This was a working van, a greasy, manly truck.

"I heard about your family. You moved," he said, as if commenting on the weather.

I nodded. "Amityville is a fitting place for two ghosts." I was trying to be droll, but Ricky didn't bite.

"Is your dad okay? Are you okay?"

The radio was playing the Eagles. Ricky flicked it off.

I always lied when people asked. I accepted their casseroles with a smile, mailed the check, reassured distant friends and relatives, teachers, neighbors when they called with that same hollow, phony tone—I'm okay, he's okay, we're doing fine.

"No. Not really. Everything's pretty terrible."

Ricky just nodded.

"You usually work on a Saturday?"

"I work every day," Ricky said. I seem to remember Danny saying he had three jobs. He was poor, on minimum wage. The working class, shitty jobs, no college, no healthcare.

> *When the stars threw down their spears*
> *And watr'd heaven with their tears:*
> *Did he smile his work to see?*
> *Did he who made the Lamb make thee?*

"'Did he who made the Lamb make thee?'" he repeated, with emphasis on thee.

"The Bible?" I guessed. Real Satanists quoted the Bible at will, I knew. Real Satanists were well read.

"No. William Blake, 'The Tyger' from *Songs of Innocence and of Experience*."

He reached under the seat and handed me a huge book, dog-eared and thick as a doorstep. It was *The Norton Anthology of Poetry*.

"'A Robin Red breast in a Cage, Puts all Heaven in a Rage,'" he quoted.

That's me, I thought.

"That's you," he said.

"Are you on break?"

"Unofficially. I just quit," he said and gunned the engine.

———

I drank two cups of black coffee and ate the gluten free Pop-Tarts my dad had purchased for me before he lost the remaining cogs of his mind. There was another reason for eating the Pop-Tarts—last night I had defrosted the refrigerator and stacked the freezer with money—100,000 reasons to be precise. I had counted it ten times. I once read a book where a poet kept his manuscripts in the crisper so that they wouldn't perish in a house fire. This would have to suffice as a solution. The money would not be banked, should not be banked, unless I wanted the IRS sniffing around. If it was a blood gift from Steve Shearer to my father, I wanted to get rid of it.

Money's just paper, it's the energy you give it that makes it good or bad, Ricky Hell told me once.

"Don't give it to the cops, just spend it with good energy, Eerie," Ricky seemed to whisper to me now.

"Your sister should have it," I answered back.

I just had to find Julie first.

———

Julie Hernandez was a common name. According to the directory, there were a thousand listings for J Hernandez in Queens alone. Then I remembered that the backdrop she was standing in front of in the video was a famous burger joint that Ricky had taken me to, a family favorite and a Queens institution: Jackson Hole on Astoria Boulevard. That narrowed it down to 145 listings for J Hernandez. I put on more coffee, sat, and made my calls. Randomly calling people in NYC is a terrifying and bizarre experience—I heard a trombone in the background of my first call and then a lot of old people speaking Portuguese, someone cursing me out in English very creatively and someone cursing me out in Spanish (coincidentally enough, something about the devil). By lunchtime, I was walleyed and ready to hang up when I heard Julie's voice after the sixth ring.

"Hello, you've reached the Hernandez family," she said. It wasn't Julie herself though, it was a recording. An actual answering machine.

"We're not home, so leave a message for Rosie or Jose—"

"Or Mami," a kid shouted and another shushed and a chorus of giggles sounded.

"Or me," she recovered.

I left a brief message and gave her my cell number, explaining I'd be available any time to talk to her.

Maybe it was picturing the whorls and loops, the DNA sequencing of Ricky's bloodline, replicating and living on in small fingers turning sticky pages and falling asleep on a mother who wasn't out turning tricks but stroking their hair as they slept that drew my tears. Maybe I had a sentimental idea of motherhood because my own mom was gone.

In the meantime, my cell pinged to indicate a new email. It was from Seth75.

Hi, Erin, is it? Don't really remember you from the Res but if you say so. Yeah Andre was my buddy and I'll go to bat for him. If you want, I can walk you through the Spot—there's an altar that was made from sticks and driftwood that the cops still haven't found. I can show you.

Go to bat? A sick joke or a slip of the tongue. Was Seth Greene another sick puppy from a bad litter? I wasn't about to meet some dude I didn't know from Adam, alone in West Cypress Road Woods. I typed back:

Perhaps we could meet at Neptune's Diner and you talk me through it. Is this afternoon possible?

He emailed back:

Y. 4:30.

I replied:

Great. See you then.

I could check out the woods beforehand, see if that altar existed. Then I remembered that Mona Byrnes lived right behind West Cypress Road Woods.

I toyed with the idea of using the element of surprise as leverage, because Mona was a somewhat slippery kind of human. I knew she'd retired and was a homebody; old school cops like Mona didn't know what to do with themselves in the real world. They were morally dubious night-dwellers who needed barstools, smoke, and criminal activity, not stamp collections or book clubs. But I changed my mind. I wanted to go in soft, play to her memories of my father. Her home phone number was in my dad's dusty Filofax.

She sucked in her breath when she recognized my voice.

"Erin Marie Sloane."

"Hi Mona. I'd like to talk to you about the Southport Three. I have some questions."

"Course you do. You want to stop by? You have the address, am I right?"

"I have the address."

"C'mon over after lunch. I walk Moscow at three," she said. Moscow, I imagined, was a dog. Like RP, it seemed Mona loved dogs.

———

It was nearly lunchtime. I dressed in a black and gray wool dress—the same outfit I wore yesterday, only this one was clean—black stockings, boots. It wasn't that I lacked imagination exactly; it was just easier to wear a uniform and I had no idea what suited me anymore. I ran a brush through my hair and examined my face in the mirror—like, I really looked at my face. Every day I went through the motions of applying concealer stick like war paint, daubing foundation and outlining my eyes with kohl, a little blush to make me less corpse-like.

Was Danny right? I mean, I'd been wearing the same eye makeup since high school, irrespective of fashion. It wasn't an accessory—it was a mask. The roundness that had plagued my face until my late twenties had become more angular, more defined as my collagen bulk slowly disappeared. The last doctor I'd seen said I looked drawn and anemic. I was childless, single, and antisocial. Maybe I should streak my hair, buy a bottle of spray tan, use bronzer.

My mother had said I had a chip of ice in my heart—but I realize now that it was more about needing personal freedom. Like RP, I was a lone wolf, only I wasn't in the position of being bound to a pack like he was. Maybe it was having someone trying to trespass on my sense of self so young; somebody violating my personal space so frequently. Danny had made me read my diary aloud to him. At times, his face would be so close to mine it was like he was trying to steal my breath. In some cultures, they describe ghosts who steal your breath and night hags who paralyze you. In Africa, they say the devil is riding you.

Simply put, I was better off alone.

My phone pinged, the sound of another email coming through. It was Aisling. Her writing made me feel dizzy and odd—the run-on sentences with no punctuation, the clipped syntax, the changing fonts and colors.

Hi Erin, I know who u R. Yes, Cormacs my brother and hes in Australia. He goes by Michael officially, cause he doesn't want to be associated with the Southport Three. I was in New York until Steve Shearer got my permanent visas canceled—I can visit but not live in US unless I go through the whole process again, he knows ppl, ppl in immigration.

Steve told Marion everything about the job, she was like his diary—but also, I have a "source" in Nassau County cant say who.

Southport 3 = Carole Jenkins is a lying slut so don't even bother-and if u do DONT mention MAC and that Danny = evil shit (but u know that)

I dont care for or about RH but he went down wrong in
history and Julie H is like my oldest friend . . . u should talk
to her. We lost touch tho, so don't have her number. I want
to bring Steve down so I'll not only talk to you, I'll fly over for
it!!!!!!!!!!

Who the hell was Marion? I read on hoping to find out.

Next was a forward from Aisling, originally from Cormac O'Malley, with a file attachment.

His email address was lostinspace@gmail.com.

The message was short and simple:

Dear Aisling, I have a great deal of consternation

(Consternation even!!)

about sending this and ransacking the past, but as you say,
Steve's got to be held accountable one day. Doing it for
Marion. Love always,

Mac

I clicked download and a Word document filled the screen.

I put my head in my hands. Another memoir. The title was peculiar: *Resident Alien.* I made a snap decision. I would read the first few pages:

Past the shapes of lightning, beneath the clouds, a dark sea of skyscrapers and buildings lit up by a million blinking lights like church tabernacles, which my sister had said before was like Jesus jumping up and down very fast; the city. Luminescent amber arteries that intersected islands of light and steel were roads and freeways, and the little vibrating objects, cars, and in the cars, people. And on and in all the islands, linked over the dark water by bridges that were as elegant as running writing, were people, more people than we could ever meet in our entire life.

Before we got on the plane, from Canada to New York, Steve told us we had to be silent. We were silent throughout the storm that made the plane pitch; Aisling drove her nails into my hand, leaving little half-moons behind, and the drinks cart nearly crashed into the lady next to us, who was moaning and dry nibbling pills like they were peanuts. Steve knew a guy in Customs, so we sat waiting in the room at JFK airport that backed onto the runway, silently, until he came and showed his badge to a large black woman with a hundred braids in her hair, and she waved us through. *Go on in.* America. It was that easy.

Marion stood waiting with a cluster of helium balloons and a placard that read "O'Malley." Marion had drawn it, I'd know her writing anywhere—the O and M too big and extravagant so that all the other letters were squashed together at the end. Next thing we knew, we were in the car that was called a Jeep, Marion holding both our hands through the front seat, and Aisling saying in a tiny voice, "I've forgotten how to talk it's been so long."

"I've forgotten how to talk," Steve said in a voice that was meant to mimic my accent, but was so off the mark we all laughed. "You're a trip, kid." Steve ruffled Aisling's hair and he whistled and beeped his horn all the way home from the airport. High up in the Jeep, not as high as the plane, we looked out at the city, the night was charcoal and there were no stars, just lights and horns and rain.

———

Steve Shearer, in living color, on the page. I decided Mona could wait. I revved up the Gotti machine to make myself a black coffee and decided to read the entire chapter of *Resident Alien*.

———

Steve's apartment was in a suburb called Queens. In the morning, we walked to Austin Street, through a steady stream of traffic. Fat bottle green and scarlet leaves crunched under our feet. We learned the names of the trees that lined the streets: green ash, Callery pear, and red maple. We crossed bridges and underpasses, looked up at fire escapes like those where cops chased criminals in the movies. People were sitting outside their apartments with boom boxes, and glittery blue-black men were ducking and weaving around basketball courts. Men in heavy overcoats with skullcaps and prayer shawls walked in pairs; an obese woman wheeled a dog in a stroller.

Queens was full of streets called blocks, with apartments and basketball courts. We learned words like "fall" and "mall" and "want." Exotic words—"Hasidic," "kosher," "bodega," "borough."

But it was the food that really got to us. Our pupils were permanently enlarged and our mouths salivated over the street foods: roasted honeyed nuts sold by vendors; pizza pies, hot saucy, cheesy slices so big you could fold them, with bubbles in the dough.

In the first week Steve introduced us to Nathan's hot dogs filled with canary yellow mustard, which had the medicinal tang of pickles, and sandwiches with six kinds of cold meat, called cold cuts; fake cheese in a can, marshmallow and peanut butter together, pizza pockets. We went to supermarkets and came out with brown shopping bags filled with Pop-Tarts, knishes, bagels, pretzels, Ring Pops, and candy bars longer than a ruler.

Marion took us to a place called Greenwich Village. Aisling called Marion Mum and Marion flew into a rage; she spent four blocks reminding us never to mention Marion's age (I found out how old she was because she left her passport out), to never call her Mum or even Mom. Aisling wept for all those four blocks until Marion bought her a Guatemalan worry doll and a Baby Ruth candy bar. She bought me a Guns N' Roses record at a store, John Lennon glasses, and leather fingerless gloves. Aisling drank hot chocolate in a café where cats sat on the tables. Marion let me drink coffee and the waitress who poured the coffee from a glass jug smiled at me and my heart jumped into my throat. The same woman asked Marion for her phone number.

Steve said that the gloves were faggoty.

"Why buy gloves without fingers?" Steve laughed, and Aisling laughed too.

We learned a new glossary of insults as Steve drove his '89 Land Rover, the Eagles on the tape deck, a baseball bat in the back of the car, and two guns strapped to him—Aisling and I saw him only take them off at nighttime. At the red lights, he brushed his hair with a boar's bristle hairbrush and looked in the mirror as he did it. No one else could touch the brush, not even Marion.

We were somewhat famous in Queens. People praised our pallid skin. They made us say words like "bath" and "ask" and "pardon" and sometimes stroked Aisling 's long red hair. We were often given free things from shops, cars honked their horns and shouted out of the car to Marion, "Lookin' fine, Blondie," and "Marry me, Blondie."

When I said Marion looked a lot like the singer Blondie, Aisling said she didn't know who that was, and neither Marion and I could believe it, so we went to the record store in the East Village and showed her the cover of *Parallel Lines*, a blonde woman in a white summer dress, with a row of suited men lined up behind her. The store clerk played us "Heart of Glass" and Aisling danced around with Marion, offbeat, until she got dizzy. Marion bought it for us on tape and Aisling was always either playing it, or singing it off-key, aloud, under her breath, getting the words wrong.

We were illegals so we couldn't go to school. We would remain illegals until a year and a half in when our immigration lawyer helped us get cards that read "Resident Alien."

Very soon it was December, but we had to say "Happy Holidays," not "Happy Christmas." Snowfall that was starched and white as a businessman's shirt, hard and painful to the touch, soon became filthy slush on the street from the exhaust fumes of the cars. It was a bit early, but we were wrapping presents we now called "gifts" in front of the small tree Marion had bought, when Marion and Steve told us we had a guest.

Cooper Deane was Steve's partner—and the first visitor we had over to the apartment. We were excited because he looked like Kurt

Russell from the movie *Overboard* and he rode up the street on a Harley-Davidson. I remember the roar of the engine as he pulled up; later how his face was illuminated by the pink and green bulbs of the Christmas tree as he bent down and ruffled Aisling's hair. He wore a brown leather jacket that smelled of cowhide and made jokes out of the side of his mouth.

"I miss Christmas, man," he said. "I'm Catholic, but my wife, Angie, is Jewish. No can do!"

Steve told a joke about a concentration camp that I knew was a Mel Brooks joke, and Steve and Marion laughed and Aisling joined in because she thought she was supposed to. It was as if I was the only one who knew that not only was it not funny, it was stealing, too. Cooper just shook it off.

"What grade are you in?" he asked Aisling, who was practically climbing on him. We'd been pretty much stuck in the apartment for so many months, we'd never met any new people. Before we came to New York, Aisling had hoped that Steve would be like Tony Danza in *Who's the Boss?* Steve had lost that smiley Danza dad-ness, or maybe he had never really had it. He didn't take me or Aisling to shoot hoops like Tony Danza did but watched us instead like a dog guarding his dinner, out of the corner of his eye, ready to growl.

"She should be going into fifth grade," Steve answered, looking at Marion like he got extra points for getting it right.

"What pretty auburn hair for such a pretty girl."

Aisling looked up at Cooper, starstruck. Her hair was not auburn but vermillion, and tightly corkscrewed. It was the hair adults praised and kids ridiculed.

Steve ordered pies—which meant pizza—and sausage and we ate, watching *Who Framed Roger Rabbit* on video, which we'd seen already.

Steve had schooled us on what to do—to wipe our pizza with napkins to absorb the fat. To fit in, we had to speak "less British." We needed to start thinking about getting into a "good college."

We only drank diet soda and never without a straw.

"We can't afford the dentist. My ex has MS, but she's basically just a lying dope fiend." Steve shot a look at Cooper when he said this, like a challenge, but Cooper just shrugged and took the peppers off his pizza, just like me.

After dinner, before Cooper left, he took Aisling for a ride around the block on his motorcycle. I watched them ride off, Aisling with a too-big helmet on her head, clutching him around the waist like a baby koala. He said he'd take me for a spin too, but I said "No, I'm right." Cooper just smiled wider, not understanding why I didn't want to ride with him. Steve shoved me toward the bike.

"C'mon, kiddo," Cooper said, his smile open and ready.

"It doesn't mean the same thing in America, to say you're right." Steve was watching me, watching Cooper.

"I'm going inside." I broke away. Aisling was still on the bike glued to Cooper, her mouth an "O" of surprise, like a 1950s biker's moll, her cheek pressed against his leather jacket, the engine idling.

"He's scared," Steve said loudly. He didn't mention our biological father was killed on a motorcycle.

On Christmas Eve, Steve took us ice-skating in Forest Hills. I watched on the sidelines. Aisling could roller-skate so she should have had relatively good balance, but she kept crashing. She waved at me, like *I'm fine, I'm fine, look at me, everyone watch me.* She attempted to shadow-skate with Marion, who was scared and clung to the wall. Steve had played ice hockey all his life. As far as I could see, ice hockey was all about flying pucks, hitting each other hard with sticks, and cheering when blood stained the ice. Steve was very graceful for a big guy, balletic even. On the ice, all his machismo and meanness seemed to evaporate; his menacing bulk made sense as he executed what I learned later was a camel spin, one leg extended in the air. Still, he wouldn't help Aisling when she fell, and I watched her sitting on the ice, blinking back tears.

Steve came over and sat next to me and smoked menthols, his breath like ice. "Aisling's got as much coordination as a drowning cat."

I nodded and blew on my hands.

"Aisling needs help," he said.

"What kind of help?" I asked, but it came out weakly.

I caught Marion creeping up to surprise Steve, with a tray of orange juice and hot dogs. She'd overheard. She gave Steve the look that she gave us when we'd broken her favorite lamp. *I'm not angry, I'm disappointed.*

She rubbed my shoulders.

"That OJ?" Steve rubbed her arm and I took one too, but the drink burned on the way down. My stomach was always acid around Steve.

"Your hands are frozen. He needs gloves," she said to Steve, as if he were to blame, even though I'd lost them.

Afterward we went to TGI Fridays for sundaes. Aisling puked up her mint-green ice-cream peanut butter triple fudge sundae in the booth.

"Is she, like, retarded or just, like, gross?" Steve asked.

"She's probably lactose intolerant." I made a five-pointed star out of sugar on the table.

"Your mom told me she wets the bed. She's ten, right?" Steve commented. Aisling *had* started to wet the bed—I had to sleep in the bathtub sometimes because of it—but it was a secret. A *family* secret.

"She's just nervous. A lot of kids do it. It's your fault anyway. Everyone knows you're a bully. You wouldn't even help her up off the ice. Our real father was much nicer than you. I wish you were dead instead of him."

One minute I was in the booth and the next, I was lifted off the seat by the force of the punch, hitting my head back onto the wooden booth. Steve explained it wasn't his fault that I drove my top teeth through my bottom lip, but he apologized for it later and paid for the cleaning of the booth and the four stitches I needed in my lip.

Marion told the nurse at the hospital that I had a fight with my sister and fell backward and then hit my head on the booth. The nurse shined a light in my eyes and stitched my lip up, right there in the corridor. A young doctor came past and did some more tests and asked me the date. My name. Where I lived. I hoped he wasn't an undercover with immigration. His voice was machine-gun fast. I looked at Marion, too fearful to talk. He got the idea I may be concussed and wanted me to stay in for observation.

Marion toyed with the gold heart necklace Steve had bought her, with a pear-shaped diamond in the middle. Her eyes were bright from crying. Men liked that.

"Can't we take him home? He's just got a headache," she pleaded.

There were people in the corridor who had been stabbed; one man had a knife still jutting out of him. An obese woman moaned, her frantic daughter pacing the hall shouting curses. An old woman had a cardiac arrest on a hospital gurney and Marion prayed a rosary for her soul and cried non-stop. As far as I could see, everyone wanted to kill each other at Christmas.

"Rest him up, Mrs. O'Malley. Not too much excitement, okay?" The doctor smiled, looking down her shirt at the same time. Aisling was waiting, still in her white ski jacket, with a pack of M&M's she'd bought me from the vending machine with her own money and a teddy from the gift store, but I noticed she sat with Steve. It was like she'd figured out if she sucked up to him, she was less likely to get hurt.

We stopped at Tower Records where Steve bought me *Master of Puppets*, and Mariah Carey's *Emotions* for Aisling.

We had to drive past Steve's ex's home, in a place called Staten Island, for something to do with maintenance. His ex-wife, the drug fiend with MS, was standing in the doorway, not in a wheelchair. She was wrapped in an expensive fur coat and her earrings were pear-shaped diamonds; her eyes were pinpoints.

"What a nice family you have," she called out, and her smile, when it broke out on her face, was like a slow, devastating fire.

Later that day Cooper Deane was shot dead.

13

Now Steve had a slain partner, Cooper Deane, who had entered the story—a felled idol for the fatherless O'Malley kids. I wondered if Aisling had read Cormac's manuscript before sending it on. It wasn't an especially flattering portrait of her; she was rendered almost like a family pet, lovable but challenging. And it struck me as a bit too stylized to be a diary; overly partisan. It had an agenda. I mean, there was nothing about Southport yet, but it was giving me a good background picture of who Steve Shearer was.

I looked up Cooper Deane's death. It was a pre-internet and pre-Giuliani crime and a time when gun crime was rampant, so there was little to go on immediately. There was a *New York Times* article in the archives about a shooting at an ice-creamery, on a snowy day in February 1993, with a few idioms about the dangers of the job. Cooper had been in NYPD Queens North Precinct. There was a blurred photo of Deane; it wasn't hard to make out his Kurt Russell good looks. Cormac O'Malley had clearly taken creative liberties with the murder of the all-American Cooper Deane when he wrote that it took place on Christmas Eve.

It was difficult to concentrate because I'd received ten more texts since I'd sat down to drink my coffee and read. Half of them I didn't open, they were a blur of menace—*Bitch, listen to me—I love you*s and empty threats, one which had succeeded in rattling my cage a little. I corralled Mister inside, locked up the house, and then went back and triple-checked all the locks and punched in the alarm code.

I normally parked on the street because the overhanging fruit tree by my neighbor's house scratched my car, which wasn't a big deal because the LeBaron was half my age, but the birds it attracted—and the bird shit—was a problem. As I left the house, I clocked a fresh oil stain on the driveway; a car had parked there recently. The oil was still wet, in the shape of a boot or an upside-down gun.

As Denise had discerned last night, my meeting had clearly disturbed Danny. I hated how jumpy I was as I started the car, how my heart crashed in my chest, how every sound in the driveway seemed too loud and cinematically rendered. So far, I had managed to ignore Danny and let him have his prolonged tantrum, but in the past, that hadn't worked so well. In fact, it had left me permanently scarred.

Cops like RP and Ox didn't believe in restraining orders but in broken legs—these days I tended to agree. I wondered if I should call Ox, ask him to have a conversation with Danny. He'd had one for me before, with a bartender turned boyfriend who turned out to be trouble back in Brooklyn, summer of '08. He'd got jumped on Morgan Avenue, heading home from a shift. Nothing too bad, a busted lip, a few stitches. It was enough for him to move to a new job in the Lower East Side and stop contacting me.

———

Mona's front yard was neat and tidy, with a winding path that was weeded so evenly it could have been done with nail scissors. She had an American and Irish flag on a pole next to the front porch and a porch swing. A pair of men's boots were lined up by the door. She was single then, I guessed—I did the same thing. A metal placard with an Irish saying was nailed above the door, alongside a Celtic cross. I think it meant something like "Bless this House" or "May the road rise to greet you" or "Come on in and get shitfaced."

"Tae," Mona's voice barked at me from behind the screen. *Tea.* It wasn't an offer, but a command. Mona had spent most of her adult life in the States, but still had the dregs of an Irish accent. The "ea" of words turned into a's; e's were o's, almost Rastafarian. Things that were small were wee; she scornfully referred to a criminal as a "hard mon" more than once. And Mona was, of course, a hard woman. She wasn't only a cop in a time when women were practically still unarmed—unwanted, bullied, belittled, and worse—she was from the North, from Belfast.

Mona's house was dark and smelled like dogs and stale cigarettes, with a top note of cinnamon potpourri. My mother also liked potpourri. I wondered if Mona liked to decoupage too. Her face was a child's drawing of a woman, two very round eyes with long lashes and a full mouth; a cascade of thick chestnut hair. In the thin yellow light of the dining room, she had a weak chin, the beginning of jowls, streaks of silver in her hair.

Still, Mona had maintained her hourglass figure. She even dressed the same: tailored jeans, white button-up Gap blouse. I could totally picture a shoulder holster as her primary accessory.

"Hi," I said.

"Hi yourself."

She led me into the dining room—there was no hallway to speak of. It was oddly formal and fitted out for a woman who lived alone—who always had. There was a dark oak family table with too many seats, cabinets with display glasses and dishware and, among the old black and white restored photos, images of two German Shepherds lined the wall.

A radio played in a far-off room.

"Those your dogs?" I seemed to remember RP telling me Mona had taken on police dogs that never made the cut.

"Yep. Whisky and Brandy," Mona called out from the adjacent kitchen. "Moscow is the neighbor's. He's a Rottweiler–Doberman." She returned, not bothering with the teapot or china cups. She held two Christmas mugs, mine was a Santa skull, full of black tea, with the bag still in.

"Let me guess, you take it black?" Mona thrust the mug at me and sat on the chair at the head of the table, folding her jean-clad legs underneath her. I sat next to her, facing a cherry-red display cabinet.

A series of drugstore china leprechauns sat next to a line of commemorative plates.

"I do, thanks."

"My dogs are dead."

"I'm sorry," I said. "About your dogs."

Mona shrugged. She wasn't going to show weakness to me, but her hand shook as she collected her cup.

"Someone baited them," she said.

I drew in a breath. "Did you find out who did it?" I knew that most of Mona's family lived on the other side of the world and her dogs were her children, the same way that Mister was mine. Grief clawed at my throat. *This could be you; this will be you.*

"They'd not still be walking the earth if I did," Mona answered, in that gravel and honey voice.

She took out a cigarette and offered me one. Virginia Slims. I accepted it.

"Ray's not dead, is he?" Most of the cops I knew referred to my father as RP or Sloane.

"No. He's getting there."

Her shoulders relaxed slightly. "Sweet jumping Jesus, that's a relief. I thought perhaps he'd passed."

"He's in a care facility. I'm fixing up the Amityville house. It's going on the market soon."

"You mentioned Southport."

"That's why I'm here. Two reasons really. One is the Southport Three. The Andre Villiers murder. I'm writing a story for *Inside Island* magazine."

Mona just stared at me, her arms folded. I stared back. She was better at this game—I looked away first.

"I know you two took Carole Jenkins' statement that night. It's signed by you and RP."

"Yeah."

"So, I want to know why RP never told me he was the responding officer."

"As you know, your dad was a dipso, so he didn't tell you, cause he didn't attend the scene. He was at Benny's with me and then some of his cop buddies got him too poleaxed to drive. He sobered up enough to make it down to the station later that morning."

I gathered poleaxed was Irish for drunk.

"But why didn't he tell me about the statement? They were my friends. Danny Quinlan-Walsh was my boyfriend."

"And Ricky," she interrupted.

"I'm sorry, is that common cop knowledge?"

"No. But your dad knew. I knew."

"How?"

"Your dad had you followed, Erin." Her voice dragged on *Erin* like a flat tire. "After Christmas Eve . . . well, he thought you were going to, you know . . ." She made a cutting motion across her throat.

"*You* followed me?"

She shook her head and stabbed out her cigarette. "Ox."

Ox. I needed to lubricate my dry throat and took a sip of the hot, strong tea.

"I just talked to him about the case. He never mentioned that." Ox had said absolutely nothing the night before about tailing me and, moreover, nothing about Ricky Hell at all. In a way it made sense, Ox was a kind of guardian angel in my life. I thought of him on that Christmas morning, helping me with my shoes. I thought of the favors he had called in for me over the years—a DUI not on my record a few years back. The bartender boyfriend who wouldn't take no for an answer. That Ox lied, even by omission, burned me a little.

"Surprise, surprise. He and RP must be cut from the same cloth. Speaking of, you have a knack for dating scumbags."

I just stared at her with scorn.

"And yet you were sleeping with a married alcoholic who was at one point suspected of murdering his entire family."

"Except one." Mona smiled. "Lucky last."

I wanted to hit her, but I thought that's what she was anticipating, and I never wanted to please my father's mistress. I stayed cool.

"They call it a sole survivor, I think."

"Last time I spoke to RP, you lived in Brooklyn, had a fancy job. Why would you come back to help a man you thought was so rotten, even if he is your only living flesh and blood?"

I couldn't answer that. Mona thought she could.

"Because you love him in the same way he loves you. RP worried about you and he wanted to protect you. And that's why he didn't tell you about that night, because it didn't matter. It wouldn't have helped you get over Ricky dying, Danny going to jail."

She sighed heavily.

"Look Erin, you survived the night of the accident and you survived that whole Southport Three nightmare and you survived . . . well, you know what, you survived. If you think about it, you're a real jammy bitch, you know that?"

"Excuse me?"

"You have a knack for surviving," she translated. "You're lucky."

"Lucky," I echoed.

"Doesn't seem to me that you are pleased about it though," she remarked. "The surviving part, I mean."

I shrugged. What could I say? She'd hit the nail on the proverbial head.

"So why take this story? Why not leave the past dead and buried?"

The slim cigarette was beginning to make me feel ill—my breathing was shallow and my heart rate began to build up.

"You wouldn't."

I watched smoke trickle out of her nostrils. Her round, polished doll's eyes registered nothing. "Yes, I took the Jenkins girl's statement. RP signed off on it. And RP hid that from you to protect you, because it was all very upsetting. Your next question?"

"Carole Jenkins' statement is, to put it bluntly, a pile of horseshit. So is her book. Another source told me RP and Steve Shearer had something going on together. Did RP take Shearer's money to corroborate this satanic BS story the kids came up with?"

"Come outside," she snapped. Her tone brooked no argument.

"Okay," I agreed. We walked through a hallway, through a rec room, and down some stairs into the yard.

"Are you wired up?" She said it so fast, her lips barely moved.

"What?"

"Your dress."

She leaned down to her ankle, where a holster was strapped. Her face set like asphalt. Mona was a hard woman.

"Wait." I didn't believe she'd shoot, but there was a margin of doubt that felt uncomfortable.

I reached around and unzipped the back of my dress. I had thick stockings on. Did she expect me to take those off too?

"You want your answers, then strip. The bra, tights, boots."

I was standing outside in 43 degrees Fahrenheit. The last time I wore a bathing suit without a T-shirt over it I was sixteen and it had been a bikini with skulls on the tits.

Mona's place bordered the east side of West Cypress Road Woods— about a mile away from the crime scene. Her backyard was the size of a small field, a chain fence erected to keep the dogs in the yard, which also kept out whatever wild things lived in the woods. Despite being so close to the place where Ricky Hell had taken his last breath, I felt safe around the trees. We often went into the woods as a family and RP would reel off the trees' scientific names. Me and Shelly would paste the leaves we gathered into a scrapbook and transcribe the scientific names: *Quercus borealis, Cornus florida*—Northern Red Oak, Flowering dogwood. RP loved trees, he loved facts—I mean he liked things that didn't talk. And like me, he didn't usually take off his shirt.

"Holy Jesus, Mary, and Joseph," Mona said, staring at my chest as I dropped my dress to the dirt.

14

"In some cultures, the pentagram is a symbol of protection," Mona offered. We were sitting in her wood-paneled rumpus room; me, with a glass of port in one hand, wrapped in a plaid blanket.

"Carved on your chest with a razor, a giant *666* and the letter *D* in the middle?"

She grimaced.

I drank the godawful port. The room smelled of mold and regret.

"Yeah, I s'pose not."

I just shook my head.

"My father once said my only future was as an exotic dancer if I kept on the way I was going. Now that option is lost to me."

"Had he known about this, he would have hunted down the perpetrator and ended him." She touched my hand. I flinched and withdrew it quickly. "You know, you didn't check my orifices. Did you want me to assume the position?"

"Come on, Erin, I'm sorry. You need to understand. Some pretty savage stuff went on. When your ma and sister died—"

"You were having an affair with my father." Despite its wood and paint palette, I nodded yes to a refill of the port.

She returned to the scar. Mona wasn't one to be rushed into a conversation. "You never thought to get it removed?"

"I've tried creams. And a derma roller . . ."

"The one on TV?" Mona looked interested. I looked around at the shelves. She clearly bought things from magazines; commemorative plates, bric-a-brac. I pictured her sitting all night in front of the television, filing those perfectly oval nails, dialing 1-800-Juicebullet and giving over her credit card details. I couldn't picture her in sweats, or pajamas. Lonely, late-night Mona wore her cop clothes, her holster.

"Yeah. I mean, there's always laser therapy, but it's very expensive. And my insurance doesn't cover the cost of removing a giant satanic symbol. There's ink in there too," I said. The fact was, I could have removed it, but it was extremely uncomfortable to show up at one of those places and have to explain how it got there in the first place. I always meant to go out of state to get it done. Then I sort of grew into it; it became part of me, like a vestigial digit. Also, I didn't like to travel.

"But yes, Erin, we had a thing. It wasn't ever going to be anything more for RP than a bit on the side. I wasn't soft and maternal enough. I wasn't book-smart yet also able to whip up chocolate-chip cookies from scratch. I wasn't *Lenora*." I didn't like her saying my mother's name, especially like that—she didn't love her. I had. I swallowed my rage with my port—it wouldn't serve me well to erupt.

"Spare me the miniature violins, Mona. He had a wife and, trust me, she was long suffering. I don't need to know the details of your affair. I only want to know if you were together that night. Christmas Eve, I mean."

"Contrary to rumor, when your mom and sister died, Ray and I weren't actually together. A hiatus, I thought. But no, it was because he wanted to make it work with Lenora. He was trying to win her back. And Lenora wasn't always waiting at home alone."

What the fuck was that supposed to mean?

Her mouth puckered. A phrase occurred to me—you get the face you deserve. Age was a great equalizer. Bitterness was sucking her dry. Or that could have been all the drink and cigarettes. Back in the day Mona was really something with her big chocolate Hershey's Kisses eyes. While the skin on her face was still taut, the large semi-lit lanterns that previously animated her were now dull. Her face was taut, but the skin on her neck was loose and crepey.

"You like to read, Erin. Tell me this, did you ever hear about a story called 'The Purloined Letter'?"

"I think I remember it. Is that the one about the monkey?"

She screwed up her nose.

"No, you twit, it's about a letter. A stolen letter. Me and your dad, we were told this story as detectives by this very screwy Supe of ours. I won't bore you with the details," she said watching my eyes glaze over, "but in the story, your man Dupin finds out the letter is right there, hiding in plain sight. See, we look so hard for answers and our brains don't allow for the possibility that the whole time, the answer is right there."

"What's your point?"

"Sometimes the answer is right in front of you," she said slowly.

I wasn't going to let her confuse me, if that was what she was trying to do. "The night that Andre Villiers died," I continued, "when you attended the scene—I called Benny's that night, looking for RP. He said, 'He's with his lady friend.' I'd paged RP. Nothing. And he didn't get home until morning."

"Yes. We were intending to meet with an informant nearby, we went to meet our guy; he never showed. Then we went to have a drink, we had a fight, namely over how much RP was drinking that night. I left, I went home. Ray stayed on at Benny's. I'm sure he stayed until closing time. After that . . . I don't know."

Benny's closed around midnight. Benny was a legendary drinker, going shot for shot with all the cops, firemen, and other shift-working dipsos he served. So RP would have been in no state to drive. Maybe he just slept in his car. I always presumed he was with Mona.

"So, that's why it was me taking the statement. And our guy, Richard was dead." Mona hung her head. "It was our fault that he died."

"Wait, what? Our guy?"

"I'm trying to tell you Erin, it's been right in front of you all this time. Richard was no Satanist. Richard was our informant."

I nearly choked on my port. "I'm sorry, what?"

"Richard Hernandez was our informant." Mona looked up at me, her face grim.

"A narc?" The word narc came out like Tourette's—it was the word Aisling had used.

"Not a narc, you dope. He wasn't a cop. He was just a kid."

"What then, a rat?" My stomach turned, thinking about Ricky and his *21 Jump Street* denims; a cuckoo, a foundling, in our death metal nest.

"More like a plant. NYPD got him to approach Shearer, got him to be his distributor, to entrap him."

"Wait, I don't understand. Go back to the beginning. None of this makes sense. Why were you and RP involved?"

"Internal Affairs approached us. You know your father went undercover narco for most of the seventies and some of the eighties with NYPD."

"Yeah, then we moved to the island when I was little," I prompted her. "And he moved to Nassau County, 7th Precinct."

It was my mom who forced it. She wanted him to stay safe. And it probably was the thing that undid their marriage. RP was bored in Nassau County—he craved danger. Maybe he found that in having an affair with Mona.

"Well, RP missed it. When they contacted us to help them with a homicide, to bring down Shearer, a cokehead, who they suspected had shot another cop—his old partner, Cooper Deane—it was the kind of covert op he needed."

The same motorcycle-riding Cooper Deane who had just entered the pages of *Resident Alien*.

"They figured Deane had cottoned on to Shearer, maybe he wanted to rat. Shearer pinned the murder on a mixed-race juvenile from Jackson Heights, who he shot dead. His name was Franklin Rivera. He would have gotten away with it too, but there was a witness. We got the job of working with the kid who saw Shearer shoot Deane dead. Franklin's cousin, Richard Hernandez."

"Ricky Hell," I said dumbly.

"Franklin and Ricky were meeting at an ice-cream shop, but Ricky was late. He watched Shearer shoot Deane and then his cousin," she said. "Ricky was scared. He wanted to help. Shearer didn't clock him and he ran. So, the NYPD decided they could use him to good effect. Your father and I had met Steve Shearer—so we could never be involved in any undercover op. But we *could* help Hernandez."

My mind was frantically trying to slot the pieces together. "Ricky was basically a kid, who watched a cop kill a cop, then his cousin—and the police *used* him and got him killed?"

"Richard was a kid—a relatively good kid even if he was planning on buying weed from his cousin that day—and he was pretty grown up. He'd been at the Queens Academy for the Sciences in accelerated classes. He'd basically raised his sister. He wanted to help," Mona insisted, brushing her hair off her face.

"Wait, hold up. Before you said Ricky saw Shearer shoot his cousin. Shearer wasn't any the wiser to the connection between the two boys?"

"Rivera was just one of thousands of kids from the neighborhood and Richard was under the radar. Despite the occasional doobie, Richard was kind of a nerd in the hood."

Richard this, Richard that. Boot-tough Mona had cared for Ricky Hell. There was something about him that invoked the maternal instinct in the most unlikely places.

"So, early on, there was a question of foul play with Steve Shearer?"

"Things didn't add up. There was a suspicion he was dealing and Cooper was clean as a whistle. All we know is Steve Shearer set Franklin Rivera up for Cooper's death, then shot him through the heart."

Like he would Ricky?

Mona went over to the bookshelf, picked up a floral printed box. It contained a glut of photos, black and white, color, some papers, and underneath a Polaroid. I sat there with my arms folded, my heart jacked. She shunted the photograph across the scuffed table. It was Ricky. He was wearing steel-framed spectacles I'd never seen before. The only thing about him I recognized was his black T-shirt.

Mona studied me. "You okay?"

I had killed the romantic in me a very long time ago. At least I had my memories, right? Wrong. She had defiled them. I fell back in my chair. Betrayal snaked around my lower intestine.

"Ricky wore glasses?" I asked.

"Hernandez did. Hell wore contacts."

In another image, he wore a flannel shirt, his hair was long—not metal long, more chin length, Keanu Reeves in style. Grunge. A tiny silver cross around his neck. His face was pitted with vicious acne scars. On Ricky, they worked. He looked serious, worried. My father sat next to him—he had all his hair then, a bad tie, and a "gotcha" expression.

"This was Richard Hernandez, pre-Ricky Hell. We gave him an alter ego, a new name. That heavy metal stuff was all part of his cover—he needed to build a rep as a dealer and a badass. We were briefing him on his backstory that afternoon. It was 1993, before summer school. He learned quick."

"I'm trying to understand the timeline."

"Your dad got him into Belmont High for a few months to cause trouble, create a buzz. He got pulled out and went to summer school at Roosevelt. By the start of school, he was pals with Danny Quinlan-Walsh and Andre Villers and dealing for Shearer. Cormac O'Malley just happened to fall into the crowd, which I think Shearer wasn't happy about. Ricky got in deep with the metal kids, but then he got involved with you. It seemed he was cracking up a bit. Flaking out. Then he was killed."

In '93, I was in tenth grade, aged fifteen. I remembered Ricky descending from the yellow bus in September, like the Aztec God Huitzilopochtli, blood on his knuckles and H-E-L-L spelled out in studs on his denim-clad back. I remember thinking I'd seen the devil himself. It was a delicious thought—a delicious feeling. We got together in early 1994, a few weeks after I turned sixteen.

The kid was on the bones of his ass—he lived off Taco Bell, ramen noodles, cookies, and the leftovers I brought him. He had three changes of clothes. He often slept in his van and showered at friends' places—or the YMCA.

"If he worked for you, how come he had no money?"

"We paid, but not much. That Wendy's job was part of his cover.

Except he just quit one day, started hauling crayfish. But he took what he was doing with us seriously. He wanted to go to college. He was on a pathway to working in law enforcement. We cleared a juvenile prior that could have hurt him."

"He told me he was from Buffalo," I said.

Mona continued, indifferent to my suffering. "Both he and his sister Julie were moved to Southport in 1993 so she could go to a better school. That was also part of the deal. Listen, Erin, I know you think we coerced him, but Richard wanted a better life. He really took to our undercover option. He had a real talent for deception. He wasn't a Holy Joe, but he had a conscience. He could have been a cop if he wanted. A detective. The fella was a bright spark."

Maybe he felt guilty deceiving me. He often seemed sad, pensive, even lonely. Sometimes I felt he was on the verge of spilling over. I had missed all his confessional cues.

"We could have gotten Shearer on multiple felonies. But for the force, in the end, Ricky Hell was an embarrassment. So was RP. All we had was a formal statement from Ricky Hell and it was destroyed. After, I wondered . . ." Mona was practically wringing her hands. ". . . if they chose us in case it all went tits up. Because we were on the out. RP was anyways."

Then she held up the prize. It was a 1993 yearbook from Queens College. "You thought he was a dropout, right? Not the case. He went to night school."

There was a gray square in place of a photo and the year of his birth was listed with a dash suggesting he was still alive.

1973. I filled in the blank.

Richard Juan Hernandez, a High School Diploma, major in criminal justice and law enforcement studies.

The quote below his name:

To be yourself in a world that is constantly trying to make you something else is the greatest accomplishment.

                                        Ralph Waldo Emerson

"Ricky was twenty-one?"

"He'd turned twenty-one on October 30. He lived another twenty-four hours."

"We celebrated his eighteenth birthday in May. He told me he was a Taurus with an Aries rising."

Mona pulled a face. "Maybe he wanted to reinvent himself."

Ricky was older than he told me. A lot older than me. I was sixteen. Was that even legal?

"Look, I didn't fight for Richard, or try to pursue it further. I know you think I'm a piece of shit, but they threatened me. Ray was already in deep trouble and I needed my job. I needed my pension." Mona went to pour me another drink and I put my hand over the glass. I was probably already too wasted to drive.

"And RP got early retirement. He got his pension."

"And his gold watch. But he fought for both. As you well know, Ray was disgraced after your mom and sister died. It was a black mark against him. He wanted to expose Shearer. It was hushed up and he very nearly got the sack. Fired, I mean."

And I had presumed he was on probation because of the constant intoxication.

"You said Ricky had a juvie prior. What was it?"

"Ach, it was a little fire, that's all. No one got hurt." Mona waved her hand up in the air, to demonstrate it was no big thing. "He had a troubled childhood. Abused. Kids do that."

Serial killers too. I wondered about the scale of the fire; the charge against him.

Mona seemed to sense my discomfort. "An arson charge would have looked very bad on those college applications."

"Aisling O'Malley, Cormac O'Malley's sister, has tried to 'expose' Steve Shearer for killing Ricky, inciting Andre's murder. She also said RP was tight with Shearer. That he took money."

"We never took any money from Shearer." Mona's voice wobbled with the force of her conviction. "I'm telling you; your dad was like a pit bull with Shearer. The case destroyed him."

"Aisling also suggested Andre cottoned on to Ricky and Steve's deal, and therefore he needed to be eliminated. What do you think about that?"

Mona shrugged.

"Possible. I mean, with Shearer and Richard. It was all very covert though. You'd have to be pretty bright to work it out."

She didn't need to say the rest: Andre wasn't. He wasn't even wily.

"It seems that somehow Shearer found out about Ricky and shot him dead the same way he did Cooper Deane. So, who blew his cover?"

"We thought that it was possibly Danny Quinlan-Walsh. He was at your house. We didn't send emails back then, we had to shred confidential paperwork, never take documents home, but he could have come across something in your dad's study. Ricky called me from the phone booth at West Cypress Roads Woods at 7 p.m. after I paged him, but when I arrived to meet him he was gone. So, the other possibility was that if Danny hated Ricky, he may have followed him and confronted him about what he was doing, who he was meeting."

I felt light-headed. Maybe that's why Danny was trying to stop me from digging.

Mona studied me. "You look peaky. You need a coffee?"

I nodded.

"The short answer is, I don't know," she called out a little while later from the kitchen. "As I said, it was a covert op. Richard was a good scapegoat and conveniently disposed of for Steve Shearer." I followed her into the kitchen. I watched her take out the Folgers coffee and put it into a stovetop perc—my father must have bought it for her. Mona had a drip coffee machine gathering dust in the corner. While I enjoyed snooping in people's bathroom cabinets immensely, their kitchens were even more telling. Did they entertain? Were they on a diet? Did they drink? I noticed she had a penchant for cutesy barnyard animals cuddling together with aphorisms about friendship, and next to a real estate agency refrigerator magnet were a few novelty magnets including one which read: "Wine, chocolate, and men—they're better when they're rich!"

She lit the gas on the stove. Frivolity, sentimentalism, feminine conspiracy—all aspects of Mona I had never seen before.

There was nowhere to sit in Mona's cramped kitchen: I leaned against the window and started sneezing. She obviously didn't dust much.

"Richard was not responsible for Andre's death. Those kids in the woods *all* know what happened. And it's locked up here." She gestured to her forehead. "Maybe Shearer bribed them." She placed the percolator on the stove. "We lost our witness and our case against Shearer when Richard was shot dead. He was a genius; he could have been anything he wanted to. He shouldn't have died."

I could see that this had been eating Mona up for years. I wasn't the type to kick someone when they were down.

"I don't know the laws for statutory rape in the State of New York, but if RP knew I was being seduced by a grown man, an informant, why didn't he arrest Ricky?"

"Erin, I want to say something to you that's going to hurt. I promise you—he did care about you, even when he was all fucked up after your mom and Shelly. But you reminded him of himself and I don't think he could handle that. And take this from personal experience— nothing was more important to your dad than the job. He couldn't risk alienating Ricky." She lit up a cigarette, baring her port-stained teeth.

"And it is considered statutory rape to have sex with anyone under seventeen years old in New York, but there's a close-in-age exemption that allows for a four-year age gap as long as the minor is older than fifteen. So, technically speaking, it was unethical of him not to tell you, but not illegal."

By a technicality, I was not the victim of statutory rape. Thus, my father didn't give a shit. They all knew, all of them knew who Ricky was, his real birthday, his real identity—and they said nothing.

"RP needed Richard. And Ricky wasn't bad to you, not like Danny was, right?" Mona said, as if she were watching the wheels turn in my mind. I wondered why she was defending my father; after all, the guy dropped her like the proverbial hot potato, leaving her to her dead dogs, Santa mugs, port, and lonely nights in front of the psychic network.

She took the coffee off the stove and poured it into two clean Pottery Barn mugs.

"The tattoos . . ."

Ricky had wings tattooed on his back, and above his heart a stick and poke 666, so, when he held up his arms, from the back he might have looked like Lucifer.

"They predated the op. We thought they were very convincing."

"Ricky sure was convincing." I sounded bitter. "I believed he was bad. It was partly the look, but also the stuff he talked about." Ricky could riff on poetry, paganism, religion, physics, psychedelics.

"He was a bright boy but troubled, as I said. People only seemed to tune in to the parts about the devil. He really took on the persona. More than we'd have liked. Every Sunday, Richard Hernandez took his sister to the 10 a.m. service at Saint Al's, Belmont."

"I remember him telling me he'd been an altar boy once. So, why did that not come out when he was being crowned Mr. Teen Lucifer?" I asked.

Mona poured a lot of cream and sugar into her coffee, left mine black and turned from the stove to face me; thrusting the mug at me. Now Mona sounded annoyed. "Because that line wasn't going to sell," she said.

She was right. Here's what did sell: Carole Jenkins' tales of animal sacrifice and psychedelics in the West Cypress Road Woods, a mixed-race Satanist inciting rich white kids to murder. Not a lost kid butchering "Smoke on the Water" on his battered electric guitar in a water-damaged hotel room, or making sure his sister took communion.

Now I knew the full truth, I reflected on what a poor faux Satanist Ricky was. He cried when he hit a deer. He held his breath when we passed a cemetery.

I took a sip of the coffee. It had a bitter chemical taste. Mona made the same face as she tasted hers. The coffee was burnt.

"Look, the kids could have been under Steve Shearer's order," Mona said. "When you think about it, they were all troubled or from broken homes. And they were high at the time, they couldn't tell what was animal or human, which way was up."

I mentally cataloged the Southport Three: Carole was an ex-beauty pageant kid and a brain donor; Cormac was clearly damaged, an illegal immigrant—his mom had married Steve Shearer and his dad was dead; Danny was adopted and his father was a creep. Mona had a good point.

"There wasn't just one call from that booth on Halloween. Cormac O'Malley reportedly called Steve Shearer to the scene around 11 p.m. From what I understand, there was a record of a phone call from the booth at that time, but obviously, no record of who made the call as it was to Shearer's car phone and not 911. But Cormac didn't trust his stepdad," I said. "I don't think he was the one who called him after all. And Carole was in some Good Samaritan's car."

"So, who made the call then?" Mona asked. The milky afternoon light streamed through the window, highlighting the silver in her hair.

"That's a really big question. So I was thinking it might have something to do with money."

I didn't trust Mona yet and I wanted her reaction.

"You swear you didn't take money from Shearer, but I found money," I said carefully. "In my father's house."

She shrugged.

"A lot." I noted the swallow of her throat, how her hand crept toward her chest as if to protect herself. Her hands were old and bony, her knuckles prominent. She wore an antique-looking ring; a citrine band. The little stones glinted at me. I thought of Ricky's tiger eye.

"I left it with a friend. A lawyer friend," I lied.

"Good. Look, I don't know anything about any money. Do I look loaded to you?" She gestured around the small bungalow. Mona had a point. Unless it all went on mail-order leprechaun and dog statues, she was not exactly rolling in it.

"Maybe your dad took some money out of the trust Lenora left you when he was losing it?"

"That's not possible. My mom rigged it so it all went to my college education and whatever remained after I graduated college went to living in the city—which didn't go far. And the payout from life insurance and compensation from the pool company was gone by 2000. RP told me a bunch of reasons why at the time and I bought it."

"He might have put some away. No offense, but maybe he didn't want you to hit him up."

Mona was being my friend—or rather, she was acting like she was. In fact, she was being polite or maybe even kind. She didn't mention my expensive stint at the hospital, or postcollege rehab. The truth was, I would have hit RP up in my midtwenties had I thought he had cash.

I sipped my coffee, tasting the possibility of the money really being mine, RP being a good man, a good father; a good cop. I wanted the warmth; it was like sitting next to a bonfire.

Mona was correct in that she or RP were not in it for the power or the money. They were in it because they had a compulsion to do the job. They couldn't do life, or anything like it. But something wasn't right. That money didn't make sense—RP's decline after Ricky's death could be explained by disillusionment, guilt even, but he was visibly mortified. He sent me away and, although you could say it was to protect me, he never looked me in the eye again. RP was broke. He was a gambler, he was a drunk. Mona was either covering up for RP or was complicit. It was what cops did—stick together. I knew I had to go to the source: Steve Shearer, the villain of *Resident Alien*. Only then could I get the real story of Ricky Hell and the Southport Three.

"'One may smile and smile and be a villain,'" Mona said. Now she was quoting Ricky quoting Shakespeare.

I remembered what my father had always told me: *It's important, Erin, to know your enemy.* Mona's new loyalty gave me a bad aftertaste in my mouth, like a salty coin. It tasted like blood—it tasted like blood money.

"I'm going to find out what happened," I concluded.

"West Cypress Road Woods are just behind you. Where better to go than the scene of the crime," Mona said. "It's three. Time to skedaddle. I got a dog to walk. Fraid we can't come with you, the great big oaf whimpers whenever we get on the trail."

15

I didn't really believe that a ghost lived in the woods; nor did I really believe Seth75's claim that a driftwood altar had survived all these years in the Spot where the kids killed Andre, and where Ricky Hell was shot, but I still wanted to find out if there were any secrets the woods were holding. And I had not walked down that path to the Spot where Ricky was killed since 1994.

I took a left at Patriot Bend, drove down Revolution Avenue, and was a quarter of a mile up the gravel road when I finally spotted the old AT&T phone booth—the phone booth of my pre-cellphone adolescence. I couldn't believe it was still there. And it was a good thing; I was losing my signal out here.

I parked the Chrysler and checked my watch: it was only 3:10. I had well over an hour to meet Seth75 at the diner. I took a bottle of water from the passenger seat and the old police flashlight that belonged to my dad; plus my phone, some mace, a digital camera, a pack of cigarettes, and a lighter.

The inside of the phone booth had a meth and butane tang and was covered in graffiti—sexual slang, aspersions about a girl named Sheryl, gang tags, and on the semi-shattered glass door, just above the AT&T logo—in what looked like blood but had the consistency of nail polish—a childish scribbling of a pentagram and the words "Riki Hell lives!!!!"

Underneath there was a crude drawing of a pipe and the phrase "Bong On!"

So, Ricky Hell lived on in the memory of idiot Southport stoner kids, who partied in West Cypress Road Woods. He'd become an urban legend summoned on Ouija boards.

Now I knew that phone was one of the last places Ricky had visited. Why hadn't he called me, even just to say *I'm not coming.* Or *It's over, Eerie.* He had ghosted me, long before the phrase was even invented. And then he became a ghost.

I picked up the handset and realized the cord was severed.

I took a few photos and stepped out into the air. I was five minutes on foot from the Spot where Ricky died.

There was an energy to the woods—something about all that oxygen—that made me, made us, heady and excitable. It still did. I felt giddy as I spotted the fat old sugar pine at the front of the trail. I had climbed it as a kid.

The autumnal afternoon half-light felt bittersweet; nostalgic. Beneath my feet, a confetti of blood orange, red, and tongue-pink colored leaves. Then the trail: a cathedral of silver birch trees. I could almost taste the cold beer, the smoke, the stars; hear the stream running, remembering the Iroquois creation story Ricky had told me when we parked out here in his van, a story he'd been told by his father, whose name was also Richard. We were on Iroquois land, the land of his people. Later he laughed and told me he'd made it up—*I'm, like, a quarter Arapaho, we're from Wyoming, dummy.*

Was that even true?

I walked the trail alone, down to the Spot, counting the steps it took—adding a Mississippi for good measure. I was thinking of how Carole ran from the Spot to the road in the dark. While it was a clear enough trajectory, high as she was, she could have gone off track and wandered as far as the brook.

When I hit ninety Mississippi I started to hear a crunching in the leaves; an echo of my own footsteps. I stopped dead in my tracks, immobile with panic—afraid to retreat, fishing my hand into my bag for the mace. Then I talked myself out of it: the woods were full of animals, noises were amplified, including the beat of my own heart and my counting.

At one hundred Mississippi my mouth was tired and I kept losing my place. Was it one hundred, or ninety when I reached the Spot? There were a few kegs, an old tire, and the remnants of a fire. That's when a figure moved fast from the side of the burnt-out fire, the rush of his body as it passed mine was a soundless energetic rip, not unlike a ghost. But he was no ghost, he was a man, both substantial in height and weight; a man, *not* a boy—but dressed as one, in jeans and a hoodie. He took off running, dashed off into the woods, the opposite direction to me.

It was one hundred Mississippi; my heart went into my bowels. He'd meant to scare me; to be seen, but not to injure me. My instinct was to stand still, as if I'd been menaced by a bear or a lion. Then I took out my camera, aimed, snapped. Adrenaline kicked in and my legs started to function. I ran the whole length of the trail back to the car, arms pumping, phone in hand. When I got back to the car, I wasn't even breathless. I took out my phone. There was still no signal—and I nearly dropped it when I spotted the spray-painted message on the hood: *Die Eerie.* Black, semi-neat cursive, spray-paint. I could smell it. I could smell Danny Quinlan-Walsh, conjure the Aramis he'd worn since '94, the Ivory soap he washed with, the familiar association I had with him: the metallic taste of blood and adrenaline.

I thought about the little song Danny had sung for me:

I want to kill her so bad, I'll kill her
For good
I'll leave her body there
In West Cypress Road Wood

And then the truth somehow collapsed in on me, like a house of bricks. Seth's first suggestion was to meet at the woods. His phrasing, I'll "go to bat for him," was classic Danny Quinlan-Walsh black humor. He knew I would not be able to resist trying to find the altar. I logged back into the "True Crime Happened to Me" website, clicked on the thread that had first caught my attention.

HSTN77—Hail Satan. And 1977, Danny's birth year. The original poster may have been Seth Greene, but I'd bet money that was not who I'd been emailing. I could ask Ox to trace the ISP address, just to be doubly sure.

There were no cars on the road, no one was around, but Danny or his accomplice was somewhere in West Cypress Road Woods. I needed help; I needed muscle. I needed Ox.

I got into the car, locked all the doors, and dialed. No answer. I started the engine and shot Ox a text.

Can you talk? It's important.

He shot one straight back.

Spinning a web.

Spinning a web was relatively easy, Ox said—it involved writing texts, or direct messages on forums to predators trying to groom underage girls. They were emotionally tough, but simple enough to pull off, except that you had to stay online for a long time to reel the creeps in. Talkies required more skill. You had to make a phone call. They were a necessary but troubling evil, all part of the process, to reassure the spider that the prey was indeed a child. Not for the first time, I pitied Ox his job; but for the first time, I also resented it.

All I wanted was to drive home, reacquaint myself with my sloppy sweatpants, Rangers jersey, and whisky soda. But what if Danny was following me? I was hardly going to call 911 and explain my history with the charismatic Satanist Danny Quinlan-Walsh. I didn't have any real friends or even any acquaintances except for Ox and Denise. I didn't want to run crying to my editor about my homicidal ex-boyfriend. So, instead I drove off, past the school and the convenience store, and then I decided to head to the Oceanside Diner where I'd been supposed to meet Seth75. I'd chosen it because it was an old hangout of Ricky's and mine, a place where we loaded up on onion rings and Cokes to soak up alcohol. This way, I could work out Danny's next move. If he showed up, he'd only implicate himself in cyberstalking me; as well as luring me into the woods, vandalizing my car.

"I am not afraid of you, Danny." I voiced the thought out loud, looking at myself in my rearview, like an affirmation. *Die Eerie* scrawled on my hood was not the worst thing that had happened to me, not even a little bit.

And that's when I noticed the red Kia behind me. At the lights, he pulled up into the next lane, a boy-man in a gray hoodie in the driver's seat, smiling pleasantly at me. Then he winked. For a guy like Danny, this was a form of foreplay.

I knew why he was trying to scare me; he wanted to stop me digging, he wanted to gag me. Then I recalled the night when I was literally gagged—first by a meaty hand, then a sweatshirt over my face. The memory made my temperature rise and my breathing became shallow. I was suffocating again now. And here he was, sixteen years later, terrorizing me in his wife's little red car—I remembered it had a baby seat and one of those stick figure family stickers on the back.

So instead of weaving and pulling off the road, I stayed in my lane. I drove carefully and legally, sticking to the speed limit. At the next lights, I made extended eye contact with him, then I pulled into a Dunkin' Donuts parking lot—Danny and I used to go there for coffee and glazed donuts before school. I anticipated he'd follow, thinking we were going to have a trip down memory lane, and he did. Another car was pulling out of the drive-through and onto Southport Avenue, so he was forced to wait for it to exit the parking lot. I waited too, and as Danny approached behind me, I reversed into the Kia with a crunch.

Think of a bone breaking. I looked in the rearview; watched Danny, his mouth forming words that I didn't need a lip-reader to understand. The airbag had been deployed; blood spilled from his nostrils. It was the first time I had made him bleed. A woman came out of the shop with her coffee tray, a box of donuts, and two kids, and walked over to Danny's Kia, seemingly to render aid, but he reversed and sped away.

16

RP said I had inherited the famous Sloane temper; a shrink said I suffered from emotional dysregulation caused by trauma; another said I had conduct disorder, a tendency to act before thinking. As volatile as a Molotov cocktail, an ex-boyfriend had phrased it. That's why I tended not to see shrinks or men anymore. I waited for the familiar wash of remorse and fear to kick in—after all, I hadn't just stirred the hornet's nest, I'd shaken it violently. Instead, I felt the most serene and centered I'd felt in years, and without any chemical assistance. In fact, I was almost euphoric. I studied my hands on the wheel; they weren't shaking. Maybe fighting back was the one medicine I hadn't sampled yet, was the one I really needed.

The witness, a harried mom, hadn't seen exactly what happened; she'd only heard the collision and she listened dubiously to my version of the story (a blind spot, I tried to reverse into the space I wanted, my foot slipped on the accelerator and not the brake) while her kids whined beside her, tugging her free arm, but the graffiti across my hood seemed to make her doubtful. She clearly wanted to get away from the crazy lady in the ghetto car, so she took down my plates "just in case" and I took down her phone number for insurance, and she went back to her car, with her kids and donut holes.

The Chrysler's bumper was dragging a little—I'd have to take it to the body shop in Massapequa where they knew RP and, therefore, were too scared to rip me off with inflated repairs and services—but it was otherwise fine, so I drove the short distance to the diner. The Oceanside Diner was 1950s styled, but with a nautical theme—there were lots of rope and compasses, life rings stuck to the walls, and the waitresses wore spray-on aqua polyester dresses. The place was empty, so the dinner special must have just ended. The booth that I slid into was covered in an aqua and silver pattern—it also hadn't been reupholstered since 1994.

They still had jukeboxes in the booths and the list of adult contemporary and R&B hadn't been updated either. I selected the Toni Braxton track "Breathe Again" and a bottle-blonde waitress with a shit ton of low carat gold jewelry and a very high ponytail poured me coffee. I always wanted waitresses to like me, I wanted to please, and stacked my plate and cutlery just right, not make a mess. They reminded me of my mom; tired, poorly tipped, scarcely acknowledged, weary; but with a lot of insight if you bothered to talk to them. My mom had also hovered around me with beverages and food, only she never received tips. This girl worked gum in her jaw and while she looked bored, her eyes were bright and healthy. She graced me with a smile as she took my order.

I drank some water, wrote a few notes in my Norman Rockwell seaside notebook about the woods, the "accident" with Danny. I also wanted to jot down my meeting with Mona and the discovery of my father's meeting with Ricky while it was still fresh in my mind. A past memory about Ricky Hell now stuck out. Denise had told me to get the poison out. Here I was, opening the wound.

THE TESTIMONY OF ERIN SLOANE
MARCH 17, 1994: SECRET MEETING AT
THE FREEPORT MOTEL

Ricky Hell and I sat on the semi-collapsed bed drinking cold Coors and watching daytime TV on a tiny set that gave electric shocks. I was missing technology class, which involved building useless household objects. I was wearing a green flannel shirt, a nod to St. Patrick's Day. On my wrist, a black leather bracelet that my mom had given to me. I fiddled with it and Ricky looked at my arm. A fresh smiley was there.

"What's this all about?" he asked, typically deadpan. The day Ricky had quit Wendy's he'd already lined up work at the docks hauling crayfish. That's how we got the dollars for the room. Typical Ricky—it was a grand gesture—he was very theatrical, but with a practical core. He would have made a great front man. Maybe he would have gone on to be one, had he lived longer.

"I wasn't paying enough attention to Danny." Normally I didn't discuss Danny, but the beer had made me reckless. I leaned in to smell Ricky's hair—it smelled like green apples, compliments of the hotel shampoo. "Danny's been slamming the acid," I said, lighting one of Ricky's cigarettes.

"No shit. And butter wouldn't melt in your mouth," he said, sarcasm curling his lips. "It's not like we haven't been doing it with him." He was staring into the mirror, seemingly trying to memorize his own disturbing beauty or, at the very least, psych it out.

The truth was, I could never tell if Ricky was high. Alcohol scarcely affected him, he always seemed in control. While the other boys slurred their words or clowned around, Ricky remained cool and imperious. A watchful director of events, easily attracting the label of cult leader. In hindsight, I wonder if he was faking it.

"I know you're all about the doors of perception and stuff but Danny doesn't—"

"Reflect?"

"Yes. It makes him, I don't know, more insecure, jealous. He gets ugly."

I fixed my hair in the mirror.

"Life is ugly. Beauty is terrible. That's why," he said kissing me on the nose, "you're a living, waking nightmare."

A Hallmark sentiment from a Satanist.

"Danny's the nightmare," I said.

He nodded and leaned back, lighting a cigarette.

Ricky said lots of things and I listened. Poetry helps. People hinder. School was a slave ship; the world was a prison. He could tell it was going to rain just by the way the leaves puckered up. He knew some serious shit about nature. He was also a romantic—when we had sex, it was connected—eye contact, hand holding, his mouth on mine. He even kissed my eyelids. He used a phrase that made me gag: making love. But it was accurate. Outside of sex, Ricky seemed to flounder with affection. He patted my head, like I was a child or a dog.

For Ricky, our stolen secret times seemed to be enough for him and I could say that this relieved me, but a tiny part of me longed for his jealousy.

"You want me to knock him off or something?" he said suddenly. I could see him snapping into a mood, which happened on occasion. He was never angry; more remote and sometimes cold. It was always when we touched on things that threatened him. His family. Getting arrested. Danny.

"Shut up," I punched his arm playfully and he recoiled as if I'd really hit him. Ricky Hell was the most easily startled person I'd ever encountered. He could not abide rough touch, sudden movement—even the sound of a bag of chips being crumpled made him jump. I had seen the foster home scars before, but more importantly I knew about the internal scars. He had a cochlear problem, a literal malformation of the inner ear that gave him intense pain in the cold, mostly late at night and in the morning, or in damp conditions, such as the Freeport Motel. His teeth were another clue to the abuse and neglect he had suffered as a kid. In Southport, expensive orthodontics were nothing—not when kids in junior high were having cosmetic surgery. Ricky had not one, but two infected, impacted wisdom teeth. He didn't fear the reaper or teachers or even the police for that matter; he feared the dentist.

"You're scared of him," he remarked, and there was bitterness in his words.

"Only because he's stronger than me," I said, which was true.

"You're a victim," he said. He got upon his knees and hovered over me, forcing me around to face the dull mirror that was above the too-soft bed. The bedspread was patterned with ivy and flowers and looked like it belonged in a grandmother's bedroom.

"I'm a realist. You know my situation," I said.

A carer for a drunk, suicidal adult, an honor roll student despite my affection for drugs and alcohol, with a WASP boyfriend who moonlighted as Bluebeard.

"Look at all the power you have, Erin. You've got this brain. And look at yourself. You could be Salome. But instead you're a servant. A punching bag."

"Fuck you, Ricky," I said, putting on my T-shirt. "You're trash anyway."

I watched him blink. Once, twice. It hurt.

"So are you," he said reasonably. "Look at your family."

I looked around for things to throw at him and then decided on my fists.

I rained down punches on him that quickly lost momentum. Ricky could take bruises and burns. Ricky was like me. We were boxers; punching bags.

He stopped my blows with one hand, gently. He wasn't even angry.

"Danny is really bad news, Erin. Your dad is too. He's not an anchor, he's a weight. He's bringing you down."

I spluttered, choking with indignation.

"Sit back, breathe," he coached me. "You and I have something in common."

"Apart from being trash?"

"We're both caught in a net," he said, one hand encircling my wrist. More maritime clichés. I thought they were so romantic.

He broke into a weird smile.

"I might love you," I said, and his smile became an embarrassed grimace.

I threw up in the bushes when his van pulled away.

————

Ricky knew my father was bad news, because he knew my father. I thought now about all the staring off into the middle distance, the way he looked at me, wanting to say something, daring himself. My teenage girl's imagination had filled in all the silences, telling myself he was psyching up to say the coveted phrase consisting of three words that I'd dared say aloud to him. Instead, the words that he'd longed to utter to me were *I've been lying*. Or maybe, just maybe, they were *Please help me*.

Ricky had night terrors—he battled invisible hands and unseen tormentors. Sometimes he talked Spanish in his sleep. One phrase repeatedly, *Tomar el pelo, tomar el pelo*.

I knew some Spanish from school. Directly translated, it means to "pull someone's hair." Closely related is *engañar*, to deceive. It was clear to me now that Ricky was pulling my hair, deceiving me, all of us. Who he was, where he was from. My head was swimming with small betrayals, little inconsistencies. *Richard had a talent for deception*. I wondered again about the night of October 8, the night of the pentagram. He was meant to come over. He never did. Ricky was many things, but he wasn't cruel. And yet, he failed to protect me that night and then on Halloween, I was sure he'd left me. And even if it was temporary, in the end, it wasn't his choice.

I wondered if Ricky would be proud of me now; I no longer let Danny Quinlan-Walsh push me around. In fact, I had just hurt him. I really hoped his nose had been broken.

"Another refill?" The same waitress was back.

"Yeah." And because I liked her, I ordered a Greek salad, which I wouldn't really eat, and a seltzer. "I like your nails," I said. They were peach-colored talons with little flamingos. My mom also loved apricot and coral.

"Life's a beach," she said, refilling my cup.

My phone began to buzz. I had two new emails: another *Resident Alien* extract and a message from a "True Crime Happened to Me" user. My stomach flip-flopped as I opened it; expecting a string of threats. But it wasn't Danny. It was another user from "True Crime Happened to Me," this time Murderbabe66 wrote:

Sorry to be the bearer of bad news, Eerie, Seth75 (Seth Greene) was in my best friend's graduating class at

Roosevelt. He went to Afghanistan and never came back,
that's why he's not active on the forum anymore. She went
to a reunion this year and he was on the memorial board.
G'luck with your story.

I dialed Ox's cell and he picked up.

"You okay?" He sounded exhausted and yet alert. "I'm still spinning a web. Almost got him."

"I'm sorry to call again, it's just that Danny's following me. He showed up at the woods, followed me, spray-painted my car. He took on someone's identity on an online forum, pretending to be a kid I thought I knew from Roosevelt to lure me to a meeting. Then we had a little fender bender."

"Whoa, Pumpkin, slow it down. Where are ya?"

"The Oceanside Diner." Even though I was independent, unafraid all my life, I somehow now wanted, no, expected, Ox to save me.

"That kid is a convicted murderer. Stay put. I'll get someone to drive you home, check out the house, stay out front all night if need be."

"I'll be okay." It came out huffy and childish. Apart from Denise, Ox was the only living soul I had any real faith in. I thought about how I would ask him if he'd been following me and Ricky back in '94, how much I should trust Mona and what she said. I was sure she was lying about the money. Then it just tumbled out.

"You followed me," I said.

"Say what?"

"Back then. When I was with Ricky. Mona said."

"Pumpkin. I don't know what that bitch is playing at." Ox sounded seriously irritated. "You know I'd never follow you, right? Not even for your dad. He asked me to look after you when you were sad, after your mom and Shelly died. A few times I drove to the school or the house to check in. I knew you were hanging out with a bad crew, Pumpkin, but that's all I knew. And we both thought the Quinlan-Walsh kid was looking after you."

I thought of my pentagram scar and laughed a little. The irony.

"If you were with Hernandez, well, that's your business. I guess we all got our own weakness."

Yep. Mine were substances, boys who worshiped Satan, and trusting anyone who showed me kindness.

"Did you know about him working for Dad and Mona? Because of Steve Shearer."

"What? That doesn't sound right."

"Ricky Hell was a plant. It was a covert op."

"No, I don't know anything about that. Pumpkin, I gotta go. Sit tight, I'll get someone to come get ya. I'll text."

"Yeah do that. Thanks a lot."

I was pissed off at myself for being frustrated with Ox. He was working and I had gotten myself into this mess; it was hardly reasonable to expect him to drop everything and rescue me. He reminded me of RP, maybe because he couldn't prioritize me and put the job to the side. Daddy issues, indeed.

I typed a quick apology text.

The reply came through five minutes later.

> Don't be sorry. But this story is dangerous and u seem upset, u do rash things when u r upset. Maybe u should give it the shove; past is past.

I wrote something back, encouraging and patently untrue, and sent it just as a fresh installment of *Resident Alien* came through.

17

RESIDENT ALIEN
BY CORMAC O'MALLEY

March comes in like a lion and leaves like a lamb, Steve said. The low light of winter days turned into spring. Aisling and I kicked each other to sleep until I got my own air mattress that hurt my back so badly I went back to sleeping in the bath.

Cooper Deane, Steve's motorcycle-riding partner, had been killed in the line of duty, shot by a neighborhood drug dealer in an ice-cream parlor in Queens that Steve had taken us to a few times. He was only a teenager and in America, teenagers had guns and killed each other for their sneakers, Steve said. Only he said it differently, with words I couldn't repeat.

Steve mentioned rumors that Deane's wife, Ange, was already with someone else. "The poor man's grave is still warm," I heard Marion say. "It's scandalous."

That word felt right—*scandalous*. I drew Cooper, slumped over the silver ice-cream dish; blood and vanilla making a raspberry swirl. I recreated him from the photo of him with Steve, sitting in a diner, wearing similar-looking jackets. I outlined Steve shooting him. Then I hid the drawing.

I turned fifteen. I got books, a shaving kit, and a voice that was a few octaves lower.

In May, we moved to Long Island, to get away from Steve's ex-wife, and rented a house in a suburb called Belmont.

Aisling turned eleven. She asked for a cat but got a pearl necklace she didn't like and new clothes that Marion had helped her pick— crop tops and short shorts, teenager stuff that looked precocious on a doll-sized human who hadn't entered puberty. While she seemed to want to look older and had even started wearing lip gloss, she seemed to be getting younger, regressing somehow. She smiled in the photographs Steve took in a way that made her look maniacally happy, despite the fact she had no friends and was given no party.

Steve, Steve, please love me.

They've been through a lot, the adults always said of us. Not Steve though. Spoiled, we were sometimes. Well behaved, he called us, when he wanted to praise Marion. Eccentric, he said over the phone to his friend. Kooky. Addams Family weird.

I wanted to make it seem like it was his decision. I brought it up over a rare sit-down family dinner of meatloaf and potatoes. Marion was trying to be an American housewife—she was even wearing an apron. She had cut her hair differently, seemed frumpier, as if to fit in with the other housewives. Flamboyant, they called her. I heard them say other things, too, when her back was turned.

"Marion gets the capitals wrong. She doesn't know anything about American history," I said to Steve when Marion was getting wine from the basement.

"Your brains are rotting from cable. And no offense to your mom, but she's not that bright," Steve said. "You're going to get your ass into a proper classroom. Summer school. Meet some other kids, who aren't your sisters. Girls," he said, raising his eyebrows.

He'd been trying to draw me into this for a bit, check if I was normal, lend me his *Playboys*. If anything, I liked the MTV punk-haired rock women, their noses pierced, ripped clothes, like fallen angels come to earth. Those women, Bambis and Tiffanys with their nut-brown hairless bodies and implants and bright pink vaginas, just scared me. I was interested in their anatomy, though. For drawing.

"Come outside for a bit," he said. When I followed him to the pool house, where his weight station was set up, he was half-heartedly pummeling a speedball boxing bag. His mouth, framed by his Tom Selleck mustache, turned up in what looked like a smile. He was smoking a joint. He had a tank top on that showed the tattoo on his chest; "Pride" with a Confederate flag underneath. There was a pink spot on his upper chest, near his shoulder, where no hair grew. He said it was where a bullet nicked him. He did push-ups every day, fifty at a time. One hundred sit-ups in all. Still, his man boobs could fill an A cup. Steve was aware of it. He even joked that Aisling was jealous of them. Marion laughed. Aisling just looked confused.

"Take a hit," he said. I took the joint from him. Despite his macho posing, I was already up to Steve's chin and his arms were relatively scrawny.

"We're going to Florida to visit an old friend of mine, Ange. She lives in a place called Coral Springs. You met her husband, Cooper Deane. You know he died. Tragic."

He said "tragic" like he was describing a traffic jam. All I could think of was Coral Springs: it sounded luminescent, a landscape of pearls and coral. "More like scandalous," I said, tasting out the word.

He took the joint back.

"Don't get cute with me," he warned. Cute wasn't a good thing. Steve called some movies cute but acting cute wasn't the same.

"Trust me, I know how to hit a guy and leave no bruises. Not that your mom would care," he added. "She gave me permission to hit you. Both of you. At least your mom believes in discipline. Everyone needs someone, sometimes," he added, like he was going all man-to-man on me. Then he began to really hit the punching bag.

———

We all drove to Florida that summer in a giant air-conditioned Pontiac, clocking up state lines and reading increasingly devout bumper stickers. The heat was dizzying—high humidity, Steve said. Even the bedding in the cheap motels we stayed in was damp. Pre-hurricane electricity in the air, sun showers in the day when we went to theme parks and shopping malls; night storms in the hotel. Steve snoring, my sister whimpering beside me, sometimes wetting the bed. This time no one said anything.

Aisling and I gorged on endless breakfast buffets and shoplifted in every gift store but were never caught. In Busch Gardens, Aisling walked out with a stuffed animal, a white tiger, under her arm. She told Marion I gave it to her. We went to the Everglades and went on a boat out to a Native American settlement where kids with braces sold hand-woven bracelets. Aisling talked to one of the boys for a long time—a heavy boy, with braces. His name was Eduardo. She had to be dragged away from him.

"He's not a real Native American, dummy." Marion told her. She was starting to pick up on Steve's pet name for Aisling. "They don't wear braces."

Marion held hands with Steve and they both wore a lot of khaki and matching baseball caps. We watched dark, slippery shapes on the banks and held our breath.

Later in the car, Aisling was dreamily stroking her tiger.

"What should I call him?" she asked me.

"Cooper," I said. Steve shot me a look from the rearview that could kill.

"I might call him Eduardo."

"That's a stupid name," Steve said. "Make it American, but do not call him Cooper."

Later we stopped at Old Town and had five-cent Cokes and Steve said to Aisling and me, "God bless the USA, huh, kids?"

I wish I'd said something about God then, how God hates America, how God was cursed and so was America, but Aisling looked so happy and dopey, staring up at Steve and saying, "Can we go over there, Dad?" that I said nothing at all. I could feel myself shrinking every minute we spent in the hugeness of the country, state line by state line, accent to accent, bistro to diner.

In Coral Springs, we quickly lost our bearings. Like Long Island, all the streets were similar and the houses looked much the same. Coral Springs was a planned suburb, and the beige and terra-cotta mansions were as neat as a row of Floridian teeth and were probably just as shiny and ivory inside.

Ange's house and the street it was on were clearly the prize of Coral Springs. It made the other sandstone and concrete houses look like bungalows. It was a good twenty degrees cooler inside than outside and smelled of floral perfume and cleaning product. A lethargic maid in a tracksuit was dust-busting near the stairs.

Ange squawked a welcome; a dog yipped from a far-off room.

The ceilings were high, decked with crystal chandeliers. At the top of a marble staircase, bookended by Roman columns, two boys stood watching. I made eye contact with the taller one, who turned his middle finger up like he was moving a dial, and both retreated to their rooms.

"Look how cute you are. Aussies. I thought you'd be so tan." She tried to cuddle Aisling, who recoiled, and then drew me in for a hug. Her breast implants felt hard against my chest; like pectorals. I had never met a real-life woman with implants—I'd only seen them in Steve's *Playboys*. Ange was brown all over and all lean muscle in shorts and a T-shirt. I could not believe that this was the woman that Cooper Deane had been married to. I'd pictured Goldie Hawn or Heather Locklear, not Linda Hamilton from *Terminator 2*.

"Ghost white, they are," she clucked.

Ange hugged Steve in an embrace that went on for longer than Marion was happy with. I could tell—her smile was stretching to the point where it looked like it would snap.

"Hello," Marion said to the maid, who gave her a look of alarm before disappearing, clearly unused to being directly addressed. Steve and Ange stared at Marion and each other before breaking down into laughter.

"You're a hoot," Ange said to Marion, but it wasn't a compliment.

"Are you guys thirsty? Carmen," she called out to the kitchen.

"The kids will have juice. Or soda. Do you want soda? We've got diet and regular."

Marion shook her head. "Just juice please, Ange."

The grown-ups decided on mimosas. It was a special occasion. Steve and Ange had not seen each other since Cooper's funeral. They touched each other absently and reminisced. Marion smiled as if she were modeling the sofa in a catalog. Aisling had brought the newly christened Eddy, her stolen tiger.

Marion looked at Steve and Ange and petted Aisling's head; Aisling petted Eddy.

"Oh, she's a doll," Ange said to Marion, licking her lips. Her words were warm, but her eyes weren't. I watched her rake her hand through a cloud of permed hair. Her pupils were massive. She worked her jaw like she was chewing on something.

"It's so cute that she still likes her stuffed animals."

Marion drank her mimosa too quickly. I knew that Aisling playing with dolls and teddies while dressed like Lolita was probably bothering her, but Marion's permanent solution seemed to be to swallow a drink or a pill alongside her worries. Carmen took her glass and brought a fresh one in, then handed us frosted glasses of Coke with painted roses on the side, loaded with ice. She'd not gotten the juice memo.

"Carmen, for crying out loud!" Ange bawled.

"*Lo siento, Señora.*"

"It's fine, really. Thank you, Carmen," Marion said, cueing us.

"Thank you, Carmen," we droned in a chorus.

"Just like twins! So cute! You have them so well behaved," Ange said to Marion. "So, welcome to Florida. Coral Springs Cascades is a planned community. We're crime free," Ange said with a degree of pride.

"What's a planned community?" Aisling whispered to me.

"Even the high school has metal detectors."

Marion nodded at this, like it was less of a worry for her

Aisling tugged at my arm and I shrugged, bored with explaining everything.

"How are the boys doin'?" Steve asked, his voice dropping. The kids were traumatized, after the death of their father, Ange told us in hushed tones: Al and Andy were on meds; Ritalin for ADD, antidepressants for depression, and something called mood stabilizers.

"They like the Nintendo all right?" Steve asked and Ange clucked her disapproval, but it wasn't real. That was when I knew that Steve had bought it for them.

"I wanted a Nintendo," Aisling protested, and Marion shushed her violently.

"You're already spoiled," Steve told her. "Mommy's little angel."

The next day, Aisling walked into Ange's room by accident and came out shortly after, with a face like she'd seen a ghost. She wouldn't talk much all day, she couldn't eat dinner with the rest of us. Aisling always had a bad stomach when she was upset. Later that night, Marion came into the bedroom, three glasses of wine in. We were watching MTV and she asked Aisling what she'd seen.

"She won't say," I said. "She's scared of you."

"What did you see?" Marion shouted. Aisling was shaking uncontrollably, curled up like a full stop. In America, they say period. Part of the way that we survive is to wrap ourselves up into little balls, to become very small.

"I don't know," Aisling said in a tiny voice. "Is Ange Steve's girlfriend?"

Marion slapped her straight across the face, which became red and swollen in an instant.

I expected her to cry but she didn't. She started to laugh. I think it was hysteria, because she wouldn't stop, and Marion hit her again and again, over the head, until I went over and held Marion's arms by her sides. I was a whole head taller than Marion and much stronger, so I was careful not to hurt her.

"Enough," I said. "Aisling's had enough."

Marion looked like I'd hit her. Her eyes were glassy and hard. She sniffed.

"Are you high?" I asked her, "Is that what this is?"

"She's ruining everything. She's ruining this family," Marion wept.

The next morning Marion wore a smile like the vacancy sign on the hotel we moved to. None of the adults commented on the marks across Aisling's face at breakfast. On the drive back to New York, Marion took little pills that made her sleep and Steve refused to stop at any amusement parks or tourist sites so we would make good time back to New York.

18

I put my phone down, pushed my uneaten salad to the side.

I was beginning to understand, if Cormac's testimony in *Resident Alien* was true, why Aisling came off a little kooky. She was Steve and Marion's punching bag; both bullied, emotionally neglected and now, physically abused. And God only knows what else happened to her. Cormac was trying to fit into Shearer's mold of masculinity to survive, though without becoming too much like him. Even though our childhoods were totally different, I knew those kids on a level. We were the same; tarnished objects that time had washed up on different shores. Here we were now, all coming together at long last.

The murder of Cooper Deane was pivotal to the story—it was Cooper's murder that was the catalyst for the chain of events: Ricky Hell coming to Southport and the murder of Andre Villiers. And if *Resident Alien* was anything to go by, it seemed to me like Steve may have had a personal incentive to kill Cooper Deane. Given he'd shot Ricky in the heart too, it could be he just liked to ice people that way. Or was it symbolic? If Steve and Cooper Deane's wife, Ange, were in some sort of clandestine relationship starting back in the nineties, it made the story of Satan in the suburbs even more movie of the week than it already was.

Coral Springs, the name of the town where Ange lived, was familiar. Coral Springs, Florida—wasn't that where Carole Jenkins was living now? Then I remembered something. Mona had a magnet on her refrigerator, just below the wine and chocolate magnet. At the time, I saw it said "Ruffalo Realty Executives" and mentally filed it away. Like Mona's purloined letter it was out there, in the open, in my face: *We buy and sell Coral Springs.* The same place Ange lived, where the O'Malleys visited. Now it seemed that Carole and Steve Shearer were both living in Coral Springs, Florida. And Mona had a magnet for Carole's business. As my father liked to say, coincidence was for the birds.

Ruffalo Realty specialized in luxury housing. When I looked them up, images of a new development in Coral Springs called Coral Palisades popped up. They were McMansions in a gated community, built in the confidence of our great swollen economy, which were allegedly being sold up quickly despite the crash of '08. The fact that Carole still had a job was amazing because the GFC had well and truly killed the property market, and the country was now in a recession, a depression even.

I thought about Mona's magnet. She could be the proud owner of one of these McMansions, bought with the blood of a teenage Ricky. Temporarily and against my better judgment, I had softened toward Mona, perhaps because she shared my flaw—a weakness for Ricky Hell. He had been somewhat of a true north for me in my teenage years, and was a monument to an uncontaminated, innocent brand of romantic love that seemed no longer conceivable. I had no compass anymore. Ricky, RP, Mona—they were all deceivers and I, the deceived.

There was a buzz from my phone. It was Ox.

"Detective Diaz owes me a favor. She's outside."

I'd been expecting a Nassau PD car, a uniformed cop, but instead I had a detective—and one from cold cases. I would need to send Ox more than an effusive thank you.

I went out to the parking lot where a woman in dark blue stood outside a dark blue Ford Contour—it was like cop camouflage. She was only a little taller than me, about 5'7, Latina, with a wide jaw and very curly black hair that she did not wear in a regulation ponytail. As Ox had said, she was young. She wore no makeup and although she looked as sleep deprived as me, she wore it well.

"Ms. Sloane? I'm Detective Diaz. Call me Marci. I'm going to follow you home, then we can talk if you like."

———

The drive back to Massapequa was slow; the traffic bumper to bumper all the way down Sunrise to Oceanside Avenue. At the turnoff, I thought I'd lost Marci, but she pulled into the driveway after me. It was dark. She took out a flashlight and started examining the damage to my hood, then checked out the bumper.

"Oh boy. You rear-ended him."

"Yeah, I kind of had to. You know, to get away."

She gave me a knowing look. She flicked the flashlight off.

"You need to pump up that front tire. And get this bumper fixed, it's dragging."

"I'll take it to the shop tomorrow."

"Whatever you did scared him off temporarily," Marci mused, visually scanning the driveway and street, then the front yard. "I kept my distance on the drive back, I wanted to see if he would try to follow you back here. Obviously, he didn't. But if I know anything about domestic violence, and I do, he'll be more pissed at you than ever for fighting back. And it will escalate."

"I think you might have been misinformed," I said, "It's not a domestic violence scenario."

"See this." She ignored me, flicking the flashlight on again, directing it at the living room and main bedroom, my bedroom. "You can see through the curtains. Take me inside." Marci beckoned me to the front door.

She began to pull at the door, putting one leather shoe against it. "This door could be busted open with a small degree of force. You'd be dead before the alarm company notified the police. You do have an alarm, right?"

I nodded.

"How are the locks on your windows?"

"Okay, I think." I had lost my post Dunkin' Donuts bravado and my hand was shaking as I unlocked the door and punched in the code.

Mister came running and I picked her up, heading over to feed her first, because she wouldn't let up. Marci left me to it, prowling around the house, calling out weak spots, rattling old locks.

She came into the kitchen where Mister was scarfing down her dinner and I was trying to put paperwork, notepads, books away—the kitchen was a kind of makeshift office for me.

"You need bars on the windows. You need security grilles and doors. I got the number for a guy who does it. He'll do an off-the-books discount for women in domestic violence situations."

"With all due respect, this house is about to go on the market. I don't have the time or money to do all that stuff." I turned to face her. It came out sharper than I intended. "I don't know what Ox told you, but I'm not a domestic violence victim, Marci. I'm writing a story and I'm being followed by a contact who is threatened by what I'm writing. He's just gone bat-shit."

"Forgive me," she said, hands up in the air a little theatrically. "I thought it was an old boyfriend who used to beat you up?"

I saw the challenge in her expression and met it by straightening my shoulders and raising my chin.

"I take it you're not going to make a report either?"

I shook my head. "I think that's a bad idea."

"That's a shame." She looked genuinely disappointed. "I know who Danny is. What he did—his crime, I mean. And Ox told me a bit about what happened between you. You might want to change your mind."

"I'm glad for all the help, truly, but I actually just wanted to talk to you about cold cases."

"Yeah, Ox said. And that's why I'm still here. I read a few of your pieces for *Inside Island*, you know. Good stuff, well written. And not too gory."

"Thanks. No animals, no kids, nothing gratuitous has been my motto. You want a drink?" I asked her.

"I'm off duty, technically; why not? You got a beer?"

"I think I might." I checked the refrigerator. There were two of RP's beers at the back of the second shelf. Rolling Rock. His favorite.

I handed Marci a can, poured myself a few fingers of Tullamore Dew and soda into a glass. We sat at the kitchen table, Marci on the side that was cleared of papers, clippings, and books, me on the side next to the water cooler. Mister had curled up on Marci's lap, which I took to be a good indication of character; Mister only really liked me.

"She'll shed," I warned her.

Marci rolled her eyes. "Please. I have a toddler and two golden labs. If I'm not covered in mashed-up banana and white dog fur at the end of the day, I'll die from shock. I should stop wearing navy, but the job doesn't really permit pastels."

I was starting to warm to Marci. She took a swig of her beer, patting Mister with the other hand.

"Have you been in cold cases a long time?"

"It's a recent thing. I got put in charge of the Murder Archive project. Ox helped us out with the tech side of things."

"You must be pretty high up."

"For a woman?" She arched her brow.

"I meant for your age."

"I'm probably older than you, girl. Ox talks about me like I'm a teenager."

"Me too."

"He's good people, even if he's a bit of an oddball. He said you wanted to know about Operation Lighthouse."

"Yeah. I know you can't comment on anything officially. I just wanted to ask about Andre Villiers. If he was interviewed about one of the other missing children, Jason Weis. I know they talked to him about Cathy Carver."

"They had a few kids to cross off the list, just to eliminate all possibilities." Marci set her beer down, serious now. "But before I say anything else, you'll probably know that it's very unlikely for a kid to have committed a *series* of crimes—also, an abduction. A *daylight* abduction," she emphasized. "As the investigation progressed, the likelihood of a teen being involved became very unlikely. He—or they—would have had to transport and dispose of the bodies. Conceal the crime. Keep a secret, for years. That takes sophistication, planning, and control."

"None of the traits Andre Villiers possessed."

She nodded. "I understand you knew him."

"I did," I said. "He choked me once. It was a joke, or like, he made it out to be one. I believe he did the same to another teenage girl, who was at the scene of the crime. She stood trial—Carole Jenkins."

Marci studied me solemnly.

"I'm really sorry that happened. I can't reveal anything about the other circumstances, but I will tell you, between you and me, that asphyxia was involved. Andre Villiers turned out to have an alibi for the Carver abduction, but the original police report had a description of a tall, husky teenager talking to Jason Weis at Waldbaum's. A description which would fit with that of Villiers."

I felt both nauseated and excited at once.

"And then there was Penny."

"Penny?"

"Villiers. Andre's sister."

I felt dazed, as if Marci had dealt me a right hook. While I had connected all the metal kids to younger siblings, I'd always assumed Andre was an only child.

"Penny was in Cathy Carver's class. She'd been moved to relatives in Bethpage around the time Cathy vanished."

"Because the parents suspected Andre was involved with Jason's disappearance?"

"I don't know the full story, but I understand she went to live with cousins to attend a school for gifted kids. I thought it was bullshit, but Villiers' folks have taken that story to the grave with them."

"So this Penny . . ." With Seth75 being a dead end, I'd lost an important link to Andre. Now there was a new one.

"Is alive." Marci gave me a knowing look. "I don't have her details, though I probably wouldn't pass them on if I did. She wouldn't appreciate it. Imagine what she's been through."

"She might want to have her brother represented in a balanced way," I argued. "He's coming across pretty badly right now."

"Erin, we must be the about the same age, because I remember the

Southport Three case. Did Andre Villiers' folks defend him in the press at the time? Did any media mourn him publicly at all?"

These were rhetorical questions.

"No, they didn't."

We sat in silence for a few seconds.

"It seems like you're saying it was all a bit of a coincidence with Andre—his talking to or knowing Cathy and Jason. Because Trey Scott was taken later."

"Yes, in 2000. And yes, Trey was killed and buried like Jason Weis. We have a profile of the killer and we do have a link to two of the victims via an online forum, which I can't discuss. So, it's very unlikely that Andre Villiers was involved in this case."

"Unless he had an accomplice."

"Possible but very unlikely. All we have about Villiers is that he was hanging around a few kids in a small town. And his sister knew the victim. And that he hurt you."

"And Carole Jenkins. She was one of the Southport Three. She wrote about it in her book."

Marci drained her beer. She had kept pace with me, I was empty. She shook her head when I made a refill gesture.

"I didn't know that. The FBI got involved, drew up a detailed profile of the killer. We have an older man, a highly intelligent, well-respected person. A sophisticated and very well-presented pedophile. But he is a sexual sadist and a control freak. The kind that doesn't play well with others. I never said this, right, and you aren't going to print it?"

"Right." I nodded vigorously.

"Do you know why he buried them shallow?"

"He wanted their bodies found."

"Yes. And they had sand in both their lungs. So you stay true to your word and your motto, right? If you attempt to print this . . ."

"I won't. I would never . . ." I couldn't finish my sentence. Marci, who looked like she could beat a grown-assed man to the ground without batting an eyelid, had tears in her eyes.

The boys had been buried alive.

19

After Marci left, I armed the security system and texted Ox to let him know I was safe. There were ten messages on my phone from a number that I didn't recognize, but was certain was Danny. I blocked the number, changed the settings to Do Not Disturb, then I poured another whisky.

I wondered how Marci managed to go home, kiss her baby, climb into bed, maybe beside another warm body, and have a restful sleep knowing what she knew. How did you live with the afterlife of those images, taste the terror of tortured, murdered kids and not chase it up with a shot, a pill, a line, whatever it was that rinsed the palate of all that horror? I was starting to understand why RP had so many vices, why he always appeared like a zombie at family dinners, why he stared too long at us kids with a look of apprehension and regret.

My fake cyber buddy Seth75 and now Marci had said Andre's folks were dead; I needed to know the details. I checked the local papers first: *The Southport Herald* was digitized from 2005 onward and *The Island Leader* hadn't been made available online until '08. I got lucky because *The Southport Herald* had covered the story; the Villiers' were big in both the church and the Rotary Club. Peter and Rose Villiers died in a head-on collision on Southport Avenue, midwinter 2006, alongside the teen driver who crashed into them. I went into the obits section: lots of religious tributes, condolences from Rotary

Club members, local businesses, the golf course they were members of. Then, as I scrolled down, I saw one that stood out: *Dearest Mama Bear and Papa Bear,* it read. *You're in heaven now. Everything is forgiven. Yours always, Penny.*

I logged into Facebook via the *Inside Island* account on my laptop. And by some small miracle, the clouds cleared away and there was the sun. Penny Villiers was on Facebook. She was a teacher at Belmont High and married with kids—her cover photo was a family picture. Like Andre, Penny was tall, white blonde, Danish looking; with two small, angelic blonde daughters and a cookie-cutter handsome husband. Unlike Andre, she was churchy: her Facebook bio was a Bible verse, Isaiah 62. New or Old Testament, I couldn't remember. Penny's birthday was February 9, 1983. Same year as my sister. Maybe Shelly would have had babies by now. Cathy too.

I noticed a green dot next to her name when I messaged—she was online. I messaged her from the *Inside Island* Facebook account. I expressed my condolences, explained who I was, my purpose, stressing the need for a balanced story and the importance of understanding Andre and representing the victim. I watched: the gray message box had a tick next to it which meant it had been read. Then a few dots that kept disappearing.

I waited, but nothing. The green dots disappeared.

———

My nighttime playlist, My Bloody Valentine's *Loveless*, was interrupted by an electronic ping. A Gmail chat window opened on my laptop. It was Aisling O'Malley:

Hiya ☺

Hi Aisling. Can Cormac skype me?
I'm wondering if I can ask him some
questions about Resident Alien?

Talk 2 me. He won't talk direct. He's sending
through another chapter.

>   Can I ask you about Angela
>   Deane (Cooper's widow)?

Her name is Angela Miller, she kept her
maiden name.

>   Is your mom still married to Steve?

MARION IS DEAD. An OD, pills and booze. We
sued Steve a few years ago. Steve denied all
guilt but paid us—should be rotting in jail.
NO attempt to resuscitate. OxyContin, you
know. It got bad. He got her hooked, told her
no one loved her etc etc. Told us she didn't
love us.

I swallowed hard, stifling a scream. Aisling and I were now living a freakishly parallel life: dead moms, diabolical fathers—girls who were raised to be punching bags. I was getting a picture of what Steve was like, what he was capable of. Gaslighting. Manipulation and extreme violence. Murder.

>   I'm so sorry, Aisling.

Thnx.

>   Do you have an address for Steve?
>   Does he live in Florida with Ange?

Yeah, how did you guess?!! He bought a
mansion in Coral Palisades.

Coral Palisades? The same housing
estate that Carole Jenkins is selling?

Read the next installment, it's INFORMATIVE.

My phone sounded—the familiar ping of an email coming through. It had no subject. The sender was lostinspace@gmail.com.

I'm just sitting down to it.

I typed in Steve Shearer *and* Coral Springs and got a hit.
The *Coral Springs Gazette* article was dated 2002.
"Local man wins Sweepstakes!" A picture of Shearer with a sinewy blonde—her face lined from the sun, like a prune, with beetle black eyes. *Shearer, a New York native, relocated to sunny Coral Springs with wife Angela, and they found their own pot of gold.*
Say what you want about Steve Shearer, the prick really seemed to land on his feet. I sucked in a deep breath. Was Ange part of the reason Steve killed Cooper Deane? Because now Deane's wife, or rather, widow—and Steve were living it up in Coral Palisades.
The story, set in the parking lots and train tracks, the woody hangouts and metalhead hamlets of Long Island, 1994, had somehow been transplanted into the gloss and the peeling façade of post-GFC Florida.

RESIDENT ALIEN
BY CORMAC O'MALLEY

Back in Long Island, something was wrong between Marion and Steve. They'd stopped holding hands in the car. Now, I saw the long-coiled phone cord under the door of the downstairs bathroom, heard Steve murmuring away at night. Marion had puffy eyes, grew even thinner. She slept a lot, read the *National Enquirer*, and cleaned before Steve got home. Aisling's stomach aches got worse, probably due to the tension at mealtimes. There was talk of taking her to a specialist but that never happened.

I didn't formally start school until mid-September. It took them months to get us registered. Then they tested me. It put me at a disadvantage, being the only new kid starting late.

As I waited for the yellow school bus, I smoked a cigarette and got shot a bunch of dirty looks from the girl who was waiting with me—she flicked her hair, rolled her eyes, and chewed gum like it was cud. On the bus the girls looked the same, in different variations—gold anklets, short shorts, tank tops, gold spelling their names across newly developed chests. The guys all had the same Jansport backpacks, Nike pumps, gelled hair, and Hypercolor T-shirts that changed color when water hit them, or black T-shirts that read "No Fear."

A dude got on a stop that wasn't on the route—outside Wendy's on Southport Avenue. He seemed to know the bus driver—they greeted each other with a high five—"¿Que tel acho, mano; Lo mismo, bro."

From the back, he looked like an armadillo, a glitter of studs on denim like armor, spelling out the word METAL. You'd think he was a skinny guy, watching him from behind, too tall and hunching to accommodate the low roof of the school bus, but he was built more solidly, I later realized. He sat rows in front of me, which was weird—metalheads, punks, and weirdos, in any country, always take the back seat. Church, class, bus trips, you sit in the back—smoke, dope, drink, observe.

"Like, what's a Danzig?" the girl from my stop said loudly, turning her focus to the dude, rudely laughing.

There was an invisible ripple in the air as the dude suddenly turned and faced us. I felt the same sick butterflies as you do when you see a pretty girl, except I was even more uneasy. He looked like Johnny Depp's younger brother; his cheekbones were Native American, but I knew he was Hispanic. He had the lips of a woman. From a black panel of unwashed hair, his eyes were like a tiger's eye stone, appearing dark, but with filaments of fire in them. The flaw in his perfection—acne craters that pitted his cheeks and gave him a tougher look. *I'm ready for juvie*, his face said. *I set shit on fire*, his clothes said. *I don't care about anyone*, his eyes said. All the same, I needed him to save me and he knew it.

His nostrils flared like a bull and I saw a series of silver rings and studs as he combed back his hair.

He stood up, hunching over so as not to hit the ceiling, filling the whole bus.

Inexplicably, I rose too, my legs supporting me despite a sudden feeling of weakness. The bus lurched and I fell forward, a head-on collision with the girl from my stop. It was like a game of marbles; then a wet crunch, a sound I'd heard when our first (real) Dad took us to a football game; the wreck of cartilage and bone.

"You broke my nose," the girl was howling and gulping blood. I smiled in disbelief, thinking she was somehow faking, but her guy grabbed me and all I could see was the dude's eyes, dancing with laughter, and his smile and it was like, I think we're gonna be friends. Then the bus stopped and he mouthed something to me and it was like the sun had come out and eclipsed the sky, but it was also terrible, like a kid's roller-coaster derailing. I'd given Randie—I knew her name now, everyone was yelling it—a broken nose. It was immediately apparent and very bad. I tried apologizing; I'd never hit anyone before, but I didn't escape her boyfriend's fists.

I remembered the shape of the dude's mouth and the words I put to music in my bedroom later—

"Let it rain down, friend."

His name was Richard Hernandez. Ricky Hell, he called himself back then.

"It was an accident," I said.

"There are no accidents," he said.

————

After my week's suspension and a terse phone call to Randie's parents, who had threatened legal action, an arrangement had been made to get me back into school. Steve drove me personally, delivering me practically to the doors of the school.

My conversation with Steve was brief. "What did you say to Randie's parents?"

He thumped me on the shoulder.

"Neva-mind what I said. Just try to fit in. Don't fuck up. Cause if you do, there are consequences." Steve chewed on the word like a sirloin steak; groomed his hair. Even when disciplining, he groomed his hair.

I nodded and tried to smile my thanks when he drove off.

First period, homeroom. I sat drawing, looking out the window, pretending not to hear the whispers:

Dude, are you a vampire?
Pssst, Freak. Randie's dad's gonna sue you.
Oh my God, Lucky Charms, you're dead.
No, his dad's a cop, stupid.

Nobody said my name. Nobody could pronounce it. Core-mock, they said. Car-mack was the other one. Poor Ass-ling.

Steve wanted me to think about girls. And they were everywhere, their deodorant and hairspray and perfumes. I studied them; I learned— decoding all the jewelry, hair tugging, lip biting, and hair flicking. It was as if the Renaissance paintings of women I had seen in books had turned into scratch and sniffs. The burnt sienna, yellow ochre, ivory black, flake white of their fleshy bodies turned into peach, strawberry, and vanilla in my nose and mouth. It was too much; too cloying. I was overwhelmed. Was it Stendhal syndrome? Or something else?

Then I saw Carole. The school had its own pool and outdoor vol- leyball team, as well as track and field and football. She was staring at the pool, coloring the tips of her bleached hair with pink highlighter. Her legs were almost completely exposed in short denim cut-offs and she had a series of bruises all over her shins and thigh, one the shape of Africa. All the guys wanted Carole; they shifted textbooks as she walked past to cover their embarrassment, they followed her around, fetched her things from the cafeteria.

Carole was a metal teenage Venus and I felt sort of sick being just being near her. She seemed to sense that and get a kick out of sitting near me.

Weirdly enough it was Carole who seemed to like me; she called me by my name, even if she misspelled it. It was Carole who passed the note:

Hey Cormack, Are you really a vampire??? Cum to the Old
Res on Creek Road this lunch. Carole Maree

I thought the signature was vaguely formal and old fashioned, but it was garlanded by rows of badly drawn skulls and, at the center, a knife with a rose.

I looked back at her and raised my eyebrows to see if she was serious.

"Meet at the west parking lot at 12. I'll be in the truck playing Hellhound," she said.

"Maybe," I managed. She looked at me like Marion looked at Steve. Like he was a badass, maybe. She smiled, showing crooked teeth, and gave me a hypermobile thumbs-up. Despite an aura of danger around her, I tasted stars and Hubba Bubba.

Carole wasn't there, but a big guy in too-tight jeans and with a little bit of a gut that made his black T-shirt expand was standing next to the truck, which was vibrating with music, the windows fogged up with smoke and bodies. He had a fully-grown mustache. His hair was nearly white—not blond but white as a mouse. All the metal kids seemed to either be bleached blonde, or white blonde. I'd dyed my red hair jet black.

"Andre," he said.

"Cormac."

"I know. We've been waiting on you."

He didn't mean today, but since school began. They'd seen me around Waldbaum's; I'd seen them.

A sense of burning panic and excitement made my mouth dry. Was it possible that Carole had been sent to ensnare me into the truck, like a honey trap, so that I'd get beaten within an inch of my life? When I had gazed into Ricky Hell's eyes last week, I'd seen something in there like those prehistoric shapes we had seen in the gloomy swamps of the Everglades, all dark instinct and appetite. But perhaps I was mistaken; I'd never known anyone who looked like Ricky before, who moved like him. Or were these the people I'd been waiting to meet all my life?

"Danny and Rick are inside."

I opened the door and a gust of dope that smelled like BO hit me—or maybe it was BO from the four bodies inside. Ricky sat in the center of the circle, taking a hit from the bong. Danny was a tall, big-jawed guy who, if he cut off his long sandy hair, would look more like a football player than a metalhead. It was his truck. Danny had a girlfriend, Erin, but she was at a swim meet. Carole was drinking a beer out of a brown paper bag. Then there was Seth, a redheaded kid, blockheaded, with gnarly freckles.

Cafeteria food was for losers, Danny said. They'd gone to Wendy's. Ricky ate ravenously: French fries, a double bacon burger.

"Welcome, brother," Ricky said, belched, and handed the bong to me. I had to take it and not cough—looking at that thick yellow smoke and skunk weed, I knew I was going to struggle.

He frowned his disapproval at my delay.

Carole saved me. "He can't smoke that. He's got a meeting with Rosenthal after lunch. He'll be expelled if he's high." Carole gave a pitying look and passed me the beer.

Danny was sussing me out. Carole bit her lip, watching him. I noticed her arm was touching his.

"You got anything stronger than pussy-assed beer?" I said, pushing it away so that it sprayed her shirt.

"Fuck, bitch, give him the Turkey," Danny said. I watched him shift his weight away from her. Carole had her arm around Ricky, even if the whole time she had her eyes on Danny. But Carole was shit out of luck—Danny was not into her, not even a little. I didn't feel relieved; more curious.

"I'm going to get expelled soon," Ricky said, almost softly. "The bus thing was like the last straw."

"He's been kicked off the bus for dealing," Carole whispered.

Ricky smiled at me wickedly and skulled the Wild Turkey, but he seemed a little sad.

"He's, like, a genius," Carole whispered. "Off the charts smart."

"Ricky?" My voice sounded too high; just dumb.

"I can hear you," he said over the gurgle of the bong.

"Ricky's a senior. So is Andre. Maybe. If they pass."

I didn't like the way Andre looked at her. I said it once Andre left the car—he had a shift at Little Caesars pizzeria.

She shrugged. "He's scary," she admitted. "Do you know the kids that went missing?"

"No," I said.

"That little blonde girl, Katie Carver? Check out the paper sometime. There's been, like, six reported runaways, but a few that are, like, abductions. Andre saw a picture of her in the paper and said, 'She's a little tease. I see her around Waldbaum's.' She's, like, ten years old! Isn't that sick? It turns out she's Andre's sister's friend."

"Eleven." Danny's ears seemed to prick up at this. "And her name is Cathy Carver. It's gnarly. Erin's dad says that the kids are being dumped in the water, because they all lived round the Sound."

"Erin's his girlfriend." Carole said the word "girlfriend" like she would "scabies." "She does dance and swimming. Extra-curricular," she scoffed. "Her old man's a cop so she's not s'posed to hang out with us. She's, like, dating Danny but rumor is they don't even fuck."

"My stepdad's a cop," I said.

"Everyone's dad's a fuckin' cop," Danny said, rolling his eyes.

"I'm a cop," the redheaded kid shouted and everyone laughed.

"Maybe it's a cop," Ricky said and stubbed out his cigarette, "who's done it."

"Yeah right," Carole said, blowing smoke through her nostrils.

All eyes were on Ricky. He relished it. He rolled up his sleeves and

I saw a brand on his arm but couldn't make out the letter. He looked old suddenly.

"Forget it," he said.

It was later that night that Carole showed up unannounced to my house, a sixer in her backpack. We sat out by the pool drinking Bud Light, Carole smoking Alpine cigarettes—menthols. I smoked Marlboro Reds because the others tore my throat to shreds. It seemed like Marion and Steve were out and Aisling was inside, playing with a doll she was way too old for.

"Weird kid." Carole crinkled up her nose.

"She's fine," I said.

I'd never kissed a girl. She grabbed my thigh, put her menthol and beer-flavored tongue in my mouth. It felt staged somehow. I thought about the oil and alpine smell of the truck, the black eyes, the ketchup-smeared fries disappearing into his mouth. I don't know if I was channeling the serpentine energy of Ricky Hell or trying to summon him, as I put my hand up Carole's shorts, into the slit of her underwear, moving my hand inside her—guided by her sighs, the sounds she made. Carole's head thrown back, her neck flushed red—and as her muscles contracted on my hand I saw that Steve was at the window. Carole had been putting on a show, only it wasn't for me. "What's up?" she said after she finished her beer, pretending like she didn't see him.

Steve came outside and blew a joint with us, bummed a beer. It was silent except for the cicadas and crackling tension between me and Steve.

When Carole said she needed to get home, Steve said, "Hang back for a sec—it's not safe to walk. I'll run you home." I said I'd go with them but Steve just looked at me. "Someone has to watch the kid."

After he came back, he said, "That chick is bad news, you don't want to get in there, not unless you want an STD. And that Hell kid and his crew? Stay away from them. That's my first and final warning."

20

I finished my drink with a shaking hand and lowered my shoulders from somewhere near my ears, which disturbed a sleeping Mister, who'd curled up on my lap. Scowling, she jumped off.

I too got up from my seat at the kitchen table and went outside, hoping the cold air might reinvigorate me mentally. My body ached, I was tired; I was wired. My leg had gone numb from sitting.

I'd had the wool pulled over my eyes so many times in the last forty-eight hours—and been battered by so many revelations about the past and what I knew to be true, I honestly didn't know which way was up anymore. I sure as shit was not going to use *Resident Alien* as a guide, because while so many of Cormac's words rang true for me, others seemed bizarre and incredulous—including the amended date of Cooper Deane's death in the first chapter, the conversation about the missing kids and Katie AKA Cathy Carver. Cathy Carver went missing late October 1993—so when the kids were talking in the truck and Danny offered a killer-on-the-water theory (which, by the way, he never mentioned to me), they were talking about an abduction that hadn't even happened.

And I was in there too, sports-playing, square-assed Erin Sloane—Danny's girl. Only that's not who I was, not even a little bit. Okay, I was once good at swimming, until I received a satanic branding that made me swimsuit shy. I remembered how good it felt to tear through the water when I was wound up like this; after a few burning laps, my muscles unclenched and the mental knots began to unspool. When I swam, it was like all my conflicts and confusions rose to the surface and by the end of thirty laps I had solutions.

I still had the same problem—a sixteen-year-old one. Danny Quinlan-Walsh. Was he out there—black-clad, with a pair of night vision goggles? I suppressed a strangled laugh at how ridiculous the image was. But also, it wasn't that much of a stretch.

To prove I wasn't scared, I reached into my cardigan pocket and fished out my cigarettes and began to walk around the covered pool, doing land-laps, trying to reconcile *Resident Alien* and the Gmail chat I'd had with Aisling. If Carole and Steve still had something going on— that would make theirs a sixteen-year-old relationship, if that's what you could even call it. If Carole was intimate with Steve then she'd been a minor—there was no question of statutory rape. So, where did Ange, Steve's wife, fit into this diabolical ménage à trois?

I considered the scenario that Carole, not Cormac, had run to the phone booth to call Steve, and told him that Andre had attacked her. I pictured a wrathful Steve coming down to the woods with a bat. After all, he had possibly killed for Ange Miller, why not for Carole? Steve could have committed both murders. He took Ricky out to protect himself. The Southport Three's testimony was all over the place for a reason— they were on such a psychedelic cocktail Steve could have coached them, coaxed them, to say or do anything, even convinced the kids to tell the story he'd fed them. But there was something else going on that night in the woods and it had something to do with the missing kids; Danny had intimated it, in his oblique and threatening way.

Inside the house, the phone was ringing. I headed back in, but it went to the answering machine.

"Erin Sloane, pick up. Your cell must be on silent. There a reason?"

Denise. I located the handset under a pile of papers and picked it up.

"Sorry, Denise. I might have put it on do not disturb."

"Guess who emailed me?"

I sighed. "Tell me what he said."

"More of the same. You totaled his car this time. But he hasn't called the cops, so I'm thinking he's guilty as shit. What happened?"

I told her about Mona and Ricky Hell, the incident in the woods, Seth75, and the "accident" with the Kia. I was getting into Detective Diaz, Penny, and all the revelations of *Resident Alien* when she stopped me.

"You're being fully stalked by Danny," she concluded. "Cyber, virtual, and literal."

"I guess."

"Is that all you've got to say? He tried to lure you into the woods. You got a police escort home. Wake up, Erin."

"Danny has proven time and time again that he can and will hurt me. And he hasn't yet. Not this time."

"I don't want to give him the chance. Erin, babe, you are putting yourself in harm's way and even if you don't care about yourself, I do."

I gulped. "Please don't take me off the story. I'm already so far into finding out the truth. I believe Steve Shearer killed his partner, Cooper Deane, and Ricky in the same way. I think he may have been with Carole Jenkins as well as Deane's wife, Angela. So he would have been sleeping with a minor. Given her age, that's rape."

Saying the phrase aloud sent fire into my cheeks. Suddenly it occurred to me that Steve fit the profile of the Southport child killer: a man in a position of authority, someone with children. A community leader; a sadist. I'd asked Detective Diaz if their perp could have acted with an accomplice, she'd said no. Andre was dead by the time the last boy was taken, so he was in the clear. What if they were wrong? Profiles weren't blueprints, they were guides.

"Steve was having sex with a high school sophomore, Denise," I said. "He'd killed in cold blood before, most likely he murdered two people. What if Steve had something to do with the missing kids?"

"Hold up, Sloane. You're getting a lot of this stuff about Shearer from Cormac O'Malley's manuscript. The whole Carole affair could be fiction."

"I've got to follow up a few more things, but Steve Shearer and

Angela, Cooper Deane's widow, are living down in Coral Springs, Florida. In a development that Carole Jenkins' brokerage sells. Something very weird is going on there."

"Maybe so. What do you want to do? I mean, the stuff about Hernandez being undercover, dealing for Steve, that's a dynamite story. You've got a living relative of Andre Villiers you might be able to talk to, who will hopefully corroborate the satanic angle as a bunch of BS. The Carole and Steve connection is interesting, it adds another dynamic to that night altogether. The Mona connection is extraordinarily tenuous, it's just a refrigerator magnet for Christ's sake. And now the missing kids—that's a quantum leap. The guy sounds like pretty bad news, Erin, but he's not Charles Manson."

"I want to go down South, talk to Carole and Steve." As soon as I said it, I realized I had already decided I was going. With or without Denise's or the magazine's blessing. "I might be safer down there anyway, away from Danny. Just till he cools down." I hated that I had said that phrase again. How many times had I waited for him to "cool down," "chill out," forgive me for whatever imagined transgression I had committed?

"If you're right, have you ever thought you might be going from frying pan to fire by going after Shearer? Especially if he is who you say he is? If you lob up in Florida and surprise him and Carole, it could get very ugly."

"Denise . . ." I protested.

"Erin." Her tone was firm but I could sense her beginning to yield. "I know your stubborn ass pretty well. If you're intent on heading down there, talking to your satanic Lolita and her demon cop lover, we can send you there. I'll book it for you, tomorrow if you want. On two conditions: one, I want you to stay with me tonight. Get away from that house, get off the island."

The phrase brought more relief than I could verbalize.

Off the island. Anywhere but here. "Yes, okay."

"And the second: I insist you exercise extreme caution with Shearer."

"I can do that," I vowed, thinking of Mister first and then the money in the refrigerator. "There is one thing I have to fill you in on when I drive over. It's kind of a big deal."

———

Denise greeted me at the door in a stretched terry toweling robe, her hair in curlers, and a mud mask painted on her face.

"Hey there." She poked her fingers into the pet cage, clucking in at Mister. Only she wasn't in there. We looked at each other trying not to laugh; maintaining the charade.

"Come in." Inside her house, votive candles were lined up on a coffee table, Warpaint's *The Fool* played on a sleek sound system. Denise had opened a bottle of good Shiraz and two balloon glasses sat atop the coffee table. The whole place was minimalist Scandinavian calm, smelling of vanilla and citrus polish.

"Sit." Denise ushered me over to an overstuffed sofa, draped with a cashmere blanket. I lowered myself and sank back into it.

She started to pour a glass of wine. "Say when."

I waited until it reached the top before I called for her to stop.

I tried to slurp the overfull glass over the coffee table so as not to spill any but managed to dribble wine down my chin and onto my dress anyway.

"Shoot. My fault." Denise went into the kitchen and retrieved me some paper towels. I dabbed my chin. The good thing about always wearing black was that it absorbed most stains.

When she returned, she looked down at the carrier. "That's a lot of loot you got there." Denise did a good gangster's moll impression. "Did he follow you?" She collapsed onto the sofa and turned to face me.

"All the way to Brooklyn." It wasn't the red Kia, though, that must have been in the body shop. It was a blue SUV; it followed me from Oceanside to Southern State Parkway. I lost him at Pennsylvania Avenue. I got the plates.

My father had given me a brainwave. Denise and I knew Danny would be watching the house, and he would follow me all the way to her house. He might even try to break into my house when he realized I'd gone to JFK the next morning. So, I'd left Mister inside the house with the guarantee that my neighbor Jude would come over the morning after I left Oceanside Avenue and take her home for the week. I gave her two hundred dollars to guarantee steak dinners and extra TLC for Mister while I was away. And I'd hidden the plastic-wrapped cash in the cat carrier—it seemed the smartest way to deal with it.

"I can put it in my safe," Denise said. "Some of it, anyway. It's more than I thought it was. God, what an insane forty-eight hours you've had."

Denise was a hugger—the type who linked arms when she sat next to you. She rubbed my arm now and I tried to allow the contact, but quickly picked up my wine.

"You're telling me." My body was beginning to unwind, the wine had gone straight to my head. I wasn't used to wine—and not only did it disagree with me, it argued loudly and violently. I was probably going to pay for this tomorrow with a thumping head.

"We're going to have to come up with a more permanent solution to protect you other than sending you away to the tropics."

"I know," I said, thinking of Marci and her warnings. "He just keeps coming." I grew more agitated as I thought of his reckless fixation on me. It wasn't love; he wanted to possess and destroy me. And it was seemingly only fed over the years, rather than starved by absence. Danny was never really touched by his crimes, he seemed unmarked by the years in between our meeting; there was something mechanistic about him—an apex predator behind the boy-band smile. "He's like that masked killer guy in *Halloween*, the one who keeps getting back up even though he's been killed like a million times. What's his name again?"

"Michael Myers. And let's dial it down a notch. Although he also killed on Halloween, Danny is no Michael Myers. For one, he's not supernatural. Don't give him that kind of power," she chastised me. "He's just a man, a big-assed, overgrown bully of a man. Bullies don't like it when you call them out."

We fell silent; the chasm wide between what I felt able to voice aloud and what she knew from the narrative on the pages I'd sent over to her. She didn't even know about the pentagram yet.

"So, playing the devil's advocate here," Denise began. "Why do you think O'Malley is sending the story in installments via his sister?"

I shrugged. "I think it's a question of trust? I keep feeding back to Aisling that we're on the same side and maybe she feeds that back to him. Cormac is sensitive, she says, damaged from the whole experience."

"I'll say," Denise clucked.

"What are you implying?" I was being perverse; I knew exactly what Denise was getting at. Cormac wouldn't speak to me directly; Aisling was feeding me chunks of an incriminating, yet stylized story that seemingly paralleled my investigation. I didn't entirely trust *Resident Alien or* Aisling. Someone with a grudge, who was so locked in the trauma of the past as she was, could be unreliable, dangerous even. And maybe that was because she reminded me of myself.

"Just that I smell a rat," Denise said.

"Okay, maybe so do I," I admitted. "I still can't believe that Andre has a sister that's linked to Cathy Carver."

"Yeah, you missed that one all right."

"I've been a little sloppy. I haven't been myself." That was the understatement of the millennium and by the way Denise raised her drink and her eyebrows, she knew it. I'd been reckless. I was eating Ambien and Adderall like Tic Tacs. I hadn't gone a few hours without a drink in the last week; I was smashing into people's cars. I was *not* in peak form.

Denise gave me a sympathetic look, halfway between a frown and a smile. "Live and learn. I booked you a JetBlue flight to Fort Lauderdale and a week in Lauderdale Lakes in a hotel. Be warned, it's not crazy fancy, but there won't be bed bugs. In fact, the bed looks pretty nice. I checked on Tripadvisor."

I thought of the Freeport, which was one of the first and last times I'd stayed in a hotel; springs digging in my back, the curtain rail falling on us, mildew flowering on the walls of the bathroom.

"I'm sure it will be just great."

"There's been something I've been wanting to ask, Erin. All this stuff about Ricky Hell." Denise unfolded her legs, so that her socked feet were almost touching me. "Sorry, I gotta stretch my legs. Is that okay?"

"Uh, it's fine."

"Now that you know he was older, not who he said he was, does it reframe things for you? Like, it's almost non-consensual too, right?"

"I'm still trying to wrap my head around it, Denise. It's a betrayal. I don't like that he lied, not at all. But I'm almost certain that, if I'd known, I wouldn't have cared. It was me who pursued him. I was wild about him."

"Really?"

"Are we really having this conversation? Is this what they call girl talk?" I finished my wine.

"It's called *people* talk. You should try it," Denise said.

"Okay, well I was." I poured myself another wine and topped Denise's up. "I don't know, Ricky was different. He wasn't like other boys. Maybe because he was a man, but still. I've not met another man like him either. He really listened. And I thought he was a true individual, even if what he was saying was phony. He always said what he felt. Now I wonder how he could have lied like that, over and over. It must have been killing him."

"It did in the end," Denise pointed out.

"I think he died because of a criminal's secrets," I corrected her. "How many others did too, I don't know."

"Are you sure you're okay?" Denise studied me and I returned a look of plucky self-confidence. "You can say if you're not."

"I'm not okay, but I'm ready."

21

All my life I felt like a ghost; never more so than in Florida. In New York, I could get away with my blue-white skin and witchy blacks; my pinched, life-worn face and off-white teeth. The laser quality of light that showed my skin for what it was; thinned and reptilian. In my compact mirror, I saw every worry and frown line on my forehead; I looked frayed, coming apart at the seams.

At the baggage desk, I encountered the apartheid between Florida natives and tourists; the pale and aerobicized; the obese squeezed into synthetic dresses and shorts, the poor minorities with their kids in cheap Asian Disney rip-offs, the pixelated features of Ariel or Pocahontas slightly distorted. I had already encountered a harem of Playboy Bunnies and Victoria's Angels masquerading as civilians. Even the airline staff were hot and tanned, with bleached, capped teeth and lineless faces.

Fort Lauderdale was about seventy degrees and climbing, and I cursed my mother's wool dress. I was uncomfortably hot, but I couldn't just rock a tank and let my satanic chest-branding fly; this was a death penalty state, chock-full of devout Christians.

My cab driver was a leathery older man who resembled Robert Mitchum as Max Cady, with lots of old ink, green-blue, creased into indecipherable symbols on his bronzed skin. I scanned him for the telltale "Loretta" tattoo and found none. He was wearing a Grateful Dead T-shirt and knock-off Ray-Bans.

"Lenny Tuna," he offered.

"Erin Sloane," I said.

I asked him what he knew about Coral Springs.

"A graveyard for the rich, huh," he wheezed and laughed.

"I'm investigating the property market. An old high school friend of mine, Carole Ruffalo, is killing it in real estate there. I think they're building a lot of new estates."

"Most of Florida got creamed after the GFC, but the rich survived it. And the property developers like your gal up there at . . ."

"Ruffalo Realty Executives. They're based in Coral Springs. The new development is called Coral Palisades."

He looked at me through the rearview with a peculiar mixture of disappointment and anger.

"Carole's not really a friend. I'm writing about an unsolved crime for a magazine up north."

"Well, I don't know your friend's story, but nobody who is making an honest living is turning a profit, especially with these new estates and their ticky-tacky McMansions. The streets are all fake-assed French names. Lotta places overcharging, taking kickbacks, you name it. You can light up in here—I ain't no puritan."

I lit up. "I'm not on her side. As I said she's not a friend. She might be involved with a dirty cop, even."

"Oh yeah?" His tone sounded approving. "Sounds complicated."

"My dad was a cop. They're all complicated."

He laughed. "I'm ex-service myself."

"Cop?"

"Former Marine. Ex-cop. Now officially a beach bum living the good life in the Sunshine State."

I rolled down the window, the humidity rising off the asphalt and warping the road. The seats smelled like wet bathing suits left too long.

"Can we make a detour?" I said, trying my luck. "On the meter. I just gotta dash in."

"Nah," he said. "Gotta get lunch anyways. I'll just pick you up at one." He winked at me in the rearview.

More texts had come through that morning from Danny since I turned my phone back on:

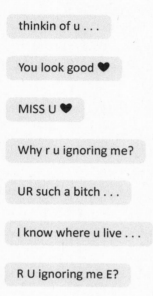

thinkin of u . . .

You look good 🖤

MISS U 🖤

Why r u ignoring me?

UR such a bitch . . .

I know where u live . . .

R U ignoring me E?

After all these years, the anxiety felt sickeningly familiar. It was close to fear, but nearer to rage now, too. I had an urge to hurl my phone in the trash can. Every fiber of my being wanted to block him, but I wouldn't until this was over—there was something he wanted from me and I had to wait to find out what it was.

The *You look good* component felt threatening—it had the horror movie threat of "I'm inside the house"—and I felt slightly light-headed as I scanned the mall where Lenny had dropped me. It was lined with palm trees; all open-planned light and glass, full of designer outlets. The impossibly beautiful or impossibly elderly queued at frozen yogurt stands.

Clad in black winter wear, I was easy prey. I needed clothes to fit in.

I took an Ambien and went from store to store for a new one of everything; makeup, underwear, new shoes, three new outfits. By about 1 p.m., loaded with shopping bags, I met Lenny and asked him to drop me at the car hire. When we arrived there, he helped me with my bags and then, after wiping his hand on his shorts, handed me a card. Tips-n-Toes nail salon, Daytona Beach.

"You can reach me there," he said. "It's the wife's place. They also got tanning beds there, huh."

"Oh yeah?" I said.

"Think about it. Stay groovy, hon." He tooted the horn.

———

When I pulled up to the White Sands hotel in a vintage black Mercedes, I was glad I'd taken the extra insurance. The hotel wasn't exactly The Plaza, but it seemed okay. It was more the neighborhood that was the trouble—blasted with graffiti and haunted by shady gangster types slowly circling the block in pimped-up cars that shuddered with bass.

The double-story cement building, painted mint and bone white, sat much like a melting ice cream, paint peeling. Inside, it didn't smell like ice cream—more like a laundromat spruced up with air freshener. The interior was significantly better than the Freeport Motel, however. The bathroom boasted a flamingo-pink bathtub with spa jets. I fell back onto the bed and, as Denise had promised, it was good. The mattress was firm and the base seemed to bear no trace of bed bugs. There was a pool long enough to do laps in outside, and it was warm enough, too. And there was a bar that it seemed would open midafternoon.

I decided to take a cold shower first and rest a little before meeting Carole. I knew she was going to be in the office until six. She updated her status at least ten times a day—*Lunchbreak Pilates owww!! School run is better with gummy bears LOL* (WTAF, I hasten to add). *Tonite is cheat night! Om Nom Nom* (referring to her diet, I imagine). I laid out my purchases on the bed.

Women do lots of things for other women: they dress for them, for instance. And in my case, stock up on Poison by Dior at the mall. I'd finished *Dancing with the Devil* on the plane and I was pissed off. As I sprayed perfume on my wrists and in my hair, I thought of Carole's Charlie perfume, the lingering smell on Ricky's mattress in the van—the same mattress on which Carole claimed, in *Dancing with the Devil*, she'd been "initiated" by Ricky. The last installment of *Resident Alien* would seem to corroborate this: Carole sidling up to Ricky, while eyeing Danny off. Why couldn't she have left Ricky Hell alone?

I put my new tailored tan skirt and white shirt over new La Perla lingerie and slipped into the patent leather stilettos.

In the tiny bathroom, I ironed my hair; I changed my makeup to high blush, nude lips, and natural eye makeup. Then I scanned my new Veronica Lake silhouette in the mirror. All that was missing was the hair. I had no time to style it further, so I just tied it up in a bun and sprayed the shit out of it with hairspray.

I checked my phone: a few messages had come through. First, my neighbor Jude. Two hundred dollars had bought me regular pics and updates. Mister looked peeved, she hated staying indoors, but she was safe.

Then Ox.

> Pumpkin, I think you should can this story. UR Ed will understand given your past. If you need money, I got u.

> Ox, it's not about the money. You know that. Will stay safe.

> I'm unhappy about the Walsh Kid. Think it's time 4 a home visit.

> Thanks Ox. Maybe go to Prestige Marine instead? His wife seems okay and I don't want to add to her trouble. And if u could keep an eye on the Oceanside Ave address that would be great.

> Why? Where are ya kid?

> I'm staying away from home for a week.
> Hotel. Cat is with the neighbor.

> Smart move, Pumpkin. Anything I
> can do to help.

I thought about it for a minute.

> Can you help me get me anything on
> Cormac O'Malley and his sister Aisling?
> I'm getting a lot of correspondence
> from Aisling and Cormac, but I can't
> locate him and he won't speak to me
> directly. And there's something a bit off
> about her.

> U got it. Forward me the email me plus
> any DOBS/addy's or anything else u got.

———

Back in the Mercedes, I was happy to note that, while it had been re-fitted with a few modern conveniences, it had a cigarette lighter and an ashtray—and a tape player. The radio dial was jammed and there seemed to be a cassette wedged in the tape deck. The Merc's air-conditioning was a bit too vintage to be effective, so I unrolled the window, took a gamble, and pressed play. Mona the rat had inspired me to smoke Virginia Slims—I tapped one out of the pack and sang along, the last person who had rented the Mercedes was into country music. A female voice came through the speaker with a voice as bell pure as Emmylou Harris, singing about a fistfight and a fickle lover.

> *I beat him black and I beat him blue,*
> *That lyin' boy who promised to be true.*

I leaned my elbow on the door, hitting the dash for emphasis as I warbled along, not really knowing what was coming next, soaking in the vitamin D and smoking, feeling generous about the Floridian driving. The chicness of the car and the approving looks from other drivers began to give me a shine; a cloak of invincibility. I sped up, gained confidence. It seemed that the Floridian heat dispelled damp and ghosts.

Danny's messages, the incident at West Cypress Road Woods, the ghost of Ricky Hell and the dead kids felt far away. Now I understood the renewed confidence in the property market after 2008. After a day in Florida, I'd already begun saying things like: "Money's no object. Put it on the AMEX." Here, I was driving a rented Mercedes.

The satnav in the car indicated that I was ten miles from Ruffalo Realty Executives. As I drove into downtown Coral Springs, I felt I'd discovered what Sweet Valley would look like in real life in an economic downturn. There was a glut of For Sale and In Escrow signs. Golf courses and real estate agencies seemed to be in high demand, but now no one was buying and no one had time to play. Brokerages and time-shares clearly desperate for business had signs that promised raffle tickets, free dinners, hell, even a car, if you bought a house. Everything was beige and stucco; shiny condos loomed next to squat frozen yogurt stores, sandwich chains, and strip malls, all warped and shimmering in the heat of the afternoon. It was probably only seventy degrees, but the humidity was at 100 percent and my thighs were glued to the driver's seat. By now I was resenting the car rental salesperson showing me the Merc; I could be driving an SUV that was like a meat locker.

Carole's office was a single-story marine blue deco building, with curved edges and a smooth-edged rectangular column running down the center like a stripe, or a mohawk. I briefly remembered RP taking me to Manhattan when I was a child and telling me the old deco buildings had "eyebrows."

I parked the car and headed inside into the air-conditioned building. Sadly, and perhaps predictably, the interior had been exorcized of all character—gutted and modernized with chrome and glass. There was a giant feature wall holding an aquarium full of tropical fish and a hatchet-faced receptionist in a tangerine dress. I straightened up my shoulders and managed a smile.

"Erin Sloane. Carole Ruffalo is expecting me," I said and sat down.

"Sure. Would you like some water? Café latte?" She pronounced this in a faux European accent.

"An espresso and bottled water?" I suggested. I hadn't had time to get a manicure at Tips-n-Toes to complete my makeover. I cast a look down at my gnawed fingernails and thrust my hands deeper into my pockets. "Thank you so much."

After the girl disappeared into the kitchen, Carole Ruffalo came through the front entrance, accompanied by a gust of hot air and a dated looking man, circa the *Dallas* era. Mr. Ruffalo, her silver fox husband. I recalled his George Hamilton tan and bleached teeth from their website.

Despite the fillers, Botox, boobs, the pert, upturned nose, and glacial eyes—her mouth remained the same, thin and sullen. Up close I could see the lemon-yellow dress she wore was designer and even I, a fashion illiterate, knew Louboutins when I saw them. She looked thinner, rich, and more inscrutable. If she recognized me, she didn't show it. She squeezed the man's arm and whispered in his ear. He disappeared into the first office as the tangerine blonde came out with the espresso and Perrier.

"A Ms. Erin Sloane here to see you."

Carole stood in the foyer, staring at her.

The receptionist looked worried and teetered on her heels helplessly. I took the drinks from her. It was extremely hot, I was very thirsty. Carole shooed the girl away, back to the reception desk.

"Eerie Erin," she sneered, looking me up and down. "A real blast from the past. You on vacation or something?" Southport lived in Carole's vowels. The voice did not match the glossy image. "You came to grab a drink?" I could hear the amusement, but there was an unfriendly undertone.

"Not a vacation. I'm writing a story for *Inside Island*. You know, the magazine? The story is about the Southport Three. I wondered if we could talk. Over a drink if you like . . ."

"Yeah well, no comment."

She turned on her heels.

"Why don't you show me Coral Palisades?" I called after her.

She stopped.

"Why? You interested in buying?"

"I want to see where Steve Shearer lives. You know, Cormac's stepdad?"

"Let's talk in my office," Carole interjected. But I didn't want to stay on Carole's turf. Plus, I wanted to see Steve Shearer and Ange's place.

"I'd prefer to talk on the drive." I dug into my bag and retrieved my copy of *Dancing with the Devil*. "Then I can ask you a few questions about your book."

"Keep your voice down," Carole murmured.

"Does Mr. Ruffalo not know about what happened in Southport?" I whispered back and she glared at me in return. The man who I presumed to be Mr. Ruffalo came out of his office. His face crinkled in displeasure, he reached out and held onto her arm protectively.

"Carole?"

"This is Ms. Sloane. She wants to see a property at the Palisades."

He quickly adapted his face into a game show host smile.

"Wonderful."

"Let's take my car," I suggested, slamming back the espresso and gasping as it scalded my throat. Carole's expressionless face moved slightly. We headed outside together. I took the Perrier with me. It had a little straw with the paper still on the end.

"Hold my calls," Carole called out to the girl without moving her lips, slamming the door behind us.

22

"*That's* your car?" Carole said, staring at the Mercedes.

"I'm trying a new look." *Bong Queen.* "I'm sorry if I got a bit mouthy back there, Carole. I'm a Long Islander, I guess. I just want to talk, woman to woman."

She laughed; it was a mirthless yelp. Then she muttered "Fuck it," opened the passenger side, and eased slowly into the seat. As we drove, I wondered if I'd missed my calling. Maybe I was a frustrated cop, like my father.

I looked at Carole in the light and realized that, despite her tan and thick makeup, her skin was quite uneven. Her teeth had all been capped. Carole took the pack of Virginia Slims off the dash and lit one without asking. She was polite enough to offer me one.

In the car, I was sweating through my linen blouse and my hands were wet on the steering wheel. Beads of sweat had gathered on my forehead and made my ironed hair spring into frizz. I looked at Carole, so cool and dry, unbothered by the situation. She wasn't perspiring. Botox must have made sweating a thing of the past. She toyed with her gold chain and displayed her throat. It was like she was flirting. Carole had barely reacted to seeing me after all these years. I mean, Carole was a cool customer, maybe she was even good at poker, but I doubted anyone was that good.

"You don't seem all that surprised to see me, Carole. How did you even recognize me?"

Carole blew out a blue ring of smoke. "You don't look all that different. I mean you're clearly older, but your face is the same. And you haven't really changed your hair. And you're still all in black. You know, Rick had your picture in his glove compartment."

Rick. I flushed. No one called him that. She was trying to distract and rile me—lording whatever feigned intimacy she believed that they shared over me.

I pushed my anger aside. "Aren't you wondering why I'm here, after all these years?"

"As you said, you're writing a story." Carole sounded like she was reading off a sheet of paper. "The Palisades is like a mile away. Take a left, keep going until you hit Coral Palisades Drive."

"Did someone mention I was coming to see you? A Mona Byrnes?"

"I may have got a heads-up from someone that you were coming here to, like, rake up the past for your little paper."

"Who?"

"It was anonymous."

"Was it Mona Byrnes?" I pressed her.

"Mona who?"

"She was the cop who took your original statement, Carole. Also, she has a Ruffalo Realty magnet on her fridge. That's quite the coincidence." As Denise had said, it was a stretch but I trusted my gut. The synchronicities were adding up.

"Not Danny?"

She shrugged at me. "Haven't heard from him since '94, and that's the way I like it."

"You know, Palisades usually means a high line of cliffs, or a fence of stakes," I said. My father, the quizmaster had told me this. "This area appears to contain no palisades, no cliffs, or inclines of any kind in Coral Springs. It is, in fact, flat."

Carole rolled her eyes.

"Whatever. It's a name."

We fell into silence until we reached the Palisades.

The mint and lavender sign welcomed us. There was an artist's interpretation of the estate: a multitiered replica of Southern-style mansions in the colors of saltwater taffy, built in a ring, surrounded by an artificial lake and a golf course. It was a fortress of a kind—a panopticon, you could call it. The security office at the front was empty. I wondered if the cameras even worked.

I turned to face her. Recalling Carole's curated account of that night in West Cypress Road Woods in *Dancing with the Devil*, I pictured her and Steve Shearer, sitting down to coauthor the book together.

"Tell me about you and Steve Shearer. You sold him a house here. And Mona Byrnes." I was bluffing a bit, but I wanted to gage her reaction.

"As I said, it's a small world. And a lot of people know of us. We have a strong professional reputation all along the East Coast and the word's spreading," Carole parroted.

"Save me the mission statement, Carole. If it wasn't Mona or it wasn't Danny, did you get an email from a woman called Aisling O'Malley telling you I was coming? Mac's sister?"

She seemed unperturbed, but her jaw clenched tighter. "No, I got the heads-up from an account called mindyourownfuckingbusiness@gmail.com."

I shook my head. If I was in a hard-boiled detective novel, I would have pistol-whipped her. If I was a cop, I would have started heating the interview up a notch. Maybe I would have hit the dash and shouted. But I was just a hack with a mania for knowing the truth, whatever that was, and an old-ass grudge.

"You know, I drove past your house with Rick and Mac once," she said, her tone changing. All the hairs on my neck stood up.

"Rick wanted to see if Danny was there."

"And was he?"

"Yes. He was. And then we all got high. You can guess what happened next."

She was trying to goad me into a reaction. I had been poking the bear, as Denise would have said.

Carole yawned and looked at her nails. From reading *Resident Alien* and *Dancing with the Devil*, and from what little I knew of her as a teenager, I gathered Carole was easily bored and craved attention. I could give her the attention she wanted. I decided to play along.

"So, you and Mac knew about me and Ricky. Did Danny?"

Carole's shoulders shrugged.

"I can't say for sure, but Ricky made us promise not to tell—like, on our lives."

"I skim-read your book on the plane. I'm wondering what happened to all that Christian redemption? You still a believer?"

Carole shrugged. "It was boring. I just gave the publishers what they wanted."

"In your book, you say you were dating Cormac O'Malley, but that Ricky was in love with you—that you were pressured into sex with him by the group. And you were a virgin. I *know* that's not true."

"Look, I hit it with Rick, yeah." The nineties jargon jarred me. "With Mac. And Danny too. You didn't know that, did you?" She blinked at me a few times, her eyes a very icy blue.

"I don't think I believe you," I said, shrugging. I really didn't. Danny was far too moral. Ricky, well, the stink of Charlie on the mattress, his open promiscuity; her proximity. Ricky may have slept with Carole, but I wanted to call her bluff. "I just want to represent you in the article in a way that's true and accurate. And fair." The heat had made me feel slightly stoned; the humidity had leached all my vital energy.

"For the sake of peace and closure, I'll help you." Carole managed to smile through gritted teeth.

Liar. But we both were. Despite how much I loathed her, we both wanted revenge.

"Just ask what you want. I've got to go back and freshen up for a client meeting."

I did a short stint in rehab and I knew soccer moms and brokers who were on the pipe. I recognized the enlarged pores, the marks and abrasions from long nails and long nights and—underneath the Lancôme foundation, her Britney Spears Fantasy perfume, and self-tanner—the

stench of ammonia and vinegar. I finished my cigarette and stubbed it.
I shouldn't even be smoking in the car; the ashtray was probably only
for display purposes.

"Ask your questions and get it over with."

"You do know Steve more than you're letting on, don't you? I mean,
you dated Cormac. You were at the house."

"Yeah. I do."

"Who called Steve out to the woods that night? I don't believe it
was Cormac."

"Look, whatever you heard, Steve is a good man. His wife, Marion,
died. Cormac's mom. He deserves some peace."

"I heard he remarried pretty quickly. Ange's first husband, Cooper
Deane, was shot in the line of duty in '92, only there was very little
written about it. And Steve was his partner. Now Steve lives with Ange."

I took out another cigarette, offered her one. She accepted with a
shaking hand.

"Who cares?" Carole said, and though I couldn't read her face, her
tone was unmistakable. I had hit a nerve.

"Do you know her?"

"I never met her."

"But you have some sort of relationship with Steve? You sold him
a house. Back then, were you . . . ?"

"Ewww." Her Long Island princess came out. "No way. He was so
old. And he was Mac's stepfather."

"And now?"

"What do you think?" Carole folded her arms.

I'd seen her husband. She liked older men, clearly. Maybe she always
had, if *Resident Alien* was anything to go on.

"I think you were an adventurous young girl who liked drugs and
booze. So was I, Carole. I'm not judging. But maybe Steve had a hold
on you and he still does. Did he convince you to lie about Ricky killing Andre?"

"Ricky killed Andre because he was out of his mind on acid and
mushrooms. So was Danny. End of story."

I tried a different approach.

"I've been developing this theory about that night. That Steve was the one who beat Andre to death, partly because he tried to strangle you, rape you even. I believe that by the way. He choked me too. Hard."

She assessed me coolly and shrugged. "Sorry."

"I didn't tell anyone. Now I wish I had. Did you call Steve out to the woods because Andre was hurting you? And Steve lost control? Shot Ricky cause Ricky had seen him kill Andre and he thought he'd tell? Maybe Steve bribed Danny and the other kids not to rat on him?"

Carole gave me a look that read *Really?* "Try again," she said.

"I think Andre Villiers was pretty evil and there was a reason he had to die. Am I right? I'm not judging. I just don't think Ricky Hell was Andre's executioner."

"Why don't you ask Aisling and Cormac O'Malley?" Carole spat out.

It took a second for her meaning to become clear.

"Aisling was twelve at the time of the crime."

"Exactly."

"Are you saying Cormac was involved in killing Andre? Because of Aisling?"

My heart went into my throat. I thought of Murderbabe66's theory on the forum.

"Did you ever hear about Andre getting Aisling and her little friends stoned?"

Her agitation was increasing. She picked at her face.

Her growing discomfort felt like claws scraping on a blackboard.

"I'm just saying the past is the past. Ricky Hell is just a bag of bones in the ground. And, let's face it, that's all he ever was gonna be." She folded her arms. "I'm done talking."

I nodded, absorbing the likeness of Danny's phrasing to Carole's. Had they conferred? Did they talk? I wanted to ask, but I knew it would have to be enough for now. When I dropped her back at her luxury office to get high, she turned to face me.

"Move on, Eerie. You could get hurt by this."

Was it a threat? She looked at me with something that resembled kindness. I watched her canary-yellow back disappear, like a bird into a cat's mouth.

———

Back at the hotel I took another ice-cold shower and played my summer of '94 mix on my phone. Motels made me nostalgic. I wanted a guilty little memory lane vacation. As Jane's Addiction's "I Would for You" came on I changed into a T-shirt and lay down on the sagging mattress, thinking of Ricky Hell, postponing reality.

"He had your picture in his glove compartment."

Carole's adenoidal intrusion was like an active construction site outside a beach house. It ruined my reverie.

What picture was she referring to? I never gave him one. He could have cut one out of a yearbook, but I doubted it. Despite the poetry and whatnot, Ricky was not a sentimentalist. He also used to talk about photographs stealing your soul or something like that. Ricky played up his Native American heritage for the girls. I understood that a little better now that I knew about his double life.

Carole had cleverly identified some deep, hidden girlish part of me that delighted in the idea that Ricky was mooning over a picture of me.

Jesus, sentimentality was making me gullible. I poured myself a whisky and seltzer and connected to the Wi-Fi. Someone had tipped Carole off and my bets were on Mona Byrnes—but Carole's insinuation that Aisling and Cormac were involved in Andre's death made me further question Aisling's intentions and her integrity. My list of questions for her was growing; the burning, billion-dollar question was obvious— what really happened with Andre Villiers?

Like Mona said, the kids probably did kill Andre, but not because Ricky told them to. Maybe Ricky killed Andre, for picking on little girls.

Money wasn't an incentive—not for Southport kids anyway. Danny once told me he had broken his dad's nose for picking on Patrick. He wouldn't say any more. All the boys came from violence; they were violence. All the girls were victims.

I heard the familiar chime of an email on my phone. Aisling O'Malley. No subject line, just a question.

Where R U?

I ignored her. I didn't want to tell Aisling I was in Florida—in any case, I had the sense she already knew. That she had, in a way, sent me here, via *Resident Alien*. Maybe she'd even worded Carole up to my visit.

It had just turned 6 p.m., the end of the hotel's happy hour. I refilled my whisky from my Jameson bottle, slipped it into my purse, and headed out to the pool area with my laptop to write.

Outside it smelled of magnolia and wet laundry. Even though the humidity was draining, I liked the intensity of the Floridian climate, the constant threat of thunder, the mineral smell of petrichor among the spilled rocket fuel and chlorine.

Half-drunk cocktail glasses and empty beer bottles lined the pool area. A couple were engaged in a sex act at the east side of the pool, underneath the palm tree. One of the Cuban bellboys was cleaning the pool with strong chemicals, grim faced. He stopped. "The bar is closed," he said, with scarcely concealed disgust.

"I know." I shook my whisky and the ice rattled. "I brought my own."

He shook his head and said something under his breath.

"*Blanquita.*"

I ignored the insult. His job sucked, I sympathized. People were generally terrible, white people especially, but they were at their very worst on vacation. I headed out to a plastic lounger at the west end of the pool area, underneath the biggest palm I could find. The couple across from me had disentangled and lit up a joint. The smell of reefer drifted across the pool.

Listening to the cicadas and rumbling of distant thunder, I couldn't have been further away from the bonfires and jack-o'-lanterns of Massapequa, or from the woods where Ricky Hell took his last breath, and the streets where those kids were taken and killed.

I heard the chime of my email. This time, Cormac had sent me an email direct. Another installment of *Resident Alien*.

23

RESIDENT ALIEN
BY CORMAC O MALLEY

That night at the Old Res, Carole undid her halter-neck and showed me her breasts. They were tiny, round as mandarins and about the same color. Her skin was self-tanned and, according to the label, should have been Brazil-nut brown. She lifted her skirt: I see London, I see France. Carole wore no underpants and, even if she did, I still would have been drawn to the bruise that reminded me of Africa. I ignored the swell of ash-blonde pubic hair, groomed into a heart.

Instead of touching her, I asked her to pose for me.

I'd never seen a woman naked before and as I laid down the lines of her shape on the paper in my mind, the excitement I experienced was mostly aesthetic.

I touched her; she touched me. It wasn't unpleasant, but it was like watching a badly dubbed movie; it was all out of sync. The only way that I managed to get hard was thinking of the diesel and tobacco smell of Ricky's truck, the way his hair fell into a curly tip, like it had been dipped in ink the color of midnight. Eyes, lips, biceps. As I was thinking of Marion's disappointment in my manliness, I heard Steve's voice in my ear: *you little queer.*

Long Island was experiencing a cold snap—the air cut like an ax, but that wouldn't stop us. The Old Res filled up with kids who formed a circle around wood and stone, squished together on old planks of wood balanced on concrete boulders, getting splinters on our asses. We sat around a bonfire fed with scrap wood, firelighters, and school-work. There were a few groups of kids from Roosevelt High; footballers, cheerleaders, a few burnouts from Belmont who brought shrooms and a baggie full of purple hearts. Two middle school girls sat with lipstick on their teeth, drinking beer nervously. They were, as Danny put it, lining up to get fucked. But Danny wouldn't be the one to do it. He seemed to have contempt for the sex act; Ricky would be the one they were waiting for. He was a boy slut, Carole said. All I saw was Ricky growing broodier and more intense; that night he was throwing rocks at the boom box, which was playing Naughty by Nature, Onyx, and The Black Crowes. One of the girls put on Slayer, Metallica; harder stuff, black metal, Swedish stuff followed. The songs formed a seamless soundtrack with the sounds of the night: a glut of cans being cracked, shit being shot, the sucking of bongs, the high-hat rattle and horn of the LIRR as it shot through Southport Station.

There was a conversation about the missing Southport kids: the little girl Cathy Carver was in the sixth grade at the same elementary school Carole and Danny had gone to.

"I'm telling ya, I talked to the cops about them kids. I reckon the kid killer is a cop himself," Andre said. His loose sloppy mouth made my stomach turn. He reached for Carole, she shrank away. He shrugged.

"Why did you talk to them?" I asked him.

He just shrugged. "I hang out at Waldbaum's. The candy and comic aisle. So did Jason and Cathy, I guess."

Next to Danny, diagonal to me, was Erin, Danny's elusive girlfriend. Eerie Erin from my art class. She used to get bathroom passes and return way too long after, her long auburn hair smelling of cigarettes and liquor. I hadn't seen her for months. I had noted her absence. I'd heard that she had been sent to a Catholic school because of some family tragedy.

"Know who that is?" Carole asked me.

"Eerie?" I faux guessed. I knew her name. We could have been friends, had she stayed on. Unlike the other metal kids, she didn't seem to be posing so much as emanating genuine pain. I feared the others, as much as I was drawn to them—their destruction and derision. I longed for level-headedness, someone to laugh with, someone to tell a secret to. Erin looked the type. She even carried books.

On the other hand, hanging out with Carole was like reading an open diary. She literally gossiped about herself. Very quickly I learned that Carole didn't trust men who didn't want to have sex with her, moreover they angered her. She had been poor once. She was seeing a therapist because she tore her own hair out sometimes. She used vaginal deodorizers, she carried breath spray, she wore smelly floral insteps, she bathed several times a day. She got stoned even more. She hated her parents and thought about fixing their brakes. The food she ate had to be certain colors. She also gossiped about everyone else and mostly because she watched everyone, she had a savant-like ability to dig out frailty and desire.

"Just after school started, Eerie Erin's dad killed her mom and sister. She and Danny were in the house at the time, but they survived." Carole's eyes looked big and wolfish; she cracked a beer.

I did not ask how.

"I heard she and Ricky have a thing. Isn't Ricky gorgeous? Would you kiss him? Wouldn't you just die if you kissed him?" she asked in a voice that came out like a purr. "Silly boy," she said. "My Lucky Charms Leprechaun," she cooed.

"He likes girls," I said, but there was an ember of hope alive in me and Carole sensed it. Carole saw me burning.

We watched Erin and Danny, walking to the side of the fire, lit up by the flames like the anti-homecoming king and queen. Rings adorned her ears, rings covered her fingers, a huge khaki parka covered her body, but you could see long, shapely legs in denim cut-offs over black stockings. He wore all black, but instead of looking metal, he looked more like Patrick Swayze in *Dirty Dancing*; sculpted muscle, legs like

Michelangelo's David. Danny's father was a doctor. He lived on the
right side of Southport, they didn't have a maid though, despite all his
father's money. I noted the way he watched Erin constantly. He never
took Carole or the other girls up on their offers for second and third
base, all the way. He was a teenage boy, but somehow, he was made
of steel. That was not to be trusted.

"Fuck off," Erin shouted, flipping him the bird as she walked off.

"She's a little bit chubby from the back," Carole said underneath
her breath.

"Erin," Danny called. "You're outta line." But he was smiling.

Ricky watched Erin leave with an intensity that troubled me.

The way I watched Ricky was the thing that I hoped nobody noticed.

Estoy ardiendo: I am burning up.

I passed out near the fire and when I woke up, it was just a pile
of smoldering ashes and I was freezing, soaked in my own cold piss.

"You're my best friend, Mac," Carole kept saying to me, over and
over, kissing my face. A daisy hung on a long chain around her neck.
It caught my eye as Carole's usual jewelry looked like it came out of a
vending machine called Skulls-n-Snakes. Her snake ring usually caught
my hair and pulled out a clump.

"Where's Ricky?" I asked over and over.

Danny just shook his head.

"He bailed, man."

———

Later that week, Steve went into the pharmacy to collect a script for
Marion and Aisling went through the glove box and took out Steve's
brush, goofing around. She was pretending to be Steve, brushing her
curls. We saw it at the same time. A silver daisy on a string—Carole's
necklace.

Aisling put it around her neck. Her smile devastated me—she
thought it was a gift for her.

Steve clocked it that night at dinner—Roy Rogers burgers and fries, eaten at the kitchen table. Marion wasn't cooking. Marion was barely doing anything, except smiling occasionally.

"It's too old for you," Steve told her.

"But it's for me, isn't it?" Aisling asked him, and he ignored her.

Marion just shrugged.

Steve made her take it off. I saw from the stiff set of her jaw he'd killed the last bit of hopeful devotion she'd been nursing for him. I watched him take the necklace to the bedroom and I stole it back from the dresser drawer when he was at work, along with some of Marion's happy pills. I didn't give it back to Carole, but I put it around the neck of Aisling's favorite teddy bear.

She understood not to wear it again.

That night Carole called.

"I lost my necklace," she said. "Have you seen it? I've, like, searched everywhere."

"No. Have you been to the Res?" I tried to sound helpful, curious.

"I had it since then."

"Oh. I wonder… I know… have you, like, checked with Steve? Like his car?"

She went silent. Carole was smarter than anyone thought—she was crueler too. It was partly why I liked her. She didn't disappoint.

"No. But I'll check with Ricky. Maybe on the back seat, you know."

24

I sat by the pool at the hotel absorbing the weirdness of being written into a scene in *Resident Alien*—gossiped about even. I was aggravated at the accusation that my dad killed my family, though I knew it was a heavily fictionalized version of events.

I had always suspected the narration of *Resident Alien* was unreliable, taking liberties with timelines and such; but the scene at the Res felt contrived to me. This disturbed me, because it seemed to me that the book was reinforcing the notion of the child killer being a cop, all the while casting a light on Andre for the crimes too—which is what I'd proposed to Denise over the phone.

The point was being driven home that Carole and Steve were fucking. Cormac O'Malley (and ostensibly, Carole Jenkins) and I all had the same taste in men. Well, one man—Ricky Hell. I remembered that night at the Res; Danny and I had fought—he'd stuck a finger in my ribs that made a stellate-shaped bruise. And if it was the night I recalled correctly, I had spent the remainder of it with Ricky at West Cypress Road Woods, in the back of his freezing truck, listening to Judas Priest.

Resident Alien had an agenda—it was slanted to persuade me to suspect Steve Shearer of multiple crimes. And it wanted me to loathe Carole Jenkins.

Which I already did. Because there was *no way* I looked chubby from behind.

Another message came through:

> WTF u got some pig to come to my work
> and threaten me? I'll END u.

Mister was safe at Jude's. Nothing of value to me was in that house. In fact, it was an albatross. Danny Quinlan-Walsh was welcome to burn it down. The money was with Denise, not that I cared. It wasn't mine—I was almost 100 percent sure it was blood money.

"I'm not afraid." I voiced my affirmation aloud. I wasn't. With my growing intelligence of Danny's real nature, what he may or may not have been involved in, any spell he had me under was gone. When I looked at his bleached teeth and pretty-boy menace, I saw what Denise saw: a bully, bloated with insecurity and unresolved anger.

My phone pinged again. Danny. Even though I'd blocked him. It came through on a different number.

> ALL THE SLOANE BITCHES ARE DEAD. EVEN
> THE DOG. LCKY UR CATS A BOY.

He was wrong, but I wasn't going to correct him.

His threat worked though. I called Jude.

"Everything's fine on our side. Mister is not happy about being kept in, but she's got extra treats. Don't worry, sweetheart," she said.

"Call the cops . . . actually, call this number if you hear or see anything." I gave her Ox's details.

I texted Danny back:

> Police are watching my place, dude. I'm
> blocking your number now.

———

I must have fallen asleep, somewhere between my third whisky and second Xanax. I woke at 4:30 a.m. with the distinct sense that something was wrong. There was no weight on the foot of my bed; no gravelly purring. I looked around and remembered where I was. The detergent used on the hotel sheets was scented with suntan lotion and frangipani air freshener. The air was as chilled as a meat locker.

I was relieved to be alone in a strange hotel room, alive and not too hungover. I often woke screaming or desperately sucking in air. Sometimes I would wake stringing out apologies in a kind of prayer. I used to dream that someone was sitting on my chest, feeding on my breath, like an incubus. Sometimes it was Danny.

I checked my phone. No more Danny messages.

There was an alert from "True Crime Happened to Me." Murderbabe66 again.

> FYI: Check out this thread.

It was in the paranormal section, no wonder I skipped it. The subjects were all ghosts in the woods—the threads were all about shapeshifting, orbs, and ectoplasm. I scrolled on and on. A lot of it read like bad fan fiction.

> I saw him. Cherry red and black hair. Looked white as real life. He was just wandering around lost.

Seth? I thought. He was a redhead and he was dead; not murdered though. Murderbabe66 had already pointed this out to me.

Then a reply:

> Yeah. I saw Ricky Hell, or what was his spirit animal. The redheaded ghost is Cormac O'Malley. He died overseas, but his ghost comes back to the woods, because he feels responsible for Andre's murder.

| **How did he die?**

| OD, I think? Last year.

I checked the thread date. 2008. So last year was '07. I searched for his death here and in Australia in 2007. Drug overdoses. I scrolled and found nothing. I wondered if he'd moved elsewhere—maybe even back to the States. Then I remembered his first name was Michael. A new search brought up a report from the Victoria Coroner's Court. A report on the death of Michael C. O'Malley. Same birthdate. Death in a McDonald's bathroom in Melbourne, Australia. Heroin overdose. I was positive it was him.

Again, like my fake source Seth75, another digital pretender had hoodwinked me. This time it was Aisling O'Malley. Not only had I not interrogated my source, I'd ignored my gut instinct (and Denise's) about Aisling—which had come to me in the same screaming red caps as her Myspace page.

I called Denise's cell and on the fifth ring I was met with a string of expletives. Then I realized it was still very early or very late. I checked the time: 4:45 a.m.

"I'm sorry I woke you up, but it seems a dead man has been sending me his memoir," I said.

"What the fuck?" Denise said and yawned.

"As you suspected, *Resident Alien* literally has a ghostwriter," I said. "I'll call the Coroner's office in Australia when they open, but it looks like Cormac O'Malley is dead. So either this is an old manuscript that Aisling's feeding me via a fake account or . . ."

"Aisling is the author," Denise finished. "What a loon." She laughed; a meaty, hearty sound. "Maybe she couldn't tell you he was dead because she's in denial. Maybe this is her way of narrativizing her life." Denise and her Dr. Phil dialect.

"What sane person impersonates a dead sibling?" I asked. "It's pretty weird. How can I trust anything she says or does?"

Maybe it was because Danny's messages were accompanying the

extracts, maybe it was the past catching up with me, but it was making my heart race. My father medicated himself so that he didn't have to listen to his cop's gut all the time—instinct gives you an ulcer. Ignore it though and you're likely to end up dead.

"Don't freak out. She's probably not dangerous," Denise said, but she sounded doubtful. "I would suggest not engaging anymore with Miss Bat-shit Crazy 2010. Locate Steve Shearer ASAP. And get back to me when you do. Then get home, get back to Villiers."

"Wait," I said.

"Shoot," Denise snapped, impatient to get back to bed.

"Danny is still sending me back-off messages."

"You want me to drive by, check out the house?" she asked.

"If you could check in with Number 12, that would be better. That's my neighbor, Jude. She's the one who's got Mister."

"I'm on my way after I go back to sleep for two hours. Just keep me in the loop and, seriously, keep telling me when Danny threatens you. Keep all the messages, even if they're disgusting."

I showered and went down to the breakfast buffet, where I picked at plain yogurt and fruit. The coffee was hot and fresh, albeit weak. I left my T-shirt off when I walked out to the pool. I had been swimming away rage and pain since I was a preteen. I'd been quite the competitor even; butterfly, breaststroke, that is, until Danny Quinlan-Walsh happened. I baptized my new high-necked swimsuit in the chlorinated water. Even though it had been a long time, I found my stride—my body became a piston, my hands were like oars. I stopped, panting. I got out of the pool after ten laps—my head almost emptied of its incessant drone and my muscles singing out, reborn. I went to a lounger with a refill of coffee. I saw there was a message from Ox.

Pumpkin, I looked into the O'Malley kids for you. Aisling has a record for stalking and harassing her stepfather—that's why her permanent residency was revoked. She's got real serious mental health problems.

Cormac O'Malley moved back to Aus in 2005. He died of a heroin OD in '07. The family are all kinds of fucked up—Mom died of an oxycontin OD.

I punched in Ox's number—his home phone, not his cell. He was a creature of habit. He'd be on *Teen Talk*, pretending to be Brittney, thirteen, from Little Neck.

"Hey Pumpkin," Ox said after the third ring, sounding cautious about the change of medium. I knew he hated the phone, but my head was spinning from the back and forth of messages and emails.

"I literally just discovered that Cormac O'Malley is dead. I'd just found the coroner's report."

"Yeah. I checked that email you sent me, and it's registered to Aisling O'Malley, the sister. She's saying that it's from her dead brother?"

"Yeah. She is."

"Just be careful with this kid," he warned. "Grief can make a person unstable. She's known to the Victoria Police. She's had an involuntary hospitalization."

"Aisling was committed?"

Initially I thought Aisling's name was pretty, but saying the syllables of her name aloud, the name aloud, gave me the creeps. My aversion to her now turned out to be for good reason. I mean, grief had certainly made me unstable—I was teetering on the ledge between life and death, reason and insanity, when I went to the private clinic after Ricky Hell's death. It sounded like Aisling had already leapt—maybe she was in freefall.

"Yeah. Speaking of the nuthouse . . . how's the Quinlan-Walsh kid been behaving?" he said.

"I'm getting more texts."

"I thought I made myself clear to that guy . . . Don't worry. I'll take care of it," Ox said smoothly.

"It's okay for now, Ox. I swear. I'll tell you if it's not." While I enjoyed revenge fantasies of Ox reducing Danny to a blubbing wreck on the ground—convulsing in his own blood, his bleached teeth ruined, his guitar hand broken—it wouldn't be prudent to maim him. Also, there was the higher moral ground, which I enjoyed claiming.

"Is he any good with computers?" Ox asked.

"I don't know," I admitted. "He used to play computer games sometimes?"

"Just wondering how he got onto the crime forum in the first place. How he knew you'd be in there. And how he keeps getting through to your number, even though you block him. You ever have your laptop out in front of him, your phone?"

"My phone is always with me, in my pocketbook. But my laptop . . . It was in my car when I was at the woods. But I'm sure I locked the car."

"I wondered if he got a hold of it, he could have put spyware on it maybe."

"Oh God," I shuddered. "That's so disgusting."

"You'll have to go through your applications. Do a scan. I might be wrong. Diaz said you won't make a report, but I think you should consider it."

"I'll consider it," I said.

"What did Diaz say to you about Lighthouse and the Villiers kid?"

"Only that it probably wasn't him. Couple of reasons. His name keeps coming up around Cathy Carver though."

"Doesn't mean he wasn't a creep," Ox said. "He may just not have done anything about it."

"Good point. Hey, Ox. There's something I need to ask you about. Was my mom seeing someone?" I cleared my throat. "Mona said something. I've been thinking about it since and I can't work it out. Lenora was pretty reclusive."

"Mm," he said.

And then the pieces fell into place—sharply. The realization was a guillotine.

"Oh no, Ox. Really?"

I shivered. I wrapped my towel around me. A young family came out to the pool area. I lowered my voice. "I just can't believe it . . ."

"Take a minute."

I couldn't help but take a minute. My throat was strangled. I felt like I couldn't breathe. Then I forged ahead with the questions that were being generated. "Did Dad know?"

"Yes, he did. He uh . . . accepted it. Look, Pumpkin."

"Don't call me that."

"Kid. Erin. It was the only time I loved someone like that. She didn't feel the same, but that was okay. Lenora was lonely. She was sad."

"Clinically depressed."

"Whatever. Look, she was a typical cop's wife—a widow in waiting. She just wanted more attention from your dad. And he was doing Mona on the side when he wasn't working all the hours that God sends."

"And drinking," I added. Mom was drinking too. Sad Mom drinking, a bottle of red at home in front of the TV, chased by cookie dough and regret, not tequila shooters and dancing on the bar at Hannigan's on ladies' night.

"I tried to help her with that. She never drank around me. I was like a comfort to her," Ox continued.

With your dick.

"There must have been an element of revenge for her there," I said, to drive the knife in.

"That too." He didn't sound in any way put out. Love will do that to you.

"I thought you liked being around us."

"I did. But I just sort of fell for Lenora. It never should have happened. I wanted a family. I tried to step into your dad's shoes and they didn't fit real well." Ox sounded at peace with it. He was a philosophical guy.

"Do you still love her?" I needed to believe this was what it was; it was too tawdry otherwise.

"Always will. But I loved your dad too. And you and little Shelly . . ." Ox wanted me to believe it. "And that's why I'm worried about you. The night Ricky Hell died, your dad told me you tried . . ." He couldn't say it.

"I was a fucked-up kid and I washed down my vodka with a few pain pills." And after I learned about Ricky's death, I tried another, equally ineffective method with an open razor, but I wasn't telling Ox the nitty-gritty. Everyone, even Mona it seemed, knew I went to a private "clinic" for a few weeks on my dead mom's dime, before it was decided I'd go to Maine, to Aunt Marnie's, to recover and finish school.

"Now, aside from Danny Quinlan-Walsh, I'm fine. You let me down. You let us all down, Ox."

"I know."

"Make it up to us. Help me find out what the connection between Steve and my dad is, who really killed Ricky Hell."

"If that's what you want," he said.

"It's what I want. Thank you, Ox," I said.

"This story means a lot to you?"

"It's more than a story," I said, and I was surprised to find it was true.

25

RP had taught me how to tail someone undetected. I'd normally be in my old jalopy, about sixty feet behind, making a sound like Mona or some other veteran smoker clearing their lungs. The Mercedes was sleek, soundless, made for the task.

All along I'd been thinking Carole wasn't all that bright. Like her brain was made of cotton candy and Covergirl—but now I was starting to glean that, as *Resident Alien* inferred, she was sharp as a nail file, or perhaps even a shank. My advantage was that Carole was very distracted this morning and she must be physically tired—she had been up since the crack of dawn, ferrying her kids to school, and working out at an elite Coral Springs gym. I know, because I was watching her, clothed in a neon orange outfit, executing burpees with a personal trainer. Exertion never showed on her face as she pulled the lat bar down, squatted under a bar, crunched, and planked. Think of a stocking over an egg, pulled taut.

While I drank my large cappuccino, and smoked half a pack of Slims, I realized that Carole was the kind of woman who understood patience. She did not put her hand through a window and require sixteen stitches when she couldn't stop her brain buzzing. She did not knock out girls in math who called her a metal slut. She did not OD when her boyfriend stood her up. She was the kind of person who waited for her moment, then ground up glass and put it in your drink, or called her baby the same baby name you'd told her about in third grade. Carole was a zoster virus: she lay dormant, and then when you were weak, she'd attack you in some profound and crippling manner.

She emerged from the gym now. Today she was driving a VW Golf, steel gray. A family car. As she raised her keys to unlock the door, her crop top lifted to reveal a slice of unscarred, spray-tanned six-pack.

Something was eating Carole. It was in her posture; the angry knot of her shoulders. She lit up a cigarette when she turned onto Main Street.

Carole pulled into a Taco Bell drive-through, where a litter of grubby children, prematurely pubescent due to food additives and hormones, loitered out front. I could hear her bitch out the server for reading her order wrong. Meth rage, maybe. I hoped the girl would spit in her soda.

Carole smoked while her supersized sodas and food were brought out by the girl in the drive-through and then she hit the gas, burning rubber. There was enough food for two or three, and wherever we were going would lead me to them. I didn't think it was for Mr. Ruffalo and her small children, given the distance from her home.

I took a right onto Pelican Crescent. A real estate wizard such as Carole would describe Pelican Crescent as downwardly mobile—and that was being generous. The paint on the semi-suburban bungalow was peeling and sagging with water damage. The wire fence around the premises added a kind of prison aesthetic. Many of the houses on the street were obviously derelict and boarded up, either because they were crack houses, meth labs, or shooting galleries—or to prevent them becoming such. It was like the whole of the GFC had hit this pocket of Florida. Lauderdale Lakes was no Coral Palisades, that's for sure.

Carole locked the car and got out, looking around. I watched her Florida-orange derriere disappear into Number 3. I saw the figure of a man at the door. He was tall, in blue jeans, T-shirt tucked in. He took the bag. He grabbed Carole gruffly and shook her, the way they do in cartoons; I pictured her teeth rattling. Despite my dislike of Carole, I experienced a spasm of pity. I fought the urge to scream at him, to march out of my car and knock him to the pavement. Then I saw who it was. Steve Shearer.

As Raymond Chandler's Marlowe might say, Steve had either made me, or was expecting a tail, because he stood out of the house, grinning like Wile E. Coyote. I was the Road Runner. Steve wanted a fight. I continued to drive, as discreetly as I could when mine was the only car on the road.

I was sure now that Carole had a thing going on with Steve Shearer. And it was taking her to bad places. Very literally.

———

I fished out the Tips-n-Toes card and called Lenny Tuna, the taxi driver. He didn't strike me as a texter.

"Ms. Sloane? The lady writer, huh," he said and began to cough up phlegm.

"Hey Lenny," I said. I couldn't well call him Mr. Tuna. "How've you been?"

"I'm keeping out of trouble. And you?"

"Not really."

He laughed. "You get a tan yet?"

"No," I said. "But thanks for asking. Do you remember me saying that I was looking for my old acquaintance, Carole, who works for an agency called Ruffalo Realty Executives?"

"Huh, yeah. As I said, I know of the Palisades estate. There was a lot of talk about it in the papers. Those people got a reputation in Fort Lauderdale. People suing and what not. And in Coral Glades."

I checked my satnav: Howard County. We were still in Lauderdale Lakes, but it came up as Coral Glades.

"I'm in those parts."

"Huh," he said again. It was a tic, not a question. "Coral Glades is bad medicine, pal. I got a buddy you could talk to though. He owns a place in the Glades; got royally screwed. Name's Marvin Abelard. Retired cop. You get yourself to the Monkey Bar and have a chat."

"Oh, man, thank you Lenny," I said, and he snorted in response and hung up. I made a vow to visit his wife's salon and give them some business as soon as I was done.

I looked up the Monkey Bar on Google Maps and there was a glut of hateful messages on my phone:

> Fucken bitch, srsly.

> I'm like, crying :(

> Sike

> Can you just call me?

> Please

Danny again. Still living in the nineties.

I ignored Danny's messages, filing them under D for Dread, and headed for the bar, which was in a semi-industrial part of Pompano Beach, with another sports bar opposite it, ominously titled Shenanigans. Both bars were badly reviewed and had two-star ratings. My favorite comment: *Bartender was drunk and belligerent. Nasty and dirty. Won't be going there again.*

Marvin Abelard was my kind of drunk and the Monkey Bar, my kind of venue.

The day was so bright and dry it was serrated, so walking into the cool cavern of the bar made me feel nocturnal, normal even. There were no customers but a muscle-bound barman with Bruce Willis good looks, who probably did stunt work, wiping the bar down with a cloth and the enthusiasm of the undead. He offered me discount Tex-Mex food mechanically and walked away before I declined. Inexplicably, I ordered a screwdriver, my mom's go-to party drink. I also ordered a bowl of nuts. I tried to work out what game was on in the background, for common ground, but it was Fox Sports, baseball, minor league, and I was out of my depth. I munched on salted peanuts and asked the bartender about the neighborhood.

"I'm thinking of buying property," I said, crossing and uncrossing my legs. I sipped the cocktail—it was basically vodka with a splash of OJ.

He looked suddenly concerned and dubious. "You aren't from around here, so I'll tell you. Me, I live in LA now."

I guessed right—he was an out-of-work actor. Or extra.

"Mom got sick. I'm out of here once she falls off the perch. Pompano Beach is the worst town for crime. It makes Detroit look like Disneyland. DC even. Had a guy in here picking his face up off the floor just before you walked in, left blood everywhere. It's in the skirting boards now." He pointed into the gloom of the bar, over to a booth where an old black man was sitting, the sole customer, with white hair and a beer in front of him, "Even Marvin got stabbed on the way here one night."

Marvin Abelard. My cop.

"Lotta crime," I commented uselessly.

"Lotta crime, lotta drugs, lotta drinking," he amended. "Lotta people out of work."

I waved at Marvin.

He frowned in reply.

"I'm actually hoping to chat to Mr. Abelard. I'm a journalist from New York," I said. "I'm writing about the GFC and the property market."

He shrugged off my lies, which sat between us, a house of cards.

"This place is gonna fold any day because of it." He slid a second bowl of nuts over to me. "Take these over to Marvin, if you please. I like to keep him eating so he stays moderately sober. He drinks Pabst Blue Ribbon and, just so you know, he's not super fond of strangers."

I ordered a Pabst for Marvin and as I approached the booth I watched his bushy eyebrows converge, like caterpillars in a sex act. His beard was gray. The whites of his eyes were almost shockingly white, but from the smell of liquor and the set of his mouth, I knew he was a drunk. He had something of my father in the sad slope of his mouth, the slight glaze in his eyes. Yet I knew he'd be able to walk out of here in a straight line.

"You're a cop," I said.

He slid his wallet over to me. I frowned. "Open it," he said, with the dropped vowels of the Deep South. I scanned his ID. His creds were there, he still carried them around.

"Was," he corrected me. "You got good instincts."

"Actually, a man called Lenny Tuna told me to talk to you. He told me you were a cop. My dad was a detective. You work around here before you retire?" Marvin Abelard was the kind of man I didn't want to lie to.

"Actually, I got fired," he mimicked me. "Because of this," he tapped his near empty bottle. "Yeah, in Miami. Got the wounds to prove it too. But I'm originally from Louisiana. What you want, girl?" he asked, suspicious. He necked the last of his beer and started on the fresh one I slid over to him.

"Mr. Abelard, I was wondering if you know anything about a former cop called Steve Shearer."

"Older looking guy, ugly-assed mustache, in good shape? I just might."

"Well, I think he's in business with a woman who runs Ruffalo Realty. They deal in luxury housing. They built an estate called Coral Palisades." I sipped on my Molotov cocktail.

"Yeah, I know 'em. They got a property scam in the Glades. Government housing. They brought the dealers in, but they won't handle drugs themselves. They just made the whole area a ghetto and turn a profit. I still live there even though it's like living in Beirut. Not ten miles away, but I can't drink in my own neighborhood now."

"I'm sorry to hear it, Marvin. I think Steve lives out in the Palisades. I'm planning on heading out there this afternoon."

"No one lives in the Palisades, girl. It's a bad Hollywood set. No power out there even. Unless he's eating cold beans and shitting in a bucket. That Shearer has a very bad rep out here. Why you after him anyway? This ain't all about the Palisades or the Glades, even, am I right? You're a long way from home. New York?"

"You're right. He's implicated in a crime where I'm from. A couple of them actually. The murder of a teenager. His own partner. And maybe, I'm thinking, some missing and murdered kids."

"Kids?" he looked at me sharply. I recapped the story of the Southport

Three and Andre Villiers; how Steve was a dirty cop who killed Ricky. Then I went on to Steve's list of felonies, including his seduction of teenage Carole, the Lauderdale Estates scam, how I'd seen him at Number 3 being delivered Taco Bell by a cowed Carole.

"What a story. If you'll excuse me, I gotta piss so bad my eyeballs are floating." He clucked. "Excuse me," he added, giving me a little gentlemanly bow as he loped off to the men's room. He came back seeming almost sober, as I swallowed the remainder of my drink.

"That's quite a story. Shearer, a guy like that, he got a taste for money, drugs, power. Maybe he likes the underage girls. But these creeps are usually real specific. They tend to stick with an age group. And a gender. Real rare to deviate. Shearer, from what you've told me, don't fit that profile. No money in kid killing. No pleasure in it, unless you're that way inclined."

I nodded. "I thought of that."

"Shearer's meaner than a wet panther, but I don't think he's done nothing to no little kids. Not out here anyway. He's doing crime though, it's just white collar, with that mean little blonde. That real estate agent. Give me that cell of yours," he said. "I don't have one incidentally. They're the instrument of the devil."

Wordlessly, I slid it across.

"I've got friends in the County Housing Authority. I can get you his real address. He don't live in no Palisades, I'm telling you."

I watched him punch numbers into the phone, from memory. His voice changed. His face changed.

"Ariana? Marvin Abelard here. Yes, I'm alive and well, girl. So, I got a question about a title. I got a property in the Lauderdale Lakes Estate. Yeah. I know. I bought it in 2001. Now I ain't got a pot to piss in— or a window to throw it out of," he laughed. "I gotta know who owns Number 3 and 4. Their sewage all up on my property. It's a hazard. I know. I know. That's why I'm ever so grateful," he crooned. Marvin looked at me expectantly. I took out a pen and paper and he made a gesture with his hand. A cigarette. I lit one for him and me.

"I'd be real grateful," he repeated. "Uh huh, uh." He scribbled something down. He hung up with a triumphant expression.

"Shearer Proprietary Limited owns a few properties on the Glades. Sound familiar? This is the address of the person they are registered to."

I read it aloud: "1005 Cable Grove Road, Beatrice."

"That's one itty-bitty town. It's got barely a hundred people in it, from memory. Howard County. Deliverance country, you know?" Marvin mimicked a banjo.

"Is that the Everglades?"

I saw dark shapes on the water. I shuddered.

"Sure is. If you go out there to confront him, don't you go out there alone, you hear?" Marvin said sternly.

He passed me a coaster.

"My home phone number." I made out his full name, *Marvin J. Abelard*, written in a spidery hand.

"Call me. You get me there or the bar here," he said.

———

On the street outside the Monkey Bar, a young family were walking, the mother and father hitting each other, while the toddlers and older children recoiled and huddled. I watched the adults fall to the ground, fighting. Even the youngest child, an infant being held by a toddler, in the same way a kid carries a cat, looked disgusted. I wondered if I should intervene, then the adults picked themselves up and carried on walking, kissing now, carrying open beers.

Back in the car, I turned over the coaster in my clammy hands. I typed Steve's HQ address into Google Maps but I couldn't find it. I tried different spellings—but I kept getting an error message. *No address found.* Maybe this was another cipher, another game. I instinctively trusted Marvin. I didn't believe he'd mislead me for any reason. Steve's place was just totally off the grid. Maybe it was a second residence, a hideout. I would possibly need an old-school road atlas or a local guide. God, I wanted to find Steve. I texted Denise an update and as I did it occurred to me I could revisit the Palisades first; see for myself if Steve lived there. Maybe I could even catch him by surprise.

26

From my vantage point of the gated entrance, in the half-light of dusk, Coral Palisades looked like a dreamy provincial French village—after a light earthquake. The sign showed that the gated community consisted of several streets, all with Gallic names. While it was close to eighty degrees, a bulk of gray storm clouds had muscled into the blue sky. The air smelled of metal and electricity. I had a takeout soda cup that was half seltzer, half whisky. It was maybe a bad idea, but if I didn't move on Shearer now, I'd lose my nerve. As it was, my Dutch courage surged and lurched. I was feeling ill; a headache hammered away softly behind my eyes. Idling at the security gate, I got out some Advil and Mentos from the glove box. Denise was calling me. I ignored her. She texted me:

> Erin, plse don't tell me you're going alone to confront Shearer. He's dangerous.

> Just checking out the Palisades now. I'm okay.

A white security guard with a crew cut emerged from the booth; five foot nothing, built like a pit bull. He had a bad teenage mustache that looked more like milk scum above the duck bill of his mouth; tracks were shaved into the side of his cranium, but I was too busy reading his body—the prison tattoos on his neck, forehead, and forearm—the readily identifiable Iron Cross, the numbers 14, 88. Everyone knew the Iron Cross was an Aryan Brotherhood symbol and while I couldn't remember what 14 meant, I knew 88 was code for Heil Hitler. Ricky had taught me that—he told me his cousin had taught him. That's who gave him his stick and poke 666.

I thought about the box cutter I kept in my purse, the mace on my key ring; I hugged my pocketbook to me, like a baby.

"Hi," I said, grabbing my press card out of my purse.

"Wait a minute, girl."

"Steve Shearer and Ange Miller?" I said. She could be Shearer now, if they were married. I wanted to gage his reaction, but a potted plant was more expressive. "He's expecting me."

"That right?" he said, finally showing. "What business does he have with you, Morticia Addams?"

"What do you think?" I said. "We have *business*."

"Whatever. But first, I gotta frisk you." Then he smiled. It was like a spider crawling across his face.

"Feel free to search the car," I said getting out of my seat, "and my bag. But don't touch me, dude."

He dumped my pocketbook on the ground, confiscating my weapons, my phone, shaking his head. Then he frisked me. I gritted my teeth and tolerated the patting down, looked at the tattooed knuckles, the tattooed hands; wishing at the very least I had my phone. I could smell his cheap deodorant, the fried chicken he'd eaten.

A red Jeep Cherokee pulled up. There was a man in the front seat. Steve Shearer wore bad mirrored cop sunglasses and a cap—there was something of the biker dude vibe about him. His body was all puffed up from the gym, but he was thinned out in the face from drugs. I noticed a tribal tattoo sneaking out of his sleeve and thought of the Confederate flag *Resident Alien* alleged he had tattooed on his body. *Pride*, it read.

"Any recording devices?" Steve called out from the driver's seat.

"Not that I can see," the guard said.

"Leave it then," he told him.

"Hey. Look at me," Steve said, snapping his fingers. He used his left hand. I looked at him.

"You wanna see inside the estate? Hop in."

"You want to take me on a tour of the estate?" I asked. No way I was getting in his car. "Okay, I'll follow you, but I'm not getting in."

The security guard stared at Steve and then me. Conspiracy passed between them. Steve Shearer was a void of a man, even if his stature and manner exuded menace. This was the man who had killed one of the only humans I had loved. I saw nothing in his eyes—no cruelty, no kindness, no compassion either.

"I know who you are. You're RP Sloane's kid."

"My editor knows where I am," I said.

"But do *you* know where you are?" he asked, raising his *Magnum, P.I.* eyebrows. I wanted to tell him he looked like the cop from the Village People.

"Like, literally or existentially?" I said.

"Get in the fuckin' car," he snapped.

"I know all about how you shot Cooper Deane and what went down with Ricky Hell that night in the West Cypress Road Woods. I got records to prove you had a business relationship with Ricky Hell," I lied.

We all heard the furious buzzing of my phone, which was on the ground, surely Denise calling me. The security guard was quickest. He collected the phone, my lipstick, and picked up a few more dangerous items (the mace, the box cutter), and threw my bag and the items unceremoniously into my car. Then he went back to his little box and pressed a buzzer.

Then he seized me by the hair and I kind of collapsed inside a little.

"Okay," I said. "But if you hurt me, you have a lot of heat coming down on you. A lot."

The guard made a noise like "Pfft" and yanked my arm behind my back—it was the arm that had been fractured by Danny in a literal push-pull argument in 1993—and I winced in both anticipation of pain and the memory of the snap. He frog-marched me toward the passenger side of the Jeep, where Shearer sat. Then he opened the door and shoved me in.

Once in the Jeep, the doors locked and we started to move. We were let through the wrought-iron gate and down a palm tree dotted lane called Clairfontaine Bend. There was a lot of cultural and geographical confusion going on here at Coral Palisades—to my left, there was a small park with Astroturf and a mini Dutch windmill. To my right, like a ring of teeth, the gleaming, half-constructed veneers of prepaid mansions that were attempting to look like Versailles. There were a few vehicles in the long winding driveways, but mostly the smallish estate homes were completely barren. It was eerily quiet. Steve and I pulled up to Number 6, an ivory mansion with an obscene fountain out the front that wasn't functioning. None of the houses, including Steve's, had lights on.

"Steve, do you actually live here?"

"What?" he spat.

"This is, like, a ghost estate." I gestured around the mile-long circle of mansions, half constructed. Marvin was right—no one would live out here, unless they were desperate. And Steve was not.

"We sold a dream and they bought it. So what?" he said almost cheerfully. Underneath his Fahrenheit, I smelled old sweat and tobacco.

"Did Mona Byrnes buy it too?"

"Who's that?" Steve winked at me.

"No, she's in on it too," I said, more to myself.

He said nothing, just breathed through his nose. He tried a new angle. "Look, I'm just a simple guy. I believe in my country and my right to bear arms."

"And money," I added. I simply couldn't resist. But Steve seemed to be tickled by the comment.

"Yeah. What did that guy say in that movie, *Wall Street*? Greed is good. Yeah, boy."

"But something went wrong along the way, right? Did you know someone knocked off Mona Byrnes' dogs?"

"What a pity. I like dogs. Christ, but you do remind me of RP. You're actually not as dumb as you look." Steve studied my face.

"Thanks."

"But not as smart as you think you are, either," he said and then he hit me, square in the nose, but as he did, I instinctively turned. Part of his class ring caught my eyelid, but at least my nose wasn't broken. He grabbed a fistful of my hair in his hand, winding it around the knuckles.

"I don't really like hitting women," he began.

And yet you just did.

"But I don't like a smart mouth making accusations either."

Because he still had my hair in his hand, because my right eye was throbbing and my cheekbone too—I decided not to be cute. Steve didn't like cute. I thought of Aisling and Cormac. Steve Shearer was like Danny, a dangerous bully. I had excised Danny, but never exorcized him. I had never gotten even with him. Now was my chance. Judging by the texts, Danny was clearly worried about what the past may uncover. Steve was too, or why would he have his guard on site and risk beating me up?

"Listen, Steve, whatever Ruffalo Realty are into, the Palisades, or whatever's going on in Lauderdale Lakes, I really don't care. Even if Mona Byrnes is involved. I'm just nosey by profession. I just want to know one thing—it's for the story. Why did he have to die?"

He relaxed his grip on my hair.

"That insect, Hernandez?" he asked, almost incredulous.

"No, I know why Ricky had to die. He saw you shoot that kid Franklin Rivera and Cooper Deane in cold blood. I know you found out your distributor was a narc. I'm also guessing that Mona is, was, dirty; that she sold him out. Or maybe it was Danny Quinlan-Walsh. But what I don't understand is Andre Villiers."

"Huh? Get outta here with that shit. That's ancient history. That's *folklore*. Why do you think those kids wanted Villiers dead? Because of what, Satan?"

"I thought maybe he was onto you and Ricky. Or maybe it was because he hurt Carole Jenkins."

"Get the fuck outta here. Read my lips: Villiers was a freak with a brain the size of a pea. The only thing he was onto was a cabbage patch doll. He liked to play with kids, if you catch my drift. Just ask Libby Jenkins."

"Libby Jenkins?" I echoed. Then I remembered her from the picture from the United Skates of America of Julie Hernandez and Aisling, a miniature Carole, with her classic Jenkins scowl.

"Carole's little sister, dummy," Steve reminded me. "He fucked with a lot of little girls. Maybe he even fucked with Hernandez's sister. RP met with Hernandez that night, right?"

No.

"So maybe your old man told him to get rid of Andre . . . who knows? Ricky was under RP's thumb, right? All I know is, when I got there all the kids had beaten Andre half to death and Hernandez was outta his mind."

"Then you shot him."

"I put him down. Do I regret it? Nope." He answered his own question.

"I don't know," I said. "Why would my father have told Ricky about Julie? That seems very irresponsible."

Unless he had some reason to want Ricky dead. Like me.

"Andre ever meet your sister? Come round to the house with your degenerate buddies?"

"Excuse me?"

"Your little sister . . . whatsername."

Michelle. Shelly.

"If he'd touched Shelly, RP would have ended him," I said.

"Really? Did he love you guys that much, you think?"

"He loved Michelle," I said. "And he knew about Ricky and me. He cared more about bringing you down than anything."

"Really? Cause rumor had it Sloane took a lot of money from an unknown source to keep quiet about some kids going missing on the island."

"He wouldn't have done that," I said. "In fact, I thought you might know something about that."

"Me? Get real. I don't know nothing about no missing kids. RP was a fall-down drunk bum, doing blow every day."

Look who's talking.

"He had gambling debts up the wazoo. He was sleeping with his partner. Did you think he was a paragon of virtue?"

Paragon was a big word for Steve.

"No," I said slowly. "But RP was old school. Old school guys get even themselves. He wouldn't get Ricky to take out his trash. Plus they never met up with Ricky cause RP was three sheets to the wind that night. Mona told me."

"You believe whatever you want to believe, I don't give a shit," he said, reaching into the glove box, taking out some cigarettes.

"Cops look after cops. That's all I'm gonna say."

He broke one and put it back in the box.

Okay.

"I smoke cause I like to. Cause I want to. Right now I don't. That's how I roll. I do a hundred push-ups a day."

Maybe he did back in '94—he still looked beefy and strong, but there was a paunch there. Steve Shearer was either still a cokehead or it had thrown his brain into a loop. Either way, aggression was emanating from him in near visible waves. "You're soft. You got no self-control, like RP. I can tell. You reek of booze," he continued. He tightened his grip on my hair and sharp pain radiated up my scalp and into my eyes.

Then he relaxed his grip. Tears stung my eyes, but I persisted.

"Where's Angela Miller? And how is Mona involved in this? If she has a piece of the pie and my dad is such a piece of shit, why not get him into it too? He likes to earn too, you're saying," I asked, keeping my voice calm.

"Bitch, you and your vegetable father got nothing and no one and if you print any of this, or you mention Ange or Cooper, or try to come near any of us, I'll take that knife from your purse, and I'll cut your fucking voice box out and feed it to him. And I won't stop there. You fuckin' ax wound," he said, shaking his head. "You make me sick."

"I understand," I said. I did. Andre, who choked women; Danny, who carved them up and hated himself for it—they were minor league. Steve Shearer would smile as he strangled the life out of me. He killed for material gain and convenience, but there was pleasure in it for him, I could see it.

"I'm not interested in writing this anymore. I'll just can the story. I only took it to find out what really happened that night. I never believed it was Ricky, you know, who killed Andre." I was bargaining, but I nearly believed it in the moment.

"You think I'll buy that?" he said. "You won't quit, I know your type. You and RP. Like little terriers."

"Dogs are the best people," I managed and Steve smiled.

"Oh, what now?" Steve released the grip on my hair. My scalp throbbed. My cheeks burned. My hair was in his knuckles. The security guard was coming up to the Jeep, had walked the quarter mile on foot. He leaned into Steve's window, breathing heavily. He had my phone in his hand, my pocketbook. There was a crack in the screen, the fucker.

"Cops are here. Behind me," he said to Steve.

"Must have been my editor. She called them," I said to Steve.

"They're driving through." The security guard looked nervous.

"Give her the pocketbook," Steve said. "Pass it through."

The guard handed it to Steve and made a face at me.

"I'm not going to say anything," I said to Steve.

"You got nothing to say. You don't even know what happened that night, but if you keep digging things are going to get very ugly for you and those you love," Steve said. "You understand? RP included."

As the cop car drove slowly toward us, I raised my hands in surrender.

"I'm all right, officers," I said loudly. Florida cops—shoot first, ask questions later.

The two cops got out of the vehicle slowly. They were uniform; one black older cop, one white younger cop; one fat, one thin. They looked like extras on *CSI: Miami*.

"Can I see a badge?" I called out.

"Can you shut the fuck up?" the white cop replied. "We heard someone was disturbing the peace," he said, looking at Steve.

I shook my head.

"License and registration," the black cop said, not to Steve, but me—the woman with the bleeding face, the obvious victim of an assault. Crooked fucking cops. I fished into my purse, saying nothing.

"You been drinking?" he continued, staring me down.

Again, I said nothing.

"You're from out of state. You are poking around in things that ain't your business. Why don't you walk out of here, get in your car, and get the fuck out of Florida State by morning? Sound good?" The black cop thrust my license back at me.

I just nodded.

The whole time I walked back to the car, I expected a bullet in my back and when it didn't come, I got back in my car and I drove. I drove for a mile and then I pulled over. And I sat in my car and shook. Then I hit the dash. Hard.

My phone screen was cracked, but still functioning.

I called Denise.

"Erin, are you okay?"

"Well, thanks to you, I am. Although the cops out here seem to be on Shearer's payroll," I said.

"Uh, come again?" she said.

"You didn't call them."

"No, what cops?"

"It was a trick. That fucking prick."

"Who? Steve Shearer?"

Steve Shearer was good. He wanted to fuck with my head. He could have me killed or arrested, he could do it by the book or in a dark alley, but he wanted to let me know he could fuck me up, good and proper.

"I'm worried, Erin. You don't sound good. And it doesn't sound very safe. What did Steve Shearer do?"

"He punched me, then he called the cops, who actually threatened me."

"What?"

"They let me go with one busted eye, half plastered. They knew who Steve was and they just wanted to intimidate me. They were, like, hired goons."

"Do you need the hospital?"

I looked in the side mirror. My cheekbone felt tender, but it didn't appear fractured or broken. The left side of my face, including my swollen shut eye, was the color of mincemeat. Through the slit I could see through there was a little blood in the iris. My vision appeared unaffected; but it was going to be a bad shiner in the morning.

"I'm okay. Nothing's broken."

"Except your promise to me to steer clear of Shearer."

That hurt, but she had a point.

"All right, lay low and get your ass home after you get a little sleep," she conceded. Then her voice got low and parental again. "I'm going to change your ticket. This Shearer stuff is far too dangerous. And no offense, Erin, you're becoming a liability."

27

Back at the hotel I got ice from my favorite bellboy and applied it to my face. According to Google, hyphema, or blood in the iris, was common with a blow to the eye. There was nothing really to do, except swallow a few Advil. I headed back into the pool area. If I didn't put my head under, I could swim off Steve Shearer, the daytime booze headache, the throbbing pain in my face.

I had scanned my computer for malware, spyware, or whatever it was that Ox had suggested might be on my laptop and it didn't seem to be there, but I wasn't the brightest of sparks when it came to anything technical.

I checked my email and saw Denise had sent me an email with the subject line "Red Eye," which was kind of funny—the flight left at 5 a.m., so I could technically still head out to Beatrice. I was still deciding if I'd go.

Twin porcelain-colored girls around four or five, who looked like they were wearing makeup, were splashing in the water with their red-headed mom who had cornrows, drawn on pencil-thin eyebrows, and a semiautomatic tattooed on her sunburnt shoulder blade. All three wore matching stars-and-stripes bikinis. I entered the pool via the deep end. One of the little girls stared slack-jawed at me.

I began a series of furious laps, enjoying the sting from the chlorine and the burn of my muscles as I tore through the water, cupping my hands, using my feet like fins. All thought was obliterated in my frenzy; my right hamstring seized, my lungs burned in a sensation not too dissimilar to a nicotine craving and, as I was rolling into my twentieth lap, I heard Carole—she was smoothly negotiating a pair of banana loungers nearby. One was in the sun, which she took. She placed a Chloe bag on the second lounger to claim it—which was game of her, given the clientele. I followed the line of her reclining body, two coral-pink stilettos were attached to a pair of legs that resembled waxed, inverted chicken drumsticks; they ballooned at the ankle and became dangerously slender, bruised.

Carole Ruffalo draped herself like an artist's model on the lounge, only she was clothed in a marmalade and lilac-colored sixties-inspired mini and matching box cut jacket, with detailed piping on the lapels. I'd seen this look on the latest cover of *Vogue* (Mulberry, pre-fall fashion). Panting and chlorinated, wrung out, I clung to the side of the pool and then hoisted myself up and walked over to Carole, who sat dry as a saltine and equally as tasteless. She attempted to crinkle her nose at me as I accidentally-on-purpose splashed her. I grabbed my newly purchased black leather Coach bag, which now just looked cheap next to Carole's (matching) Chloe bag. I pretended to scrounge around for my cigarettes and hit play on my recorder app.

"Classy place," she commented as the cornrowed mom lit up what smelled like a doobie. It was happy hour again at the White Sands. Floodlights illuminated the pool area; there was a growing chatter of Spanish-speaking bar staff; an amiable soundtrack of rattling ice and laughter as they prepared strong, cheap cocktails for the gringo guests.

"Yikes," Carole said. "What happened to you?"

"Steve Shearer. But you already know that, right?"

"Dry off and let's have a drink and a little chat," she said without moving her lips.

I don't know if Carole possessed a sense of humor, or if I was projecting, but when I returned from the cabana, she'd ordered two Long Island iced teas.

"The only problem with living in Florida is all the Latins," she said conversationally.

Lovely, Mona's voice deadpanned in my head. I had my phone on record, so I could play this to Carole's clients, some of whom, I'm sure, were rich Cubans.

Carole had relaxed enough to kick off her heels. I had wrapped a towel around my hair and went into the ladies' pool cabana to change out of my swimsuit into my American Apparel sweatsuit. Then I sat next to her, knees to my chest. The waiter brought the drinks over to us, gator-green eyes fixed on Carole, looking both cowed and lustful. I slapped down some singles that were a bit damp and he scowled at me and cursed. Carole waved him away.

"So, Carole," I said, arranging my limbs on the banana lounge and sitting on my fists, so I wouldn't slap her. I watched her drink from her iced tea and decided to swap them when she wasn't looking. I wouldn't put anything past her. "What about you, Steve and Mona, and Coral Palisades? Mona Byrnes is an investor, or was. Things went sour, clearly."

Out of the corner of my eye, I saw the cornrowed mom clamber up to a banana lounge a few feet away from us. The same waiter brought her a weak-looking piña colada. I hoped she'd apply sunscreen.

"Mona Byrnes?"

"We've been through this, Carole."

The little girls splashed each other. One girl shouted that she was fixing to fuck the other up. Although they seemed able to manage adult content, they were a few feet away, so I kept my voice down.

Carole scanned the banana lounge and looked at me knowingly. Mona all over again. I wasn't about to strip in the White Sands pool area.

"I'm not wired," I said.

"Wouldn't trust you as far as I could throw you," she said.

"Likewise, babe."

We sat locked in a hateful contest of eye contact. That is to say, I radiated hate and received nothing in return. Any animation, curiosity; any playfulness in Carole had been crushed by drugs, by bad men, by life. I thought of the light coming through the stained glass of St. Mary's church, my mother's collection of Murano glass from Venice—the beauty emanated from the one-dimensionality of the glass, the color itself. I unzipped my hoodie, revealing a supportive cross-my-heart bra, the color of midnight blue—a nice contrast to the raspberry and white scar tissue on my chest.

One of two little girls had been watching, picking at her nose, teasing her sister. Her face crumpled like she was going to cry. Maybe she wasn't so tough. I mouthed "sorry" at her.

"It's a keloid scar. You know what they say about people who keloid scar?" I said to Carole.

"They're real ugly?" she smirked.

"They've got African heritage somewhere along the line," I said.

She spat out a chunk of ice.

"And below?" she said, looking pointedly at me. I pulled down the sweatpants, revealing matching underwear, no visible scars, no African skin tone—and no wire.

She shrugged.

"I'm not a rat, Carole."

"You're a writer," she spat.

"And you're a corrupt real estate broker and possibly a white supremacist," I countered, sipping the tea, which was all bottom-shelf spirits. I could taste Hawaiian Punch. Carole followed suit and winced. Then she turned her phone on; Mariah Carey's "Dreamlover" played loudly. She was trying to drown out any recording I may have been undertaking in my pants region. "And you were never really a metalhead."

She rolled her eyes.

"Have you seen Danny since '94?"

"That loser. Please. He never even got off the island. Look, I never think about that place, those people. Mona Byrnes is a client. She invested. She lost out. Maybe she's bitter. But whatever."

She kicked off her heels and I was shocked to note her toes were un-pedicured; gnarled looking.

"Aisling O'Malley told me that you and Steve were lovers back in the day. That you and Steve and Ange are into some criminally bad shit. Property scams, fraud, you know—the American dream."

"Oh yeah." Carole crunched on her ice, her expression completely blank. "I'm a businesswoman. Like, what's in all that for me?" Carole sounded like pure train-tracks-rat-Long Islander. It came out like: "Faw-mee."

"Steve. Meth."

She threw a look that was so disdainful that it was nearly embarrassing.

"Drugs are ghetto. I'm not into anything like that. If Steve and Ange are involved in something nasty, that's their funeral."

"I don't believe you, Carole. You're a threesome of sorts, aren't you? Or maybe you're, like, just the third wheel?"

That was a low blow, but I had to try and divide and conquer, tug at Carole's insecurity. Guilting her wouldn't work. The only weak spot in Carole was Steve. He clearly had a hold on her; she'd been somehow spellbound by the second-rate fake father-figure Lothario since she was sixteen. And from our encounter, Steve was clearly on the edge of reason. Carole was too hard to read for me to really judge, but I knew that she was using. Money was a buffer against the heavy and fast erosion of meth—there was the purchased gloss and shine of health from IV vitamin treatments, teeth could be capped; pits and cracks in the skin covered. Paranoia, hallucinations, and going clinically nuts—well, there was no insurance policy, no way to buy your way out of that.

"I think Steve killed his partner for Ange to, like, be with her. Imagine a man loving you so much he killed for you." I was starting to sound like Aisling O'Malley. I was sure it wasn't true, but it sounded good. "I know you said that you never got involved with Steve, Carole, but I know that's not true. He used you. And he always has. He hurts people. That's how Ricky got involved in Southport in the first place. Ricky saw

Steve kill his partner and his cousin, Franklin. So he was working for Nassau County, undercover," I continued.

"You're coming off crazy, Eerie. I mean, I heard stories that you were all fucked up because of what happened with your mom and sister and that, but I didn't realize you'd gone totally nuts. Steve and me together? Steve, like, murdering Ricky because the kid went *21 Jump Street*? Look, just know this. If you keep scratching away at the past, there's going to be a problem. It's defamation, you saying that Steve assassinated Ricky or he ordered it. And your poking around the Palisades, hating on my business practice. That impacts *me* personally." Carole cracked her jaw.

"Don't forget the Lakes," I added. "You three will go down. And you won't be with Steve. You and Ange will be in prison playing gyno with Aileen Wuornos or someone for the next twenty years."

"She was a serial killer. And she fried," Carole snapped her umbrella in two.

I knew that, of course.

"All this is really about Ricky Hell, right? You're not really going after us."

"Right. Like I said to Steve, I'm not interested in any of that," I lied. "I was just being nosey. It's my job to be a snoop."

"I mean, *if* I know anything about anything that even matters. That's why I'm here—I'll answer your stupid questions if you back off. Look, Andre Villiers was a very bad kid. A rotten apple. This story . . . is about him, right? My sister Libby . . ." she began and took a drink. I watched her larynx bob up and down; she was on the verge of tears. She was (spontaneously, genuinely?) emoting.

"Your sister Libby," I prompted her. "Andre hurt her?"

She drank noisily and lit a cigarette. I had touched a nerve. "He tried. I think he lured them out to the woods, got them all stoned. Cormac's sister too. Remember Linda Bauer? Gross chick that got creamed by the train freshman year?"

"Pretty hard to forget something like that," I said, incredulous at Carole's brutal description.

"Yeah, well; Andre said he raped her, but like Danny said, you can't rape a girl like Linda."

Black spots began to swim before my eyes. I wanted to punch Carole out for what she'd just said, but also the rape confession made me breathless, in a kind of body memory way. I could feel Andre's hangnail, his big thumbs, smell the tomato soup and weed on his breath. I knew that he was turned on, that choking me was a prelude to something, but somehow I stopped it with that punch.

"Danny and I, Mac, we all thought we'd teach him a lesson. It just got outta hand. We were in the woods, getting stoned in the back of the truck. We were all on mushrooms, so, like, it's jumpy, my memory, you know? Ricky was there, he left for a while. It was me and the other boys, drinking beers and kind of talking about it, and then it was like we all knew and we all decided at once."

Group consciousness, she meant—collective consciousness. Carole sipped her drink. The sun was setting. The Florida sky turned into a pink, bile, and yolk-colored bruise. More people were talking, laughter. The music changed; more easy listening. I was getting close to the end of my drink, so was Carole. I wanted her to keep talking. I waved over at the waiter and held up my fingers, pointing at our glasses. He nodded.

"Was there a discussion?" I lit a cigarette and offered her one. She just stared at me.

"Not exactly. We'd all talked about it, like all the time, over summer. Like, me and Danny, Mac, we were like, let's kill him. Let's end him. It wasn't serious at first, it was like he was annoying . . ."

I winced and finished my drink. Carole looked at her nails and grimaced. Then she took the cigarette.

"But then Libby came home and told me what that pig did to her. Touched her. I told the guys, they were like, fuck it, let's do it. That night we started to play a truth or dare game, so that—"

"Someone would dare you to kiss him," I suggested. I felt sick.

"Actually, it was the other way around. He pinned me up against the truck." Carole drained her drink. The waiter set down new drinks.

I handed over another heap of soggy singles so that he wouldn't interrupt Carole's confession. She went quiet for a minute.

"Carole, this is not on tape. It's not even on the record," I lied. I just wanted to know if Ricky had been the one to "batter up," as Danny reported he had in court. I wanted those gruff, tobacco-colored hands free of dirt and blood. I noticed that Carole had not used Ricky's name once when she talked about that night.

"The truth is that he came from behind. Cormac," Carole amended.

"Cormac went in first?" I didn't hide my surprise. Cormac seemed so gentle—with his New Romantic bangs and comic books.

"And you were underneath Andre?" I guessed.

Carole seemed to pale under her tan.

"He was like a dog with rabies, foaming at the mouth. He was licking my neck, had one hand here," she gestured to her breast. "Had my pants down in seconds and I'm, like, panicked, thinking . . . this is it."

"Danny and Cormac . . ."

"They didn't need no excuse. They . . ." She hesitated. "We hated him."

"You ran away then," I prompted her.

"I called Steve. Andre was going to, like, rape me, Eerie."

I nodded. I didn't believe in an eye for an eye, but his murder would not keep me awake at night.

"The whole Satan angle was the media's fault. And all the kids doing interviews. Steve told Danny the way to plead, to get less time."

"Less time killing for kicks as opposed to vigilante justice?" I asked her. She shrugged.

"We shouldn't have said that. But the books, movie deals, all that. It was . . ."

"Lucrative. Satan sells," I concluded. "Thing is—that phone booth was quite a long way from the Spot. As far as I know, you never did track at Roosevelt. Plus, sounds like you were in no shape to run and call Steve."

So who was? Someone who was athletic? Danny? Was he dealing for Steve too? Did he want to get rid of Ricky and not just because of me?

"I think Steve had been coaching you all summer. I think he was in your ear. I think someone told Steve about Ricky being a narc and he came down and executed him. He wanted Ricky removed and Andre was a really great way to achieve that."

"You're wrong," she said, but she was smiling.

"You didn't care about Cormac at all, did you? You left him there."

"Mac hit Andre, his choice," she retorted. "I did make the phone call. And when I went back, Mac was crying and shaking. Danny was, like, covered in blood and . . . stuff. Like, head to toe. Like, it was the goriest thing I'd ever seen. He'd gone in and just wailed on him."

"And where was Ricky?" I asked.

"Ricky? He was, like, barfing," she said, something like disappointment came over her face. She ground out her cigarette.

"Ricky didn't touch Andre. Mac said he went white as a ghost and started shaking all over when they were beating on him. He threw up. He kept saying he was sorry. But Danny, Danny was, like, smiling and laughing. When Mac hit Andre, Danny asked Ricky to turn up the music. I think Danny had smoked PCP. He was tripping so hard. Nothing he said made sense."

Maybe when Danny said he didn't remember what happened in the woods after a point, he was telling the truth. Maybe he didn't make the call after all.

"Did you watch Steve kill Ricky?" I closed my eyes thinking of Ricky, white-faced, shaking, knowing that something terrible was going down, again.

"I didn't see anything. I don't know about the others. I was trippin' out, crying, scared. I, like, wet myself. When I heard the gunshot, I just ran, didn't even wait for him. Mac, I mean."

Part of me wanted to knock her brains out with a bat, but the problem was I felt sorry for her. Groomed by Steve Shearer, assaulted by Andre, she watched a kid be beaten to death, and her boyfriend go bananas. Even at sixteen, Carole was a nasty piece of work, but no one deserved that.

"It wasn't about Ricky. It was to save Mac," she said, baby blues welling with tears. "Mac hit Andre first. If Ricky told on him, then

Mac would probably get the death penalty. The story was Ricky did it and we were accessories only, scared of Ricky's power or, like, under it. Steve came in and put Ricky down—stopped him." Carole even used the same words as Steve. *Put him down*, like a dog. She'd swallowed the story herself. All those kids—Danny, Cormac, Carole—they'd all celebrated the violent spectacle; they'd cheered for Andre's slow death, maybe Ricky's too, like Romans at the Colosseum.

New York State didn't have the death penalty until '95, when lethal injection came back in vogue and was then rescinded again in 2007. I knew this, most people knew this, but maybe Carole was trying to play me for a fool. Just like Mona. I remembered the line she'd fed me about the picture in Ricky's glove box.

"Is that what Steve said?" I injected sympathy into my tone.

"Yeah," she said, draining her cocktail. The gurgling sounds at the end were like a death rattle.

Carole stretched and reached over me to get my cigarettes. The movement was liquid, sensual.

"Look, I'm sure Ricky didn't suffer, all right? I'm sure it was real fast."

It seemed that the temperature had dropped from the low seventies to the high fifties in a matter of minutes while we drank in the balmy frangipani and chlorine scented air. A javelin of lightning had been hurled through the sky, which, in the day, had been full of titan white cumulus clouds and now, an ominous mob of muscular charcoal-gray shapes.

"I thought you'd run off by then," I said and Carole just nodded. She picked up her jacket and shoes. She stood up, as if to leave.

"I heard that it was quick."

"Right."

I didn't know what to believe anymore. At least I knew Ricky hadn't incited or participated in Andre's murder. I could write that story.

"How long have you and Steve been together? This whole time? How do you feel about Ange?"

"I feel good. You're planning on coming out to Beatrice to meet her, right? I'll make it easy on you. Why don't you just follow me?" she said, pausing by the poolside.

"I don't usually drink and drive," I lied.

"This is Florida. I'll wait in the parking lot. You got ten minutes. By the looks of it, you probably won't take that long to get ready."

She turned as if it was an afterthought.

"Stay close behind—it's not on the grid. No GPS."

———

In the lobby of the White Sands, "Crocodile Rock" was playing. I watched the cornrowed mom arguing with her two soaking wet kids, pink with sunburn, tears, and tantrums. She yanked hard on one girl's arm and the other child let out a wail, as if the injury had been done to her.

"Oh Lord, is there gonna be a cyclone?" she asked the short Spanish bartender, with the green eyes, who was now at the front desk. She wasn't from here, she was Southern—a Texan maybe—from some arid, uncyclonic state. I read her T-shirt as I got closer—"Pornstar."

"It's just a cluster storm," he replied. "We're at the end of the season, Ma'am."

"What's that," she asked, mouth hanging open.

My dad, the autodidact (he couldn't even pronounce the word), had told me all about multi-celled storms.

"It's not a cyclone. A cluster storm is when a group of cells move as a single unit, sort of like a gang. Each cell is a different stage of its thunderstorm life cycle and gets a chance at being the gang leader. The younger cells tend to become the upwind, the western or south-western edge of the cluster, and the older guys go to the center. This one's on the way out, the older guys are on the downwind, east or north-east," I said.

They stared at me.

"It's not a cyclone," I repeated and went toward my room. I changed out of my sweatsuit, into jeans, I slid my cell and credit card into my pocket. I put on Converse and a jacket, braided my hair tight, put a Mets cap on over the braid, removed my earrings—like a teenage hood heading into a fight, which I ultimately was. All the surviving members of the metalhead Southport kids were there, except Danny—I knew he was there in spirit, cursing me.

28

Back in the parking lot, I sat in the car, with shaking hands flat on my diaphragm, breathing in and out as slowly as possible. Rain beat down, at first softly and then marble heavy. It could have been romantic in a different context, but the howl of the wind and the sense of impending doom was something out of my many nightmares. I fiddled with the radio dial; still stuck. The night had a sheen on it, like someone had exhaled onto a mirror and then wiped it clean of condensation.

I felt like my stomach was being dragged, and the lake of my bowels invaded by distressed waterfowl. I began a self-pep talk that sounded a bit like: *You're a cop's daughter. You can do this. By any means necessary.* Then I lit a Slim and examined my nails, waiting on a cue from Carole.

A text pinged in, from an unknown number.

> Do you like surprises?

Then I saw Carole's VW Golf bunny-hopping along in front of me, trying to exit the parking lot. All week I had watched Carole drive. She was cocky and defensive, a real New York driver.

I gunned the Mercedes into action; the VW Golf sped through a red light and I waited. My phone began to ring. Denise.

I answered. "I'm following Carole. Something's wrong with her. She's all over the road."

"What? Erin, where are you?"

"Following Carole. We're going to Shearer and Ange's joint. I gotta go."

I could hear Denise shouting something as I hit end on the call.

We headed straight onto the highway, the car seeming to straighten out and drive in a line. After twenty minutes on the road with my churning belly, we passed the town called Beatrice and then the GPS seemed to die. The road became dirt and gravel, the scenery a semi-rural slum of shacks and stray auto parts, a sign reading "You are now entering Gator Country" and then a hand-painted marker saying "Cable Grove RD." It resembled a frayed rope tossed into a field and the road itself felt knotty, lined with rock and gravel. Out here, near the gloom of the Glades, away from the highway and the rest of the county, the only sound was the rain on the roof of the car and my own heart beating furiously. I recognized the erratic flutter, a bird tangled in a Venetian blind, knocking itself out on the glass.

I drove slowly, the light from the VW, the harvest moon, and the porchlights of a few distant houses were all I had to go on; the last thing I needed was a flat from an animal trap or a sharp rock.

———

The VW came to a lurching stop in front of an old Florida-style cracker house, the wood painted cream and periwinkle blue. Underneath the iron roof were the words: "Steve's Place." Maybe it had once been an airboat hire or a shanty bar but now it was peeling, cracking, and overgrown with old world climbing ferns. I walked out and floodlights illuminated the entry—a wraparound porch, bare-assed wooden boards, unvarnished and unadorned by furniture. There was what I presumed to be gator skin hanging from the porch awning. In the distance, I saw dark water—the house backed onto a jetty.

The VW's driver's door opened. I saw Aisling O'Malley, red curls spilling onto an orange raincoat, holding what looked like a .38, with a pink handle. I was going to wager a guess it was Carole's gun. Carole liked pink. Then something fell out of her raincoat pocket with a clatter—it was a claw hammer drenched in oil, but as I looked closer, it was sticky looking, wet with gore. I guessed maybe Carole had tried to use the gun on Aisling and Aisling's hammer had won out.

I guessed correctly. Carole fell out of the passenger door and onto the ground, on hands and knees; hair whipped by the wind. She was making wretched, gulping, sniffing sounds as she crawled—Aisling had broken Carole's nose, badly. Carole had become primitive in her own fear, her knees shredded, her hands groping on the gravel. Even if Carole was the bait and mastermind of Andre's demise, even if she was the one who'd dealt the first blow to Andre, the image of Carole, a corrupt broker, a murderess even, in shredded stockings, bleeding from her surgically enhanced face, was surprisingly unsatisfying. I was inherently moral; blame it on all those years of Catholic education. I was sick of people being hurt. Steve Shearer, however; Aisling could go nuts on him.

"Aisling," I said, exiting the car very slowly. "Look at me."

"What?" she snapped, facing me, raising the hammer. I flinched. I had a box cutter, but no real weapon. Aisling was only about 5'3 and 90 pounds soaking wet, wearing a pink T-shirt that said "Sugababe" and blue bootcut jeans that swum on her, but she harbored enough psychotic rage to beat Carole's face in with a hammer. I raised my hands in an act of surrender.

"I'm on your side."

Her face and arm relaxed. I noted her Skechers were pink and had a platform base. Her body, her whole look, was that of a preteen from 1996, which I suppose she was. The Aisling I'd seen online had been washed out, aged; rage gave her a slightly feral degree of youthfulness. She was thirteen again; her skin was very pink, her lips were red, her glossed stained teeth were bared. Carole was younger, too—gurgling and kicking on the ground, regressed to a state of infancy.

A man appeared at the door; Steve, in a Giants T-shirt, grinning, his two arms raised in a hello or surrender. Aisling pointed and shot.

Steve looked down and brought his hand away from his abdomen; dark
and wet with blood. There was silence, then Carole started screaming.
Someone or something shot out at me, from behind, dragging me into
the black. I had no time to turn to see my attacker.

———

From the floodlights and view of the moon on the water, I figured I was
out back of "Steve's Place." The sounds of Florida nature—frogs humming, chirping, and rattling, subtle and larger animal disturbances on
and in the water—were drowned out by the gale-force wind. I wondered if it could tear off the iron roof as it battered the spiky fronds of
the palms and wild tamarind. Either way, I was seemingly safe from
the elements, wrapped up tight in a blanket, like a baby in swaddling. I
freed my right arm and felt the surface of what I was lying in; whittled,
flaky, splintered wood—a faded teal rowboat.

There was a throbbing pain at the base of my skull, and when I put
my hand to it, it came away red. There appeared to be no obvious open
injury, though, so it must have been a small gash. Aisling O'Malley
swam into view. A small figure, spirals of red hair.

Legs, I thought. Wiggle them. I willed them into action, but it was
like the message was blocked. I simply couldn't move them. And there
was a smell that troubled me even more than the fact that my limbs
weren't responding to my brain. I was soaked in something. Gasoline.
Any relief at not having wet myself dissipated. I was in a boat, drenched
in gasoline; a Viking funeral waiting to happen. Carole was unconscious,
bound, and gagged, curled at the foot of the boat. I wondered if Aisling
had dragged me out here to kill me.

Then I heard a creaking on the boards. Oh fuck.

"How many times have you broken a man's bones? How many times
have they broken yours?"

"Six," my own voice replied. *Six, Six, Six.*

Fuck this shit for a joke, Erin, move.

I needed to get out. My pocketbook was missing. Wait, I hadn't brought it. My phone had been in my back pocket. Neither my phone nor my card were there. I sat up. "What happened to my legs, Aisling?"

"Chill out," came her voice, a weird mash-up of Australian, Irish, and American. Like Cormac. *Transatlantic.* She smiled and I saw a missing tooth on the left side of her mouth. Her lips were chapped and indented from her overbite. When she sat on the side of the boat and touched my legs, I felt nothing, just her candy-apple red hair—she must have dyed it redder—tickling my arm.

"You thumped your head good and proper." She squatted on the jetty, catching her breath.

"How?" I managed.

"Ange shot you."

"I can't feel my legs."

"It was a dart gun. The kind they use on gators. It hit you in the back. A nerve block, I think. It should wear off."

The fact that I was in the Glades in a storm with a maniac had nothing on my paralysis and the fact there was gasoline everywhere.

Aisling patted my arm.

"Don't freak, Erin. The feeling will come back, promise. I got Ange for you, I missed the femoral artery, which is what I was aiming for—got her hip; painful but not fatal. She can't walk, I'm sure of it. Steve's on the porch. The stomach's the most painful place to get shot."

"You have a lot of medical knowledge," I said.

"I trained to be a nurse," she replied. "Mental health, specifically."

I had experienced a nerve block before, when I broke my wrist, or rather when Danny did—the week before he carved the pentagram. They call that an escalation of violence. I'd been an hour late to meet him at the diner. He pushed; I pulled. The result was a Colles fracture.

"Can I get up?" I asked. "Try to stretch my legs?" Aisling nodded. I tried to pull myself up with my arms, but my legs were too heavy. I could see where we were more clearly now: the rowboat was on the edge of a floating jetty; one push would set the boat into the water.

Aisling was sitting in the center of the jetty. There was a walkway that spanned a few feet. A gangplank, you might even call it.

"Sorry about the gasoline. I got it all over you, but it was Carole I was aiming for."

I looked over at the wretched, now semi-conscious Carole, who was stirring. Aisling had done hospital-scale damage to Carole. Her puffed-up face was pink and she was folded over like an hors d'oeuvre, a pig in a blanket. The angle of her arm made me think maybe her collarbone or arm was broken. If Aisling wanted her dead, it was going to happen. Unless I stopped it.

"That's not the Glades, you know. It's where the sea starts. Isn't that neat?" she said, looking out over the water. "Any gators, you think?"

"Alligators don't like saltwater," I said. "They're swamp dwellers."

"Whatever." She seemed agitated. "So, you haven't read the final chapter of *Resident Alien*." It was a statement.

"No, I'd like to live to do that. Steve's got a security crew," I told her. "It's best we get out of here, like now."

"No cellphone reception," she said. "It's just him and Ange out here. And Carole, of course."

"Speaking of, my cell is missing."

"Ange took it." Aisling blinked as she said this. "And no one's going anywhere. I hope I didn't kill Steve. I want him to watch this."

"I'm going to throw up," I said and heaved. She made no movement to help or hinder me. I tried to project the bile away from my body, into the water.

"So, what have you learned since you've been out here?" Aisling asked me pleasantly, as if she were a tourist guide. She got to my level and sort of squatted next to the boat.

"Steve, Ange, and Carole, they're all investors in Coral Palisades. Then they brought my dad's ex-partner, Mona Byrnes, in on it, but Carole or Steve, or both, screwed Mona over. I think Steve threatened Mona or something, when she said she'd bring the heat on them. Killed her dogs maybe."

"*They'd not still be walking the earth if I did,*" Mona had said. But it wasn't true. She did know who and it was eating her up.

"I think Steve had something on Mona and he corrupted her," I said. "I'm wondering if he did the same to my dad."

"The Steve Shearer Effect," Aisling agreed. She examined my face, like a therapist. "Dads aren't great, are they?"

I shrugged. "Not really. Look, Aisling, Carole was being manipulated and controlled by Steve from a young age."

"Hold on a minute," she said, holding up her hand. "Carole Jenkins is a lying—"

"Slut," I finished for her. "I know you're not a fan of Carole, neither am I to be honest, but immolation seems a little . . . extreme." The gasoline that was doused over me had collected in a reservoir at the bottom of the boat. Carole was the collection point; the repository. I wiggled my legs. The nerves were firing, I was ready to stand. Carole moaned at my feet, seemingly conscious.

"Steve likes to act, so I'm giving him a bit of theater." Aisling smiled. "Don't worry, you won't go up with her. I need you alive, to tell our story. You've read *Resident Alien*. Carole was in on the Andre murder all along. She probably would have been banging Danny, but you were going out with him. Even though you didn't like him."

"He was beating me up. For real," I said, trying to make eye contact with her. "Remember my previous answer per the broken bones?"

"Love is like that, isn't it though? *If love be rough with you, be rough with love,*" she quoted dreamily. Then she ran her hands over her non-existent hips and grew grave.

"Violent delights and violent ends, is that what you mean?" I asked, finding the quote among my high school English remembrances of *Romeo and Juliet.*

"And Ricky, you slut." She winked at me, to indicate she wasn't really judging. She seemed impressed. Her eyebrows executed a Groucho Marx wiggle. "That said, I personally never cared for Ricky Hell. He was a wannabe Satanist and a fake cop pretending to be a teenager. Look what he did to my brother. He seduced him," she continued.

I wanted to know how she knew about Ricky's double life. Was

Steve the "secret source" she'd been referring to when I first spoke to her about the police conspiracy?

"I knew he was a phony. But when Steve found out that night, I really knew."

I bit my lip, held my tongue. Maybe I was learning to be quiet. Or maybe I was just learning it was better to stay afraid; on guard. I tried to steer her back to the subject at hand. All my senses were heightened, the sound of Carole's jagged breathing, her moving at the bottom of the boat like a bug scuttling in wet leaves. As much as I hated Carole, I didn't want her to burn alive.

I tried to think fast, through my cotton wool concussion.

Even though she'd told me I could get up, I felt like it might be dangerous to make any sudden moves. "I'm going to try and stand now," I warned Aisling. I stood up slowly, on shaky legs that nearly buckled. I climbed over the edge of the boat and sat down on the jetty. Relief at being out of the gasoline-soaked coffin washed over me. However, I was still highly flammable—my shoes were soggy with gasoline. Aisling crouched next to me, keeping an eye on Carole.

"I chose you, you know. To tell our story," Aisling whispered. "I emailed your editor."

I remembered Denise, that day at the Lyrebird. Some true crime nut had emailed her.

"I was there that night," she continued. "I followed Cormac and I was hiding in the woods. He was in trouble; I saw what he did. He killed Andre because Carole told him Andre had hurt me too. She put Cormac up to it."

I gulped. "I heard he tried to get you guys stoned. You, Libby, and Julie."

"I never did it! I wouldn't," Aisling shrieked. I'd hit a no-go zone.

"I'm sorry," I said quickly. "I really didn't mean to pry."

"Ricky arrived," Aisling continued, lowering her voice. "Gunning for Danny for some reason. Then a car pulled up and I heard the gunshot. In the end, if I'd been braver, if I'd said something, if I'd done something. But I couldn't. I was scared."

I swallowed heavily.

"You were just a kid. No one blames you. Especially not me."

"And all my life I've been paying for it. Cormac paid for it too. He killed himself with drugs, he couldn't handle the guilt. And all my life, I've been in trouble because of Steve, because of his choices. And Carole. I've got nothing to lose. My mom's dead, Cormac's dead. When they were killing Andre, Ricky was paging someone. Maybe it was you? I suppose Ricky loved you."

Hope rose inside me stupidly for a second and then instantly deflated.

"No. It wasn't me. Maybe it was my dad. But I think . . ." I paused. "I think that Ricky loved me as much as he could. We were kids. It wouldn't have lasted."

The planks creaked and I looked up to see Ange walking along the jetty; there was a dragging, thumping sound as she walked, the dragging of her wounded leg—or rather her hip. The lights above the jetty illuminated her. She was in jean shorts, a button-up top. She'd ripped off one shirt sleeve, made a tourniquet. Her shorts were soaked in blood. Aisling and I rose at the same time and Aisling turned around, as if expecting her.

Ange pointed a rifle at Aisling.

"You little twat. You shot Steve." Ange's Queens twang was like a garrote. One eye was the color of Hershey's chocolate, the other reminded me of Andre Villiers'; a milky film was transplanted over the iris. Scar tissue webbed over the lid and grew up the eyebrow, like ivy. It was like she'd been dipped in fire and put out. The scoured and melted browned skin slackened and pulled taut on her right side.

Ange nodded to Aisling. "Sit down in that boat. Next to Carole. Untie her."

Aisling just folded her arms across her bony chest. She had Carole's gun tucked into her jeans.

"Where's Steve, Ange?" I asked.

"He's out the front," Aisling answered for her. "He'll die probably. I shot him. I shot the devil."

Ange choked back a sob and spat blood instead.

"Untie her," she said to me. She kept the gun on Aisling.

I looked out past the gangplank, back toward the house. I could see lights, as bright as Fourth of July fireworks, but not loud, just flashing—no sounds, no sirens. The cops were here. They had about sixty seconds, by my reckoning, to get to the jetty before Ange killed Aisling.

I knelt to Carole, removed the gag.

I was aware that I kept looking up at Ange, I wanted to ask how she'd been burned, but I didn't dare. Aisling seemed to pick up on this.

"These guys have a thing for fire," she piped up.

I noticed it then. A silver Zippo in Aisling's palm.

"They bought up houses in downscaled neighborhoods like the Lakes and made a ghetto." For emphasis, Aisling turned to Carole, who screamed at the sight of the lighter. "Then they set people's homes on fire for insurance money. But playing with fire means you get burned, right Ange? It's common knowledge you got barbecued on purpose. Three's a crowd, you know?"

Ange rolled her good eye, but I could tell Aisling was telling the truth.

"Shut up, bitch."

"Did you know, Ange, that Carole has been sleeping with Steve all these years? And now, I mean, well . . ."

Ange cocked the rifle. "Not true."

Aisling leaned in and touched my cheek. I could see the soft down on her face, all over the shriveled apples of her cheeks. Anorexia. She'd clearly been sick for a very long time. The smell of her breath was like she'd been sucking on rotten meat.

"You'll get the rest soon." She flicked the Zippo and the flame was visible.

Aisling's eyes were half closed. I thought of *Resident Alien*; of Aisling's wretched, love-starved life—she'd been banished from America, all her family was dead, and her whole life had been defined by the hate she felt for the man who was the engineer of her suffering. Now she looked almost beatific; peaceful. Aisling reached in her waistband for the pistol, but there were two short, sharp, rhythmic pops as Ange blew two holes in Aisling's torso—the force knocked Aisling into the boat, still holding the lighter. For a second all I heard was the rush of flames and then the two women went up with it, but the banshee scream was from a fully conscious, gasoline-soaked Carole, who was, like Aisling, being consumed by the fire. Carole's body jerked up straight and then it flopped around as she burned. Then she stopped screaming. And the noise of the police running down the gangplank sounded strangely light. Or maybe it was my concussion; cotton wool was packed into my head and the volume and brightness had been turned down.

The cops were on the jetty now, shouting at Ange to put the gun down; shots were fired.

I was dissociating, I suppose. The flames appeared even as my lids were shut; I still heard Carole's screaming. I could smell smoked meat and blood; burned fabric scored my nostrils. I puked up cocktails and bile. Aisling was silently burning, and her story had died with her. Except, of course, it hadn't.

29

I sat on the bottom step of the front porch that was tacky with my blood while a medic applied sterile gauze to the right side of my head; it stemmed the bleeding from the small rent, which the medic said might need stitches. The area where Steve and Ange had been shot was being cordoned off. The medic began shining a flashlight in my eyes, questioning me in much the same way Aisling had. *What's the date? How old are you? Who is the president?* I answered but I was finding it hard to concentrate; despite my splitting headache and my blurry vision, adrenaline was pumping through my body. I was getting more and more agitated—all I could think was that I needed to call Denise, but my cell was missing. I wanted to go home, or at least back to my hotel and take a shower—but where were my keys?

It was still night, and floodlights illuminated the tiny property, which was crawling with human activity now. White-suited forensics traipsed through the house and trailed around the back. Numerous uniformed officers, and what looked like FBI, were searching inside and coming out carrying bagged evidence. Evidently, many of the bags contained guns. The media had started arriving; news vans full of reporters were being kept at bay by a row of uniforms.

Aisling's blackened body, covered by a sheet, but with the platform sneakers peeking out under the blanket, was wheeled past me and into the coroners' van. Ange, or at least I presumed it was Ange, followed. Then Steve was wheeled out, miraculously alive. He was handcuffed to the gurney and it rattled; his body twisted and convulsing. He had an oxygen mask on, but I could still hear him roaring; it wasn't pain, it was his sheer fury at being caged.

He was screaming something at me. He even lifted the mask. Still, I couldn't make it out entirely. "Your father's friends take bribes! I took the heat. You don't know shit!"

The medics loaded Steve into an ambulance manned with three cops.

"What was that all about?" the medic asked me.

I shrugged, "I don't know." But I thought I did: maybe he was confirming Mona did take a bribe for Ricky.

I wondered where Carole was. Perhaps still in the boat—maybe it was harder to extricate her—whatever was left. I began to hyperventilate just thinking about her unearthly screaming; the caustic amalgam of burning flesh and hair; it smelled like a box of old matches and burning fat on the grill. The fear she must have felt as she waited to be burned alive. No one deserved a death like that.

"Can I borrow someone's phone, please? I need to call my editor," I asked the medic. I thought about the crooked cops who threatened me. I didn't want to be here anymore.

"You gotta go to County," she said, ignoring me. "You need to be seen to."

Then my panic began to dissipate as I tired and my words began to slur. "I can't go to the same hospital as Steve Shearer."

"You've got a head injury. No arguments. You've got to go to County."

———

I must have blacked out: the next thing I remembered I was in the hospital. The police said they found fragments of a cell phone, charred beyond repair. So, Aisling had taken it after all. My ATM card must have been on her too. I had repeated everything I knew to both the detectives in charge of the case and the FBI agents who I had been told had been poking around the Beatrice operation—Steve wasn't just into real estate scams. I also told them what happened at the Palisades with the dirty cops and they didn't seem all that surprised. Finally, someone brought me out to the ward phone.

"So imagine my surprise when I get a call from a Southern sounding gentleman telling me my star reporter has stumbled into a Southern Gothic version of *Hamlet*," Denise said in place of hello.

"Something's rotten in Howard County?" I managed.

"I meant more the body count and all the ghosts and shit. But that too."

"Marvin called you."

"You know, I was totally against you finding Steve Shearer. This whole sub-story is a disaster," Denise chided. "And yes, the Southern gentleman was someone named Marvin Abelard. It was him who called it in—and called me; how he got my number, I don't know . . ."

"Marvin Abelard?" I managed. "So, that's how Howard County and Broward County got the heads-up? Steve was in the cops' pockets."

"Maybe so, but Steve Shearer and Co pissed off a lot of cops, Marvin tells me. And the FBI were obviously aware of him. Marvin said he went to visit you at the White Sands because he heard about the amount of arsenal Steve and Ange had at Beatrice. Then he saw Aisling break into Carole's VW and smash her in the face with the hammer, when he saw you take off after them he made the call."

Marvin had saved me. But he wasn't in time to save Carole, to save Aisling from herself. Ange and Steve, well, as far as I was concerned got what they deserved.

"Have you spoken to the cops?"

"I've given my statement, albeit under opiates and with a head injury. I even received some hearty congratulations from the FBI. My visit has been a catalyst for a pretty good clean-up of white collar and gun crime and maybe even the local police. Except Aisling was caught in the cross-fire." I remembered Aisling's rotting smell as she moved in close to tell me something, goading Ange to shoot her—mingled with something chemical, sour, like a baby's spit-up, and her hairspray.

"Aisling was sick. I think she wanted to die. I think she never intended to leave America alive. It was like suicide by cop, but in this case it was suicide by Angela Miller."

Denise stayed silent.

"I know it's just . . . I feel so horrible. And Carole. God. I keep replaying it." Carole might have toed the line with the Ricky Hell murder, but she didn't pull the trigger.

I needed something—a hug, reassurance that I didn't get everyone killed, some answers. Denise supplied the reassurance.

"You didn't light that fire. You just tried to find out the truth. They were going to end up killing each other. It's you who got caught up in the crossfire. Even if you were poking around where you shouldn't. Like I told you not to."

"I know."

"Does the hospital say you're okay to fly home?" she asked.

"Yeah, I got an MRI. I passed out for a little while in the back of the ambulance, but it's just a concussion. I got a few stitches. They made me take blood tests in case the dart Ange shot me with was dirty or contaminated. Steve is at the same fucking hospital, in surgery. He's critical, apparently. The shell hit his colon. The odds weren't on his side, was how they'd phrased it, but guys like Steve always beat them."

Acid bile filled my mouth as I thought of Steve's parting words.

"Steve said something to me like, I did it for your dad and his friends. What did he mean?" It was like a question mark, in a bubble over my head. "Aisling said Ricky paged someone before he died. She thought it was me, but it wasn't. Was he paging Mona? Or my dad?"

"We might never know. Mona isn't going to talk. RP, well, he can't. You said RP gambled. It might have been a gambling win that he forgot about," Denise said, unconvincingly, bright sounding. "I'm going to pick you up from the gate in about eight hours, so get some rest."

30

At LaGuardia, I was going through baggage claim when I spotted Denise's big, black-clad body. I was expecting her open arms, a fierce hug. She was red-lipped, but that was the only vibrant thing about her. I didn't want to absorb the pity in her eyes, I drowned out the downward inflection in her tone, looking at my shoes, my head full of noise, still aching. I set my bag down.

I knew that look, that tone. "Mister," I said finally.

"No. Your father. I'm so sorry. They couldn't reach you," she said.

"My phone is dead," I said, almost accusatorily.

"He just slipped away in his sleep. They said it was real peaceful, babe."

Typical RP. He gave everyone hell but slipped off on a fluffy white cloud.

"But Mister's okay?"

She nodded slowly and squeezed my hand.

"You knew when I called you."

"I'm sorry, I couldn't say it over the phone, Erin."

My shoulders sort of sank and then I hugged her. She recoiled almost in shock and then squeezed me.

"It's okay to feel relieved."

———

Given the way he'd left the NYPD, they weren't about to give my father a departmental funeral, even if he'd wanted one. He hadn't. His will, which I never knew existed, strictly prohibited a viewing and stipulated a private cremation take place at a funeral home in Suffolk County. He'd requested a scattering of ashes over the Sound. It turned out he was also quite the lone wolf in death, not wanting to belong or lie down next to anyone. The house was willed to me and any pension and monies left over went to the Humane Society. I feared I would never know where the money came from. There was no grief; only waiting questions.

Due to the body count, what happened in Florida was already a media sensation. Carole was made famous again by immolation—a kind of celluloid saint. Hers was a big splashy funeral; reporters swarmed the cemetery and pictures of her went nationwide; an image of her young kids and grieving husband on the cover of every paper. Ange's funeral evidently went by with a whimper, only one of her sons attending. No one claimed Aisling's body, so she was cremated by the state. I located family in Ireland to advise them of this and left it in their hands. I finally received a message from an Orlaith O'Malley that they had arranged to send for her, saying they would not repatriate her back to Australia, but to Ireland, where she was born.

Aisling, she wrote, had been a most beautiful baby girl, no matter what she'd grown into.

Aisling had finally found her place.

I sent Marvin a case of Pabst via the Monkey Bar, alongside an eighteen-year-old bottle of scotch as a thank you.

Marvin wrote me an email—via the bartender at the Monkey Bar's account, no doubt dictated by him.

The gifts were unnecessary, albeit appreciated, Ms. Sloane. It was my pleasure to render aid. I am sorry about your father. Best to draw a line under it and write The End. Let sleeping dogs lie. They bite when disturbed.

—M

Denise offered me an extension, grief leave or whatever she called it, but I registered her relief when I refused it. She knew I would. The story hadn't even been written yet and there was nationwide interest—talk shows, syndication, a book deal. The uncovering of a sordid interstate or trans-state property scam in the search for the answer to a seemingly meaningless sixteen-year-old crime. The socioeconomic and racial angles of Ricky Hell's murder—well, they were just the icing on the cake. But we couldn't file yet. I wanted to talk to Julie Hernandez before I did that. At least I knew she was okay. On my insistence, Detective Diaz had done a welfare check the week before, drily reporting that Julie and her kids had been in the Midwest somewhere and had just arrived home. And that morning alone, Danny texted me about thirteen times.

There were expressions of concern:

> Read the papers. Heard about your dad.

> thinkin of u.

> Sorry.

> worried about u.

Cue requests for return calls:

> Call me back, Erin. K? Plz.

Cue incandescent rage and expletives:

> u think ur fkn better than me? I am a married man n have a wife hotr than ull ever be. Ur alone and fkced up. U Freak.

> WHORE

Cue threats:

> This isnt a threat U know what I can do to you?

And then, as always; remorse:

> Call me bck. Please. Please.

> I'm sorry, I'm sorry.

> Luv u, Eri.

> Babe?

And then there was Penny Villiers. Andre's little sister.

———

I was writing, taking breaks to sort through RP's possessions and box them up, when a message came through my *Inside Island* account.

Okay, Erin. I'll talk to you. This is my cell.

Penny Villiers.

I dialed it.

She didn't say hello, she just launched into it. "I read about you in the papers. I'm ready to talk. I just dropped my daughter off at her piano lesson, near Lake's entry. I've got an hour max."

I looked at the clock. It was 3:45.

"I can meet you at Oceanside Diner at 4:15."

I sped most of the way down, part of me wishing I'd suggested the Lucky Shamrock around the corner. I was on the wagon, however, while recovering from my concussion. Plus, Penny seemed religious; there was a lot of God stuff on her Facebook. And she was ferrying around elementary schoolkids, so she probably wouldn't want to do a shot while talking about her brother's satanic murder.

Penny recognized me immediately, probably from the papers. She looked like a teacher. She was dressed in gray and pink, soft wools. Even though she wasn't smiling, her energy was that of warmth. Her skin was a similar raspberry tone to her sweater—flushed and wholesome looking. On the other hand, I still had a fading shiner and bruising to the left side of my face; I'd covered it up as best I could with makeup.

She sat down in the booth next to me and asked for an herbal tea when the waitress came over. I ordered black coffee.

"I thought I was going to chicken out on the way over. I had to do it now, you see." While I knew Penny was Shelly's age and a few years my junior, she seemed older; her poise, her diction was somewhat quaint. Old fashioned. Maybe it was because she was a teacher, maybe it was because she was a proper adult and I was barely passing for one. She tapped her fingers on the Formica tabletop nervously, and I studied her wedding and engagement rings, her immaculate nails.

"I understand. I'm so glad you came."

"Wait." She held her hand up. "Before we talk, promise you won't record this. I'll talk to you, but I want control over what you say."

"Of course," I said. "I won't even take notes if you don't want me to."

"What do you want to know exactly?"

"Why didn't you live with your family, Penny?"

"Because it wasn't safe," she said, and then she started to cry.

"I'm sorry."

The waitress silently placed the tea at the table while Penny and I both foraged around for Kleenex. She found one first. She didn't touch the tea, wiped her face.

"I wish I had a drink right now. I'd kill for a Chardonnay."

I reached for the menu to see if they served wine, but she shook her head. "No, no, I'm driving. When you said you wanted to talk to me about Andre, I knew you wanted me to say something in his favor. I knew that. You want to represent the victim? How about this: if Andre was killed as a sacrifice to Satan, well maybe he deserved it. My brother did terrible things."

Her last statement was like a slap across the face.

"Andre might have been murdered, but he was never a victim. My parents, well, they wouldn't do anything about it. My parents are dead now, so I can finally say how I feel."

"What do you mean 'terrible things,' Penny?"

"He was a nightmare." Penny was angry now. "He ruined my childhood. My friends would never stay the night because he was grossly inappropriate to every young girl he met. My parents wouldn't send him to therapy, military school, whatever. So, as you know, I was sent away," Penny choked back tears. "To cousins in Bethpage. My parents sent me away to protect me. I know it in my heart. And he went down whatever dark path he went down."

"The satanic stuff. Was any of that real, Penny?"

"Andre didn't believe in *anything*. God or the devil. My parents, however, they were fanatical. They thought he was possessed. The more they fretted, the worse he became. He played it up. He did it to torture them. He got arrested for shoplifting and property damage. He was violent. He hurt animals. Our family dog, Ludo—he fed him chocolate on purpose and he got so sick he nearly died. Andre did drugs; he sold them, I think. Then he was interviewed about Cathy. She went missing. We were friends. I knew your sister, too. God rest her soul." Penny smiled at me. "That's probably why I agreed to meet you. And how I recognized you in the paper, because you look so much like Shelly."

"Thank you," I managed. I remember reading Shelly's middle school yearbook tributes, gushing pledges of eternal friendship, girlish outpourings of bottomless sorrow by girls who I thought cynically would not remember Shelly's last name by freshman year. I guess I was wrong.

"I've kept the Villiers name. People still ask me if Andre is a relation. And I always say no. I keep it for my mom and dad. The same way you've kept yours."

"Penny, with regards to Cathy Carver, did you suspect Andre was involved?"

"Cathy . . . Well, he used to walk past her house. He was always staring at her. She stopped sleeping over. They never found out who took Cathy, did they? Cathy's old nanny was called Rosa. Rosa is probably long gone, but you might try and find her. Cathy's parents won't help you. They've lost their minds with grief. They hate the media." She finished her tea. "I have to go."

31

After Penny left, I quickly read up on Cathy's parents. As Denise had said, the case had a touch of the JonBenét Ramsey tragedy: Cathy was young, blonde, wealthy. She disappeared from her home. The police initially suspected conspiracy. Her father did not participate in the search on the water (hydrophobia, even though they lived on the water). The mother came off as icy and cynical. They both refused interviews with the media. There had been divorce rumors; money problem rumors; whispers of the father sleeping around.

I remembered I had been inside Cathy's home once. It has a foyer because it was less of a home and more like a mansion. I came to the door to collect Shelly and peered in—drinking in the chandelier, the immaculate ivory carpeted staircase, the childless quiet—as if the girls had been disappeared.

A door knock approach may be a misfire, but I looked like my sister and she and Cathy had been friends. Maybe I could convince the parents I could help solve their daughter's unsolved disappearance, somehow. Or at least I might get a chance to talk to their staff, maybe get a contact for Rosa, the nanny. I jumped into my car and took Southport Avenue to Lake's Entrance. I parked the Chrysler at the lake, walked across the road and raked a hand through my hair, smoothed my skirt and rang the doorbell.

"Yes?"

A South American woman came to the door in sweats and a worn Abercrombie & Fitch T-shirt. She looked to be in her fifties. I peeked inside. Two Dalmatians with red leather collars were straining to get to the front door.

"Hi, I'm Erin Sloane. Is Mr. or Mrs. Carver home?"

"Who are you?" She held the dogs back and swore in Spanish.

"I'm from *Inside Island* magazine. I'm interested in writing a story about Cathy. I wondered if—"

"About Cathy?" the woman's impassive face broke into concern. "No, no." She began to close the door on me.

"Look, I knew Cathy. I know Penny Villiers, her good friend. My little sister Michelle Sloane was also friends with Cathy. Michelle's dead too. She was murdered in '93."

She visibly softened. I internally crossed myself for this lie, hoping Shelly, if she was anywhere, would understand it was for the greater good.

"I'm only a few years older than they would be now and I want to write about what happened to them."

"Wait a minute." She shut the door in my face.

She came out, pulling on a duffel coat with a faux fur trim. She pushed the dogs back in the house.

"We'll walk. Quick. I'm Rosa, Cathy's old nanny. I stayed with the family, look after Mrs. Carver now. She's very sick."

"Is Mr. Carver around?"

Rosa gave me a look that was at once fiercely protective and disgusted.

"You leave them out of it, she's sick and he's gone. I'm the only one she has now. I hate what you people do, only I talk to you because I loved Michelle. She had a nice, heart-shaped face, like you."

For the second time today, Shelly had somehow saved me.

Rosa looked at me like she was trying to see the similar goodness in me, a light that had naturally emanated from Shelly, and both she knew and I knew it wasn't in me.

We walked together, in silence, across the road to the lake.

The sky was starting to darken; the wind was up. Rosa rubbed her hands. A jogger flew past us. At a safe distance from the house, Rosa finally spoke. "I told the police over and over that Cathy was doing something weird."

"What do you mean weird?"

"The maid told me that Cathy was being abused. Cathy was a little kid; you know, she was a young eleven. But she'd come home, little bottles in her pockets. She's upset. Then one day, I find . . . blood in her jeans. Her mom say she shave her legs. Her mom say, 'No, no, don't tell anyone.'"

Little bottles. She meant minis, the kind that dipsos like me carry around in their pockets.

"Blood on her jeans where exactly?"

"You know," Rosa gave me a stern look. "She'd not even gotten her period."

"The police don't know about this?"

"No. They don't know about the blood."

"But you're telling me."

"People have forgotten her. The police—they do nothing. I haven't forgotten. She was on the computer a lot. I think she meet an older man, who creep around the kids there. The police know that."

"Did you ever see a young guy around her, a tall blond guy? He was eighteen, about 6'3." I handed Rosa the senior's portrait of Andre from Carole's book. She used her cell to illuminate the photo.

"The Giant. Yes. I see him. Always riding his bike around the house, always at the lake. But I tell the police, back then. They said it's fine. He was just a troubled boy."

"Did Cathy ever mention him to you?"

"Just that he was Penny's brother, she didn't like him. She said he gave her creeps. She called him the Mean Giant. She didn't like to stay over Penny's house anymore."

I thought back to Shelly's nightmares and I wondered if she had stayed over at Penny's, had been afraid of Andre too. The thought that Andre might have hurt Shelly entered my conscious mind and I shoved it back, roughly.

"But one time, he gave her stickers and maybe she changed her mind."

"Could there have been any other men at the house, anyone else you could think of who could have hurt Cathy?"

"She was lonely child." She shrugged. "Dreamy. And she was pretty. She was like a little bird. She sang a lot. Birdie, I called her. Always singing and happy. Anything could happen to a little girl like that in this world. All the men are a suspect."

I walked Rosa back to the driveway and she disappeared into the grand entry without a goodbye; her words ringing in my ears.

All the men are a suspect.

32

I had just gotten back to Oceanside Avenue and was disarming the alarm when I heard the phone ringing. I had resigned myself to letting the machine pick up, but I sprinted to the phone when I heard the voice.

"Julie," I guessed. I breathed out. I hadn't quite realized the extent of my concern for her; hearing her voice was like an opiate. I felt stoned with relief.

"Yeah," Julie said. "You the one who got the police to check up on me?"

I heard a child yell in the distance. "No, you can't have a Little Debbie, Nene, it's dinnertime." She was met by a wail of indignation. I remembered how much Ricky loved Twinkies and Little Debbies. If it glowed in the dark and didn't biodegrade, he wanted it.

"I just asked them to do a welfare check. I was worried. Aisling O'Malley—"

"Yeah. I read about it in the paper." Her voice was thick with emotion. "Crazy fucking girl. I can't believe she's dead."

"I have some old photos she scanned and sent me. You guys at the roller rink. I can email them."

She laughed for a second. It was strangled.

"For real? Aisling was so funny and goofy. Had a good heart. She had a hard life. I didn't realize how much so, until I was older, you know?

All I saw was the big pool, the rich stepdad . . . Just make some copies, mail them to me." Then her tone went flat, uncompromising. "I can't do email. I don't do online anymore. You already got my address. Just send them."

"Julie, I want to exonerate Ricky. I know part of you wants to help me even if it is painful. Do you know anything about what happened with Ricky and Steve Shearer?"

"I knew that Ricky was working with the police, I knew it was because of drugs. I know he wanted to be a cop. The funny thing is, before he got in trouble, and started dressing like that, he looked so straight, like such a goody-two-shoes. He ironed his jeans."

I snorted with laughter. Or maybe I was crying. Surely not.

"Ricky grew up in Kansas. That's where we were just at—visiting my dad in Salinas. He was living with Dad. He came back to the city when he was like fifteen. Then he got in trouble, went to juvie. That was in Buffalo."

So that explained where Buffalo fit in. And the Midwestern accent; his weird affinity with nature.

"I got a box of Ricky's things, some photos and stuff. I'll send it to you, it might help," she said. "I gotta go. I got kids to look after. I don't want to be a character in your story. It's not personal. Just do what you gotta do, but leave me out of it."

She set down the receiver. I followed suit. Then I called Marci Diaz.

———

Detective Diaz sat at my kitchen table drinking coffee while I told her my theories about Andre and Cathy Carver; recounted my interview with Penny Villiers. I played her Carole's tape-recorded confession, looking tense and furious. And then I played her my conversation with Danny at the diner.

"Carole's 'confession' is good, but you know it's probably inadmissible in court. It's a covert recording. And all the parties—Andre, Carole, Cormac, Aisling, all the witnesses to Ricky's death—are dead."

"Except for Danny Quinlan-Walsh and Steve Shearer," I reminded her gloomily.

"Danny's pretty much said nothing on this, except that he doesn't really remember what happened and he doesn't really give a shit—he's dangling a carrot in front of you. You've got compelling information on the Cooper Deane murder. Maybe not enough to open an investigation into Shearer for that, but we'll consider it. We can prove that Ricky was Rivera's cousin and Mona might go on record about Ricky; but she probably won't. Nassau County will continue to deny he ever worked for them. And I can't find a formal record of Richard Hernandez working from the 7th Precinct."

"Julie Hernandez said her brother worked for the police. She might even have something to evidence that in her records."

Marci shook her head. "I doubt it. Probably not bank records or anything concrete. It's not the first time there's been a cover-up in Nassau County or the history of policing, and it won't be the last. The story might bring heat on them. Howard County told me Mona is listed as an investor in the Palisades, which proves she knows Shearer. But it also means she's just one of many folks to put down a deposit and lose out. If you can trace a big sum of money to her or your dad around that time, that's another story," she said.

I drank my coffee too quickly. I had still excluded the fact that I'd located the money, because I wanted to find its source myself. Now I regretted not telling her.

"And the kids. Lighthouse, Nassau County, they do not want *Inside Island* printing anything about the murdered and missing kids in the story—you might face criminal charges if you do."

"I know."

Marci stood up. "I gotta get back to work."

I walked her to the door and she asked me how Danny was behaving.

"New number, but he still sends an average of ten texts a day, but no drive-bys. I'm out of here by the end of the week. Ox thought Danny might have put spyware on my laptop, but it seems to be clean."

"Someone or something is giving him your number. Is he good with computers? Ox should have this figured out. It's like hacking 101."

"He's distracted," I shrugged.

"Well, hit him up again. It shouldn't be happening. As you may already know, Steve Shearer is in an induced coma so we can't question him until he's out of the woods—*if* he gets out of the woods; he's got sepsis. We'll question Danny again about what happened that night with Ricky, but until we have proof there isn't a lot I can do on my side. Just know Danny might flare up shortly because of that."

I shook my head. "Flare up?"

"Expect the worse."

———

When Marci left, I had to feed Mister, so I began the task of chopping up livers and she resumed her habit of nipping at my legs through my sweatpants to hurry me along. I was listening to Slayer's "Raining Blood" because it reminded me of Ricky. I had long quit crying; I think it may have been after the night Ricky died. I thought I had wept so much in those couple of years that I had exceeded a quota of sorts.

I didn't cry when RP died.

But now sobs racked my body; I was physically unable to stop. I was howling, inconsolable, my nose running. I was wretched.

I don't know if it was because Ricky was gone now; the story was being written and still I might not be able to formally exonerate him for Andre's murder. Maybe, despite all the corruption and collusion and dirty cops, I still believed in the long arm of the law. Or maybe it was Danny and the fact that no matter what I did, no matter how many phones I dropped in the water, he would never stop trying to hurt me.

I thought about Ricky's face next to mine, his breath that smelled of Juicy Fruit and Marlboro Reds, the weight and silk of his naked body against mine. He said into my hair, "Saints smell like carnations." He smelled like clams and green-apple shampoo.

"What do devils smell like?" I asked.

"Roses," he said immediately.

Then I remembered a time on the water, watching boats. Danny's family was fishing over the side.

Little Pat, fleshy lipped, in a blue polo shirt and Z Cavariccis, spotted a dolphin.

"Dolphins are perverts," Danny whispered into my ear, pinching me. His belt buckle stuck into my leg. "I wish we had a harpoon."

That day Dr. Quinlan-Walsh taught me how to catch a fish and Danny watched, unsmiling.

"I love fish, but the smell is what gets to me," Danny's mother said, wringing her too-large hands. She went into the galley to make iced tea.

"Fish is good when it doesn't smell or taste like fish," Little Pat said.

"I can think of another thing that's like that," Dr. Quinlan-Walsh said. "Right, Erin?"

Danny spat into the water and pulled me back into a tight hug.

"Danny says Erin smells like roses," Patrick told his father.

"What a lucky boy Danny is," Dr. Quinlan-Walsh smiled.

Danny pinched my arm so hard it left a bruise that even his mom noticed.

It was like Ricky was breathing in my ear.

Eerie! Wake the fuck up!

Ricky knew evil had another face. Sometimes it looked like beauty, sometimes it looked like love—or indifference, cruelty.

I thought of the pentagrams the boys were obsessed with; power and protection. I thought about Danny; his issues with sex and his long-held virginity, his aggression and cruelty.

Danny's father, Big Pat, was weird, sexually inappropriate. Danny was scared for me to be alone with him. Dr. Quinlan-Walsh lived on and loved the water. All the kids went missing near the water. Danny had told me at the diner it was cancer that took his father. I went online and searched for his obit. There was something about an accident—the phrase "vehicular suicide" jumped out at me.

I heard the doorbell and grabbed my father's Glock.

When I saw who it was through the peephole, I shoved the Glock in a dead potted plant and wiped my face with my sweatshirt. I opened the door, wrapping my shawl around myself.

"Hey Ox," I said, hugging him. He responded in his usual fashion—stiff and unresponsive.

"Nice surprise," I said. "I haven't heard from you for so long." Meaning, I'd texted when I'd been unable to call him to tell him RP was dead. And he'd texted back that he was out of town.

"Sorry. I was out of cell reception for a few days. I'm so sorry about RP, Pumpkin." He didn't have his usual six-pack, which none of us could drink, pizza, that only he ate, or bunch of gas station flowers. He had a box tucked under his arm. His hair stood up at an odd angle and he shrugged off his leather jacket and shuffled in, ox-sized, and took my dad's favorite overstuffed armchair. His jeans were sagging, his gut spilled over his too-tight button-up shirt. His boots were dirty. For a second I wondered if he'd been on a bender, then I remembered he didn't drink.

"You been cryin'?"

I shook my head. "Cutting onions."

He handed me a box. It was marked *John*. It was unmistakably RP's writing; one foster parent taught him to write calligraphy. The DT shake was there though.

"Lawyer sent me this. It was with RP at the home, alongside a whole bunch of old letters from your mom and him. I guess that was his final fuck you, maybe. I thought he'd forgiven me, but I guess not."

I shook my head. "Sick."

"You should have them. You got a tape player?" I did. I went into the bedroom to retrieve my old Casio boom box. I'd carved my initials into the hot-pink plastic surround with a pocketknife. We tested it out with an old cassette, and it didn't warp or unravel.

Then Ox popped in the cassette. The scratchy reel started—we both sat watching the tape player, knowing that the tape could still unravel—knowing that what was being heard could never be unheard. A confession? A song?

"What does the tape say?"

"Nothing. Just the date. June 3, 2003."

A muffled ring.

"Your father was pretty paranoid. He recorded all his incoming and outgoing calls," Ox explained.

"Figures." I felt ill. I didn't know how deep my mistrust, my fear and loathing for my own father was—it had roots though. I could feel my whole body shaking.

There was a background sound—a low, bronchial wheeze; the blip of a machine. I made out a name through the jungle of medical sounds and Judge Judy screaming insults at a cowed defendant in the background.

"You okay, Mrs. Weis?"

It was the first time I'd heard RP's Brooklyn gutter-dragged tone in months. Despite myself, I choked back a sob.

"Yeah, I'm on the oxygen now."

Candy Weis. Jason's mother.

"I'm sorry."

She sucked in air; once, twice, three times. "Yeah, yeah. I wanted to see if you'd gone over the original police report."

"It's missing."

"The first report?" She laughed bitterly. Then I heard her light up. Emphysema, on oxygen, but still smoking.

"Filed and lost on the same day." RP sounded a little cold.

"We told them we suspected whoever took Jase was a local high school student. That kid got his head beat in, Andre? He was seen talking to my kid at Waldbaum's. Then another time, Jase came home with a pack of Garbage Pail Kids stickers. I didn't like 'em. I was religious back then. I confiscated them, even."

"Villiers was on the list of men questioned about Cathy Carver, but he was cleared." Now RP's tone was kinder, but weary. "Trey Scott was taken by the same man as Jason, Nassau County are positive about that. And that was 2000, Candy. So that rules Andre out."

He couldn't talk burial with a victim's parent, but the subtext was this: Trey was found a mile away from Jason, buried the same way. Unless it was a copycat. Or there had been an accomplice.

"Andre was seen talking to Jase at Party Perfect. Then the cops forgot all about Andre. And then I remembered the stickers. Predators groom kids. They give them gifts . . . Andre was seen with Cathy there, too, wasn't he?"

I remembered Party Perfect. It was the only shop in twenty miles where they sold Lisa Frank stickers and oilies—stickers that were liquid crystal; you touched them and they changed color—and of course Garbage Pail Kids stickers.

"He was spotted talking to her. That's all I know."

"All the same, I want to know why they eliminated him. He was a victim in the papers. That freak. That albino fuck. He was spotted loitering at Whitman Elementary. What do you think he was doing there? Playing fuckin' marbles?"

"You're right—there's no reason for Andre to be at Party Perfect or the school for that matter, even if the kid had a low IQ and a screw loose. But as I said, Trey Scott was abducted and murdered in 2000, after Andre died. Jason and Cathy were a school district apart, but was there any way they may have met? Jase do extracurriculars?"

"Computer club. No athletics. Religion at St. Al's."

I went to St. Al's back then too. I had presumed Candy was Jewish, from her surname. All of us public school Catholic kids went to religion class at St. Al's. Andre, Danny, and I. Cormac. Aisling. My mom had been a teacher there.

"Did Jase do the Wednesday night religion class?"

"Of course."

"Who was his teacher?"

I tried to swallow, but the lump in my throat became a bolus.

"Dr. Quinlan-Walsh. His wife took over last year. And his son now."

"Danny?"

"Lord no. Holy water would have burned him up. No, Patrick. Lovely boy. I stopped volunteering, but he visits me sometimes. Trying to get my faith reignited. That family has suffered . . ."

"Dr. Quinlan-Walsh," RP repeated. I heard my father cough, I could almost see the wheels turning. It was June 2003. I was on a diet of cocaine, benzos, and booze. I weighed about what Aisling had—ninety pounds. I partied all night and I think I left the house during the day only to get coffee and a toasted sandwich from the bodega. That was the only food I ate. The only thing I read, over and over, was a book about South American mythology. My father wasn't good at much, not good as a father, a husband, even being a human, but detection was his forte. He was great at that. After he got kicked off the team, or benched, he became a private detective. And he was good at that, despite being blasted, blazed—whatever. I remembered him in the eighties, with his hands in the earth, planting sunflowers for my mom to cheer her up. Everything good had left him by the time he made this call. He was now a very bad man.

"He used to take all the kids out for pizza. You know, whoever did it, I'm gonna find out and murder him. God don't do justice no more," Candy stated, as if she were reading the weather bulletin. "Don't call here, not unless you know something."

The tape kept whirring until I leaned over and turned it off.

Ox finally spoke. "If it was Dr. Quinlan-Walsh, it makes sense that Danny has been warning you off the story. His father had the opportunity. He was respected, he worked with kids. The kids would have willingly gone with him."

He was a community leader. He was a sadist.

"And maybe why Danny hated Andre," I finished.

Danny's father was dead. But secrets never stay buried. They sleep inside us, eat us up from the inside out.

"Stay away from Danny, Pumpkin. We'll get it to the authorities. But only if you want to."

RP Sloane, wasted twenty-four hours a day, was no fool. He found out the truth about secrets—they pay.

"If I want it to?" Southport was rising in me. I felt ice cold; I was burning up. "Get out of here with that shit. I'm not my father, Ox. I don't want blood money—it's at Denise's. Go get it, take it to your crooked friends."

He got to his feet, his big belly showing as he hiked his pants up. I thought of the bulk of him as he gave his famous bear hugs and I remembered how Shelly used to call him Yogi when she was little, after Yogi Bear. He even did a pretty solid impression of him.

Suddenly I realized something—Ox had all my new numbers. He had all my information. He'd been dragging his heels on this cell phone mystery.

"Did you give Danny my number? To keep me scared? To scare me off?"

Ox shook his head slowly, and the accusation had blanched his face of color and expression. "All I do is protect you."

"Really." I folded my arms.

"I'll turn it in. Don't do anything stupid, Sloane." He was grave, but not angry.

Sloane. That's what he used to call my father.

33

Danny picked up on the second ring. It sounded like he was in a bar—I could hear the drone of sports on TV and glasses clinking in the background.

"Sorry about your dad." He sounded almost resentful. "You want to talk?" His voice always sounded hoarse when he drank. It broke at the end. He must have been smoking a lot too. He coughed; it was thick with mucus.

"Yes. The diner?"

"No," he said. "My office. No one will be there."

"That sounds extremely lonely and deserted," I said.

"I'm not going to hurt you," he said.

"I've heard that one before." I laughed and he joined in, mirthlessly.

"Hey, so I know some things about your dad and the missing kids," I said. "Plus some stuff about you. I've left a tape for my editor, should any harm come my way."

"Pop . . . he . . ."

Pop. I forgot that they called Pat Senior "Pop"; it was so hokey at the time, I gagged.

"He did bad things to those kids, maybe at St. Al's?" I prompted him.

"I only wanted to keep you safe."

He carved a giant pentagram on my chest so that I'd be safe.

It dawned on me that today was October 8, which was the anniversary of the pentagram.

I applied a slash of Stop Traffic Red on my lips. I put RP's old service revolver in my purse.

It wasn't smart, what I was doing, but I was with Candy on justice. You had to find out the truth and make your own justice. And I had to make it right. I sat down and sent my final extract to Denise, explaining what I had found out, where I was going. I was facing the monster from my past, the son of the real monster, sixteen years later. The timing was uncanny.

THE TESTIMONY OF ERIN SLOANE
OCTOBER 8, 1994: THE NIGHT OF THE PENTAGRAM

Since the broken wrist, Danny had been overly solicitous, eager to nurse me. I think that night he wanted to make me dinner. But once he was there, he was also sullen, with a face like a wet weekend, as Mona would have said. He poked around the house and my possessions, asking leading questions. I had gotten a page from Ricky, which simply read *13, 69* which meant I would probably put Metallica on and dance around in my underwear for him later at the Freeport Motel, Room 13, and this would end in said sex act. For now, I was studying.

I lit a roach, turned the music down, picked up *Richard III*, and looked out at the window. Beethoven was playing in the background because it aided my concentration. In the illuminated window, among the moody blues and greens of the flickering television, there was a face looking in at me. I shrieked like a Hollywood scream queen. I had been drilled and coached on this; practically prepared since birth for the bad man to come through the window (which was locked). I carried mace, a box cutter (still do). I also knew how to shoot a gun; had done jujitsu. It was the same feeling that I had the night my mom and sister died; the warm, wet blood on my face and the burning sensation of my feet in the snow. In the same kind of decibel range as the snap of a bone, Danny literally put his fist through the glass—he was wearing wool gloves—and punched a neat hole. My first thought—Dad's gonna be so pissed. The second—Danny's literally going to kill me.

The next few minutes were all about the broken glass, Danny opening the window almost politely, climbing onto the bed, commandeering the joint. I thought at first he was laughing, but he was actually crying, or at least his eyes were leaking fluid. His whole body was shaking.

He opened my bedroom door and looked in the house. He checked the wardrobes, under the bed. I grabbed the mace, ran to my dad's room but he held out a foot and tripped me. There's a scar above my eye, two millimeters long from the collision with the door. No stitches.

I realized right away he was on acid, because he talked a lot about the devil, the devil being in me. And for some odd reason, his eyes always leaked when he was on hallucinogens. The way he was gnawing his jaw made me think he had also taken a lot of speed, maybe crystal. It was going around at the time. It was in fact PCP.

"I'm just trying to protect you," he said.

He busted open a man's razor on the floor of my dad's bathroom. Maybe it was a lady's razor. Maybe it was pink.

He cut himself first.

"I am going to be in your life forever," he said. "Whether you like it or not."

It was something his dad said when they fought.

"Not if I can help it," I said.

"Are you in love with Ricky Hell?"

And I did the worst thing you can do in that situation. I laughed at him.

———

I don't know how long it took, I don't know what happened to time—ten minutes, twenty, a half hour. The pain was hot and jagged, searing, it had an alphabet and chronology, a timeline of its own. His breath was like he'd been sucking on quarters, his eyes weren't blue, but a kind of silver. There was something about his face that kept shifting. It was either madness or possession. His cries were not like a man, but a cat calling out an enemy. More than anything I wanted him not to touch me with his hands. All I know is, he decided that the D would protect me. The pentagram was additional. It was fifteen minutes, I think. Five for the star, ten for the D—and it shows. The pentagram is more faded these days. The 666 was a surface scratch, half-hearted. Still, he wouldn't have known that Ricky had a real one. Or maybe he did, maybe that was the point.

He took ink from my calligraphy pen, tipped it onto the wound.

When he left, I made it back to my room, soaked in blood and ink, sweat from the pain. I bundled up my clothes, my sheets, and threw them out. I screamed as I cleaned myself up in the shower, disinfected the wound, taped myself up with medical gauze.

And what did I do next? I told everyone, my dad and Ricky, that I had glandular fever. My dad would never take me to a doctor; in fact, he barely even noticed. I found antibiotics in the house from an old script. I went to bed for a week.

I never went to the Freeport Motel. Ricky found out about it the day before Halloween. I just couldn't hide it from him any longer. And clearly, he couldn't face me after it happened. Maybe he was mad at me. Maybe he blamed me. Maybe he pitied me. Maybe he loved me. Maybe he confronted Danny about it. I don't know why he didn't show up for Mona and RP. All I know is, I took too many pain pills and too much vodka because I thought he'd left me. And then Ricky left the world for good. When I found that out, I tried again, the next time, a bit harder. So I went to the clinic and then was shipped off to Maine.

Why didn't I tell about what Danny did to me? Why didn't I go to the ER? My dad was a policeman for God's sake. He had taught me to shoot.

Maybe it was because, even though I had a knife to my jugular, I knew I was stronger than Danny and I was ashamed because he had cornered me, carved me up like a Thanksgiving ham.

I was ashamed of my victimhood, of my weakness. Also, most of my family were dead. I didn't want to make a fuss. In short, I was afraid.

———

This October had started mild but turned icy; there was a bite in the air from the Sound that went into my bad wrist. I was brittle with fear.

It was now completely dark outside, the only car in the parking lot was Danny's Range Rover. The storeroom was bright inside from industrial strip lighting, but with warmer globes, giving the place a rich, creamy glow. A security light was triggered as I approached the entry. I looked out onto the boatyard and beyond; the water was still and dark. The storeroom was unlocked and there was a sense of a disturbance in the room—RP had experienced this at homicides, he said crimes left a psychic imprint. The hairs on your neck stood up as you walked through—it was animal instinct, he said. Danger.

Danny's office was open, the steel chandelier lit up the desk. All the photos on his desk were shattered. His wife, his child, his Sharper Image gadgets were on the ground, the Scandinavian wood splintered. I was a stronger animal than Danny, I told myself.

He was slumped in the chair, not facing me.

"Danny," I said, "turn around."

He wasn't moving.

It was Patrick, Danny's little brother, who was in the chair when I spun it around. What a cheap trick.

I felt the air move as Danny's fist went into my gut, winding me instantly.

Monkey see, monkey do.

After I caught my breath, still panting, swearing at Danny, ducking and weaving, I connected my fist with his high cheekbone and it shocked my arm all the way through to my funny bone. I socked him hard, but with my bad wrist, and it wasn't a good one. I screamed in pain. He reeled, but smiled blearily, his pupils fat, like he was on ecstasy. But it was anger and anger is one hell of a drug. He grabbed my bag and I pulled it back.

"It looks like someone has been knocking you around," he said, pointing to my black eye. "Ow." He patted his cheekbone.

I ran behind the desk and picked up a letter opener. "Correct. I got punched out, shot with a dart, partly paralyzed. I saw several people get shot, and even burned alive. Carole Jenkins, in fact. Then my dad died. What's next?"

"Your father died," Danny repeated. "Now you're an orphan."

I kneeled, put my fingers to Pat's neck. His pulse flickered under my fingers. He moaned, stirring back into consciousness.

"I only knocked him out," Danny said, annoyed.

"I'd like to get him help," I said. "He needs help."

He kicked Pat, square in the ribs, like he was responding to me. I winced.

"Pat and my mom made me go back to the hospital. Pat tried to fire me. My own brother."

"Did you stop taking your meds?" I asked, injecting sympathy in my tone.

"No. I've been going out a lot. They staged an intervention and I got mad. I just smashed up the kitchen at home."

He gestured to a rip-off Eames chair, the color of burnt caramel. "Take a seat," he said. "Give me the letter opener."

I eased myself into the seat to appease him.

He sat opposite me. His Versace tie had blood spatter on it. Danny would have a shiner. Even if I died, I got one in—finally. My father's gun was in my purse.

"It's all yours." I threw the letter opener on the ground and while he was cursing me out, scrambling to pick it up, I hit record on my phone—in that way, I was my father's daughter.

"You told me your father died of cancer, but that's not true. Why did Big Pat kill himself?"

"You didn't need to find out any of this."

"So you sent me messages, to put me off."

"I wanted to talk," he said seriously. "What I always wanted was to protect you. My dad had a list. I thought you were on it."

"Okay," I said. "You thought if you carved a giant pentagram on my chest that I'd be safe. That makes sense."

"Like, I was high. God, Erin, I missed you." He began to tug my wrist, like he was literally trying to pull me over the desk by one arm. It was my once-broken one, the one that was now fantastically painful. I relaxed into it, went limp—our last push-pull ended badly.

"He was their doctor. He knew the signs. They were abused kids," Danny said almost softly. "My dad helped them escape. That's what he said. They were better off."

"Better off dead?"

He looked at me blankly, his whole body a question mark.

"The boys he took to the Sound, I think, but he let Cathy go. Canada somewhere. She's alive, Erin. She could be a mom now." I could see the desperation in his eyes. He wanted to believe it, wanted it to be true.

"Was Andre Villiers involved somehow? Tell me."

"You tell the cops about that money?" Danny asked. His ham-sized fists were so tightly clenched they were puce.

"I had to."

"Your dad found out when he started investigating for the Weis family. He blackmailed my dad."

"Yes, I know."

"You know shit," he wept. "Cathy was in the basement, crying. I gave her one of my sister's stuffed dogs. The next morning, she was gone . . ."

Dogs are the best people.

"Big Pat paid RP to keep quiet about it. RP agreed. But RP kept squeezing. Dad drove himself into a tree. Then my mom got sick. It destroyed my family. You know, at trial, he was a different guy, your dad. He just got more and more crooked, I guess. The gambling."

The booze, the coke, the doubles. My dad had made so many deals with the devil that even he, black-hearted as he was, couldn't pay up. He went downhill from there.

"I know. I'm sorry, Danny." I offered him a weak smile, my eyes bright with tears. Men liked that. "What about Andre?"

"Andre had to die, because he was evil," he said. "He hurt kids. And Ricky, well, he asked to meet me by the phone booth. He showed up early and wanted to fight me. About hurting you, I guess. I knocked him out. Thought I killed him." He smiled boyishly. "He was unconscious for like an hour. But like, mostly fine."

So that's why he missed meeting RP and Mona.

"And there's something else. That night. Someone came to the woods. Before Mac's stepdad. That friend of your dad's. Maybe because your dad was hammered. He shot Ricky in the face, screaming that he was a rapist. Then Steve came and shot Ricky in the heart."

"Ox?" I said. It wasn't possible. It couldn't be true.

"Steve said, 'Guy was doing me a favor,' and then he finished him off."

Then I thought of Steve on the gurney. *Your dad's friends.* He wasn't just talking about Mona and whatever money she'd invested in the Palisades. He'd thought Ox helped him, so he helped Ox. Maybe even he'd asked Ox for money to cover it up—or maybe Ox buried something that Shearer wanted buried. Maybe it was Ricky Hell's records. Steve had been dancing around something that day at the Palisades; saying I didn't know shit about my dad, I didn't know shit about that night. Turns out I really didn't.

It was at that point Danny realized I was probably recording and reached across the table and grabbed my bag from me, breaking the strap as he yanked it. I was starting to hyperventilate. He didn't see the revolver, thank God, but extracted my new iPhone and shook his head. He grabbed my wrist, his thumb driving into the webbing of my thumb, into my wrist bone. Then he pressed stop on voice recording, hurling the phone against the wall. He dug around further in my bag, where his fingers must have found the metal.

"Were you planning on hurting me?"

His lips puffed out. His tongue lolled in his mouth, obscene and purple tinged. Inadvertently, I thought of Carole on fire. The tongue of those burned alive can reportedly protrude, flex. I blocked the image. "I mean, aren't we going to fuck first? We got to. Don't you want to?"

Danny lunged across the desk, landing in the broken glass, grabbing my hair, some of it in his knuckles. His knuckle hit my eye, which had only just recovered from where Steve Shearer had hit me; the indent of his class ring was still there. Danny's free hand was around my throat. His eyes bore into mine, and his face drained of all color. I thought I heard something snap.

I forked my fingers and drove them into his eyeball. There was a sound like a dropped squash, a sickening squelch. I didn't know what it was for a moment. Pat had risen, Lazarus style, hitting Danny over the head with one of those ugly Scandinavian lamps.

Unlike the cartoons, the lamp didn't just knock him out. The base of the lamp collided with the back of his skull. Blood poured out but Danny seemed beyond pain, grimacing; half in and out of consciousness as his brother held onto him, crying, while I called an ambulance. I watched the shadow of fear pass over his face, a visible panic, and I wondered if it was the faces of the kids, of Andre, that he was seeing.

"I think I get it now," he said. Then his muscles contracted and relaxed.

Time stopped.

———

It was early evening and I was revisiting RP's favorite cop bar, Benny's. It was his hangout with Mona and Ox, the cop family he cared about more than us. I sat in the gloom of a booth that reeked of overtime and Old Spice; a double in front of me, untouched. I felt sick to my stomach. I hadn't eaten, showered, changed out of my blood-splattered clothing after waiting for the paramedics and giving my statement. Luckily, it was always nighttime in Benny's and my choice of wardrobe was as dark as the secrets I had just ingested. Marci, who was not on duty, had heard what had happened and come down to the station to pick me up. She now sat opposite me, a Bud Light in front of her. She peeled the label while she took a work call. I knew it before she said it, but I waited for her to speak.

"He's gone. He was DOA, they started his heart again, but it was no good."

I nodded dumbly. Danny the invincible; dead on arrival. I thought of the Quinlan-Walshes and their Bible verses on the wall; religion classes. Next to Steve Shearer, Dr. Quinlan-Walsh turned out to be the devil in Southport; and Pat and Danny, Cain and Abel.

"I don't know how to feel. Like, I'd like to say I'm relieved, but I'm also not sure I believe you."

"That sounds about right." Marci rubbed her eyes. "You're in shock. And I'm pretty sure that's a stage of grief."

"Right. Denial." I nodded and drank the whisky. It burned.

"We're excavating the Quinlan-Walshes' backyard for Cathy Carver's remains. There's going to be a lot of media attention. Just so you know. And with the whole Andre Villiers murder, things have just gotten a lot more interesting."

"Ox," I whispered. I didn't want to say it aloud. I remembered the smell of his worn leather jacket, his bear hugs; the loyal brown eyes that never averted from mine. His voice was always smooth, never wavered with untruth. I would have bet my life on his honesty and devotion. It had shaped my life.

"What about him?" Marci watched me carefully.

I looked down at my smashed phone. An email had pinged through.

It was from lostinspace@gmail.com. Aisling had obviously set up an automated email, cued well in advance, in the event of her death. It wasn't a message from beyond the grave. Like Denise had said, none of these happenings, none of these people—Danny, Aisling, Cormac— were supernatural. And it wasn't the end of the story.

EPILOGUE

**RESIDENT ALIEN
BY CORMAC O'MALLEY
THE FINAL CHAPTER
OCTOBER 31, 1994**

The sound of the woods, the Res, the Spot are rushing sounds: Penn Station-bound LIRR train whirring and chiming as it exits the station. Then there's Hellhound throbbing away, beers popping, bongs rattling.

Mostly I'm listening. Mostly I'm remembering, when the darkness lets me. No cats, no dogs. Ricky saw three crows overhead that day. Ricky had a Magic 8 Ball and we turned it around and asked questions like "Am I going to get laid tonight?"

"Outlook not so good." "Ask again later." "Better. Not. Tell. You. Now."

Tabs of acid, shrooms, speed that was kissed by angels; no devils. Hits from the bong.

Something was there, in the woods, it was moving through them. Through me. Something wicked this way comes.

I was on my knees puking from the mushrooms when I saw them. Two sets of shoes, Converse, aqua—Danny, his calves were thick—and

Ricky's work boots. There was a bristling energy, a fury between them. I could hear hissing words and then shouting.

There was a pause in the night, a rip in time. It may have been ten minutes, it could have been hours.

My hands were cold; I was shaking. Danny was saying something to me like "The devil's inside, the devil's inside," and I never believed any of it until tonight. I couldn't see so well but it looked like Carole was with Andre, on the top of the car. Her legs fell open like a doll. Her mouth was an O of agony or ecstasy. I didn't know. I was so high, everything was turning into something else, it was two people, humping, moving, transforming into the beast with two backs. Andre was on her and he was hooting something. Then Carole was screaming.

I was on my feet and I was standing over Andre. I had the bat in my hand. It was hot and sticky. There was hair and part of a tooth on it.

It was Danny standing over me saying, "Everything's going to be all right."

And then a big bear came out of the woods and he was so angry—he moved fast, screaming fire and shooting stars at Ricky, and Ricky turned into a crow. Steve had his foot on my back and he said, "You tell anyone what you saw and you're as dead as that kid over there."

That dead kid was Ricky. That dead kid was Andre.

Steve was in the gloom of the woods, holding Carole, and then suddenly she took off running and Steve took the bat from me and said, "Batter up, play ball. You actually did good, Mac. You did real good."

What? I did what?

I thought of the lights as we flew into JFK, dirt in my mouth, the stars were knives, darting out of the sky and stabbing me over and over, and he asked me, "What did you see, what did you see?"

I swear I never meant to really hurt Andre, and then Ricky was gone—in the air, above us all.

Steve, he kept hitting me until I said I saw nothing. I saw nothing, nothing, nothing at all.

ACKNOWLEDGMENTS

Deepest gratitude to Shane Salerno and the Story Factory—thank you so much for your integrity, perseverance, and faith in this book—and me as an author and to Blackstone for helping me take this story into the States, where it all started.

Thank you to Curtin University for accepting me into the doctoral program to complete this novel as part of my creative project. I especially thank my supervisory team, Susan Bradley-Smith and David Whish-Wilson, for their wisdom, support, and encouragement.

I would also personally like to thank Hannah Richell; the Richell Prize continues to nurture and encourage emerging authors and honors Matt Richell and his legacy.

I had a lot of help from my friends who were either early readers or who helped with edits and submissions—sharing my joys and freak-outs; for permitting my absences from important occasions and for getting excited with me about the book. I thank my family, at home and overseas. To my mum, for instilling a love of books in me and taking me to the library, often multiple times a week; to my father for getting me into true crime, and both for believing in me as a writer. My love goes out to all my Irish family for your ongoing love and support.

I wrote this book in Perth, Western Australia and Melbourne, Victoria—Whadjuk Noongar and Wurundjeri land—which was and always will be Aboriginal land. I would also like to acknowledge that my book is also set on Indigenous land in North America, largely on the land of the Iroquois people and the Seminole people.

Lastly, it would be remiss of me not to acknowledge how much this book has been shaped by trauma. I would like to recognize survivors of child abuse and domestic violence and those who did not survive. On this note, I would like to acknowledge my therapist, Bridget, who has helped me both to continue to write and to stay alive, by having these difficult but essential conversations.